The All Nations Team

Michael Jasper

UnWrecked Press

The All Nations Team

Cover art by TomWang112 | Dreamstime.com

ISBN: 978-0692635261

Published by UnWrecked Press

Also by Michael Jasper

Chapter One

The final season of the World's All Nations team began with the terrible sound of a baseball striking a human skull.

A sound not unlike that of a book slamming shut.

Not a fancy leather-bound bible sitting in a rich white man's parlor, mind you. More like a small prayer book that's been snapped under your nose by your wife after she catches you dozing during the sermon again. An unholy sound, destined to haunt your nights and steal your sleep.

The lethal impact occurred as night approached in the final innings of my team's second exhibition game of the 1918 season, at the tail end of a long winter.

I remember the cold wood of the bench under me, and the competing smells of sweat and dust and flannel uniforms in my nose. Despite the shooting pain in my knees, I made myself get up and pace in the safety of the visitor's dugout.

In those moments before that popping sound shattered the night, my thoughts weren't on the game, but on the season's conclusion: settling down at last at the end of my travels next to a warm fire, surrounded by grandchildren I'd yet to meet, a book of stories in my hand instead of an incomplete roster.

My old heart kept trying to convince my thick head that I'd made the right choice in answering the letter tucked into my uniform pocket.

My thoughts raced and diverged like horses on a track. And as a result of my distraction, I took my eye off the ball.

Only for an instant, I lowered my gaze to my empty hands—imagining retirement, an ending—just long enough to miss the quality of my pitcher Donaldson's throw.

But after over fifty years of playing, nothing could stop me from looking when I heard the ever-promising pop of a bat making contact with a ball.

That pop brought me back to the game, just in time for the *second* sound of impact.

Next to the plate, the batter from the Kansas City Maroons was already down on one knee, the stub of his broken bat cradled in his dusky hands like a fallen bird. His eyes bulged white as eggs as he stared at a spot just outside our dugout.

In front of him, the area between the batter's box and the pitcher's mound held a thousand splintered slivers of wood that formed a jagged halo.

Silence coated the Kansas City ballpark. I felt the chill of the winter-tinged air as the wind changed direction, bringing with it the smells of popcorn and pine tar.

That day had been the first of April. April Fool's Day.

Thinking back on that moment now, I can still taste my own anger and bitterness, tempered by the strong bite of guilt. If I allow myself, I can even hear that sound, ringing in my ears, loud as a gunshot.

A prayer book snapping shut. A life stopping in mid-stream.

Worrell. You took your eye off the ball, you foolish white man. I wanted to tell you to get in the damn dugout. I should've dragged you in, though I never would've dared to even touch you in those days.

Nobody could have foreseen this, not even our prescient centerfielder Mack. Even if Mack was—as I suspect now—somehow responsible for what had just happened to our head coach. When I looked out into the brown stretch of dead grass that passed for centerfield, I saw Mack standing twenty feet in front the crooked white-picket fence of outfield, his skin gray in the fading daylight, his eyes...

His eyes—

No.

Let me stop a moment. I'm getting ahead of myself.

To recount this history properly, I must go back to *before* the line drive that went screaming past our dugout.

Before the endless series of foul tips, before the bunts and the squeeze plays, even before my distraction with that letter. Back before the crowd screamed for a win against my team and the air thundered from hundreds of boots and shoes and cold bare feet pounding on the ground and the wooden bleachers.

No, I need to start with the early innings of that second game, with my last face-to-face talk with head coach Abraham Worrell.

"George," he called to me at the bottom of the third. "Come here, please, and explain something to me."

The sun was already sagging toward the horizon behind us, above the six levels of bleachers and the line of bare oak trees beyond that, but still high enough to stab my outfielders in the eyes.

Worrell gripped our roster tight in one hand as I stepped closer, inhaling his soapy odor; he was always clean, without perspiration. The man was thin as a rail, blonde hair cut short and parted sharply. He stood just as tall as me, but I always felt like I had to look up whenever I talked to him.

"Who put Mack after No Small Foot in the lineup?" he said in his soft, scratchy voice. His words brought back a familiar tightness to my chest.

What I wanted to say was: Why, Mister Worrell, sir, since it's only you and me coaching this team, well, if it wasn't you, then it would've had to be me, now wouldn't it, sir? We could blame the Huns overseas, if you like. Or maybe an enemy spy lurking under the bleachers, for that matter. And while you may not have noticed that Mack has been hitting with twice the power of our Cherokee catcher lately, I *did* notice, and I made the switch. So perhaps we can quit pussyfooting around and get back to the game, sir, since we are down by two runs already?

What I did say was: "That was me, sir."

Worrell shook his head, now fatherly toward me with his smile, though the man was barely half my age. Patronizing, like so many of his kind before him. His eyes held nothing more than a gleam of contempt.

"George," he said. He was now holding tight to his trusty bible underneath the wrinkled-up roster. "Let's not make such decisions without consulting first. With his speed and ability to get on base, Mack should *always* be batting second or third. No Small Foot bats cleanup. That is how it is."

His hands tightened on the roster and the bible, and his watery eyes narrowed.

"You know that. Do *not* tamper with my winning combinations, —"

I could hear the missing word of his final sentence hanging in the air: "boy."

Worrell bit down on the word like a gob of spit before it slipped out between his straight white teeth and exposed him for the kind of man he really was.

I wanted to grab him by the front of his starched, spotless uniform, one hand on the big A and one on the big N, and press him against the metal of the dugout fence.

How does it feel, I'd shout into his pale face, to be always meek as a child at my age? To be unable to speak on your own God damn behalf? How does it feel now, to be helpless?

But all I did was turn and walk away from him without a word. My knees twinged with pain as my metal spikes bit into the cold, tobacco-stained ground, gouging out clods of dirt in my wake.

I did not wish for his death, then. But I did not wish him good health and longevity either.

The bottom of the inning began, accompanied by the five gongs of the big bell at St. Mary's Episcopal Church.

Maybe if I left this two-bit stadium here at the ass-end of winter, and just started walking until I arrived at the return address printed on the folded-up letter from Lizbeth in my pocket, then she could speak to Maddie for me, and we could all be together again.

But, as always, I stopped at the far end of the dugout, knees aching and chest pounding, and turned back to the game.

I couldn't think about Maddie right now. Twisting my fingers into the chicken wire of the dugout fence in front of me, I exhaled in a slow-forming cloud and gazed at the field and my players scattered across it.

My players. They were never Worrell's.

From behind the plate, No Small Foot the Indian flashed a sign for the next pitch to our colored southpaw on the mound. A burly Mexican man stood at first, a white woman at second, and a lanky amber-skinned fellow from the Philippines played shortstop. A Jew covered third. In the outfield, a compact Japanese man waited in left field, a light-skinned Negro with a trio of brown and white feathers trailing out of the bottom of his cap paced back and forth in right field, and the man I knew only as Mack prowled center.

The All Nations Team, the posters called us.

We were one of a kind, the only truly mixed team in those days filled with the constant, numbing echo of war from the other side of the world. If J.L., our team's owner, hadn't gathered these players for our team, they'd be working twelve-hour days in Chicago slaughterhouses or Pittsburgh steel mills or California orchards, or they'd back in their native lands, living in a slum or a tent or a shanty, trying not to starve to death on a daily basis.

Or more likely, they'd be stuck in a trench on the Western Front, aiming rifles instead of bats as they tried to hold back the German onslaught. But our team owner had a cousin in the draft offices, and he'd pulled some strings to shield most of my men from the draft. That was J.L. for you: a good man, even if he was white.

I considered all of them my players, though I'd always be their assistant coach, serving Worrell or some other white man. The unspoken fact was that a man like me could not coach a team with white players on it.

We'd already had two other white head coaches like Worrell since the team began in 1914. Our original head coach left with most of our share of the gate receipts before the last game of that first year, and his weak-spined replacement parted ways with us when we lost our Pullman car and most everything else that came with it near the end of the 1916 season. I can't even remember their names anymore.

As for me, I'd been here from the start: reliable assistant coach Grunion.

Still burning from Worrell's scolding, I gave No Small Foot behind the plate the sign for one of Donaldson's wicked curves. I limped past Jose Mendez, our Cuban pitcher, as he recovered after tossing over a hundred and fifty pitches in our first game that day, a 5-1 win. Each step I took sent needles of pain into my knees, but I refused to sit down. One of these times, I'd sit down and never get back up again.

My team—and the game itself, with all its amazing catches and minute strategies and close calls—were pretty much all that kept me going at the age of sixty-four, or, as I liked to think of it, sixty-*sore*.

"Come on, Donaldson," I called out. "Toss it in there."

I paced for a dozen more pitches before my sixty-sore-year-old body stopped cooperating. I had to rest.

The moment I sat down on the splintery wood of the dugout bench, the Maroons batter clubbed the ball deep into center, for what looked like three bases, easy.

I didn't bother getting back to my feet, however. Our man Mack chased the ball down in a dozen long strides, plucking it from the air with his gloved right hand as if it were a firefly. He'd made an impossible catch look easy. Again.

My smile dissolved when I looked at the chalk scoreboard above the home dugout and saw that we were being out-hit by these meat packers, factory workers, and day laborers. The Kansas City Maroons led three to one thanks to an unlikely home run that passed over our rightfielder Grant's head.

As the third inning ended, my team jogged to the dugout accompanied by scattered boos and hisses from the crowd. Even here, in our unofficial home town of Kansas City, the All Nations were seen as the villains, the team the fans loved to hate. I could allow the spectators that luxury, especially if it made them forget the bloody war in Europe for just a few hours. I was used to always being a visitor, and sometimes a villain.

But what I hadn't grown used to was losing, even in an exhibition game against colored players. I stood up and spat my plug of Red Man into the garbage barrel, suddenly furious that we were playing like such bush leaguers.

"Damn it all anyway," I said as I met my players filing back into the dugout. "Let's get off our sorry asses and knock the stuffing out of that ball, before I knock the stuffing out of each and every one of—"

"That's quite enough, George," Coach Worrell murmured from the far side of the dugout. My mouth snapped shut as Worrell continued speaking, soft as a saint. "Now, let's get some hits this inning, gentlemen, Miss Nation."

Worrell and his churchly ways. Why, to my knowledge, the man had never uttered any word stronger than "Dang" in his life, and he didn't even chew tobacco. That behavior only got you so damn far in this game.

And the little prayer book snaps shut, right under my nose.

Our rightfielder Charlie Grant raised my flagging spirits by taking my surly advice to heart. He pounded his first pitch deep into center field. Charlie raced around the bases, a blur in gray flannel, the three feathers stuck into his cap fluttering behind him like tails. He slid headfirst into third a heartbeat ahead of the throw, evoking a range of insults from the now-nervous crowd.

"Damned speedy redskin" was the tamest of the taunts.

"Atta boy, Charlie!" I called out, giving first the crowd, then my other players a pointed look. I pulled out a fresh gob of tobacco to tuck into my cheek. "Glad to hear *someone* was listening."

Dusting himself off, Charlie gave me a crooked grin as he adjusted the feathers under his cap. I nodded at him and swallowed a curse aimed at the white owners of the majors that excluded my people from the majors.

Even oddballs like Charlie, a colored man who once claimed he was a redskin after posing as "Chief Tokahoma" to make it into the big leagues a decade ago. He'd kept up his Indian act even after being exposed as a Negro by Sox owner Charles Comiskey and kicked off the team after only one game. He still insisted we call him Chief.

At the plate, the short young man nicknamed "Jap" Mikado stepped back to look at me to see if the squeeze was on.

My lips formed a bitter smile as I glanced at Worrell sitting with his chin in his hand, studying the other team like a doctor examining a patient. I turned back to the young man I insisted on calling by his real name, Goro. I ran a finger over the bill of my cap, wiped a hand across my chest, and scratched the side of my nose.

The squeeze was indeed on.

Goro stepped back into the batter's box and the pitcher released the ball. At the last possible instant, Goro squared up and dropped a beautiful, dribbling bunt that limped toward first base.

Goro bolted out of the batter's box as Charlie sprinted headlong down the third base line toward home. The bunted ball rolled onto the infield grass and died just as Charlie slid across home plate with a war whoop.

The first baseman, pitcher, and catcher for the Maroons stood over the ball, staring at it with their arms at their sides, as if trying to comprehend its sudden appearance there.

Kansas City Maroons 3, All Nations 2.

"Now this is turning into our sort of game," I said, pounding on our Cherokee catcher's broad back until my hand stung.

"Ol' *Chief* got a lucky break," No Small Foot muttered, working his threadbare catcher's mitt open and closed. He glared with squinting eyes at our panting rightfielder outside the dugout.

"Easy, there, John," I said. I spat a long stream of tobacco onto the ground, drawing a line in the dirt between the two men.

As Charlie swallowed a celebratory gulp of water from the ice bucket in the dugout, Rodriguez stepped up to the plate. Rodriguez was a big, round-headed Mexican who claimed that he lost a battle with the butt of a rifle during his country's revolution. He'd also claimed from the start that his first name was Buddha. He even had the smooth, hairless head to go along with the name.

What could I do? I called him Buddha, as did the rest of my team.

Perhaps it was blasphemy to those who believed in such things, but I wasn't one of those people. Not anymore. These days, I didn't believe in much other than the game and my players. The years had taught me that much.

I rubbed my arms to warm them in the cool air, and suddenly I had to sit back down again. I lost my breath and nearly swallowed my plug of tobacco.

No, I thought, as my vision went red. Not again.

I blinked to clear the blood from my vision and pulled myself up to my feet again. Had to be the damn cold around here. I couldn't wait to head south tomorrow for our first series of road games in warmer weather.

Rodriguez clubbed his first pitch straight up and back, foul, and I followed the hissing trajectory of the ball back into the bleachers.

Just like that I was caught, entranced by the dozens of dark faces in the crowd.

Sometimes, between innings, I would start counting them all, fascinated by all those lives gathered here for our game—the women in their feathered hats and long dresses, ankles demurely covered, and the men in their dark suits and dusty bowlers and fedoras. I wondered what kind of families these people had, what sort of homes they lived in, what class of dreams and passions guided them in their lives. I was never able to count them all.

And, as always, I entertained the wild thought that *they* might be out there as well: Maddie, Jacob, and Lizbeth. Impossible, I knew, but that never stopped me from daydreaming about it.

I was still gazing out at the crowd of colored men and women when a clear, confident voice spoke up next to me.

"You know, Coach, they *will* all show up at a game one of these days this season. Your family."

A wave of blood darkened my vision again for a painful instant. Now that the foul tip had been retrieved, I turned back to the game. Our Mexican Buddha gave the pitcher his best scowl while he choked up even higher on his chipped brown bat, adjusted his cap on his bald head, and dug in with the glitter of metal spikes.

I finally turned to the source of that familiar voice: Mack, who was now staring directly up at the low-hanging sun through the dugout fence.

"My family, Mack?" I said, spitting more tobacco juice and drawing a grimace from my odd centerfielder. "You can't know that."

"If only I could be more precise," Mack said as he picked up three scuffed bats and swung all three of them in a slow arc, "but you know, Coach, your family *will* attend one of our games. All of them, though not together in the manner that you might expect."

Mack's eyes seemed to catch the rays of the wintry sun, the whites around his brown-tinted irises almost glowing now. As he continued talking, my tongue felt glued to the roof of my mouth.

"Maybe not this month or next, but soon. And not before we lose quite a few of our own people right here on this team. They'll show up just in time, though, your family, along with many others, some of them unwanted and unwelcome. But all of them just in time. That's what I see."

"*Mack*," I protested, but he'd already stepped into the on-deck circle, leaving me—as always—with a handful of questions and a heart full of dread.

In the late afternoon light, Mack's skin looked darker than my own. I could've sworn that at other times the boy's skin looked as pale as one of our white players. I'd long ago given up trying to tell if Mack was white or colored.

The next pitch to Buddha went high for a ball.

Losing our own people? And just in time for *what?*

The kid always left me feeling flummoxed, as if he had jumbled the order of his words and left it to me to rearrange them properly.

As if reading my thoughts, Mack turned to me suddenly from outside the dugout. I caught a coppery whiff of his aftershave, and his eyes were abnormally bright.

"Have I been wrong before?" he said, his face now tinted red with emotion. "Like now, Coach. After Señor Rodriguez gets his hit, I'll knock the ball over the Butler-Flynn Paint sign in right. No joking."

Faced with Mack's unblinking gaze and shifting skin tones, I had to look away.

As if on cue, Buddha fouled the next pitch back into the stands. With his swing, a long, flatulent sound erupted from him, and the crowd broke into raucous laughter. With Mack's odd prediction still rattling around in my head like loose change, I bit back a smile.

Sometimes my colorful players were too much. If the crowd remembered *anything* about this game, they'd surely recall the farting Mexican.

I looked back at my centerfielder in the on-deck circle. Tall and lean, with broad shoulders and wide-set eyes that narrowed like a hawk when he was up to bat, Mack had been with the team since J.L. had formed it in 1914. I usually laughed at Mack's serious manner and his stories about the stars of baseball to come, men of all colors and nationalities; all playing together much like the All Nations did now. The kid had an imagination like nobody else I'd ever known. But today I found it hard to smile at his predictions.

Finally making solid contact that didn't go foul, Buddha drove the ball to the fence in deep center on two bounces. He thundered to second, breaking wind every few feet. Ahead of him, Goro made a beeline around the bases to tie the game at three apiece.

"*That's* my team," I said, grinning and rubbing my chest, which had gone tight in the past few minutes, thanks to my chat with my centerfielder.

Mack dropped all but one of the bats he'd been swinging and undid the top button of his collared jersey. His eyes caught the sunlight for an instant as he tipped his cap at me on his way to the left-handed batter's box.

As predicted, he knocked the first pitch over the billboard-studded wall at its deepest in right field.

"You make it look easy, kid," I said after he returned to the dugout. He was barely winded from rounding the bases.

His home run had passed ten feet over the painted image of a big black bucket with "Butler-Flynn" emblazoned on its side.

And you scare me sometimes, I thought, and not for the last time in that season.

At the bottom of the ninth of that second game, three outs away from a victory—and barely five minutes before our head coach took his eye off the ball for the last time—I sat heavily on the bench, hands itching to pull the letter from my pocket to read again about the end of this season. We led five to three, and the air grew cooler with each pitch. Except for Mendez, the dugout was empty next to me.

Outside the dugout, Worrell played catch with Boles, warming up. Worrell often insisted on pitching the final outs of a game, using every trick in the book to compensate for his lack of power. His favorites involved tobacco juice, bits of sandpaper, and even chewed-up licorice to slick up his pitches and make them harder, if not impossible, to hit. Whenever Worrell closed a game, the ball ended up black as my own skin.

Worrell, you foolish man. You never saw it coming.

I glanced out at the noisy crowd in the graying light, attempting to rally their beloved Maroons. The colored men in their dark suits could barely stay in one place, pumping their fists into the air or waving their hats above their heads. Someone leaned on the horn of one of the half-dozen Fords parked behind the bleachers.

Next to the men, the women had pulled on their overcoats to keep warm, and whenever they clapped, they'd touch their hats with delicate hands as if to make sure they were still there. Beautiful ladies.

I caught myself smiling, thinking of Maddie in her favorite blue dress, so many years ago. When I returned my attention to the game, the rumpled letter from my pocket was in my hands.

"Steeerike one!" the ump called, a black blur as he punched his fist. A wall of boos from the revived crowd answered him.

I glanced down at the name on the letter. Lizbeth, my daughter.

Whenever I was home, I used to tell her stories about the plantation where I'd lived as a child, working the fields alongside my family and friends for Mister Satler, along with tall tales about baseball that she never enjoyed as much. I blamed Maddie for that.

I'd been wondering about Lizbeth all this past winter, ever since receiving her letter at Christmas. She was married and a mother herself now, living her own life, according to her letter. She'd found me, after all these years. It took me a week to write her a letter in return, and another week to actually mail the thing.

Months passed, and I heard nothing in response from her, until opening my mailbox today to find this letter.

Donaldson finished off the first two Maroon hitters on six pitches, throwing as hard now at the end of the game as he had at its start. Worrell's shaky pitching services wouldn't be needed, after all.

The home team's fans remained standing, but their cheering had dwindled away. They could sense a loss in the air.

Outside our dugout, Worrell and Boles stopped playing catch and took a knee to watch the showdown. I caught young Boles fingering a bump on his forehead, a knot so big it pushed the bill of his cap up at an angle.

The white boy, still in his teens, was always getting hit by pitches, which I blamed on how he crowded the plate and how he ran his mouth on the mound. Of course, most *white* pitchers we faced were able to throw strikes to Boles and avoid beaning him altogether.

I watched Donaldson kick his right leg as high as his own head and then twist through his windup to uncork a curveball out of his left hand. The ball dropped like a bomb toward the plate.

The young hitter swung so hard—and missed by so much—that his feet became tangled and he fell to the dirt. A sigh traveled over the crowd.

The hitter kicked his way back up to his feet. He armed sweat from his forehead and took a quick series of swings with the bat as if to remind himself how the whole process worked. Then he placed one foot, then the other, back into the box like a man stepping into an icy ocean. He gave Donaldson the tiniest of nods.

Donaldson responded with another high kick and the hard blur of a fastball. This time, the hitter got a piece of the pitch, sending it back over the stands. Nearly five seconds later, a tinkle of glass tickled my ears. That had to be one of the houses on the next block.

The kid had strength, not to mention guts, to be standing his ground against John Donaldson, one of the best southpaws around—colored, white, or otherwise.

And so the duel began. By the fourth foul tip, the crowd was on its feet again.

"You got it, Eddie!"

"Stay alive, Edward!"

"Make 'em work for it, Eddie!"

"Ed-die!"

The ump called for time, waiting for one of the panting kids outside the fence to return the game ball to him once more.

"Hit it far, Eddie," the kid in faded overalls called out after tossing the ball to the ump. "An' hit it *fair*. We're all beat from chasin' the foul ones."

As the crowd barked laughter, I heard a foreign sound: Worrell's voice, calling encouragement to Donaldson on the mound. Usually Worrell had precious little to say to our colored players. I wondered if my ears deceived me.

Donaldson caught the returned ball from No Small Foot and wiped his brow, which was now furrowed by Worrell's sudden attentions.

Something struck me then, a strange prickling feeling, like the sense that you've just said the wrong thing and killed a lively conversation. The way the kid at bat was clobbering the ball had put me strangely ill at ease.

The ball could go *anywhere*. Fast.

Not necessarily a revolutionary thought, after so many decades of playing this game. But Worrell and Boles were sitting not twenty feet from the batter, exposed outside the dugout in the fading daylight.

I should get them to come inside, I remember thinking.

Then I thought of Worrell's talk with me earlier. The way he dismissed my attempts to lead the team more efficiently to a win. How he'd wanted to call me "boy."

Let it come, I thought. Let the ball go where it may.

Judging from the pounding roar now coming from behind me, every person in the crowd was stamping their feet on the bleachers or the ground. They stopped the instant Donaldson launched the ball.

In the sudden silence, Eddie made his best contact of the night, hitting the ball so hard he shattered his bat. Like an explosion of wooden fireworks, the broken bat showered the infield with slivers of wood, distracting everyone for an instant from where the ball had actually gone.

The sharp, popping sound that followed came from a spot directly next to the All Nations' dugout.

My hands clenched, crumpling the letter in my grip.

At that moment, I simply couldn't turn to look to my right. Instead, my gaze traveled from the countless shards of wood on the infield to Mack in centerfield. The young man dropped his glove as if *he* had been the one who'd been hit, and in the unnatural hush covering the ballpark, I could hear his mitt drop onto the dead grass surrounding him.

Mack. You should've seen this coming, son.

As I stared, a gauzy white light spread around Mack's darkened face, spilling out from his eyes as if he had a white-hot fire inside his brain. And the only way for that heat to escape was through his eyes.

My vision went blood red on me again. I felt myself slipping, falling.

Despite the distance between us and the haze of my own bloody vision, I could see Mack slowly nod at me.

I felt a stabbing pain in my chest, and the tobacco went bitter in my mouth.

Mack. What do you *see*?

Then I blinked, and the strange light disappeared from Mack's eyes. The frozen, timeless moment ended.

I needed all the strength in my tired old body to finally turn to the right, where head coach Worrell still stood, left hand tight against his temple, mouth forming indecipherable, soundless words.

Then, as if he'd been waiting for me to look his way, Worrell fell. He landed face-first in the dirt, five feet from the shelter of the visitors' dugout.

The park burst into motion and sound. My players rushed to Worrell, while the crowd exploded with shocked screams. Footsteps pounded all around me now, on the ground and on the bleachers behind me.

"Coach," Boles murmured from next to Worrell. "*Coach?*"

"Coach!" Buddha Rodriguez cried from first base, hands clamped to his bald head.

I realized he was calling me, not Worrell.

"Coach! *¿Qué debemos hacer?* What should we *do*, Coach?"

All of my players turned to me. I spat my plug of tobacco onto the ground, gagging from its suddenly foul taste, and dropped my tattered letter.

I was going to warn him, but I didn't. I should have pulled him inside. He was half my age, and now he was dead, the life driven out of him by a ball faster than a bullet. Nobody should have to die that way. Not even a man like Worrell.

And now my players were looking to me for guidance. To lead.

I dragged my heavy feet through the dirt outside the dugout, thinking, *I did not want this* with each step, my knees aching in time with my thoughts. My future plans faded like old ink on dried-out paper.

Did not want it.

At last, out of breath and tight-chested, I reached Worrell's unmoving, prone body, with my players all huddled around me.

The man wasn't getting up; I knew this as sure as if Mack predicted it. Like a door slamming shut. A prayer book snapping closed.

Abraham Worrell, the All Nations head coach, was dead. His spirit would begin haunting me later that very night.

Chapter Two

Until I met Maddie, I never took much stock in religion. I remember the hymns my mother would sing to us during those hot nights under the tin roof of our quarters in South Carolina. How I tried to keep still but went right on sweating on my blanket, wedged between my two older brothers. Mama sang of a balm in Gilead, of O-Mary-don't-you-weep, of Moses fittin' the battle of Jericho.

But they were just songs, stories to help us fall asleep and get through the day's labor. I didn't really put any faith in them.

Father, on the other hand, refused to talk about religion while we lived on the plantation. Not until much later, after we'd gotten our freedom and moved to Chicago, did the old man stop looking away when the topic of believing entered the conversation.

Then he'd listen in with a sudden intensity and start asking the kind of questions that would be difficult for anyone but a preacher to answer, and that would sour the mood for everyone.

Around that time, I started getting paid to play ball—not much, but at seventeen, I didn't require much—and ended up in Kansas, of all places. Where I met Maddie.

Working next to her in a Kansas City laundry one snowy winter between seasons, I would tell her stories about traveling the country and playing baseball, and she would tell me about Jesus and his desire to save our immortal souls. The way she talked, you'd think Jesus was a close personal friend of hers.

I admit, the combination of her closeness, her pretty face, and her melodious voice, even there in the noisy bustle of the great washing machines, made me *want* to believe. And if my faith made me more attractive to her, so be it.

Not even a year later, in 1875, I married her in the tiny church she'd attended since she was born. I was so full of the giddiness of love and the breathlessness of our lives opening up together that I promised Maddie I'd attend church every Sunday, even when I was on the road with my team.

She would take my hands in hers, and we would pray, and that would be enough for me. I felt man enough to fight like Moses at Jericho, so long as my Maddie never had to weep like Mary.

That was then.

If I were that same man now, over forty years later—a man of *faith*—I'd be whispering a prayer instead of watching my breath cloud in front of my face like a mask.

I'd be taken by the Holy Spirit in the presence of the dead white man in the pristine gray uniform, laid out in the square bed of a Ford Model T pickup, his lifeless body cushioned with my players' gloves and hats. Maybe I'd even get a sense of his soul, brushing past me on its way to the afterworld.

If I were a better man, I'd *feel* something for him, out of the goodness of my heart.

But, standing alone just outside the dugout, staring not at the truck and its lifeless burden, but at a darkened baseball field, I couldn't feel a thing other than a bellyful of guilt and a glint of relief.

As the pickup bearing his body finally sputtered off into the night, I swore I could hear his dry laughter drift toward me like a cool breeze against my cheek.

A moment later, the owner of the All Nations team approached me with his battered hat in his hand, walking with the slow stride of a pallbearer. His blue eyes were ringed with circles of sadness, like a hound dog returning home after a long, unsuccessful hunt.

I'd known J.L. Wilkinson for decades, going back to the days when we played in exhibitions against each other in the '70s and '80s. He'd been the new young white pitcher dogged by accuracy problems, while I was the veteran colored hitter who belted the ball deep into the outfield for extra bases whenever we met.

Then the so-called "Gentleman's Agreement" of 1887 ended those meetings. As far as I knew, colored men would never play ball with white men again. Not in a Major League game—the only kind of game that truly mattered. All we had were exhibition games in small fields scattered across the country, diamonds like this nearly deserted one here in Kansas City.

"*You* are the new head coach, George," J.L. said, stopping right in front of me. It was not a question.

In spite of the chill in the air, I could see sweat on his bald forehead as he looked up at me. He smelled like fried food and dust.

"I refuse to take no for an answer."

"No," I said anyway, feeling a tremor in my chest that ran down both hands. I didn't want to be the colored man who replaced the newly dead white man. "It's not... not my place, sir."

"What is this 'sir' garbage, George?" I could feel an edge to his voice, like sandpaper under silk. "You're not thinking of, well, going against my wishes, now, are you?"

I tried to smile, but couldn't. I kept seeing Worrell fall nose-first into the dirt, his left temple bulging and purple. He didn't even try to catch himself.

All in the blink of a distracted eye. All my fault.

"Sorry," I muttered. "I just—"

"Can't believe it. I know. In all my years of baseball, I've, well, I've *never* seen anything like that. He never saw it coming."

The strange ache in my chest that I'd felt earlier in the game returned, along with a stream of dark thoughts: What must it feel like to be alive one second, and dead the next? What had the poor man felt? And when did all feeling stop?

"George?" J.L. said, stepping closer as if to catch me. I'd been swaying, shifting my weight from one foot to the other, as if I were in the batter's box myself.

"I'm all right. Just a bit overwhelmed, that's all."

"I understand," he said, then added, "Coach."

"Thanks." I could barely hear my own voice for the growing buzz of the crickets around us. The cold night air infiltrated my sweaty uniform, as if sensing an opening and charging in.

Worrell was gone. Dead.

And I was head coach. At last.

"Do me one favor, though," J.L. said, his round face colored in the weak light by a familiar shade of frustration. "Tell Grant to lose those damn feathers, would you? We're *not* a gimmick team or a novelty team. People need to take us seriously, well, for who we really are. All of us. Including Grant. No more hijinks."

"Yes, sir," I said automatically, thinking of Charlie flying around the bases, feathers waving. How he'd ignited our rally, back when Worrell was still alive.

I heard that popping sound again and tried not to flinch.

I stood there with J.L. in the chilly darkness, not needing to speak. Our team owner was the only white man that I could truly consider a friend. Though I'd never call him "Wilkie" like his other friends or one of his many cousins.

He was a fair man for a team owner, making sure my players promptly received their portion of the gate for each game. He even understood my knee problems and didn't expect me to play like most coaches and managers did on other short-handed clubs. I hadn't picked up a glove for an actual game in years.

I exhaled, feeling the some of the pent-up tension drain from my tight shoulders and clenched jaw.

"*That's quite enough,*" a voice whispered from somewhere down the first base line, ruining my moment of composure. "*Boy,*" the voice added, this time from the vicinity of the pitcher's mound.

I froze, grinding my teeth once more. I looked first at J.L., but he was still staring down at his small, empty hands, and then I looked out at the empty bleachers behind us. We were alone.

When I risked a look back at the field, though, I could've sworn I saw—for a mad instant—a lanky white figure in a strangely glowing gray uniform, winding up on the mound, kicking high, arms akimbo.

But when I blinked and looked at the mound again, there was nobody there.

Just my tired brain, playing tricks on me.

"Look," J.L. began, toeing the dirt with one not-so-shiny black shoe. He hadn't noticed any of my contortions next to him. "I'd understand it if you wanted to, well, delay the start of the road trip. I can talk to my cousin down in Shreveport and see if we can't postpone—"

"*No.* We need to play." I swallowed, tasting more dust as I remembered my place. We were friends, but he was still white and I was still colored. "If that's all right with you, that is."

"Of course." J.L. said. "I'll do my best to see you gents off tomorrow, bright and early. That is, well, if I can get my flivver to crank in the morning. That car hates the cold." He shook his head, put on his hat, and turned to go. "Get some rest now, Coach. It's been a rough night. A terrible night."

As the cool blanket of night covered Exposition Park, I watched J.L. fire up his mud-spattered Ford Speedster. Most of the spectators, not to mention all of my players, had come here and left on foot. Flivvers were not so easy to come by for the rest of us, and our team bus was in the garage, waiting for our season of barnstorming to begin.

I'd watched my players leave while I was talking to J.L., some heading home with their families, while others went off

29

with friends, most likely to find a tavern. All of them wore dull expressions of disbelief and loss on their faces. They reminded me of the grainy photographs of the soldiers in the trenches of Europe. Shell-shocked, they called it.

The game itself would remain forever one out away from completion. In my first act as head coach, I listed it in my records as a loss.

Back in the visitor dugout, with all my belongings packed up, I pulled out my pouch of Red Man, wincing at the profile of the feather-wearing Indian on its label. When I tasted the moist tobacco, I gagged. Like varnish mixed with dirt. Ruined.

Sputtering, I threw the whole works into the garbage barrel next to the bench.

Then I saw the letter.

I picked up the crumpled envelope I'd left on the churned-up ground next to the barrel. With a grunt, I tore it in half and threw the pieces into the barrel, on top of my pouch of spoiled chewing tobacco.

Enough with the letters. No more sitting up all night composing them in my head as sleep escaped me. No more waiting for responses that never came. No more getting my hopes up for some sort of reconciliation, after all this time.

With the letter disposed of, I could think about heading home at last; the team bus left tomorrow at five a.m. for our games in Shreveport. Our travels were about to begin I should be home, enjoying the comfort of my own bed.

Over the rightfield and centerfield walls, across the street from the ballpark, rectangles of light glowed yellow and warm from the rows of two-story houses. As I gazed at one of the windows and listened to a distant gramophone churning out a waltz, I wondered about all the people out there I'd never know.

Was a baby crying on the other side of that window? Was a father playing with his kids in that light? Was an old man or woman eating alone in that house?

And what about Worrell? Did he have a porcelain-skinned sweetheart somewhere in the nicer part of the city, wondering when he'd return?

Something skittered across the dirt outside the dugout, though it was now too dark to see anything. I nodded and squinted in the dark, as if I'd been waiting for this, now that J.L. was gone.

"*That's quite enough, boy.*"

I held my breath as the dry voice of our former head coach floated through the night air toward me. Of course it was Worrell. There was no sense in denying it.

"*You think she'd want to talk to you?*"

The voice came from the pitcher's mound, and it froze me where I stood in the dugout. My old, arthritic hands began shaking. I tasted salty sweat on my lips.

"*After all these years, and how you treated her, and the rest of them?*"

The voice was in my ear now, coming from behind me. My heart thumped against my sternum, painfully.

I whirled, feeling foolish for chasing after my imagination like that, and paid the price with twin stabs of pain, one for each knee. I inhaled at last, but my breath remained short and choppy, like a panicking swimmer too far out in the waves.

"*Especially,*" Worrell's bodiless voice taunted, "*your boy. Boy...*"

I'd half-convinced myself that someone actually was out there, floating above the brown grass of the infield, but in the light of the waning moon I could discern that the mound was clearly empty.

For a maddening few moments that seemed to last half a lifetime, I felt like I was surrounded by a whole team of angry, spiteful spirits, all of them echoing that last word: "*Boy.*"

I waited for the disembodied voice to continue its scolding derision, but the only sound I heard was the wind and my own ragged breathing.

I was alone. I remained in the dugout, hoping that one of my players—Buddha Rodriguez or No Small Foot or even Mack—would come back and rescue me.

But ten silent minutes passed as I stood there in the darkness of the dugout, and no one appeared.

At last, chilled and aching in my old joints, I changed out of the scuffed pair of spikes that now belonged to the new head coach of the All Nations team and let my tired, sore legs carry me the sixteen blocks back to the small, mostly empty house I called home, and I did not once look back.

The next day, when the team bus rolled over the southern border of Missouri into Arkansas, I couldn't have felt more relieved. Outside the dirty windows, the land had turned to rolling green hills instead of the endless miles of flat black pastureland. The bus rattled down yet another gravel road, a route that our driver Blount insisted was a short cut.

The *bus*. That was a bit of a joke. This vehicle was actually a refurbished Double-T flatbed truck with four extra rows of unforgiving wooden seats and a reinforced metal frame.

The players' bags and equipment sat stacked onto the front seat next to Blount, along with the rolled-up tents and stakes we used on nights when a hotel was unavailable or too costly. I couldn't count the number of nights I'd slept in a tent on the same field where I'd play ball the next day. That was just a sacrifice you made to help your team succeed.

My players and I sat three to four to a row behind Blount. On each side of the exterior of the bus, bold black letters proclaimed the bus property of "The World's All Nations Barnstorming Team" (a title that would've been even longer if Blount hadn't run out of room and paint), and the roof was made from a chunk of billboard we had plucked from the road late one night.

This bus was a far cry from the Pullman car we once used to ride the rails in luxury just two seasons ago. But times were tough, and J.L. had to cut the expenses wherever he could.

Looking up at the fading circus broadsheets still affixed to the billboard ceiling made me think about the Chautauqua I'd taken Maddie to when we were first married. After paying our dime to get in, we'd sat at the back of the big brown tent. All afternoon we watched a parade of performers that included an opera diva, a ten-man band, a Plains Indian, a band of jugglers, and a magician.

While Maddie made a sour face at some of the more colorful performers, I reveled in the variety. So many fascinating people, with so many specialized skills. I felt like a rube, a simpleton who only knew how to smash a ball with a piece of hickory.

They saved the fiery inspirational speakers for last, as dusk approached.

"Find your happiness!" the first speaker had shouted, his voice already growing hoarse, his pear-shaped face red and shiny with perspiration. "You don't need to rely on your preacher, your teacher, or the latest "Perils of Pauline" double feature! Will you be able to say, on your deathbed, that you have found your happiness in life, and that your time was not all wasted?"

Maddie had not been particularly pleased when I'd told her my happiness in life was from baseball more than anything else. I should've known better, but back then I simply didn't think. I must've been such a disappointment to her. No wonder she left.

A hard lurch of the bus nearly knocked me out of my seat. Rubbing my chest and blinking memories and dust out of my eyes, I turned to look at the mix of light and dark faces crowded next to me and behind me on the bus.

Chief Charlie dozed on the end of the seat next to me, while behind him the lower part of my second-basewoman's face was obscured by a newspaper shouting "Germans Launch Another Offensive Against Allies." Above the paper, the blue eyes of the woman we knew only by her nickname of Carrie Nation were wide with a mix of shock and rage, a look similar to the look she wore whenever she went on about how women deserved the right to vote.

I felt a stab of sympathy for Carrie, even if she was a white woman, and as such, I didn't dare say more than a word or two her on a good day. J.L. had signed her on a tip from one of his many cousins spread out across the country. She'd never told me her real name, but whoever she was, she was strong enough to stand on her own against whatever curve balls the world threw at her. Even a world filled with marauding forces and mounting death tolls overseas.

Next to Carrie, Mack dozed. His skin was brown as a bruise today, catching and distorting the weak light of morning in its usual way. I looked away before he opened his eyes, remembering the unholy light coming from them at yesterday's game. I was in no mood for any more predictions.

Boles, Mendez, Goro, and Phil the Philippine all slept in the third row, like a bunch of oversized, snoring schoolkids.

In the last seat, squeezed between a snoozing Buddha Rodriguez and a frowning No Small Foot, John Donaldson looked up and caught my eye. I could see the furrow in his brow from here.

Oh boy, I thought.

An instant later, Donaldson got up and began squeezing through the tiny aisle of the bus, one hand on the ceiling and the other on the backs of each seat. He paused next to me, looking down at the space by the window where Worrell usually sat. He gave me his usual shy smile, about to speak.

I beat him to it.

"How's the arm, John?" I said, nodding at the empty seat.

"Hey there, Coach," he said, dropping onto the hard seat with a good-natured groan. Despite the fact that he'd just turned twenty-seven, he looked no older than seventeen. "It's good. Though these bumps Ol' Blount keeps hitting won't let me get any rest."

"Yeah. I think he aims for the ruts so he can test the bus's suspension." As if in response, the makeshift bus slid around a bend in the road, motor roaring as the wheels spun.

"I got it! I *got* it!" Blount shouted from the driver's compartment in front of us, like an outfielder chasing down a high pop fly.

We all held on for dear life, including the sleeping players—they knew the routine, even asleep. The air quickly filled with the stink of burning oil.

"So how are *you*, Coach? You okay?"

"I'm all right." I sighed. Might as well get this over with. "So... What's on your mind?"

"Coach," he said, glancing behind him for a second. He exhaled. "I really wish we could've stayed for Mr. Worrell's funeral."

I hid my surprise by looking through the dirty glass of the makeshift window next to Donaldson. The early-morning light painted the unfamiliar landscape golden.

I didn't have a single qualm about skipping the man's last moments on this earth before they planted him in the ground like a pale, bitter root.

"I understand. But we could all use the money from these games. The show has to go on, I'm afraid."

Donaldson didn't look convinced. In any case, I wanted to add, I doubted they would've let most of my team inside the white funeral parlor so we could pay our respects.

"Can't get paid if we don't play, I guess," Donaldson said at last, watching me. "Probably what Mr. Worrell would've wanted. So. You *sure* you're okay, Coach?"

"Just thinking about who's going to pitch tonight, now that we're short a relief pitcher."

I felt my smile melt away as the young man gave me another one of his piercing looks.

"He was a good man, wasn't he?"

"I'd like to think so," I said quickly, but all I could recall was Worrell's soft, judgmental voice. His patronizing tone.

That's quite enough. Boy.

"For the most part," I added. "I just wonder if he's at rest now."

"What do you mean?"

I suddenly wanted to check under the seat to see if Worrell had left his bible with his name inscribed into it, or if maybe Worrell himself was under there, hiding and waiting for just the right moment to spring out.

The ball *popped* off of Worrell's skull once more in my mind.

And then... silence.

"I keep speculating," I said, feeling like a weight had been removed from my chest, "about what happens when you die."

Donaldson sat up, stirring up wild motes of dust.

"Coach, you got something to tell us players? You're not sick, are you? We can't afford to lose you, too."

"No, just wondering, is all." I tried to keep a poker face as I asked, "What do *you* think happens?"

This wasn't Mack, I reminded myself. Donaldson has always been one to shoot straight.

"Well," Donaldson said. "I think a person's got some explaining to do before they let him through those pearly gates."

"Explaining? For what?"

He waved his hands, his long, delicate fingers spread wide like nets. "All your misdeeds in your life. Maybe you got to make amends. I heard some preachers talk about that purgatory, which is probably a lot like riding this old bus, on our way to the next game, 'cept we never know when or if we're going to get there. Or maybe it's like prison, doing time for your crimes."

"And then it's on to the harps and the choirs of angels?"

"Oh, I hope so, Coach," Donaldson said with a laugh. "And I hope there's some ball to be played up there, too. Otherwise eternity could be one long, boring bus ride. And just our luck, all us coloreds would have to ride in the back."

That got a reluctant laugh out of me.

"So if heaven is a baseball game, what's hell like?"

Donaldson couldn't help but shudder, which he tried to cover up with by shrugging.

"Beats me. Maybe it's just something preachers and parents made up to keep us marching the straight and narrow like those soldiers overseas, going off to the war."

I rubbed my chin and thought of all the dark headlines emblazoned across the front of Carrie's newspapers in the past few days.

"Sometimes," I murmured, "I wonder if hell isn't what people do to each other when they're alive."

Donaldson's eyes widened for a moment as he contemplated this concept. Was he thinking about the war as well, or was he anticipating the cheap, rundown hotel in Shreveport we'd be staying at tonight—if we were lucky—or the back rooms of the restaurants we'd eat at before our first game tomorrow?

"Maybe," he said with another quick glance over his shoulder. I realized who he was looking out for, now—our centerfielder. "Maybe you should talk to ol' Mack about it, since he seems to know all about the future. Me, I try not to think about dying too much. It's sort of like my fastball on a bad night—out of our control."

I couldn't have said it better, so I simply nodded.

Donaldson shook my hand and forged his way back to his seat at the rear of the bus.

I took a long, deep breath of warm air and gazed at the fading, peeling logo of the Barnum and Bailey circus pasted on the makeshift roof of the bus. I felt like we'd already left behind the cold Midwest and entered the warm humidity of the South. And in the South, all the rules were different. Who knew what was to come in the days and weeks ahead of us?

Out of our control.

Donaldson was right—I needed to talk to Mack about these things.

But not right now. I didn't feel up to Mack's random answers to questions I'd never asked.

Instead, I leaned back and closed my eyes on the washed-out images of sword swallowers, camel riders, lion tamers, and trapeze artists.

Within three breaths, I was asleep and dreaming.

I was a kid again, running through the fresh-cut grass while the hot Carolina sun beat down on me.

I didn't even notice the heat, because Nate had just knocked the ball over my head again, and for a few shining moments, my entire world revolved around getting that ball and throwing it back to Father.

I'd forgotten everything else: the uninsulated shack I shared with my parents and two brothers along with another family, the cuts on my fingers and arms from picking cotton, and the chains worn at night by the bigger men on the plantation.

Panting from the heat, I knew I was smiling as I charged after the stitched, lumpy ball, now falling from the air at the end of its arc.

"Look at that nigger boy *run*," a gravelly voice called from the side of the field by the tobacco barn. "Like a damn jackal."

The world spun as my nine-year-old self pulled up short at the sound of that voice. I stopped so abruptly I nearly went sprawling into the summer-browned grass ringed by the rows of cotton.

My breath went hot in my lungs, and I became aware of my bare feet and naked chest, as well as the eyes of the white men in their chairs over a hundred feet behind me.

The ball never felt as heavy as it did by the time I reached it, and my throw to my shirtless, shoeless father took all the strength in my wiry left arm.

Mister Satler, the owner of the plantation as well as all the slaves playing on this rough version of a baseball diamond, sat on top of his wooden picnic table watching the game in his dirty gray suit, orchestrating the players like the Southern soldier he was trained to be.

On his left sat fat, white-haired Mister Oldham, belting out his cackling laugh. Directly next to Mister Satler was a colored woman wrapped up in a lacy white dress, her back straight and her face expressionless. I never learned her name.

While I was gaping at them, a third white man, all skin and bones in a white suit, sauntered up to the picnic table and sat next to Oldham, shaking his head as if he couldn't believe such a sight. The three men were all laughing at me and my father and the other slaves, as if we were no more than attractions in a traveling side show.

All of this I could see without squinting from the grass of the outfield that my father had cut that morning behind the two Satler horses. To the best of my young memory, the master had never beaten a slave, and the man had been the first to show me how to play baseball. His oldest daughter had been teaching me how to read, a skill I'd treasure almost as much as my knowledge of this wonderful game.

But my mother and father hated the man, so I did too.

I wanted to run from the flush of shame heating my skin, yet I knew I'd never make it to the rows of cotton that ringed the outfield: Mister Oldham had his rifle resting across his lap like a lethal black cane.

I wanted to run and to keep on running, but on that day, I went back to the field and continued playing for the enjoyment of the white men watching us. I swung the splintery bat with tears gathered in my eyes, and my bare foot bled when I caught it on one of the metal bases.

In my *dream*, however, I ran.

I turned my back on the white men and the baseball game and sprinted toward the cotton field, determined to escape down the countless roads leading away from here. I knew that another world, a better one, had to lie beyond those rows of prickly white cotton.

I ran, the wind screaming in my ears, my body electric with fear. I just had to reach the cotton field, and I'd be gone. I ran, and in the blurring of the fields around me, I swore I saw other dark figures running as well.

First one, then three, then a dozen dark figures, arms and legs churning. Maybe more. Following my lead. We ran for all we had, for our lives.

"*Shoot him,*" a harsh, scratchy voice called from behind home plate. The voice of the third man, the stranger. "*Kill that coward. Shoot them all.*"

The other runners and I were ten feet away from freedom when I heard the distinct click of a gun's hammer. I wanted to look back, but I didn't dare.

I pushed myself until I thought my heart would burst, the other figures screaming and running all-out in my peripheral vision, but none of us could outrun the explosion that followed.

My eyes snapped open with the booming sound of the team bus backfiring.

The wheezing vehicle had come to a rest at an intersection, but my heart continued hammering. My hands were locked onto the seat edge under me, and I forced them to loosen their grip as a wave of cold, dank air blew over me.

I looked over at the window seat next to me and felt a hand grip my heart through my breastbone.

Worrell sat there, in his old spot, staring at me.

An ugly blue and brown knot almost the size of a fist bulged from his left temple, pulling his left eye into a crooked squint. The stitches of a baseball wound through the swollen lump of his fatal wound like train tracks on a map. His normally white teeth as well as his uniform were stained with blood.

Shoot him. The voice had been soft and full of judgment and contempt. That had been *his* voice. *Shoot them all.*

I made a feeble attempt to speak, but my tongue was glued to the roof of my mouth. I very well might have expired right there, unable to breathe in the sudden cold, if Old Blount hadn't saved me by hitting another hole in the road. The bus lurched and I closed my eyes involuntarily.

When I looked at the seat next from me, Worrell was no longer there.

He'd been replaced by Mack, my centerfielder, who was staring at me with a knowing look on his dusky face.

Mack's strangely bright eyes widened, just for a moment. Warm, fresh air blew over me from my cracked window, and I got a whiff of Mack's coppery aftershave once more.

I found myself waiting for an unholy light to start spilling from Mack's eyes again. I wanted to duck to avoid the baseball or bullet or explosion that was about to strike home on me. Head, chest, or belly?

But all that happened was that Mack gave me a quick nod before looking up at the makeshift roof of our bus.

"I know, Coach," he murmured with a yawn. He rested his head on the back of his seat and closed his strange eyes. "I know."

A moment later, he was snoring.

I lacked the energy to ask Mack any questions about what exactly it was that he claimed to know.

Instead, I breathed deeply until my heart's violent beating returned to normal, only to feel a strange heaviness fill my chest and arms. The bus still hadn't started moving again.

No, I ordered my old body. *Don't give out on me yet.*

Exhaling slowly, I leaned forward to look outside the window next to Mack. I saw a pair of white boys gaping at the bus as if waiting for tigers to burst from its doors.

Behind them was a tall store window with "Shreveport's Finest Hats" emblazoned across the front, the words disappearing as the sun pulled free of the clouds to ignite the entire pane of glass.

A moment later, the boys were chased away by the store owner, a rail-thin white man with pins and needles sticking out of his mouth like tiny cigarettes, a hat in each hand. He could have been Worrell's twin, especially the way he gave the bus a disapproving look before storming back inside.

Blount revved the engine, and we shot through the intersection at last.

Chapter Three

You know, Coach, this team will be forgotten by history," Mack told me on the day we first met.

This was in Kansas City, at the start of the 1914 season. I'd been watching our team's head coach—two coaches before Worrell—conduct batting practice from the pitcher's mound, the rotund white man grunting louder with each pitch he delivered.

I looked over at our new recruit. His skin was pale as a boy off the boat from Ireland.

"Beg your pardon?"

"The World's All Nations," the young man had pronounced, "shall perform feats that no person watching our games can or will ever forget. But our accomplishments will be lost unless something is done."

"Nice to meet you too," I'd said, laughing. "So how can we prevent this, son?"

Mack simply stared at me instead of answering right away, his brown eyes widening the slightest bit. I wonder now if maybe I did see a touch of that strange white light spilling out from them on that day.

"Do the one thing that all of us disparate men do best— play ball together. As a team. That very well may be enough. But we'll need *your* help. I'm telling you this now to help prepare you for that eventuality, Coach."

Then he simply wandered off to pick up a bat and set up at home plate. That was the first time he'd left me at a loss for words as well as at a loss for comprehension.

The first time, but not the last, of course. Not by a long shot.

* * * * *

Now, six years later, with the sun smoldering high above us, Mack stood next to me again.

Our team had *not* been forgotten by the world. At least not yet.

We were still around, in Shreveport now, in the northwest corner of the boot that was Louisiana.

Mack and I watched the infielders practice while our two other outfielders played catch. Today Mack's skin was brown as the dirt of the infield, and he was staring at me once more.

"You've given up chewing tobacco," he said at last, inhaling deeply. "Good. The air is much cleaner around you now."

"Yes," I said after a pause. What the hell was I supposed to say to that?

"You know, Coach," he said in the same way he started all his predictions to me, "one day in the future, most baseball games will be played at night. The ropes dividing the stands will be gone. No colored stands and no white-only stands. No Japanese or Chinese section, no Mexican or Philippine section. Just Americans, watching their teams play a game of ball. So many teams, and every one of them mixed, like ours. It *will* happen, if..."

He trailed off, turning his gaze toward the sun.

Tired of waiting for him to continue, I looked away in frustration.

Now that he'd mentioned it, I wished I had some tobacco, even if it the stuff did taste like dust to me these days. I thought of Maddie's complaints after I tried kissing her after a day of baseball and plug after plug of Red Man.

"Oh, what the hell," I said at last, skin prickling from heat and frustration. "What miracle will cause this to happen, Mack?"

"If people can remember the example this team is setting right now," he said, still staring right at the sun, "or even just remember that it *existed* without any of us killing each other, all us players from all over the world, from hither and yon, then those people can continue what we started. Baseball can belong to everyone. But if people forget us, I sense the game will become a novelty, played only by whites. By the end of a few decades, it will disappear. And something else will be lost along with it, something precise and beautiful."

I tried to laugh at all that, though his words rang true.

Mack lowered his gaze and looked at me with a strange grin.

"But it doesn't have to be that way. We can bring dignity back to not just the game, but to humanity, just by staying intact and enduring. *This* team. It must be this team, Coach."

I thought once more of the light spilling from Mack's eyes, wreathing his head. My heart flip-flopped, and I blinked away the redness that tried to fill my vision.

"Mack. Why must you give *me* these hints about the future? Can you not share them with someone else?"

He answered with a shrug, and then silence.

Pop, pop, pop went the sound of baseballs hitting gloves out on the field.

Pop went the sound of the baseball hitting Worrell's skull.

"Can you tell me, then," I said in a low voice, rubbing my chest once more, "can you tell me how much time *I've* got left?"

"Coach." Mack stepped closer to me inside the dugout, out of the sun, his skin darkening even further. "If someone told you the exact date of your death, what would that really accomplish? Would that knowledge have helped Coach Worrell? And anyway. You've still got plenty of time, plenty of life yet, and a great deal to teach us all. And more than a little bit to learn, I think."

45

I was leaning over so close to Mack that I could smell his too-sweet aftershave. He'd turned his head from me again so he could stare up, unblinking, at the sun.

"Tell me more," I whispered.

Mack didn't even flinch. "I've made enough predictions about you and the team for today," he said. "I can't say any more, Coach."

I wanted to grab him and shake him until the answers spilled out of him like stolen coins. But I was suddenly afraid of what he might do in response. Those eyes of his...

"Don't you have a game to get ready for, son?"

Mack lowered his gaze and gave me a quick half-bow before he spun on his spiked heel, leaving me alone once more to try to digest all he'd shared with me.

What would that really accomplish? And would that have helped Coach Worrell?

I thought of the strange apparitions I'd seen on the darkened field back in Kansas City, along with the other figures running with me in my aborted dream this morning. Had they been running with me, or chasing after me, like Worrell seemed to be doing?

I allowed myself one last shudder before I turned my attention to the present again. It was almost noon and I had a game to coach. I picked up a blank sheet of paper and a pencil from the dugout bench, casting a quick look out at the growing crowd behind me.

One glance was enough to tell me that we were back in the South. We actually had *two* crowds. Sitting on one side of the greasy yellow rope that separated the crowds, behind home plate and the Shreveport Sports dugout, the white spectators laughed with one another and called out encouragement to the members of their team.

I even saw a white man holding up a Brownie box camera with both hands, counting to eight as he made a picture of the white portion of the crowd.

The clamor of voices from that section felt too loud to my ears when I turned to the colored stands behind our dugout.

The people seated here were far quieter, though they too were crowded elbow-to-elbow on the rickety wooden bleachers. A few people nodded at me solemnly, while most looked away.

It was an all-too-familiar story told in blacks and whites.

I inhaled the clean scent of cut grass and ignored the dull, familiar pain in my chest. Still trying to put Mack's words out of my head, I watched a dozen baseballs cut paths across the field as both teams warmed up for my first full game as head coach.

Looking back at that day in Shreveport, with the split audience and the rising heat, I should've seen it coming.

But I was too busy fashioning my roster and savoring all the details of the ballpark. I wanted to remember everything about this moment. The grass was bright green and freshly cut, and the chalk lines were sharp and straight. According to J.L., this field had been built just two years ago, and the twelve-foot-high outfield fence, coated in advertisements, looked twice as tall as the fences we'd seen at countless other fields.

"Going to put *un béisbol* over that," Buddha Rodriguez said as my team filed into the dugout, pointing a thick finger at the wall. He was answered by the laughing jeers and rolling eyes of his teammates around him in the dugout.

A loud rustle of paper caught my attention from the white section of the crowd. A set of pale fingers held up a newspaper that read "Germans Use Paris Gun to Kill Dozens on Good Friday."

The words made my breath catch in my throat and the smile evaporate from my face. I wanted to go out there and grab that paper to read more of the horrific news of this unending war.

Or, even better, instead of reading the paper, I'd just grab it from the white man's hands and tear it to shreds. People came to our games to escape the bleak dispatches from Europe. How dare he bring that paper, and the war, to our exhibition games?

I looked down at my roster, but couldn't read it for the shaking of my hand. This damn war was going to infect us all. It would take a miracle to keep my players out of it. Or magic. Probably both.

Waiting for the tremors to leave, I thought about how, back in the day, Maddie and I had carried on an ongoing discussion—one that usually verged on becoming an argument, especially toward the end—about miracles versus magic. Maddie's faith was always stronger than mine, even in those early years of our marriage when I had been filled with the zeal of a new convert, so she remained quite emphatic about the likelihood of miracles.

Miracles I had trouble with, but magic, well, I could believe in *that*. I saw plenty of it in baseball. Wondrous things happened on the diamond that I could never foresee, whether it was a wild pitch smothered impossibly in the dirt by our mostly blind catcher, or a home run foretold by our centerfielder before he even got in the batter's box.

That's what kept me coming back to this game I loved. The unexpected moments of magic.

Even if one of those moments almost got us killed that day.

Play ball!" the ump shouted, and I forgot about Maddie and our discussions of the unknown as I turned my attention, at last, back to the game.

I'm sorry to say that my team got off to an inauspicious start. The Shreveport Sports were semi-pros from the Texas League, and they should never have posed much of a challenge to us. But three All Nations batters went to the plate at the top of the first inning, and all three came marching back without a hit. Even though most of us had slept last night on the floor of the hotel kitchen downtown, this wasn't like my team.

As the game progressed, I noticed a tension in my team, especially my white players. Out on the field, they kept ducking their heads at the slightest sound, as if caught in the middle of an unsavory act more despicable than playing with a mixed-race ball group. Maybe it was due to the divided crowd, half of them too boisterous, the other half much too quiet.

Carrie at second and Art at third kept themselves busy inching forward, then creeping back, their eyes hidden under the shadow made by their caps. The knot on Boles' forehead had receded enough for him, perched on the mound, to pull his cap down low over his flushed red face.

I swallowed hard as Boles' knot made me recall the wicked bump on the side of Worrell's head that I'd dreamed up a few hours earlier on the bus.

I nodded at No Small Foot behind the plate, though I doubted the big man catcher could see the gesture—he was mostly blind in his right eye, and his vision seemed pretty questionable in his left—but he hunkered down behind the batter anyway and began flashing signals at Boles on the mound.

Soon I was caught up in the opening strategies of the game, and I hardly noticed when Donaldson got up and walked over to the jug of water. He took a drink from the dipper and offered it to me.

After I took a quick sip—"Strike two!" the ump called, to scattered boos from the white side of the crowd—Donaldson took the dipper and sat next to me with it still in his darn, slender hands.

We watched Boles rear back on one leg before unleashing his towering fastball with a grunt. The Sports batter didn't even get to finish his swing before the ball slapped into No Small Foot's tiny mitt.

One out, bottom of the first.

"They lynched a man here last night," Donaldson said.

I'd gotten so caught up in the game that I found myself cheering on Boles the loudmouth, and I almost missed what

Donaldson had said. The smile froze on my face. Boles made the second Sports hitter pop up to Buddha at first for the next out.

Donaldson continued, not looking at me as he spoke.

"A colored man. He was walking down the wrong side of the street on a Friday night, and he looked at a white couple in a *disrespectful* way. They strung him up at the edge of town and hung him. Right here, in this town, Coach."

At the far end of the bench, Mendez had taken out his cornet, which he sometimes played for the crowd after our games. His coal-black fingers tapped the trio of bronze valves in a silent song. Old Blount was sawing logs next to him with his feet up on the splintery bench, a line of drool leaking from his mouth.

Old Blount. The man was probably a decade older than me, though like so many of us former slaves, he had no record of his birth. He may have been younger than me for all I knew.

"Heard it from my aunt who lives down here. Never mind today's paper. Wasn't in there. I checked."

I once again noticed that there wasn't a trace of the usual fun-loving behavior breaking loose from the colored stands behind us. No shouting, no singing, no laughing; just a strained silence.

Now I knew why. We were sitting on a powder keg, waiting for someone to ignite it.

"Think you might've had a point about hell, Coach."

The sharp crack of the bat kept me from having to respond to Donaldson. The white crowd roared with the hit, setting my teeth on edge.

The hit ball climbed in a sharp arc toward deep center.

"It's going over!" a raspy, almost hoarse voice shouted from the white bleachers. "Home run!"

Judging by the angle of the ball, I would've agreed with the owner of that voice—if Mack hadn't been playing centerfield. As always, Mack was smack-dab in the middle of the action. And with a cold trail of certainty running down my back, I could see what he was getting ready to do. If I were still the betting man I once was, I would've put my money on our centerfielder, not the ball.

"Oh, Coach," Donaldson said, his voice almost a moan.

"Yeah," I said. "Mack's got it."

The ball was going to clear the fence easily, by close to ten feet if my eye hadn't lost its ability to judge distances. But I doubted the young white hitter from the Shreveport Sports would get his four-base knock. Not on this hit.

You see, the reason I put Mack in center was that nothing ever got by him, no matter how hard the ball was hit, no matter which part of the outfield the ball went. Unlike Worrell, the kid never took his eye off the ball.

Well, I have to admit, *almost* nothing got by Mack—only three batters in the past five seasons had ever homered off his centerfielding magic, and Mack had claimed that those three colored hitters would all end up in something he called a baseball Hall of Fame one day. I'd only laughed at the idea, then.

I wasn't laughing now as Mack charged at the twelve-foot-high fence in deep center.

Mack's got it, I wanted to tell the hitter. Maybe next time, kiddo.

"Better wake Old Blount," I said. "We may need to get to the bus, soon."

Two strides away from the wooden fence, Mack launched himself forward and upward. I leaned as far as I could out of the dugout to follow the lithe young man's slashing movements.

Mack planted the metal spikes of his left, then his right, and then his left foot again into the wood of the wall. His body surged up almost four feet with each vertical planting, passing billboard-sized ads for Hunter Rye and Ajax under his left foot, Cross-Cut Cigarettes and Bushmill's Whiskey under his right.

Still moving as fluidly and dangerously as quicksilver, he set his right foot on top of the fence and propelled himself up until his gloved right hand stopped the ball.

Ten feet above the fence, defying gravity as always, he launched the ball toward Boles on the mound, and then he kicked his legs over his head and flipped twice before landing soft as a cat on the grassy outfield, knees bent and arms flung wide.

Boles caught the ball on the fly and dropped it, pulling his hand free of his glove and massaging it from the impact of the throw, cussing the whole time.

The inning was over. The chaos in the white section of the stands, however, was just beginning.

The white men sitting closest to the home dugout were already on their feet, shouting that they'd been robbed.

I glanced back and saw a tall white figure slipping through the crowd, his build somehow familiar to me as he bent from one ear to another, gesturing at the field with his long arms. Then the figure was lost in the clamor and chaos of the other white men as they leaped to their feet.

"Circus act," they called Mack's acrobatics, along with "Cheating nigger" and "Goddamn monkey" and countless other insults we'd all heard so many times before.

After a long moment of shocked silence at what Mack had just done, the colored half of the crowd had burst at last into spontaneous cheering and applause. At the sound of the insults from across the bleachers, the colored men stopped clapping and stood up as well. The wick leading to the powder keg had been lit.

"You sure about that lynching?" I said to Donaldson as the cheers faded and the shouting intensified.

"'Fraid so," Donaldson said, giving me a look of such sadness that the young man's face looked as old as the one I saw each morning in my shaving mirror. Mendez, cornet in hand, was poking Old Blount to wake him. "Should we make a run for it?"

"Just wait," I said, watching Mack approach us from centerfield, smiling, with a glint of light in his eyes. Instead of filling me with dread, however, that light gave me a surge of confidence. "Yes. Let's see how this plays out."

By this time, all the members of the All Nations had jogged back to the infield, but none of them had made a move to the bench. They stood just outside the dugout, armed only with their baseball gloves and their hard-traveling ways.

The shouting white men pushed toward us and the single entrance opening onto the field, which was right next to our dugout. I thought I saw the rail-thin white man from the hat shop in that crowd, tall as Worrell and looking just as mean, his mouth still filled with needles and pins.

The white men were cursing and pushing past women and children, as if their anger had been rekindled by being reminded that colored men—not to mention men of other backgrounds and nationalities—still existed in *their* world, soiling it for them.

"*Tear them apart!*" a caustic voice yelled, cutting through the other shouts and curses.

The wave of anger spilling through the crowd took me back to the days after the fourth of July of 1910, back in Nevada, when Jack Johnson trounced Jim Jeffries to become the first colored boxing champion of the world. Johnson's victory was no miracle—the miracle was that he'd been able to hold up Jeffries for as many rounds as he did.

All baseball games in the area were postponed due to the fight, including the game for the colored team I was coaching at the time. I got caught up in one of the riots, and one of my players had been almost beaten to death in an alley.

"Don't be too proud," the newspapers had editorialized to us celebrating black men back then. "Don't let your heads lift too high because of this lone victory."

Too proud. Can you believe that?

I'd hoped such a thing would never happen again, but then, I'd always been a fool. That same frenzied look I remembered from the crowds in Nevada now filled the eyes of the white men approaching our dugout.

"Have a seat, gentlemen, Carrie," I said, stepping up to the entrance to our dugout with the tiniest jolt of pain in my old knees. My voice sounded much calmer than I could've hoped it would be. Or so I hoped. "This isn't our fight. We're just here for the game."

As if spurred on by our brave stand, a line of men formed in front of the colored bleachers. Faces that ranged from night black to brownish-tan to high yellow now turned to the outraged band of white men storming their way to the All Nations dugout.

I quietly began passing out bats, motioning for my players to keep them down, out of sight. We'd make one last stand here, if we had to.

"Let 'em play, I tell ya," a deep, drawling voice called out from the colored stands. I could have sworn I'd heard that voice before, years ago.

That distinct voice sounded just like Derby Molton, one of my former teammates from the deep south, but that was impossible. Derby had died in a train wreck when we were both in our thirties.

More voices joined that first deep voice from the colored side. "It was a fair catch, can't argue with that."

"Put away the rope for once," another voice added.

"Let 'em *play*!"

All of my players held a bat except for Mendez. I hadn't noticed until now that my burly pitcher from Cuba had pushed his way out of the dugout and onto the field. He now stood on the pitcher's mound, all alone. The sun glinted off something metallic in his big, dusky hands.

I was about to yell at him to get out of there, but then he took a deep breath, and a piercing wail filled the air.

The angry voices were temporarily silenced as everyone turned toward the field. When they saw Mendez, my players dropped their bats at the same time, creating a scattered drumbeat.

Mendez held up his shining cornet as he gathered in another breath. When he blew into his battered instrument this time, a spicy, New Orleans-style rendition of "When the Saints March In for Crowning" covered the field with notes as fat as Thanksgiving turkeys.

By the end of the first verse, which I recalled had something to do with being reunited on a new and sunlit shore, I could almost feel the air being released from the balloon of indignation elevating the white fans. They coughed and elbowed one another, as if waking from a tumultuous dream, and started turning from the cluster of colored men blocking them from our dugout.

Both groups inched back to their seats, singing or talking about Mack's catch or nodding their heads in time to Mendez's music. Many of them did quick dance steps as they made their way back to their spots on the bleachers.

Just like that, the situation was defused.

Just like magic.

"O lord, how I wan' be in that number," that deep, familiar voice belted out from somewhere behind and above me.

I had to smile, thinking about my old friend Derby. Maybe he had some kin in the Shreveport area. His death had been so sudden and unexpected that none of us on the team truly could comprehend that he was gone.

At the end of the third verse, Mendez lowered his horn with a big smile. On his way into the dugout, he walked past Mack, whose eyes were wide and white again, almost glowing. I tore my gaze from my centerfielder.

"Hope you don't mind I played now 'stead of after the game, Coach," Mendez said, a nervous smile on his coal-black face.

"Not at all," I said, patting him on the shoulder as the rest of my players came up to do the same. "Your timing was perfect, son."

"Play ball!" the umpire shrieked.

Those familiar words brought more relief to me than anything I'd heard in ages. I exhaled for what felt like the first time in ten minutes and rubbed my throat, imagining what the lynched man must have felt last night as the rope pulled tight with a sudden jerk and the world went black.

How would he have felt if the rope had broken, or the knot had come loose, just in time? I had a pretty good sense of how that may have felt.

I stood at the entrance to our dugout and turned in a slow circle, trying my best to take it all in so I could remember every detail—the shouted threats of war, the impossible beauty of Mack's catch, the rage and determination of both crowds, the shining sound of Mendez's cornet. I wondered at all the things people do to each other when they're alive.

Was it magic or madness? Miracles or nightmares?

"*I can tell you,*" a soft voice tinged with anger—or was it frustration?—whispered from behind me, turning the back of my neck cold. "*I know, now. I can... educate you, boy.*"

I almost spun at the sound of those words, but I refused to take the bait again. My knees wouldn't allow it.

"Don't bother," I whispered, thinking once more of Mack's impossible catch. Luckily, my players were still huddled around Mendez and didn't hear my mad chattering. "I can figure this out on my own."

As the touch of cold on my neck dissipated in the midday sun, I looked up at the bleachers behind me and watched the men and women—whites on the far side of the rope from me, the colored folk closer—talking and laughing as the game resumed. Just a few minutes ago, the two sides had been ready to tear into one another.

Maybe Maddie had been right about miracles, after all. Maybe a miracle would be enough, a starting point for something bigger here in the South, and perhaps even everywhere.

Which made me wonder: what other miracles and works of magic did the world still hold for this old, worn-out, faithless man? What more did I have left to discover in my dwindling lifetime?

As it turned out, my education at the hands of the strange, unpredictable mix of the World's All Nations players had already begun.

Chapter Four

One thing I've learned in my fifty years of playing ball around this country was that if you put a group of players together on a bus, dugout, or cramped hotel room, they'll talk more than a bunch of hens waiting for a wayward rooster to return. Gossip was often the glue that held a team together in the long hours of travel and waiting between games, and my All Nations players were no exception.

Apparently, Donaldson had told the others of the discussion we'd had over a week ago on the bus about Worrell, and heaven and hell. That had to be why, halfway through our first game against the Elks of Rocky Mount, North Carolina, I barely had time to flash signals to No Small Foot while my team was outfield.

Donaldson's fellow pitcher Mendez hound me, chattering the whole time in his staccato voice about his beliefs regarding faith and the afterlife. Information I never solicited, thank you very much.

"There is the *Orisha*, you see, who serve *Olorun*, or *Olódùmarè*, and they protect us like, well, like you hear people talk of guardian angels, right? Maybe the Coach Worrell should've given an offering to the *Orisha*. They are everywhere, you know. We see them in the flash of lightning, in the stones, in rivers and lakes. All over the world. Even right here in this baseball diamond. *Comprendé*, Coach?"

I took off my cap and fanned myself with it in the mid-May heat of the South. My eyes ached from lack of sleep— my dreams had been especially unsettling last night in the hot, crowded tent we'd set up on this very field last night.

Something about falling from the sky as fireworks exploded all around me, the same dream three nights in a row. At least I woke up each time before I hit the ground.

After watching Boles fire a fastball across the plate that the batter tipped right into No Small Foot's gloved hand, I turned around. Mendez was two steps behind me, gazing at me with an expectant—and slightly impatient—look on his dark face.

"*Comprendé*, Coach?" he asked again, tugging down the bill of his cap.

I gave him a nod, but Mendez continued following me and chattering away. One of these days, I vowed, I'd get Mendez to teach me Spanish; something was surely getting lost in translation here.

"You see now how the *Orisha* can help us, if we give them the sacrifices they desire? They like chicken, you see. Maybe we could call to an oracle to see how the Coach Worrell and his soul is doing, or maybe we could hold a ritual and sacrifice a chicken or two for good luck someday—"

"Yes, of course," I said. I glanced at the scoreboard with a barely stifled yawn and saw we had just a one-run lead. The crowd was listless from the heat behind us, clapping every minute or so as if doing penance.

"Sure," I added, with what I hoped was authority.

My head ached from Mendez's theories about the guardian angels of Santería, and my knees complained from all the pacing I was doing to unsuccessfully avoid him. I was going to have to have a talk with Donaldson for getting me into this.

At last the third out was made on a shallow fly to center that sent Mack sprinting infield, until he was ten feet from second base. He beat both infielders, Carrie and Phil, to the ball by half a dozen steps. Without pausing he jogged on a dozen or so long strides, right into the dugout, grinning and nodding at me.

I would've gladly listened to some of his nonsensical predictions about the world in the years to come instead of talking about religion with Mendez. All that talk brought back too many memories of Maddie for me, not to mention a growing sense of shame at the faithless man I'd become in her eyes.

But I still wasn't out of the woods of player confessionals.

I spent the tops of the fifth and sixth innings talking—if you can call it that—with Phil the Philippine, my shortstop. As Phil threw an impenetrable volley of words my way in his native tongue, his breath smelling of fish and tobacco, I looked around, wondering if maybe Mendez's *Orisha* guardians were listening to this and, if they were, could they possibly help me out?

I simply couldn't comprehend a word Phil was saying. Something about walking down a winding path and the sun shining in your eyes, I think. But I was just guessing; his English wasn't so much broken as random as a handful of sand that was constantly slipping through your fingers. Phil spoke the wordless language of baseball, and not much more.

When he paused to take a breath, I finally nodded at the long-armed man with the dark amber skin and put a hand on his shoulder. Boles had just popped out to first for our third out of the sixth inning.

"I understand now, Phil. Thank you. You can go play ball. Go. *Please.*"

At the top of the seventh, I was starting to feel a bit ill from the heat and my fatigue, when Charlie Grant sidled up to me, already talking.

"It all has to do with the Great Spirit, you see," he began, as if continuing a conversation we'd started a few minutes earlier. Giving off a rank odor of sweat and unwashed clothes, Charlie ran a hand through the feathers I was supposed to have demanded him to stop wearing. Knowing his history and his slightly unbalanced mind, I just couldn't do it.

"The Great Spirit's who we believe in, you see. He's to my people what God is to your people, of course, except he visits me every now and then, in the shape of a giant eagle. That's where these feathers came from. He dropped in on me when I was in the majors, when I first realized my true nature."

Charlie looked away, a sudden storm brewing in his dark brown eyes.

"Before that bastard Cap Anson," he spat, "and that fool Comiskey stuck their noses in my business and had me kicked out, calling me a *Negro*, of all things. I've never been so insulted."

"Now wait a moment—" I began, now breathing through my mouth, but Charlie kept talking.

"I was going to be a real player, on a real team with real transportation—the fanciest cars and best train compartments—instead of all *this*." He waved a disparaging hand at his faded uniform, the black letters on his chest worn away by too many dives across right field, too many headfirst slides into third. "Even my time with the Page Fence Giants was better than this. Now those gentlemen knew how to travel. All *we* have is our joke of a bus."

"Charlie," I said, smacking his arm, but the man wouldn't stop talking. "Charlie! You're on deck! Get out of here."

Without batting an eye, he grabbed a piece of wood from the dozen bats spread out in a line in front of the unfenced dugout.

"I just wanted to play ball," he continued. "If they had to make me a redblood so I could play with the best in the world, why, they could call me Chief. If I had to believe in the Great Spirit and sleep in a teepee, I'd do it. I tell you, Coach..."

"I give up," I muttered, turning away from Charlie so I could watch Carrie Nation crack a line drive into right. Her hit nearly took off No Small Foot's head as he barreled from first to second. But somehow, our stout, mostly blind catcher managed to duck under the screaming ball, round second, and chug on to third.

"Tell you more later," Charlie said, on his way to the plate, giving me a jaunty grin and a wink.

Immediately, the crowd began taunting him, hundreds of hands patting open mouths as they made crowing battle cries. Wincing at the sound, thinking of Mack's words—"But if people forget us, I sense the game will become a novelty"—I flashed the signals to Charlie and No Small Foot for the suicide squeeze we'd need for an insurance run. We'd give them something to talk about after this game was history, something to remember us by.

As far as I could tell, however, Charlie was receiving his signals from the Great Spirit.

He neglected to bunt and instead swung away, hitting a lazy pop-up to right to end the inning. No Small Foot was left running down the third-base path toward home. A thundercloud would have paled next to the furious expression on my Cherokee catcher's face.

I gave No Small Foot a warning look that I knew he saw, bad eyes and all, but doubted he would heed. Luckily, Charlie was already in right field, pulling on his glove. I could see his lips moving and his head shaking back and forth as he talked to himself out there.

In the dugout next to me, No Small Foot unleashed a low series of curse words as he retrieved his beat-up mitt and homemade catcher's mask, which looked more like a padded birdcage than a protective guard for his face.

The day grew hotter and more humid, and the stands continued to fill with fans that had arrived on foot, many of them carrying picnic baskets and blankets. All the women wore their finest hats, and they led their men and children to the grassy sidelines and the outfield, where the slope of the land allowed them to easily see the action over the low, unpainted fence. All of the spectators deserved a better game than we were presenting them.

The Elks were a colored semi-pro team, so the people in the stands and spread across the grass today were, without exception, colored; whites rarely attended when we played teams that were not also white.

I felt my usual sense of relief at this, especially after the ugly scene in Shreveport last week. I smiled at a pair of young kids, a girl and a boy, trying to keep up as their parents headed for the grass on the first-base side. The little girl's curly black hair stuck out on either side of her head like a pair of Charlie's crazy feathers.

Lizbeth's hair had been even curlier than that, I thought, tight corkscrews that Maddie was always trying to tame with hats, brushes, and occasional scissors.

I shook my head at the memory. Not today, I told myself, not in the middle of a game. Even if I was dog-tired and working on too many broken nights of bad sleep than I could count. I couldn't take my eye off the ball again, not for a foolish dream about reuniting with my family.

I had a sudden urge for a player to come annoy me with some foolish talk about heaven, hell, or purgatory.

But nobody spoke to me again until just before the bottom of the eighth. With my team leading now by two runs and every player sweating and gasping for breath in the thick, humid air, No Small Foot stepped up and gave me a long look with his good left eye.

"Where's your chew, Coach?" he said, his constant squint narrowing even further. "Don't like Red Man no more?"

"Must have left it at home," I muttered.

No Small Foot inched closer and pushed his battered catcher's mask to the top of his head, so that his mask looked like a makeshift raft traveling down the dark river of his long black hair.

"What's that fool Grant been talking to you about? I know he ain't been listening to you coaching, the way he left me hanging at third in the sixth. His mouth's been running like a dog in heat."

"Personal beliefs, John," I said. I figured an honest approach was best; I was too old to be sneaky anymore.

"Shit," No Small Foot said.

He hit himself in the leg with his catcher's mitt, creating a burst of dust that lingered in the air like a cloud. He whisked it away with a wave of his gnarled hand.

"He's *no* Cherokee. He ain't from any tribe I ever heard of—hell, I can see that with my bad eye!"

I smiled at No Small Foot and pointed at home plate, where the ump was waiting for him so they could start off the last at-bat for the home team. No Small Foot grunted in response and pulled down his metal mask.

"Don't believe a single word," he said before departing, his voice muffled but still loud enough for most of the crowd to hear. He ended up jogging halfway to first before the ump called him over to home plate. How the big man caught every pitch and never let the ball past him remained a mystery to me.

Boles ended the inning, and the game, on a strikeout, a weak pop-up, and a trio of fastballs that the last Elk hitter didn't even bother trying to swing at. We came away with a win for the first game of our doubleheader, but my mind wasn't on victory. I was thinking about that dry, whispering voice back in Kansas City, and my haunted dream of the plantation as we entered Shreveport.

Had that been Worrell each time? And had he somehow been at the Shreveport game, inciting the white men in the crowd? Or was I simply starting to lose what few marbles I had left?

All questions, no answers in sight.

Feeling a wave of fatigue roll over me, I put away my roster and pencil. Instead of plotting out the next game's strategy, I grabbed a seat down at the far end of the dugout, closest to first base.

I had an hour before our next game. As my players lined up for a chance at the water barrel or escaped the dugout for some shade and possibly some local female companionship under the magnolia trees behind the bleachers, I closed my eyes and went immediately to sleep.

At first, I encountered only the blissful dark of a dreamless, bone-weary sleep. I thought I just might remain in that senseless state forever, but something began picking at the fabric of my sleep, like a termite at the frame of a house. Soon the termite had invited all his friends over, and they brought with them strange images: falling eagle feathers, lines of plucked and headless sacrificial chickens, and gods that slowly rose up from the rocks of the path below me. Not a single familiar icon among them—no crosses, no men with beards and mournful eyes, not even a white lamb.

And as I dreamed, I once again heard that voice that had been dogging my heels and ruining my rest ever since our April Fool's Day game against the Maroons.

"*Are you about done,*" that voice said from somewhere ahead of me on the roadway littered with rocks and feathers, "*attempting to figure all of this out on your own?*"

There was a pause, followed by a snide, drawling, "*Coach?*"

Turn away, I told myself in the dream. He's not really here.

"*Do you see any branches on this road?*" Worrell said with a dry laugh. "*There's no turning away.*"

He stood in front of me now, still wearing his dusty uniform stained on the left side with blood. He held a sticky, brownish-black baseball in his right hand. One spiked shoe rested on top of a pile of dead, plucked-clean chickens. The obscene lump on his temple was a garish purple and red color.

I looked down and saw a trio of eagle feathers in each of my hands. If only I could use these six feathers to fly away from here, or to at least tickle myself into wakefulness.

"*This path is one-way,*" Worrell continued, "*and I daresay you are approaching its terminus. I am certain your players have reassured you of what you will find there, at the end of your road. Coach."*

I didn't want to, but I had to look. Behind me was nothing, the rocky road dropping off right at my heels. I let go of the feathers in my hands, and they too were eaten up by nothingness.

Worrell nodded and rubbed two greasy fingers over the lumpy baseball in his hands. The bloody pile of sacrificial chickens under him had turned into a pitcher's mound. I clamped my mouth shut, refusing to let him goad me into speaking to him and acknowledging his control over me.

I contemplated simply stepping off the path and into the arms of Mendez's gods, but the blackness on either side of me was too vast. I didn't dare.

"You have been continuing to win in my absence," Worrell said, kicking a leg and leaning into his windup. He froze like that, on one leg, and glared at me. *"Not a single loss this far. I wouldn't have given you credit for such a string of wins, boy."*

His unexpected, left-handed compliment surprised the words out of my mouth.

"I didn't mean for you to get hit," I blurted out, off-balance on the rocky path that seemed to grow more narrow with each passing moment.

Somewhere in the distance, I could hear footsteps approach, either from behind Worrell or behind me. I was so disoriented, I simply couldn't tell.

Worrell let out a barking laugh and twisted his lanky body through the rest of his windup, but he never launched his greased-up junk ball at me.

"That's rich," he spat, holding out his unpitched ball as if showing it to me. His voice was heavy with disdain, but the expression had softened in his face. He looked less certain of himself, for once.

At that point, I realized I could see through him. A pinprick of white light grew behind him, growing like a train approaching in the distance.

"Guilt isn't one of the seven deadly sins, you know..." As he spoke, I could hear more footsteps now, and the distant gurgle of many voices. *"But maybe it should be number eight."*

"Don't get me wrong," I said, "I never said anything about feeling guilty."

I was surprised at how good it felt to speak my mind to Worrell. I should never have waited until he was dead to start doing it.

Worrell made his best attempt at a sneer, but only succeeded in looking like a spoiled child. He continued fading as the light behind him grew brighter.

"I'm watching you," he said as he pointed a nearly-transparent finger at me, and I felt my heart clench. White light filled the void behind him and then engulfed him, but his harsh voice remained.

"We're all *watching you. And I daresay... We don't... approve..."*

I woke with a start, chin on my chest and drenched in sweat. Next to me sat No Small Foot's discarded mitt and mask, though he was nowhere to be found. I just hoped he and Charlie hadn't run into each other out by the food stands, unsupervised.

Worrell's strange words from my dream echoed in my head along with the pounding of my blood. I blinked sweat from my eyes and caught sight of Phil the Philippine sitting under a magnolia tree, talking and gesturing emphatically to a confused-looking Art Houdini and Jose Mendez.

Like walking down a winding path and the sun shining in your eyes, I thought. Judging from my dream, Phil just may have been on to something.

Behind me, the town band began playing a gospel song, and I had to smile. It was a tune I'd first heard on the plantation, except the band had sped it up so it sounded more like a jig than a dirge.

"*There is a balm in Gilead,*" a pair of familiar voices sang out at my back, one low and baritone, the other reedy and overloud. "*To make the wounded whole. There is a balm in Gilead—to heal the sin-sick soul.*"

As the song continued, I turned and saw Donaldson and Boles perched on opposite sides of the bleachers behind our dugout. Both of them were singing along with the band. When they heard each other's voices, their mouths snapped shut almost simultaneously, without looking at the other.

Listening to the music, I felt the last dregs of my dream and my fatigue melt away. My sweat cooled me in the mid-day heat, and I nodded as a capless Rodriguez walked past me in front of the dugout. I sat up straight when I saw that the big man was carrying four sausages wrapped in bread in one hand and a greasy bag of popcorn in the other.

"Easy, there, son," I called out. "You've got another game today, and it's starting soon."

"*Tengo hambre,*" Buddha Rodriguez said around a mouthful of meat and bread. "Hungry, Coach. Need to stay strong. *Mucho hambre.*"

I stepped out of the shaded dugout at last and inhaled the familiar scents of magnolia blossoms and fried food drifting over to me. My belly rumbled, though my appetite had dwindled sharply in the past few weeks. Above me, the Carolina sky was clear and bright, the air thick with humidity.

I took another heavy breath of the hot air, amazed at how each park had the same feel, wherever it was located. No matter how poor or small the community, the grass on the field was always manicured, the lines always chalked with care and precision, and the oversized signs on the outfield fences always freshly painted.

All that changed from town to town were the people in the crowd and the names and logos on the signs. There was a sense of rightness to that.

Behind me, the younger male spectators milled around, smoking cigarettes and flirting with the ladies, while the older men puffed on cigars or took a quick pull from small, hidden flasks.

One of the women still sitting in the half-empty stands, most likely hoping to inspire the jealousy of the lanky young man in a dark brown suit next to her, waved her handkerchief at me with a big smile. I gave her a smile before looking away, marveling at how long it had been since I'd properly flirted with a woman.

Too long, old man, I told myself, my old knees suddenly weak. Besides, you'd just embarrass yourself if you tried. Maddie would laugh at my feeble attempt, if she were here. I *was* still married to her, for all intents and purposes.

Before I turned back to my roster, I caught sight of a few white faces lingering at the edge of the bleachers closest to our dugout. There, working his way back to his seat and balancing a plate of pulled-pork barbecue in his hand, was a familiar round-shouldered figure.

"J.L.," I called out. Usually the owner of the All Nations team showed up at games closer to home, so I was surprised to see him here. I certainly hoped he was scouting for some new players. We needed them, badly.

J.L. waved at me with his fork and gestured at the open seat next to him.

I paused, the smile frozen on my face. Surely he didn't want me to sit next to him in the white section. What would the people around him think?

But before I could leave the dugout, I heard the thump of two bodies colliding, followed by the sound of fist meeting flesh, a sound I'd never be able to forget.

I spun too fast in the midday heat and nearly reeled on my feet when I saw two of my players wrestling in the dirt around home plate.

"I'll show *you* the Great Spirit," No Small Foot shouted, sitting on top of Charlie. His black hair hung like a curtain over his face as he leaned close to our rightfielder to shake a fist in his face. "Right here, you lousy faker!"

"Get off me!" Charlie shrieked back, throwing dirt into No Small Foot's good eye and trying to squirm free.

"Break it up!" I shouted as I moved toward the two men wrestling in the dirt. No Small Foot clubbed Charlie in the eye with another dull smack. With my next step, my right knee gave a deep twinge.

Luckily, my players got there before me. Phil and Mendez did their best to pull away the growling No Small Foot. Meanwhile, my third baseman Art Houdini had put some sort of headlock on Charlie, rendering the darker-skinned man motionless.

All five of my players were coated in mud as the dirt from the field mixed with their own sweat. Charlie's right eye was starting to swell shut.

"Take them into the dugout," I said with a glance back at J.L. in the stands. Why did he have to be here to witness this?

Worrell had to be laughing and laughing somewhere nearby.

"He insults my heritage!" No Small Foot said.

The big man pulled hard in his attempt to break free from the men holding him back. The wiry Phil wasn't about to release his grip, but Mendez got his spikes entangled with those of No Small Foot. Both of them went down in a clump. Mendez hit first, landing with a yelp.

"Damn it all anyway," I hissed, ignoring the pain in my knees as I pulled No Small Foot off of Mendez. Our Cuban pitcher rolled to his feet holding his pitching arm. His eyes were closed, and his mouth was clamped shut in a tight line of pain.

"Get in the dugout!" I roared at the other players. My vision was tinged with red as I turned back to Mendez. "Jose? You all right, son?"

"I'm okay," he said. "I think I just... need to rest my arm... a bit... Don't worry. I can still pitch."

"Careful," I said, leading him back into the dugout. Fortunately, the fight had gone out of No Small Foot, otherwise I would've ended up with a roster filled with the walking wounded, like a heroic platoon of soldiers torn apart by the onrushing Huns. The big Cherokee was unstoppable when he lost his temper.

"I'll deal with you two later," I told him and Charlie before I stuck my head out of the dugout. "Is there a doctor in the house?"

Luckily, a man had already pulled himself free from the crowd of people standing at the fence and watching the fight. J.L. followed the colored man into the dugout, and they gathered around Mendez.

I took a step back and was rewarded with what felt like an ice pick of pain jabbing into my knee. I dropped onto the bench next to No Small Foot, gasping for breath.

"I'm a Cherokee, you see," No Small Foot muttered to Phil the Philippine, who was standing guard over him. Phil nodded sagely as he patted the downcast Indian's shoulder, though I doubted the islander understood a word of what our catcher said. "I am no holy instrument of a Great Spirit or a God, as they say. I just try to live properly and to avoid doing wrong in my lifetime. That's all I was trying to explain." No Small Foot looked over at me. "Coach, you have to understand that."

"I'm not sure if I like the way you use your *fists* to explain your beliefs," I said, watching the physician from the crowd use a pair of towels to stabilize Mendez's throwing arm tight against his chest. I looked back at No Small Foot. "Doesn't the world have enough fighting the way it is?"

"*Coach,*" Carrie Nation said in a sharp voice. "We have got a problem over here. Another one."

"Now what?" I groaned, following the angle of Carrie's pointed finger.

Forgotten on the edge of the infield, three feet from first, Rodriguez lay crumpled on his side like a discarded paper bag, a half-eaten hot dog in his right hand.

"Buddha's down!" Boles shouted, charging out of the dugout.

"Please do not be calling him that," Goro muttered on his way past me. "Please do not."

"He's *shivering*, Coach," Boles called out from where he and Carrie were hunched over Rodriguez. That was Boles for you. Always trying to be the hero while getting someone else to do the dirty work.

Pushing away my petty thoughts, I limped out to our fallen Mexican flanked by the white boy and white woman. I had a flash of dreadful insight that nearly made me stop in my tracks as I recalled how I'd left the dugout that night in Kansas City to limp up to Worrell's unmoving body. Buddha looked just as lifeless.

Something was plaguing my team. Maybe we were *cursed*.

But this time, from five steps away I could see that the downed member of my team was still breathing. We hadn't lost anyone else. At least not yet.

And so, I couldn't help myself—I gave Buddha a soft kick when I reached him. He responded with a groan and a loud breaking of wind.

"Heat stroke?" Carrie asked, grimacing as she helped him sit up.

"Could be," I said, but I was cut off by loud belch from Buddha, sitting in the dirt, legs spread wide, like a gassy baby after a particularly vigorous feeding.

"Let's get him to his feet," I said, breathing through my mouth.

With the help of Carrie, Boles, and Art Houdini once again—not wanting to lose another pitcher, I ordered Donaldson out of Buddha's path when Donaldson tried to lend a hand—I was able to bring our moaning, shivering first baseman back to the dugout.

As Buddha slurped up some water, the doctor looked him over.

"He looks fine," the doctor said a few moments later, waving a hand under his own nose to clear the fog of Buddha's flatulence. "Just overheated and ate too much. A touch of heat stroke mixed in with dyspepsia. Probably in that order."

What a motley crew, I thought, surprised at how relieved I was that Buddha and Jose were going to be okay. And Charlie's right eye was swollen completely shut now. We'd be without the services of all three of them today, no doubt. I dug into my pocket for my roster so I could start making changes for the next game. How did I ever get to be so blessed?

"Hey Coach," Boles said. "Who's gonna play first for us?"

The question hung in the thick Carolina air until all eyes came to rest on me. I looked from my scratched-out roster to my players surrounding me in the dugout. Faces black and white, yellow and red, and all hues in between.

And then Mack was there at my side, eyes bright, a small smile on his thin lips, and a battered homemade cigarette in his mouth. A white cloud of foul-smelling smoke wreathed his head in a way that made fresh sweat break out on my arms. He'd conveniently disappeared during the chaos, I noticed.

The umpire was calling for our first hitter, and I stood there in the dugout, knees aching, as my team waited on me, needing me to take charge once again.

"You know what to do, Coach," Mack murmured, barely loud enough for me to hear. "All part of the team's destiny."

At least I thought that was what I thought I heard him say.

To hell with it. I gripped my roster and ripped it up. Like so many of my letters to members of my family I'd written in the past decade, I threw them in the garbage. Then I grabbed Mack's smoke and ground it into the dirt, glaring first at him and then the rest of my players.

"Let's give these folks what they paid money for," I said. I waved at the ump and pushed Art out of the dugout toward home plate with a bat. "Let's give 'em a baseball game, not a boxing match or a vaudeville show."

Worrell, I thought, you can laugh all you want, but we've got a game to win here, right at this moment. I certainly hope you *are* watching.

"All right," I called out, on the verge of laughing at both the situation as well as my own giddy enthusiasm about the upcoming game. I knew I was going to pay for this later, and I didn't care. "After Houdini, I've got Mack on deck, followed by Carrie, then No Small Foot—and if any of you lay a hand on one another, I'll throttle you myself."

This is my team, I thought. Let's do something memorable here today.

"And for Christ's sake," I added, glancing once more at our grinning centerfielder on his way to the on-deck circle, "someone get me Buddha's glove. We've all of us got a game to play."

Chapter Five

*M*y *Dearest Maddie:*

I am writing to you in the early hours before dawn, sitting in what was once a hot bath. A glorious bath, here on this most rare of occasions—a night in a hotel. I have just enough room to sit up straight, with this candle my only light. But I feel that I earned the right to this bath, even if the smell of magnesium sulfate is not the most endearing of odors in the world, and the water already grows cold.

Now Maddie, you know I'm not one to complain, but my knees ached so badly last night I couldn't sleep. So I've been soaking in this tub and thinking of you and waiting for the pain to go away, though I fear it never will. Not completely. The pain is not limited to just my knees, you see.

I wonder where you are right now, at this moment. What are you doing? And are you happy there? Do you think well of me, in spite of all I've done?

I can imagine your voice right now, saying, "Why should I even think of you, after all these years without you? Why should I care if your knees ache, Georgie? Especially now, with the war and so much suffering around the world?"

The answer to your questions, my dear, would have you laughing if you hadn't forgotten that skill years ago. Maybe you've relearned it, after all this time away from me.

You see, my team had a bit of a personnel problem yesterday. First, my catcher and right-fielder got into a fight about the real meaning of the Great Spirit. In the process they injured one of my best pitchers, Jose Mendez. Almost broke the elbow on Mendez's pitching arm.

Such an arm, too. Rumor has it that Mendez once killed a teammate when he accidentally hit him with a pitch in the chest in batting practice. And now he may never pitch again, all because of a fight between his teammates. Some example we are setting, I must say.

Then my first baseman, the slightly unbalanced fellow who claimed he was wounded in the revolution in Mexico a few years back, choked on his lunch and passed out from the heat.

And so, with Coach Worrell gone (struck and killed by a foul tip, in case you hadn't heard the news), my pitcher Mendez injured, my right-fielder Charlie unable to see out of his swollen eye, and Buddha fighting to stay conscious on the bench, I put our white pitcher Boles out in right.

I'll give you three guesses as to who got to play first base.

I'm not sure if you actually care about the fielding skills of yours truly, but I am not too proud to admit that I let no ball get past me that game, even the wild corkscrew throws that Houdini launched my way from third. I kept waiting for one or both of my knees to give out and leave me writhing in the dirt, but my old body actually held together. No errors in sight.

There I go again. My apologies, my love.

I know you don't like all this talk about baseball, Maddie, but I do want you to know about something amazing that happened during that second game of our doubleheader.

After just two innings, the Rocky Mount team found our weakness. Their hitters targeted Boles in right, and with good reason—the kid has no depth perception. In hindsight, I should've just left Charlie out there with his one good eye. Because Boles would either charge at a ball that would end up going over his head and bouncing off the outfield fence, or he'd stand waiting on a ball to drop into his glove only to have it land twenty feet in front of him. He was getting beat up, and so were we.

So when Boles misjudged yet another pop-up and paid the price when it caromed off his thick noggin and knocked him out—not an easy task, believe me—we threw ourselves on the mercy of the crowd.

We asked for a volunteer.

What the crowd gave us was a young fellow barely five feet high. The youngster's name was Buck Leonard.

The kid fit in with our style like a natural. All gangly arms and bony legs, he marched up to the plate with our biggest bat and swung away, even when the players from his own home town threw at his head and tried to convince him he didn't belong out there with the grown men.

But Buck stood his ground and smashed any ball close enough the strike zone for him to hit. A natural.

And we needed him. In that last game, with all of us running out of steam and half of us injured on the bench, the Rocky Mount Elks gave us a run for our money.

We had to use every trick in the book: I showed Buck how to drag a bunt from the lefty side of the batter box, and he made it to first twice on that one, while Mikado and Houdini showed him the joy of double steals. We ran squeeze plays all day, but by twilight, everyone was too exhausted to do more than jog the bases as night crept up on us.

Except for Buck. Nothing could stop him.

Batting left with one of the sweetest swings I'd ever seen, the kid got hits in four out of five at-bats. The other team started trying to walk him toward the end, but he'd chase the ball and make good contact each time, except for the one time when he accidentally stepped on the plate and was called out.

Of course I tried to sign the kid on to the team by the end of the game. Nobody told me that Buck was only ten years old. I just thought the young man was short for his age.

Ten years old. Unbelievable.

When I was ten, I was living for the game on the plantation, playing ball in the too-short hours after the work day was over, before the sun sank into the Carolina landscape. I remember wishing that the sun would sit on the horizon and just hold there, forever, so the game would never end. When I was ten, slavery still bound my people, though *the Emancipation Proclamation had been on the books for over a year. Slavery's end was fast approaching, though.*

Perhaps my centerfielder's latest prediction would prove true, and Buck wouldn't face the same kind of life I'd faced.

"So many teams, and every one of them mixed, like ours," Mack had said, out of the blue.

And if that prediction came true, that would mean Mack's other prophecy might come true as well, the one about—

But I'm digressing again, I know. Nevertheless, my love, my hopes of signing Buck got dashed yesterday.

The kid shakes my hand and gives me a smile, and then he says, "Maybe later, sir. I've got to finish grade school first."

You could've knocked me over with a feather.

And I've rambled on, my love, for far too long. I have so much more to tell you, but the water in this tub has grown stone cold, and the morning light creeping across the bathroom the wall tells me it's time to dry off, get dressed, and load the bus so we can travel to our next game.

I still wonder when I will talk to you next. I hope it will be sooner rather than later.

All my love and memories,
George H. Grunion

Cold, dirty water.

I sat there in the cooling water of the metal tub, naked, rubbing my writing hand, and stared at the pile of moist pages resting on the chair next to the tub. I'd lost myself again in the past. At least it was the recent past this time—yesterday's game and its odd, wonderful events. A game whose unexpected surplus of ticket sales had enabled us to splurge on a hotel for the first time on our road trip.

I heaved a sigh before getting out of the water, thinking about Worrell for some reason. How in that odd dream of mine between games, he'd claimed to be *watching* me. But he never showed up during the chaos of No Small Foot's attack on Charlie, or even when Buddha passed out. And who was he watching us with? The thought that he'd found companions in the afterlife was more than a little bit disconcerting.

As if echoing my thoughts, I heard through the open window of the hotel bathroom the distant gong of a church bell. It sounded four, five, six times.

I toweled myself dry and tried to read my blotchy handwriting on the pages next to me.

Just one last letter, I'd thought before climbing into the bath. One last letter, and maybe I'd even mail it this time. Like an old drunk, vowing to have just one last drink.

"I am a fool," I whispered. I gathered the ink-covered pages that had occupied me for the past two hours and dropped them into the gurgling, draining water of the tub.

I didn't watch to see if the words I'd just created on the soaked, curling pages would dissolve into nothingness like my fading memories of my family. I knew all I'd written would all be gone by the time I'd dressed and began the long process of gathering up the members of my team dispersed throughout this hotel. In fact, I was counting on it.

The real name of our Japanese leftfielder was Goro Mikami, but everyone on the team but me simply called him Jap. His last name had been mispronounced as "Mikado" so often that it stuck. J.L. claimed he kept saying it wrong because of some Gilbert and Sullivan play, but I had to take the team owner's word for it. My players and I were too busy playing ball and trying to make a couple dollars to make it to many operas or stage shows.

Just like I did for the rest of my players—except Carrie Nation and Mack, whose real names I'd probably never know, no matter how often I asked—I refused to call the young man by anything but his true name.

As he spoke to me on the bus, Goro's small, clean hands moved through the air to clarify his most recent point. He was determined to learn our language and culture, and he sat next to me under the pretense of discussing some of my various hand signals from the past few games.

That chat quickly turned to topics more spiritual in nature. I should have known better.

"Everything in the world," Goro said, "has *kami*. A spirit. Even rock, even animal, have spirit. Not just men. That why, ah, with Shinto, we have much respect. For all things outside, ah, in the world. Mack understand this, out in centerfield. He *always* respecting sun, honoring it. Smart man. He, um, stare at sun quite a bit."

I listened to my player's halting words along with the splattering sounds of our team bus getting coated in mud. We'd left Rocky Mount and Buck Leonard behind weeks ago, traveling north and west into the rocky edges of the rainy Appalachians, playing games every step of the way, headed for games in Tennessee and Indiana.

After that, we had four games in the Windy City on Independence Day with the Chicago American Giants, a team everyone considered to be the best Negro team in recent years. I was looking forward to seeing Rube Walker's team of bold hitters and fearless runners again on the Fourth of July. And I figured that we just might have the manpower to take a few from them this year, with Donaldson pitching at least one, more likely two, of those games.

I was punished for my distraction from Goro's story by nearly cracking my head on the roof of the bus as Blount dropped us into a huge hole in the road.

Yet another Blount shortcut. This time it was a dirt road through a narrow pass in the mountains, a road thick and slick with mud from the rain that had started as soon as Blount cranked the engine that morning.

I watched Goro's immaculately clean, almost delicate hands, putting the numbers out of my head and instead thinking once more about the lovely ladies in Rocky Mount at our game. The women had ignited a memory inside my head about Maddie and her hats, back in the days before she left.

Maddie loved her hats, I remembered. She had a pink one that she liked to wear whenever we were "stepping out," as she called it, a wide-brimmed boat of a hat with a trio of fresh flowers always pressed stem-first into its brim. She'd left the hat with me the day she took the kids and moved east, away from Chicago.

The day they left, she'd shielded both Lizbeth and Jacob from me with her ample hips, holding them tight against her as if I'd try to steal them away from her. The look on Jacob's tear-stained face was a mix of betrayal and what I foolishly hoped was sadness at leaving me.

Then they were past me, and all I could do was listen to the fading sound of their footsteps.

"There *is* life... after a life."

At the sound of those words, a sudden chill turned my skin to gooseflesh. It put me in mind of that whispering voice insinuating itself into my dreams at night. Worrell's lingering spirit, following me to torment me for not saving his life. Haunting my sleep, but absent from my waking hours this past week. I had to take comfort wherever it was given, in his case.

I looked over at Goro, his small, dark eyes narrowed with concentration and frustration as he tried to explain further. He didn't seem to notice my lack of attention. He threw a dark look behind us at Rodriguez, who'd been eavesdropping. Buddha gave Goro his widest, most innocent smile and rubbed his shiny bald head like a brass lamp.

"This life," Goro continued, chewing on his lower lip as he tried to lasso the right words floating around in his head, "is, ah, one of many. I not think like most other Shinto in Japan, you see."

He spun in his seat, lightning-quick, to see if Rodriguez was still listening over his shoulder. Buddha pretended to be sleeping. Goro sat back down with a sheepish look on his face.

"Please not tell anyone. I believe people, ah, come *back*. Their... *spirits*."

Yes, I wanted to say. I was well aware of how they came back. But why was it those we didn't want or need that decided to come back?

Goro continued on without me, rocking along with the bumps, eyes narrowing with every grunt and snore made by Buddha behind us.

"If spirits everywhere, then they always have new place to go, see? Some come back human, some come back—" he shot another look back at Rodriguez "—animal. Like a, ah, copying cat. Or... a bird that mocks."

I gazed at Goro with his straight black hair, which he always kept neatly cropped and combed forward, and his strangely lashless eyes. Caught up in my thoughts of my wife and her favorite hat, I realized I had no idea what my leftfielder was talking about.

I wracked my brain for the last thing Goro had said: A bird that mocks.

"A mockingbird? What does a mockingbird have to do with dying, Goro?"

"That only... example, Coach Grunion, sir," Goro spluttered. I realized that the Japanese man's ire was not directed at me, but at the grinning Rodriguez behind us.

"I think I understand," I said. "So there's nothing to fear about dying, for Worrell and the rest of us, because we all come back in some other shape. Right?"

"Death is a, ah, *fear*," Goro said after a pause. "But death also give..." He rubbed his chin, his mouth trying out the right words until he came across the right one: "*Hope*."

"Because that's not the end," I said, trying out one of my own theories on the afterlife. I couldn't help myself; the topic was endlessly fascinating. And for a man my age, quite relevant. "But just another beginning?"

"Yes!" Goro clapped me on the shoulder even as the bus lurched to the right, out of control for a heart-stopping moment. "Death is only part of life. Our, ah, *spirit* never die. It just take new... form?"

I nodded. It made me wonder—if such a thing as another life were even possible, did we get to choose what we'd *be* in the next life?

I turned to ask Goro when Buddha Rodriguez interrupted us.

"*Worm,*" Rodriguez said, his voice loud and jarring over the rocking of the bus.

He gave a loud belch followed by a sharp laugh, as if he were drunk. Or maybe he'd never recovered from his heatstroke a few weeks ago. His breath was foul enough to make my eyes water. I turned on him, half out of my seat.

"What are you talking about, Rodriguez?" I said. Next to me, Goro's small, clean hands had become small, clean fists.

"I'd want to come back as a worm," Rodriguez said, still chuckling. "A worm at the bottom of a tequila bottle."

"Rodriguez—" I began.

Goro beat me to it.

He leaped onto the bus seat and launched himself onto Buddha with a screamed word that sounded a lot like "*Banzai!*"

Goro struck Rodriguez twice in the face before the other players could separate them. He was still shrieking at Rodriguez in his native language when No Small Foot and Art Houdini pried him away from the bigger man.

"See what you started?" I hissed at No Small Foot, wanting to clout him one upside the head. Instead I held on tight as the bus rocked over a bump so jarring I saw red again. "Now you've got everyone fighting, and we can't afford anyone else getting hurt."

I winced when I felt sharp jabs in my knees as I half-sat, half-stood on the rocking bus, gripping a player in each hand. I hissed in a breath and spoke through clenched teeth.

"Jap—*Goro*—shake Rodriguez's hands. Both of you put this behind you. Make peace. 'Cause we *need* some peace in this world. Shake, damn it."

I blinked the last of the redness from my vision just in time to catch a look from my centerfielder, sitting at the very back of the bus. Mack's gaze was turned upwards, as if searching out the sun through the solid roof of the bus and the clouds above that. Two slivers of white light slipped out the bottoms of his eyes, like a shuttered lantern cracked open for an instant.

As if on cue, the bus lurched once more in the mud, and came to an abrupt stop, stalling. Without the roaring of the engine filling my ears, I could hear the rain beat down on the roof like hundreds of tiny feet stamping on the stands.

"Everyone out," I said, looking anywhere on the bus but in Mack's direction. "Looks like we've got some pushing to do."

We rolled into Nashville at eleven thirty, half an hour before our scheduled game was to begin. My players jogged around the field and did jumping jacks to get the blood flowing through their cramped limbs as the sun baked off the last bits of humidity from the air. We had half an hour to get ready, while the Nashville players had been preparing for us for days.

The game itself wasn't pretty to watch, but we eked out a victory over the all-colored team, and then we packed onto the bus and headed off for the next game two towns over at four o'clock. J.L.'s scheduling on this leg of the tour was brutal, but we all needed the extra money.

I encouraged all my players to go all out every game, to swing for the fence and take chances stealing bases and angle for fancy catches in the outfield. That was the only way to bolster our reputation and bring more paying spectators to fill the coffers we split with the home team after the games.

Rodriguez complained about feeling lightheaded before the four o'clock game, which he blamed on Goro's punches to the head on the bus. He claimed they had aggravated his old war injury.

As a result, I played first for him yet again, bad knees and all. I spent every free moment during the game thinking about an early start to the bald man's next life as a worm. And I got no hits in any of my at bats, damn it.

That was my sorry state when J.L. met up with me at home plate, after our third and final game of the day ended. Though I was frustrated about our thin roster, I knew better than to raise my voice to him here in the South.

"I understand your plight," J.L. said. "I've got my scouts looking for a good replacement for Mendez on the mound, and some help with your infield. But money's tight. Hope we can, well, keep Mendez on the payroll if his arm doesn't heal. Attendance is declining. People don't have much extra money these days. I think we need to play more—"

"Don't say it," I said, wincing.

"—More all-white teams. That's where the money is, I'm afraid. They can draw from a bigger group of people with more cash to spend on games. Our cut of the gate at these colored games is just a fraction of what we could be making." J.L. held up a chubby hand. "I know times are tough. Reminds me of the 1890s, how we all had to scrape to get by. At least there's no depression going on now. Well, not yet, anyway."

"I know," I said with a slow nod. "I just hate saying no to these colored teams who want to play us, even if they don't have a lot of money. It feels wrong to not play everyone, especially the colored teams."

We always split the gate with the other teams, and every colored team agreed to a fifty-fifty portioning of the money. The all-white teams almost always felt they deserved a larger slice of the ticket sales pie. We were denying many colored men wages that would last them a month or two—our games were almost always well-attended.

J.L. fell silent at that. We watched the players lugging bats and our water jug back to the bus, piling them on top of our rolled-up tents. It was a far cry from the loads of equipment we once had, from the portable bleachers J.L. had rustled up somewhere to the extra gloves and bags of bright white baseballs we used for practices.

When my players finished loading the bus, most of them took a seat in the lantern-lit bleachers along with the band from town. Nobody was ready to climb back aboard just yet, not with half of the crowd still in the bleachers, flasks being passed and songs filling the night.

I even saw Mendez up there, holding his cornet with his left hand, his right arm still wrapped in a sling. Next to him, No Small Foot played a trill on his flute while Buddha tapped out a beat on his homemade drum.

"There is one other thing," J.L. added as the band and my players began a jazzy, snappy version of "Good Night Ladies." Players from both teams clapped and sang along. "We could use a big win in our series against the American Giants in Chicago. I've got some friends with money riding on those games, and, well, I've got a little bit on them myself."

I gave J.L. a curious look, wondering if I'd heard him right.

"We could use the cash, George. The team is pretty strapped. What I wanted to ask you was—do *you* want in, too?"

I felt a rushing sensation overtake me, different from my occasional bouts of breathlessness on the field. I hadn't gambled on a game in ages, and never on my own team. Surely he hadn't just asked me to do so as well.

"If the games pay off for them," J.L. continued, "I'd bet I could talk my friends into financing a recruiting trip for us this summer, after the Fourth of July. Think you can beat them?"

"Recruiting?" I asked, ignoring his question. Both of them. "We could definitely use more players, that's for sure. Where would we be going?"

"Somewhere farther south than we've ever been. We can find guys who'd play for us, for cheap. Quality fellows."

"I'm afraid to ask where," I said, brushing dirt from my uniform pants. J.L. and his big plans. "So you want us to travel some more, during our two weeks off? Wouldn't we be better off scheduling more games, or hell, just resting? Will this trip be worth it?"

"I understand everyone being tired," J.L. said, and gave me one of his winning smiles. "But it *will* be beneficial. I have hopes that times are changing, George, and for the better. Even, well, even with this damn war in Europe."

J.L. stopped, his blue eyes going wide as if struck by a sudden thought.

"No one's gotten it into their fool head to actually sign up for duty, have they?"

I shook my head, and hoped I wasn't lying to him. I'd seen some patriotic fervor in some of my men, especially young Boles, but also Donaldson and even Carrie Nation at times.

"Good. The war's there, not here. And in any case, I think I've got the transportation all set up for our trip." A car horn broke into the music coming from the stands. J.L. waved at his traveling secretary Gilmore behind the seat of his idling flivver. "I've got to go. Just keep up the outstanding work. Good luck with the Giants in the Windy City, and, well, let me know if you want in on the—" he rubbed his thumb with his forefinger and winked "— action."

"Yes, sir," I said. I watched our team owner leave the field and step past the bleachers. The band was breaking up, with lots of laughter and hand-shaking and emptying of flasks before my players headed for Blount's bus.

Soon, in the space of just a few minutes, I was alone once more in an empty ballpark.

I waited for Worrell's now-familiar voice to creep into my thoughts or slither into my ears, but the dead man remained silent. I almost wished he *would* come to talk and spout more empty threats and nonsense about my coaching skills. His absence during the past few weeks threatened to unsettle me more than feeling his cold fingers on the back of my neck and hearing his taunting whispers in my ear.

Perhaps he'd started his next life, as Goro had suggested, maybe being reborn as an animal or a bug or, more likely, as a new human being. Hopefully, a better man. Or woman.

On my way to the coughing and sputtering team bus, I found myself thinking of eagles and mockingbirds and worms and my *own* spirit.

So many theories about the intangible aspects of life and death. Each one of my players seemed to believe completely different things, though all of them came back to someone having a soul or a spirit—that invisible presence a person has that was worth saving.

Which made me wonder: Did I even *have* a spirit? Or did I gamble it all away on baseball and lose it, just like I'd lost my family? And if it was lost, could I ever win it back again?

I had no answers to these questions, so I squeezed my way into the bus, and we hit the road once again.

Chapter Six

On a balmy afternoon on the third of July, we arrived in Chicago, weary from the road and with almost half the season under our belts already. We checked into what to a well-off man would see as a flea-bag motel in a questionable neighborhood on the South Side.

To my players and me, it looked like the height of luxury, compared to pitching our tents on the ball diamond where we'd play later the following day. J.L. must've had some confidence in his bets he'd made against the Giants.

In a rare turn of events, we found ourselves with time on our hands, so I decided to spend a cool afternoon with the team exploring the streets closest to the newly built Weegham Field, soaking up the sights. The twelve of us must've made quite a sight, dressed up in our nicest suits and somewhat battered and dented hats.

"They're talking about calling it Cubs Park now," Art Houdini said, walking ahead of me with Carrie, Donaldson, and Mendez. He tucked his kinky brown hair under his wool hat. "I've heard it can seat eighteen thousand spectators. Can you imagine that many people, all coming to see us play? And it cost two hundred and fifty *thousand* clams to build."

I loosened my tie and stared up at the big red sign and imposing white-and-gray height of the stadium on West Addison. My heart ached with the thought that most of my players would never even be given a chance to play here.

Hell, right now I'd be hard-pressed to be able to afford a ticket to see the Cubs, the team that had replaced the defunct Federal League Whales.

But J.L. had reminded me just yesterday about how I too could talk to one of his cousins here in the city and put some money down on the game. Just one little bet. I deserved that much, didn't I?

"Box seats here will run you a whole dollar," Art continued, as if reading my mind about money and the numbers. "A regular seat's two bits. A nickel for a hot dog. And the best hitters and pitchers probably pull down ten grand a year. Ten grand! Can you imagine?"

I walked north along the outside of the whitewashed wall of the stadium, trying to outpace my desire to make that one last bet. I busied myself with memorizing the details of the new edifice. Flags and team pennants waved from far above wooden and metal stands that were easily four stories high. I swore I could smell the cut grass even on this side of the park.

"The Whales—what a terrible name," Art continued. He had most of the team gathered around him now, all of them leaning close to hear his soft voice, full of wonder. "Now the Cubs, that's a good name. They even let the fans *keep* the Cubs' homers instead of making them return 'em so they can use the balls again. Can you believe that?"

As Rodriguez and Mendez made simultaneous sounds of disbelief, I glanced back at my short, muscular third baseman.

"How do you know so much about this place?" I asked him.

"Read about it in the papers," Art said with a shrug. "I usually skip over all the bad news about the war in Europe and the like, and go right to the sports section. But my brother—"

"The King of Cards?" Boles interrupted from the back of the pack of players. He stepped forward, a sarcastic grin on his ruddy face. His tie was already undone, and his jacket swung open. "The master illusionist?"

Art cleared his throat, and the crowd of players started to move apart to give Boles and Art space.

"Yes, *that* brother. Harry has been to a game here, and he memorized the history from the plaques inside the entrance. It's a trait we both possess—photographic memories. I can recall every place I've ever been, every page of every book I've read."

"Of course," Boles said, his grin widening. "That's how you remember all those pitchers and which ones have the best slowballs and screwballs. What are you batting these days? A buck fifty?"

"Boles," I warned. "That's enough. Can't you just enjoy the scenery?"

"Oh I *am*," Boles said, grinning at a passing woman who quickly turned her parasol on him. "I just get tired of the Jew's far-fetched stories. He ain't kin to Harry Houdini. He just stole the man's name to use as his own."

Art nodded, as if to himself, and then he turned to Boles. The boy had a few inches and at least thirty pounds on him, but Art only smiled at the chuckling teenager.

Before I knew it, Art waved first one hand, then the other in front of Boles so fast I barely saw it happen. When he stepped away from the younger man, I heard the tinkling of four small buttons hitting the sidewalk. Boles was left grabbing for his pants while his suspenders dangled loose on his chest. The rest of the team burst into laughter at the sight.

"Not kin at all," Art said, tipping his cap at me on his way past. "Of course, you *must* be right, Master Boles."

With one hand on his pants, Boles made to go after Art, but No Small Foot stepped between them. Nothing in the world was going to get past our big catcher. Nice work, John.

"He's gonna pay for those," Boles muttered, kicking loose buttons into the road, but his voice had lost its heat.

Everyone gave the stadium one last look as we continued walking, with Boles and No Small Foot bringing up the rear.

Now that Boles had mentioned them, everywhere I looked I saw pretty women, all of them walking arm-in-arm with dapper men. We passed in front of stores so fancy that I didn't dare look inside them for fear I'd get lost in the extravagance and never escape. I felt embarrassed of my ten-year-old suit with its shiny knees and dated fashion sense.

Just one bet, a soft voice whispered in my head, bringing with it a sudden chill, *and you can buy two new suits, with money left over.*

I started walking faster, hoping to outrun that nagging voice in my head. That voice sounded quite a lot like the voice that had been slipping into my dreams every night. I wondered if he'd caught up to the team again after we'd lost him for a few weeks on our tour of the south and now the Midwest.

I stopped to catch my breath at a newsstand, and my players kept on walking. Hoping they could get by without a chaperone for a few minutes, I picked up a copy of the *Tribune.* I parted with my last nickel to pay for the paper, listening to two men talking behind their papers.

"Wilson's a fool if he thinks he can throw our boys at the Western front and keep the war from spreading to our shores, Sully. Not the way the Europeans have let the Huns run roughshod over them. We shoulda stayed neutral and never got involved last year. Wilson's a fool."

"Nah," said the other man. "He knows what's best for us. Germany wouldn't dare bring the war here, not with our doughboys moving into France. We'll blow his subs right out of the water. We're in it now. We won't do this halfway. I say we take the fight to them, and show 'em what we're made of."

"I say it's not our fight," the first man said. I realized I was eavesdropping a moment before the two white men lowered their papers to glare at me standing there. They gave me a quick once-over before walking away, papers tucked under their summer jackets.

The headline of my paper read "U-Boats Attack Allied Shipping Again." Below that was an article about British dugout life near the Somme, with an illustration of soldiers digging a trench eight feet deep.

I shuddered, thinking about having to spend time in such a structure. Too much like an early grave.

"May I read that when you are done, Coach?"

I turned to see my second-basewoman gazing at the paper with worry lining her face. She wore men's pants, an oversized tweed coat, and a wool cap in spite of the warm weather. Carrie always preferred to hide the fact that she was a woman when the team went anywhere together.

She figured that the mix of white and colored, Japanese and Philippine, Cuban, Mexican, and otherwise would raise enough eyebrows as it was. She didn't want to make any more trouble than the team made just by existing.

"The paper, Coach," Carrie said. "I want to know about what is happening in England and the front lines. It seems to not be going well." She gave me a guilty look, as if she'd said too much. "I have... family over there."

Sometimes, when Carrie spoke, I'd hear the traces of what sounded to my untrained ears like an Eastern European accent. If she had German blood in her, she'd want to cover that as well as any links to the "bloodthirsty Huns." I certainly didn't want paranoid people who were convinced that their neighbors and even their friends were spies following Carrie and waiting for the right moment to charge her with treason.

"Let's catch up to the others," I said as we left the newsstand behind. "And you can read my paper now, if you'd like."

Carrie had the paper out of my hand before I could finish my sentence. Newspapers and anything else that cost money was considered a luxury.

Doesn't have to be that way, boy, a scratchy voice whispered.

"Worrell," I whispered, standing alone on the street now. I felt a half-smile on my face and quickly rubbed it away with the back of my hand, along with the cold sweat from my face. "What do you know? You're dead."

Gambling is not a deadly sin, either, he added with a dry chuckle, and then the chill dissipated.

Shaking my head, I walked faster until I caught up to my team, a block ahead of me. I began herding them back to where Old Blount had left the bus, close to the ball field. I didn't need to be thinking about gambling right now, with our four biggest games up the year stacked up for us tomorrow.

On our way back, I walked next to Mendez, who had at some point during the walk peeled his right arm out of his sling. He gave me a guilty-looking smile as he gingerly exercised his arm, folding it open and closed.

"Ever think about playing first base?" I asked him, casting a meaningful glance at Buddha walking on the sidewalk ahead of us, balancing a sandwich from a sidewalk vendor in each hand.

I was only partially joking. I'd been playing quite a bit in the past two months, and I still hadn't gotten a single damn hit.

The young Cuban brightened. "Maybe, Coach. Though I've got my eyes set on second or short, once I heal up for good, if you don't mind. If the doctors say I can't pitch again, that is."

"We'll see what we can do, son. Don't worry. You'll always have a spot on our team."

So long as the money holds, I added silently.

When Weegham Park came back into view, and my knees were starting to feel the same old aches as always—I blamed it on all this walking in my fancy shoes—Mack dropped back to walk with Mendez and me.

"You know, you're going to be an unbelievable shortstop," he said to Mendez. "Watching you field and turn the double play, people will wonder why you ever pitched. But, at the same time, they won't forget your pitching. It'll be a perfect situation for you, Jose—embracing the present, while never forgetting the past."

"Ah, I see," Mendez said, shuddering as if he'd gotten a sudden chill here in mid-summer. "Thanks, I guess."

Mendez took longer strides until he caught up with Donaldson and No Small Foot ahead of us.

"Guess he didn't care for your prediction," I said to Mack, who was smiling in a distracted way.

Mack shrugged. "That's fine. He's got a lot of future in front of him."

"Unlike some of us." My heart was suddenly beating wildly. If my vision went red again, I'd have no one to blame but Mack.

"You have plenty of time, Coach," he said. "It's the team itself that is running out of time."

"What do you mean?" I said in a low voice, and then stopped. I had to backtrack a few steps when I realized that Mack was no long walking next to me.

My young centerfielder had stopped to stare up at the bright new stadium across the street. He blinked rapidly, as if he had dust in his eyes, and his skin tone had darkened with the fading daylight. Mack turned his gaze up directly at the sun.

"You know, Coach, this place won't be known as Weegham Park for long. Soon it be Cubs Park, yes, but then it will have another new name. *Wrigley.* Yes," he said, nodding and blinking. "Yes, I like the new name much better than Weegham. Even if it's the name of a chewing gum."

"Forget about all that," I snapped. "What did you mean about my *team*, Mack?"

Mack looked at me for a few awkward moments in the fading light as if he didn't recognize me. I took a step back, hands instinctively curling into fists.

You are not the man I think you are, I thought.

"Coach," he said again, turning his face back to the sun. "You know, we're going to have some more hard times soon, but we've got to keep the team together. You know, this *is* the final season of the All Nations."

I looked from Mack to the tower-like heights of the new stadium, not believing his latest prophecy. My chest was tight with this illicit knowledge, though deep down, his words did not surprise me.

"This can't be the end of the team, not this year. How do you know this?" I held up a hand. "No. Don't answer that. I don't want to know. But what does all this have to do with my family?"

"It's all connected. *Everything* is connected. We just don't see those connections until it's too late and you're at the end of the line. Unless, of course, you're always looking ahead instead of behind."

"Sure," I said. "If you say so. And as for the future, why, I'm more worried about how we're going to hold up tomorrow, playing four games against Foster's Giants as shorthanded as we are. I can't even think about next *week*, much less next year."

"You know, Coach," Mack said, still gazing at the sun as it dropped toward the horizon. "A new player will be joining soon. Even if we do lose someone else in the process."

Without another word, Mack began walking away. With one hand, he undid his red bowtie and pulled it free of his starched collar. The undone tie unfurled in from his hand like a red flame as he strode off toward the team bus without another word.

I stood alone next to the impressive bulk of Weegham Park, soon to be known as Wrigley. As I watched my team push their way into the bus, I decided to skip making any bets on the games tomorrow. Even if I could use the money—we all could—I didn't dare risk losing a moment's concentration during the game. Worrell's words in my head, whether they were real or imagined, had helped me decide. Unlike our former head coach, I could not afford to take my eye off the ball.

The decision made, my steps felt immediately lighter as I made my way back to the bus. Just about everyone was aboard now, except for Charlie.

Our slender, light-skinned outfielder sat perched on the rear bumper of the mud-spattered bus, smoking a cigarette and staring off at the setting sun with his back to the new ballpark. His eyes were dark under the brim of his battered hat, and his three eagle feathers stuck out of the side pocket of his suit jacket. He only wore the feathers during games now.

I was twenty steps from the bus when I heard the whine of a car making a too-sharp turn behind me, accompanied by the screech of tires. Before I could turn to see what was happening, two gunshots rang out.

"Oh God!" I heard someone call out, a voice I wouldn't recognize until later. Boles. "Everyone down! Save yourself!"

I was already running to the bus, my back hunched low as if I was trying to duck the tag from a second baseman. We would not lose anyone here, not on the streets of Chicago. Charlie still sat on the bumper of the bus, cigarette clamped in his frowning mouth.

"*There they are!*" a voice shouted out, both far behind me and somehow right in the middle of my head. A familiar voice. "*There are your culprits, soiling your fair city!*"

The car ground its gears as the men riding in it shouted obscenities and roared drunken laughter. A bottle exploded in the spot where I'd been standing a moment earlier.

As I ran, I hoped my knees would hold up long enough to get me to Charlie and the safety of the bus. I could barely breathe.

"*Down,*" I tried to yell at my rightfielder. All that came out was a hoarse rasp. I kept trying. "Get down, Charlie, damn it!"

"Get out of our city!" someone shouted, and I turned in time to see an onrushing black Ford Roadster. The car had its top down, and two men stood on the back seat. "Go back where you belong, niggers!"

Above me, Art slipped out through a window, feet-first, a bat clenched in his hands. Donaldson and No Small Foot burst out of the side door just as I reached it. No Small Foot grabbed me while Art launched his bat at the car.

As I waited for another gunshot, Donaldson threw a baseball at the car.

In the instant before the bat and the ball struck the glass rectangle of the windshield, I got a good look at the men in the car. Their white faces were twisted with rage, and they wore collarless shirts and crooked driving caps. They looked like oversized schoolboys except for their bottles of liquor and the tiny black gun in the hand of the man in the passenger seat.

I caught myself searching for a long, gaunt face among the four in the car, but all I saw were round, red, corn-fed Midwestern faces. Nothing like Worrell at all.

When the windshield shattered, the men covered their faces and ducked for cover in the seats. The driver veered off, and the car missed the bus by a handful of inches. I waited for it to stop or crash into something, but the Roadster continued picking up speed as it roared down the street, and I heard no more shouts or gunshots.

"Everyone on the bus," I gasped, "before they come back."

I shook No Small Foot's hand and clapped Donaldson on the shoulder. His curly hair bouncing free of his cap, Art jogged back with his bat, looking amazed that it was still intact.

"My lucky bat," he said, giving the barrel a small pat with his delicate white hand. "That ought to teach 'em a lesson."

Art and Donaldson kept asking me if I was all right, but I pushed them back toward the bus and yelled at Old Blount to get the engine going. Everyone was back on board when I realized we were missing someone. I went back outside and found Charlie still sitting there on the rear bumper, smoking. I hurried back to him, waiting for the roar of another car or more gunshots.

"You okay, son?" I asked Charlie, my heart still racing as I panted for breath. He hadn't moved from his spot during the whole altercation. I looked for blood, some sort of wound. His eyes were distant, as if he was imagining himself someplace other than here. I couldn't say that I blamed him.

Instead of answering me, he simply dropped his lit cigarette to the ground and climbed into the bus.

Rubbing my chest, I stepped on Charlie's still-smoking cigarette. Tomorrow's fireworks—during and after all four Independence Day games—would be enough to keep everyone on their toes, and Chicago certainly didn't need any more fires.

I spent that night in the small hotel room I shared with Donaldson and Mendez. All three of us had trouble falling asleep. Not only were we not used to beds, but we kept talking about the events that had ruined our walking tour of Chicago and our appreciation of Weegham Field.

Someone had *shot* at us. I couldn't fathom that. According to the colored doorman of our hotel, a white saloon-keeper had reportedly been killed by a colored man earlier that night. To retaliate, a group of white men in an automobile had driven around, shooting at groups of colored men.

"Bunch of *toughs*," the doorman had said, rubbing his curly white hair under his red cap with an angry gesture. "From their so-called 'athletic clubs' down by Roosevelt and Sixty-third. Showing their courage by taking shots at people. Hell, I heard that white barkeep died of a damned heart attack. No colored man ever touched him. I don't 'spect much good will come of this, no sir. Next there'll be riots, mark my words."

At last, after hashing out the incident one last time, discussing the accuracy of Art's bat and Donaldson's baseball, my players were all able to relax enough to catch some sleep.

But for me, I couldn't yet fall asleep. I was thinking of the games tomorrow, and all that was riding on us winning the four-game series.

We could do it, I thought, staring into the darkness at the vague outline of the ceiling, which felt much too close. Even if Foster's Giants were practically invulnerable, I knew we could beat them. At least we could win three out of our four games. That was a spread I knew we could cover.

With that thought, I drifted off at last. But my sleep was poisoned with haunting images, not of white men in cars, but Germans in their airships. I'd seen many drawings and a few grainy photographs of them in the papers, and I couldn't believe such awkward-looking, bullet-shaped machines could actually fly.

But there they were, in my dream: a fleet of zeppelins cruising over Lake Michigan, rolling in from the east like storm clouds armed with bombs. Their approach had been silent and steady, eating up the sky with each passing second. They arrived with the rattle of gunfire as the city's defenders on the ground and perched in buildings tried to puncture the ships' hulls, to no avail.

Even though I was standing hundreds of feet below the dozen dirigibles, I could see the deadly bombs attached to the metal bases of the zeppelins like tiny offspring. I turned to run back toward the false refuge of the brick buildings of Chicago, but my knees gave way on me. I fell to the sidewalk, once more a feeble old man, seeing stars from the impact of chin meeting concrete.

"Stay down, boy," a voice murmured, dripping with contempt. *"Don't let your sinful pride lift your head too high, even in victory. Just. Stay. Down."*

The guns firing up at the zeppelin attack went silent as the bombs dropped through the air from their impossible height. The bombs created a pressure inside my ears that was so great I could only turn my face and my bleeding chin back to the ground, my arms crossed over my head in futile protection.

I could hear laughter fill the skies, first just Worrell laughing, then he was joined by other mad voices barking with a mad glee that made me want to cry out to silence the sound of it. He was no longer alone, I realized. He had his own army of spirits backing him up.

Then the dream shifted, and I was *inside* one of the zeppelins.

Faceless men shouted orders all around me, in a harsh language that had to be German. Every voice sounded, impossibly, like Carrie Nation's, except for one, which my dreaming mind refused to recognize.

A strange heat covered me, along with a humming that I felt in my teeth more than heard with my ears. I smelled foul gas and burnt rubber. The city burned below us, the bombs hitting with deadly accuracy, punching holes into the ground and gutting buildings.

As vertigo overtook me, I could only hang onto the ropes on either side of me for dear life. Then the zeppelin began to shudder. A heartbeat later the big airship began to drop.

"*You killed me,*" a soft voice hissed into my ear. "*And stole my team from me... boy. Now it's my turn. You're going down with the ship. Going down, and staying down.*"

I spun around on the springy floor, losing my balance as the zeppelin lurched again, dropping so fast my ears popped.

"No," I said in the empty metal cage attached to the dirigible's undercarriage, but my word was lost in the roar of engines. When I blinked, the smell of soap filled the air.

I turned again, and Worrell was standing in front of me, arms crossed, not even the tiniest bit off-balance in the failing airship. There was that garish, purpling lump bulging from the side of his head, growing as if from his left temple. His eyes were mostly whites, almost glowing.

Like Mack's, I thought immediately, and then Worrell's dry laugh scratched at my ears.

101

"*I'm sorry,*" he hissed. "*What did you say to me... Boy?*"

"No," I said, suddenly less than five inches from him. Our noses were almost touching. "You don't. You will not call me boy, ever again. You are dead, and I hold sway over you now, here in *this* world."

Worrell rocked back on his heels, eyes wide for an instant before he caught himself. He chuckled, the sound like sliding into third on gravel. And then, amazingly, he nodded.

"*But you forget,*" he said. "*This is not your world. This may be your dream,*" he whispered, voice fading as the sound of the zeppelin engines began to rumble louder and faster.

"*But this is my domain, and I've come to reclaim my team, boy. And this time, I'm not alone.*"

I looked out the window of the plummeting zeppelin and forgot about the disembodied voice. The burning city rose up to meet me, and a strange calmness washed over me.

This is how it will end, I thought. I'll know what happens soon enough.

The zeppelin suddenly lifted nose-first into the air. My heart dropped into my belly as the ship kept rising in a powerful upsurge. We lifted up and flipped over in a perfect arc. I heard the engine knock three times as it fought for control, then silence.

The earth below me spun in a slow circle, and just as my eyes adjusted, the zeppelin hit the ground.

I felt and saw and knew nothing more.

Nothingness.

And then, three sharp knocks. In my hard hotel bed, I sucked in a sudden, desperate breath and pushed both hands against my chest, as if trying to stop the galloping of my heart.

"Hotel," I croaked. "I'm in a hotel."

The trio of knocks, just like those in my dream, had come from the hotel door. In the cots next to me, Donaldson and Mendez shifted in their sleep, but didn't wake. I took relief in the movements of my players, their deep breathing, signs of life, not death.

I crept over to the door and cracked it open. A young colored boy stood there blinking in the shadowy hallway, holding up a thin envelope.

"I'm s'pposed to deliver this to Coach Grunion. Is that you? My boss made me run it up to you soon as it arrived."

I nodded, still thinking of zeppelins, and felt the earth tilt once again when I saw the handwriting on the unstamped envelope. I closed the door on the boy's disappointed face, too distracted to grab a nickel for his tip.

I threaded my way through the dark room, past the three beds and into the bathroom. My chest ached almost as badly as my knees as I closed the door behind me and clicked on the electric light.

With the bulb buzzing in the wall next to me, I slid a finger inside the envelope and gently ripped it open. Only then did I flip over the envelope for a closer look at the writing on the other side.

"*George Grunion, of the All Nations.*" Lizbeth's handwriting—I'd read and reread her lone letter to me back in December enough times to recognize it. No stamp, which meant the writer had delivered this in person, to the hotel.

"Open the letter, old man," I muttered, as if ordering my still-shaky hands into action. My thick fingers fumbled for the single piece of paper inside the torn envelope. On a piece of yellow hotel stationary, Lizbeth had left a short message in black ink:

"*Welcome to Chicago. I would very much like to meet with you after your games tomorrow. I will be in the diner next door with my husband. I pray you will understand if we do not attend your games. I greatly anticipate seeing you again, Father. All my best, Lizbeth.*"

I read the note half a dozen times before my eyes began to ache from the bright light and my fatigue. She was here, in Chicago. My little girl. And she wanted to see me. I couldn't believe it. It felt like some sort of prank or a bad joke played at my expense.

I thought of all the letters I'd written—to her, to Maddie, and even to my boy Jacob—but never sent. I should've contacted them sooner, instead of waiting for them to write to me.

I folded up the note and turned off the buzzing light. I stood there in the dark, blinking stars from my eyes and listening as my breathing slowed from ragged to heavy and deep. At last I eased open the bathroom door and crept back to my bed in the dark.

Just before I lay back on my pillow, though, I realized the true cause of my nightmares. It wasn't the headlines from the paper I'd given Carrie or the carload of armed white men that caused my bad dreams, nor was it Worrell.

What haunted me was—as always—Maddie, and the children she'd taken from me.

Perhaps, I thought, closing my eyes, tomorrow would be my chance to begin making amends, in person, at long last.

I refused to obey the orders of Worrell's dream-voice to stay down. I would *not* go down with the ship, not without a fight.

Chapter Seven

The sleeves of his borrowed Giants jersey looked ready to burst at the slightest movement, and his golden front tooth glinted in the sun whenever he smiled. Towering over the other colored men on the Chicago American Giants, he was hard to miss, and the Giants had some big fellows to start with, like John Henry Lloyd and Bingo DeMoss. Their coach and owner, cigar-chomping Rube Foster, was no slouch in the size department either.

But this man was bigger than them, bigger than life, with a laugh that echoed around the diamond and doused my hopes for victory today.

We were going to be fighting for our lives today against the Chicago American Giants, whose roster now included the former heavyweight champion of the world, Jack Johnson.

And not ten minutes ago, just outside our team bus, on a last-minute impulse—one I was already regretting—I'd just wagered all my forthcoming paychecks for the month of July that my All Nations team would take the four-game series from the Giants.

"What the hell is *this*?" I demanded as my team entered the visitors' dugout after their pre-game calisthenics. Most of them, like me, were unable to take my eyes off the champ. Young Boles even walked into the post of the dugout entrance while staring at the big bald colored man on the field, adding another lump to his head.

Within ten minutes, I'd gotten the whole story from Donaldson, who was pals with one of the Giants pitchers.

Johnson had been on the run ever since he'd been charged with violating the Mann Act for transporting his fiancée across state lines for what a judge called "immoral purposes." I couldn't believe there was such a law, until I heard that Johnson's wife was white. Then it all made sense to me.

He'd been living outside of America ever since, though he'd just returned for a few days to attend the funeral of a relative. The cops had been on him in a heartbeat, until Rube took him in.

In spite of my worries about the upcoming games, I managed to relax long enough to take in the huge, still-growing crowd behind us. For a moment I saw a female face that I swore could've been my Maddie, or maybe even Lizbeth. My chest tightened up, just as the band wrapped up another song.

Then the crowd shifted, and I lost sight of the woman. Surely that wasn't her; she hated the sport. And Lizbeth had said in her note that she wouldn't be attending the game, so it couldn't have been her. Just my imagination.

I stepped out onto the field again and nodded at Rube and the champ ambling back to their own dugout. I found myself frowning with irritation at the band's version of "Over There," made worse by the accompaniment by our skinny white pitcher Boles as he warmed up next to the dugout. I heard him muttering, "Make your daddy glad, to have had such a lad," as he unleashed another fastball into No Small Foot's glove.

I'd heard enough.

"Let's go, men," I shouted, tipping my cap at Carrie Nation. As my team gathered around me, I realized that we were missing someone.

"*Charlie.*"

I cursed myself for being so caught up in trying to figure out the champ's story and staring at the crowd like a moony teenager.

"Boles!" I hissed.

"What?" He gave me an innocent look, but I'd seen him flinch. He knew something was amiss. "What'd I do now?"

"Where's Charlie?"

"That crazy loon? Who knows. Maybe he's out looking for more eagle feathers. Look, I got to get ready for the game."

"Not if Charlie doesn't show up. Because if he's not here, I'm putting *you* in right field in his place. Again. Remember how well that went last time? Not too fun, was it?"

Boles' cocky smirk was replaced by a bright sheen of fear.

"But I'm *pitching* today. He was just here, wasn't he?" Boles turned to his teammates, desperate. "Houdini, didn't you see the Chief just a minute ago?"

Art shrugged and tucked his dark curls under his cap. "Beats me. I'm just a dumb Jew ballplayer who thinks his brother can do magic. What would I know about anything?"

"Listen, guys," Boles said, looking from left to right in a panic. "Who here saw Charlie last?"

"Better check the stands," I said. "Art, get warmed up. Mendez, I hope your arm's feeling better, because I'm putting you at second and moving Carrie over to third while Art pitches. Got it?"

Mendez gave me a bright smile and nodded, while Carrie responded with a distracted nod. Houdini was already dragging No Small Foot out to the bullpen to warm up.

With the way things were shaping up, I'd soon be back on the roster again. I glanced out at the stands and saw men my age, grandpas decked out in their Sunday best, and wished for a weak moment that I was out there, resting my sore knees and medicating them from a flask in my hip pocket.

But then I returned to my senses. Sixty-four wasn't *that* old. Plus, I always got a hit or two on the Fourth of July. Whatever it took to cover that bet I'd made.

As I was scratching out and scribbling names on my roster, Mikado grounded to first and Phil the Philippine struck out; Cannonball Redding had his stuff today. Mack hit a dribbler to third that he barely outran, only to have No Small Foot strand him after three called strikes. The bat never left the shoulder of the squinting Cherokee; he needed spectacles like no one's business, but I was not going to be the fool to tell him that.

"Ump's strike zone is bigger than you and me put together, John," I said in a voice loud enough for the rest of the team to hear. I watched Jack Johnson lumber in from second base and head right for the Giants' pile of bats. I swallowed with a painful click. "Gotta be aggressive at the plate. All of you, including Charlie. Soon as we find the three-feathered fool."

B ack in my playing days, unlike most of my fellow players, I always looked forward to Independence Day every year. We'd give the crowd their money's worth with lots of baseball and add more cash to the team coffers by charging a tiny bit more per game. I'd always gotten at least two hits per game on the Fourth. My best was ten hits in four games in Philly, way back in 1877—over forty *years* ago. The Fourth was always my luckiest day of the year.

At least, until this year.

Charlie never showed up for the first game, so I grudgingly stuck Boles in his place out in right field, just as I'd threatened. Rube's hitters immediately took advantage of Boles all game. I should've known better than to put the kid out there in right. Before the game, Foster's Giants had put on a show of their accuracy for the crowd—each player would step up to the plate and bunt the ball right into Foster's cap as the big coach moved from one spot in the infield to another, sucking on his cigar.

If the Giants weren't placing the ball precisely where they wanted it into the outfield, they were using the tried-and-true Baltimore chop to drive the ball down into the dirt near home plate, so that nobody could tell where the ball was going on the rebound. Usually the ball shot high into the air, giving the Giant hitter time to reach first. At first base, Buddha Rodriguez was hit three times in the chest as he tried to field a chopped ball.

As I've said before, the ball could go anywhere in a baseball game, and the Giants proved that to us all game long. And Art Houdini, with all his best tricks up on the mound, was getting tired already.

Rodriguez, complaining in Spanish and then English about his aching chest and the heat, barely made it through the first game, stumbling to the dugout and dropping onto the bench each inning as if the distance from first had been miles instead of feet.

He finally went down for the count after he ran after a pop-up ten feet from first and tripped over the glove left there by the Giants' second baseman. In all my games I'd never seen someone do that. Just our luck.

So, once again, I took Buddha's glove and played in his place, though I didn't have my usual Independence Day luck. I failed to get a single hit.

It goes without saying that we lost that first game. Between games, as a small army of colored kids crowded around Johnson, asking him to sign slips of paper for them, I sat sweating in our dugout, wondering how I was going to afford to eat in the weeks leading up to my first paycheck in August.

Next to me, Buddha sat capless in the dugout, attempting what he called "meditation," which looked like sleeping while sitting up to me. He hummed softly in the empty dugout, the thumb of each hand touching the middle finger.

"You sure you can't play this next game?" I asked him.

I gave him two minutes to answer, but his only response was more humming, interrupted by a long breaking of wind.

"I *really* need to find Charlie," I muttered, breathing through my mouth.

As I got to my feet, I felt glad that I'd had the foresight that morning to wrap both my knees with material from an old pair of pants, knotting it tightly for support. My knees felt strong, but my toes were starting to go numb.

I walked with barely a limp out of the dugout over to where Mack was playing catch with Goro in the outfield.

"Mack. Where do you suppose Charlie has gotten to?"

"Why do you ask me, Coach?" Mack threw an effortless strike to Mikado a hundred feet away. His skin was a grayish hue today. "I see the future, not find lost sheep."

"I don't have time to mince words." I took a quick breath and forged ahead with my somewhat crazy idea. "Mack. Can't you, ah, *see* where Charlie is a couple minutes from now? That'd be the future."

"Why, Coach Grunion," Mack said, handing me the ball and gazing at the sun. "Your ingenuity always inspires me."

He blinked slowly, three times, eyes aimed skyward. Watching him, I felt a shudder run through me, like electric current.

"You know, Coach," Mack murmured, "I *do* see Charlie. The poor fellow's walking down a gravel road not long from now, wearing just his feathers and his skivvies. It's what No Small Foot would call a *vision quest*."

"A what?" I almost dropped the ball. "I don't have time for vision quests or anything else. I need my rightfielder back!"

Mack was still looking up at the sun, but now he'd started sniffing the air.

"Cigars," Mack said, nostrils flaring. "What a scent they have! Someone in the stands must have just lit one."

"Mack. Pay attention here. We were talking about Charlie. Where is he?"

"Gone," Mack said. "He was upset last night, after that carload of fools nearly ran him down and shot at us. Claimed that was the last straw."

An eerie light flickered in Mack's eyes now, covering his gray face like a second skin. I stepped back, away from him and that unholy glow.

"And you know, Coach, he'll never play ball again." Mack sniffed again, and I thought I saw a tear slide down his shimmering face. "His life will spiral downhill in such a way that he ends up in Cincinnati, alone and disillusioned and without his feathers."

Mack was whispering now, gazing right at me, eyes wide and glowing.

"While he sits in front of his apartment building, relaxing, a passing car blows a tire and jumps the curb. Charlie Grant dies fifteen, maybe sixteen years from now when the car strikes him. Maybe last night's incident with the men shooting at us from their car only put off the inevitable."

I stared at Mack. Words failed me.

"That's just a guess, though," he said, blinking away the strange light from his eyes as he took the baseball back.

"I see. Sorry I asked." I walked with Mack toward the dugout, inhaling the green smell of the outfield. "Think you could get that accurate someday for one of *my* predictions?"

Mack shrugged and closed his eyes for a long moment, still walking and sniffing the air for cigars. I thought I heard the hint of joviality in his voice as he murmured, "One of these days, Coach. One of these days."

My roster had never been very deep even when I had Charlie playing right and Coach Worrell doubling as a manager and a closing pitcher. Now, with Charlie absent, Buddha riding the bench, and Art Houdini recovering from his shellacking in the first game, I not only had to play first base, but I also had to play referee in the second game, when No Small Foot stood in Jack Johnson's path after the champ's third home run of the day. I got between them just in time—Johnson was rearing back for a roundhouse that would've sent my Indian catcher far into next week.

Yet for this second game of the day, my All Nations rose to the occasion. I moved Mendez from second to shortstop, exchanging places with Phil, and he turned out to be a whiz at short. In right, Boles lucked out with Donaldson's pitching; no balls made it out of the infield, much less into the corner of the outfield where Boles cowered in Charlie's usual spot.

At last, in final inning, with a slim 2-1 All Nations lead and two outs, the heavyweight champ of the world came up to bat, with the tying run at second.

I slid a few steps behind first base and inched closer to Phil at second, giving Johnson plenty of the respect he deserved. That was when I caught sight, once again, of a familiar figure in the crowd.

"Maddie?" I whispered, the name slipping from my lips before I could catch myself. I flinched with the pop of ball in glove; Donaldson's first pitch against Johnson went a bit high, giving me a chance to pull myself together.

Just like Worrell, I'd taken my eye off the ball. Worrell had paid for that mistake with his life. And here I stood, making the same damn mistake.

The ump, whose vision must have been worse than No Small Foot's in front of him, called it a strike.

She's not here. Pay attention the game, you old fool. She has no reason to be here. Not anymore.

I risked another glance at the crowd and was rewarded with twin spikes of pain in my knees as I leaned forward, anticipating the angle of Johnson's hit.

Donaldson stepped off the rubber strip on the pitcher's mound to catch his breath. He'd only given up one hit and one walk in the whole game, but that hit had been a towering home run to the big man now dug in at home plate, and the walk had been to the player at second right now, a base he'd stolen as soon as he'd had the opportunity. No Small Foot hadn't even attempted a throw, not with the champ blocking the way.

Donaldson narrowed his eyes, nodded at No Small Foot, checked the runner at second, and twisted up into his windup.

Johnson let the low pitch go by him for a ball: one and one. No Small Foot made a disgusted sound from behind the plate, but I couldn't tell if it was directed at the ump or Johnson. The former champ grinned his golden smile as he looked down at No Small Foot and spat near the catcher's foot.

"Come on now," I called out, mostly to Donaldson but also to my catcher, who'd been madder than a fire ant ever since finding out Chief Tokahoma had disappeared. "Play it smart, gentlemen."

Donaldson didn't even bother checking the runner at second this time. His curve flashed from his hand, almost as fast as his fastball, and Johnson swung a foot too high and a split second too soon. One ball, two strikes.

As the crowd inhaled in surprise (and No Small Foot snickered from behind the plate), I caught myself looking out at the spot in the stands where I'd seen the slender, cinnamon-skinned woman with the slightly hunched shoulders.

She was wearing a pink hat, decked out with red and white flowers. That had been Maddie's favorite hat, and seeing it here, today, made me break out into a cold sweat.

But then all of the spectators had stood, chanting Johnson's name, and the woman disappeared.

Johnson caught a piece of Donaldson's next pitch and sent it up and back, crashing through the awning of a hot dog stand. It landed in an explosion of yellow mustard.

I punched my left hand into my glove and slid back another few feet. I gave No Small Foot the signal for another curve and fought the urge to look once more into the stands.

She's not here, old man.

No Small Foot shook me off and gave his own signal: fastball, low and outside. I didn't have time to argue;

Donaldson was already in the last stage of his windup, sweat exploding off his arm as he released his pitch.

The ball cut through the air toward the plate, a gray-white bullet.

Johnson's dark, deep-set eyes went wide. He flexed his huge arms—the same arms that had knocked out countless men of all color—and swung.

The world exploded as bat met ball.

I had only enough time to wonder at how much Johnson's hit had sounded like the bat-shattering, line-drive foul ball that had killed Worrell.

And then my body was moving directly into the path of the ball.

My knees felt full of gravel as I dove for the line drive in the gap I'd left between me and first base. I threw my gloved right hand across my body as hard as I could, feeling the ligaments of my arm and shoulders stretching, hearing the creaking and popping of my knees, inhaling coppery dust, reaching reaching reaching for the ball, and somehow I managed to snag it in my threadbare glove.

It went into my glove without a sound, not even a tiny pop, and the power behind the hit ball spun me twice around in a mad counter-clockwise circle until I ended up on my rear end. I end up sitting in the dust of the infield, knees screaming in pain, the air knocked from my lungs.

But I had the game-winning catch clenched tight in my stinging hand.

At that very instant, if I could have gotten to my feet on my own power, I would have gone back to my hotel room a happy man, knowing that the All Nations had *finally*—after over four and a half seasons of trying—beaten the Chicago American Giants.

Instead, I pulled the ball from my glove and exhibited it to the world, deflating the crowd while earning some grudging applause of my own.

And then I dropped onto my back to stare up at the empty, cloudless sky as I tried to find my breath again.

My young players ran over to me, hands empty after chucking their gloves into the air. I shook my head in disbelief as I slowly sat up. My gaze traveled into the stands, searching for that lone dusky face in the crowd that I'd never expected to see again.

Then my team overwhelmed me, lifting me up to my feet and shouting in my ears, and I lost her again. With every win came a loss of one sort or the other. The story of my life.

You could say that a miracle occurred between our second and third game on that day, right before the law showed up to ruin everything. J.L. Wilkinson arrived just after I'd doused my head with a ladle full of lukewarm water, and he brought with him a new outfielder. Already dressed in the faded gray woolen shirt and pants of the All Nations uniform, the new player was built like Goro "Jap" Mikado, but he was taller and thinner, and his dark eyes took in everything as if he were memorizing details like a crackerjack reporter.

"Coach Grunion," J.L. said in his usual low-key manner. "Meet Jiang Ming-Kai. Rightfielder, from China by way of sunny California, where he grew up. He's so quick, well, he can throw runners out at first on a grounder to right. Saw it myself, two days ago in Frisco. Jiang, this is George Grunion. Who knew you'd need a rightfielder so quickly, eh? Funny how that works, isn't it?"

"Who knew, indeed," I murmured with a glance at Mack, who had shrugged and turned his gray face once more toward the sun. I wiped water from my face and dried my hand on my pants leg before shaking Jiang's hand.

"Please," Jiang said, his accent heavy but not overpowering. He held a leatherbound book in his hands. "Call me John."

"Good to meet you, Jiang," I said, hoping I did okay with the pronunciation of his name. I couldn't stop looking at the fancy symbols marching up and down the cover of my new player's book. Jiang opened the book and created more of them as we stood there, using a tool that was half fountain pen and half paintbrush.

"This is *your* name, Coach George," Jiang said, pointing at a line of symbols that looked like tiny dancing houses. "That okay-fine?"

"Yes." I felt a goofy grin on my face. My *name*, I thought. "That is definitely okay-fine. So, Jiang, you ready to play?"

Jiang nodded and carefully set down his book. He sprinkled a tiny bit of a sandy substance on the symbols he'd just drawn and blew on them before closing the book.

"Good," I said, and directed my voice at my first baseman dozing in the corner of the dusty dugout. "Maybe Buddha here can actually earn his keep and play in this game?"

"*Buddha*?" Jiang's widened as he stowed his book under the bench.

"I'll explain later," I said as the rest of the team filed into the dugout to shake Jiang's hand and introduce themselves.

I had just added my new player to my roster when, like fast-moving thunderclouds, a platoon of cops arrived on the other side of the backstop. I hadn't even heard them coming.

"We hear there's a fugitive from justice here," a round-faced white cop said from behind me, his voice cracking.

A sudden silence in the dugout and stands greeted the man's words.

"Ah wish ah could help ya, son," I said, falling back on the Southern accent that I'd mostly lost in my past five decades in the Midwest, "but all ah've got heah are ballplayahs."

Boles snickered at that, and the cop turned his gaze on my players while his colleagues—two of them decked out in black suits and hats—stepped out onto the field. The young cop's face was twisted with confusion as he took in the multi-hued array of faces turned toward him.

"How do... what are—"

"We're the World's All Nations," I explained, my accent disappearing, my tone softening. "A mixed-race ball club. All my men—" I gave Carrie a warning look "—are here legal and square. No fugitives in this dugout, friend."

The young, round-faced cop appeared to struggle with the concept of players from just about every race under the sun working and traveling together as if it were normal. He gave a slow nod.

"I heard about you. I just didn't think you guys were real..." He shook his head as if waking from a deep sleep. "In any case, we got a tip from someone, well, someone a bit odd, who told us about the game today. And who's playing for them Giants out there."

The young policeman looked out at the field, where the other cops were moving toward the home dugout, much to the dismay of the hissing crowd. The spectators who had been shocked into silence by my final catch in the second game were now shouting at the cops. I felt like I was back in Shreveport, right after Mack's impossible catch.

"It was the darnedest thing," the cop said. "This fella wore a uniform like yours, 'cept he had these big feathers in his ball cap and his shirt was all unbuttoned. He come up to us and told us Jack Johnson was here, playing ball for the Giants. The fella wouldn't stop walking, either. Just kept heading south, pulling off his shirt but still wearing his spikes, clacking on down the road."

"Ain't that the darnedest thing," I murmured.

Charlie. Chief Tokahoma. I'd kill him, if I could ever find him. But then again, the man was, in his own way, already dead.

Inside the fenced-in area of the other dugout, partially hidden in shadows, the Chicago American Giants stood huddled together, forming one single mass of ballplayers. Each man was almost indistinguishable from the other. I felt two lines of sweat slide from my forehead to my eyebrows, but I didn't dare lift a hand to wipe it away.

The policemen in their blue uniforms, along with the two unsmiling men in black suits, began to walk across the field. They were aiming for the home dugout. So far nobody had drawn a weapon, but I could feel that time quickly approaching.

It really was Shreveport all over again.

"Listen," I hissed to my players. "I know the big man beat us up in the first two games, but we can't let him get hauled off like this for some damn-fool law. We need a *diversion.*"

Mendez and Donaldson were already on their feet, nodding, and the others soon followed, even Boles and Phil, whose amber-skinned face was a wide map of confusion and eagerness.

"Everyone grab whatever equipment you can," I said. "I'd suggest a bat or two."

"You want us to club the *coppers*?" Boles said, wide-eyed.

"No," Mack said. "We're going to go out on the field and get in the way so Johnson can make a break for it. If the Giants do it too—and you know, they will—the field will be too full of players and bats and balls and gloves for them to catch up to the champ. And coach is getting ready to—"

Before Mack could finish his prediction, I made my move, and I hoped my players would follow my lead. I stepped up to the cop in front of our dugout and clicked open the gate.

"Watch out, son!" I said as I pushed the cop ahead of me into the on deck circle. The young man's arms felt far too thin in my big hands. The All Nations team followed us, and a crowd of spectators poured through the gate after us. My players charged onto the field, throwing bats and balls and any other loose bit of equipment in front of the other cops. The Giants, however, remained inside their dugout.

"Come on, Rube, let 'im go," I whispered as the other cops turned on my team and reached for their holstered weapons.

The Giants coach suddenly stepped out of the dugout, and all fifteen of the Chicago American Giants bolted onto the field, hunched over with towels covering their heads.

"They all look alike, don' they?" I said to the young cop next to me, giving him as innocent a look as I could muster. "Shore is hard to tell 'em apart, ain't it?"

The towel-wearing Giants ran in every which direction, some straight across the field, others running directly toward the policemen trying to pick their way through the obstacle course of bats, balls, gloves, caps, and even shoes.

From the gates next to either dugout, colored men in their Sunday's best—along with some of the feistier women—charged into the infield, joining up with my team to create more barriers for the policemen.

The cops simply weren't able to stop the players zigzagging all over the field like a clown team that had forgotten its act.

As for Johnson, I caught one final look at the champ, running from the law. There was no disguise that could hide his majestic frame for long. The big man cut across centerfield, long legs pumping high, eating up five feet with each stride. As he ran, his towel slid off his bald head and dropped to the grass of the outfield like a discarded flag of truce.

Quick as can be, Johnson was up and over the eight-foot fence. I imagined his gold tooth glistening in the summer sun as he turned for a moment on the other side of the fence and gave us a victory smile.

I laughed with relief and let go of the cop's spindly arms.

"Don't stop 'til you hit Canada, my man," I whispered, still looking at the spot where Jack Johnson, the colored man who was larger than life, the former champion of the world, had disappeared.

Chapter Eight

The crowd needed close to fifteen minutes to settle down and take their seats again after that, and I guessed that most of them would go home feeling that they'd not only gotten their money's worth from today's games, but that they'd also played a role in helping an innocent man remain free. What better reward could one expect from a day of baseball on the birthday of our nation?

As for my team, I managed to convince Buddha to play the third game, prying him from his spot on the bench. He *needed* to play, and I needed to rest up and try to get one more glimpse at the mysterious woman in the crowd.

I figured I could pinch-hit for Buddha or anyone else showing fatigue later in this game or the next. That way I could still try to get at least one of my lucky July Fourth hits that had thus far eluded me.

As it turned out, my team didn't need me. Mack and No Small Foot cooperated with a double, a stolen base, and a sacrifice fly to squeeze out a run in the eighth that the Giants, without the recently departed Johnson and his home run skills, could not match. Boles kept a leash on his wildness and a muzzle on his mouth while he was on the mound, and as a result he allowed only three hits in the entire game. With one game left and the daylight beginning to fade, the All Nations led the series 2-1.

Between games, a local amateur ball club took some batting practice. While my players dispersed, the crowd behind me thinned. And I'd caught another glimpse of that pink hat with the red and white flowers, twenty rows back on the third base side of the stands.

If she was here, I wanted to talk to her. Maddie owed me that much.

Before leaving the dugout—the *safe* dugout, a tiny voice reminded me—I slipped off my metal cleats to avoid puncturing anyone's feet in the crowd. As I trudged through the crowd, my socks already brown as shoes from the dust of the field mixed with my sweat, people clapped me on the back, though some men gave me venomous looks when I eased my way around them.

The crack and pop of bat on ball peppered my ears from home plate.

"You didn't have to leave," I'd tell her soon as I reached her. "I never meant to hurt him, just teach him a bit of respect. I was a fool, hitting him like that. I've changed."

I stopped for a second, more sweat trickling down my face as I inhaled the sweet and sometimes salty odor of other perspiring men and women, baking in the sun. I flinched as a practicing batter made contact again, and my head swiveled instinctively to the field. Line drive into left center.

Before I turned my attention back toward the spot ten rows away, I caught sight of Mack, standing on the bench of our dugout, fingers embedded in the dugout fence. He was watching me.

I nodded at him, but he just shook his head, as if to say, "What are you doing, Coach? *Why* are you doing this now?"

"You wouldn't understand," I muttered, and pressed on, ignoring the odd looks of the spectators cheering on the local boys at bat below us.

A few rows above me, I saw the hat again and pressed forward, heart hammering so hard I could feel it in my ears and taste copper on my tongue. I didn't even look to see where the next hit went on the diamond.

I dodged a pair of old timers arguing about how dead the ball was these days and then I saw her, looking right at me.

All the saliva in my mouth dried up, my fingers went numb, and I froze in my tracks.

After all these years, she could still stop me cold from over fifty feet away. Why did I wait so long to come after her?

I lifted my right arm, still aching from catching Jack Johnson's earlier hit, and felt my lips try to form her name.

"Mmm—" I began, at the same instant the latest batter cracked a hit. I never heard anyone yell a warning, but I'd been assured later that everyone around me had done so. At that moment, all I could hear and see and feel and think was Maddie, *my* Maddie, right here in front of me after so long away from me.

"Mmmmaaadddd—"

The line-drive foul tip hit me in the back of my skull and knocked me flat on my face.

Some people claimed they saw stars when they got hit in the head. But what I saw that day was the stars turning themselves inside out: millions of imploding spots of light all disappearing into an infinite blackness. And it kept happening, over and over again, like explosions in reverse.

My body was weightless, and I had the sickening sensation that I was falling—not down onto the wooden bleachers below me, but *up* into the vast emptiness of the night sky, where all the stars had now gone out, and nothing waited for me but the uncaring void of the universe. Falling upwards.

In that black nothingness, I heard the dry, scratching laugh of a man who seemed unfamiliar with the act, a disdainful, contempt-filled sound. The man never seemed to cotton to the act of laughing.

"*I cannot believe you are still employed by the team,*" Worrell said. "*Surely your owner could have found a suitable replacement for me by now.*"

The back of my head suddenly filled with pain, like a spreading bloom of fire in the spot where my hair had grown thin. That damn voice.

"I've been talking to... others like me. They're not too happy with you playing ball while they're being shot at and planted in foreign soil."

The man made no sense, but I was unable to do anything but listen to his ranting. The pain in my head paralyzed me.

"We're watching you. Do the honorable thing and let the team fall apart. Or there will be consequences," he added, and began to laugh.

I thought I heard other voices as well, laughing along with him, as if he'd told the best joke ever and they couldn't help themselves. Deep voices, all of them somehow familiar.

I thought once more of the voice I'd heard in Shreveport, who I'd been convinced had been my old friend Derby. Which was of course impossible, as I'd been there when they put him in the ground, fifteen years ago.

"Worrell," I said at last, his name bitter as tobacco on my unconscious tongue, "I don't believe in you. Never have."

"That does not matter. What you believe no longer matters, boy."

I opened my eyes and saw the dead man gesture at the black sky above him, with a hand that was quickly become ethereal.

"For I am no longer alone. I have been... Recruiting, too."

After his hollow voice had faded, the blackness was split apart by what appeared to be a flock of headless chickens and pigeons, flying in perfect synchronization with an armada of zeppelins above them, all of them apparently heading for the glowing, growing moon taking shape at the edge of my befuddled vision, expanding like a baseball rushing at my head, everything expanding and expanding.

But that whole scene was too breathtakingly peculiar to contemplate, so I decided instead to simply wake up.

* * * * *

When I opened my eyes, the first thing I saw in the clear, dark blue sky was the sun, sitting a foot above the park, a red baseball about to be hit into the air by the white bat of the foul pole.

To my relief, there were no chickens, pigeons, or zeppelins to be seen. I heaved a long sigh, glad to be back in the world again, and immediately groaned from the flood of pain from the back of my head.

I sat in the dugout, my spikes on the bench next to me, a wet towel wrapped in ice tied to my noggin. The start of the fourth game had been delayed as the umps checked on me again to make sure I wasn't going to keel over on them.

Like a damned fool, I took my eye off the ball and paid a price for it.

According to Boles, he and the other players had carried me back to the dugout from where I'd been felled by the foul tip, and I'd sprawled out there like a dead man for almost ten minutes. When I woke, the first thing I'd said—again, according to Boles, for I remembered nothing—wasn't my wife's name, but "Mack."

He'd been watching me as I slipped through the crowd. He hadn't wanted me to find her, if that indeed had been my Maddie. The bastard.

Don't ask me how he could've done it, but he was responsible for that foul tip, just as he was for the one that had killed Worrell.

Now that the umps were sure I wouldn't die on them, they started the final game of the Fourth. I removed the chunk of ice from my head and set it next to me on the bench to melt. The pain in my head settled to a low ache.

As soon as I did, Mack walked past me to pick up a bat. He turned and gave me a quick nod, and my heart gave a painful twinge. I exhaled and rubbed the knot on my head, and then bent down to put my shoes on again.

Behind me, the crowd had swollen to twice its original size. Apparently, word traveled fast through the south side when the Giants won, but when they lost the news *flew* through the neighborhoods. Everyone was buzzing at the prospect of the Giants losing another game to this motley crew of multiracial players.

I wasn't much heartened when Cannonball Redding struck out the All Nations' best hitters at the top of the lineup, 1-2-3. On the other hand, Buddha had decided he felt strong enough to play another game, our new rightfielder Jiang hadn't missed a single ball all day, and Donaldson's pitches were popping even though this was his second game pitched today.

I could even handle Boles' bragging on the bench next to me, praising his success in the third game as he soaked his arm in ice water and bragged about how he'd saved my life between games.

I got to my feet and took one final look out into the rows of spectators behind me. Just as I'd expected, the woman in the pink hat was gone, replaced by wave after wave of shaking hands and bobbing heads.

But I knew who I'd seen. Maddie had been here.

Far below where I'd imagined her seat, someone in the stands was waving at me. Three rows back from our dugout, J.L. sat with Gilmore, his right-hand man, a soft-spoken white fellow with thick, round lenses obscuring his eyes. After all these years of coaching the team, I'd never remembered Mr. Gilmore's first name, even though I'd been told it countless times. I nodded at them, sitting together in the no-man's land where the white section met the colored section, then watched Donaldson fire in another heater for a strike.

For the Giants, John Henry Lloyd was up to bat. He stood on one foot and knocked dirt from his uplifted spike. I tried not to look at the bulging muscles of Lloyd's thick arms.

We needed a curve here. I touched my forehead (which made my sore skull ache even more), sliding the first finger of my left hand down one side of my nose and up the other, swiping across my chest with my right hand, tapping my belt with my left, and finally, sticking out my tongue as if to touch my nose, the signal for one of Donaldson's impossible-to-hit curves.

In the middle of my slightly lightheaded contortions and dancing, I remembered something vitally important: I simply loved this game.

The final game had turned into a pitching battle between Donaldson and Cannonball Redding. The struggle was made all the more spectacular by the fact that both pitchers had already logged nine innings in a game earlier today. Both men looked more like marathon runners than pitchers, but nobody could steal a hit off either man. It was amazing to watch. The innings flew past.

At the start of the ninth inning, with only the top-most rind of the sun visible above the horizon, I came across my centerfielder again. To my relief, his skin was no longer bronzed, but somewhere between gray and dusky.

"Mack," I began, ignoring the sudden shaking of my hands. "What happened back there, between games?"

"Coach?" Mack looked over at me as if hating to take his eyes off the setting sun. "I'm not sure I know what you mean."

"That foul tip. Did you have something to do with that? Just like..." I swallowed. "Just like Worrell?"

Mack stared at me for a painful couple of seconds, and I regretted my inquiries immediately. He hadn't been himself the past few games, keeping to himself, rarely speaking, always trying to sneak in a cigarette between innings. I'd ground out a dozen contraband smokes from him in the past week alone.

"I can't control where the ball goes, Coach. However, I do know *this*. This is not the time for you to meet up with your family again. Especially not your wife, by herself."

I glanced around at the other players, who were engrossed in watching Boles at the plate, talking non-stop to the opposing pitcher.

"What in the hell are you talking about?"

Mack gave me a strange smile before he turned his gaze toward the setting sun. As I watched, the young man's skin turned from its sickly gray color to a deep burnt orange color. Surely it was the bump on my head affecting me. Or so I hoped.

"You know, coach, no other group of men—and women," he added, with a look in Carrie Nation's direction, "have ever worked together in this fashion. As *equals*, Coach. Led by a man with black skin. White men and women, taking orders from you. Somehow, you make it work. Like right now, for instance."

I rubbed my chest as I listened, feeling my heart quicken its pace. I hated even thinking about it, but I'd woken up this morning with the fingers of my left arm completely numb. And I was always losing my breath at the worst possible moments.

"This team has no precedent, you see," Mack continued, just as the ball ricocheted off Boles' right shoulder and went sailing into the stands. Boles left the batter's box, wincing, and threw his bat toward the dugout on his way to first. In his anticipation to knock in the winning run, Mikado leaped over Bole's flung bat and sprinted to the plate.

"But you said something about my wife—" I began, then both of us turned to the field at the sound of ball meeting bat. Mikado lined a shot into deep right, igniting a burst of speed from Boles at first that I'd never seen before. The bruised pitcher-turned-rightfielder never stopped until he slid into home a step ahead of the throw. We were up by one run.

"As I said, this team is unprecedented, and will remain so for... for many years. For decades, even." Mack's gaze turned from me to the sinking sun. "You know, the team will almost survive long enough to see the war's end, though we will lose players to family, to the war, and to unexpected accidents. For one last game with those who must not be named."

As he spoke, his voice became even more monotone, almost lifeless.

"So you see, the team *must* be remembered, Coach. Just hold them all together. History will take care of the rest. And those who need to find you, will find you."

I stepped away from Mack and his wall of words to shake Boles' hand as he came puffing back to the dugout. When I turned to say something more to Mack, he had moved to the other end of the dugout, his gaze aimed at the horizon as the sun began to disappear.

At the bottom of the ninth, still thinking of Mack's litany of prophecies, I watched Donaldson befuddle the best hitters of the independent Negro teams on nine strikes. Three straight strikeouts, after eighteen tough innings pitched. Donaldson collapsed at the mound, only to have his teammates swarm over him, just as they'd done to me, five hours and two games earlier.

And that was how, on the strength of John Donaldson's arm, with the night swallowing up more and more of the remaining daylight, the World's All Nations team defeated the Chicago American Giants, three games to one. It was enough to make my sore head spin.

As if on cue, darkness fell, covering the field until it was cut to pieces by the headlights of the stunned spectators. Nobody spoke or even tooted their horns in farewell. My own players—the victors—were too tired to sing or play a tune on their instruments. We simply fell, exhausted, back into the bus.

But we'd accomplished something here today, though. Something for the history books. And then there was my bet, and the money coming my way. At the long odds established for us, it would be a whole hell of a lot of money. Unbelievable.

If only I had known then that this would be the pinnacle of the season, and all our games to follow would begin to roll quickly downhill from those glorious Independence Day victories.

My team's slide downwards, as well as my own descent into hard times, began to truly pick up speed less than two hours after the final game ended, starting with the meeting scheduled with my long-lost daughter Lizbeth.

Chapter Nine

After a quick bath, I put on my suit from where I'd left it, next to the open window to air out. Properly attired in this other, less-comfortable uniform. I left my hotel room, already running late. I was made even more tardy after an encounter with J.L in the lobby, where he was nearly dancing a jig at our wins and the money coming our way from our bets on the team.

"Did I ever doubt you and the All Nations?" he cried out. "Well, just for a moment, right after you caught that foul tip with your head during batting practice. But then you got up, and all was well. And all will *be* well, George! What a day. What a day!"

His enthusiasm was infectious, and he quickly had a crowd of players and spectators from today's games gathered around him. Soon everyone was reliving the catches and strikeouts and home runs from today's battle, and was finally able to slip out the smoky lobby unnoticed.

All will be well, I thought. If only I could believe that.

At half past nine, I found the stranger who was my daughter in the diner next to our hotel, and she was not alone. I knew I had to contain myself, but after the day I'd just had, with our huge wins and the thought of the money coming my team's way, I couldn't help but act a bit like our owner when I saw the couple sitting in the booth of the otherwise-abandoned cafe.

"Lizbeth Grunion?" I called out, ignoring the jabs of pain in my knees as I navigated around metal tables and chairs in my path. "I don't believe it," I whispered, out of breath as I arrived at their table. "You haven't changed a tiny bit."

"And this," said the woman to the man next to her, "is my father."

Her demeanor was serious enough to make me want to take a step backward, but then she smiled. She had turned into a lovely woman, with her mother's crooked smile and my mother's sharp brown eyes.

"And if you think, Daddy, that I haven't changed since the last time you saw me—when I was barely sixteen—then you'd best get your eyes checked."

"That's my girl," I said, taking her outstretched hand. I shook it instead of giving in to the urge to kiss it. One small step at a time.

"George Grunion," I said to the man with to her as he unfolded himself from the booth and stood up to tower over me. "Pleased to meet you."

"Thaddeus Martin," he said. "Looks like we're in-laws, sir."

"Allow me to buy your dinner," I said after extricating my hand from the silent man's grip. We sat back down again, and the waitress took our orders. Suddenly ravenous, I wanted to eat everything on the menu, but I settled for their night-time breakfast platter.

"We heard about the game," Lizbeth began, reaching to take a quick, almost nervous sip of coffee. "Your team is the talk of the town, beating those Giants like that. How's your head, by the way?"

I grinned and rubbed the bump on the back of my skull. "Takes quite a bit to dent this old head of mine. And I'm always bowled over by the feats of my team. Amazing fellas. They deserve all the credit." I could tell I was starting to blather, so I forced myself to take a breath. "I wanted to thank you for your letter last Christmas. That was a very pleasant, unexpected surprise."

Thaddeus turned to look at Lizbeth, and I swallowed hard. I don't think she'd told him about that.

"I'm glad you liked it," Lizbeth said, sipping more coffee. "And thank you for your letter in response."

131

I busied myself with dumping sugar into the steaming cup of coffee the waitress had just set in front of me. I was a source of tension between my daughter and the stranger who was my son-in-law. Had she even told him of the invitation she'd extended to me in her letter? I doubted it.

A plate crashed to the floor somewhere on the other side of the swinging doors leading into the kitchen. All three of us winced at the sound, which seemed exceedingly loud in the empty diner.

"Sorry about that," the waitress said as she came back to refill coffee cups. "New dish washer back there."

I glanced back past the half dozen empty tables and saw an oval-shaped face poking through the middle of the two doors to the kitchen. A pale white face, painfully familiar, and it was smiling at me.

"*Enjoy your meal, coach.*"

I nearly spit out my mouthful of coffee out onto my daughter and son-in-law as I realized that Worrell was in the diner. He'd found me again, after almost a month away.

I blinked, looked down at my coffee, and looked back over at the kitchen. This time, all I saw were the doors swinging in opposite directions until they came back to rest, closed.

After another, more successful sip of coffee during the awkward silence that had been stretching out, during which Thaddeus checked his watch only once, to his credit, I looked back at Lizbeth, my face hot.

"Strong coffee," I said with a laugh. "So tell me about *you*. What have you been doing here in Chicago all these years. Any kids? Do you like it here?"

"We have a daughter and son. Their grandmother is watching them, though both kids claim they're too old for such supervision."

"Ah," I said. I wanted to know more about her children, their names at the very least, but my mouth sometime got ahead of my brain and my own common sense. "I see. And how *is* your mother?"

"Feisty as always," Thaddeus said with a laugh, before Lizbeth could speak. "Sorry," he murmured. "Her mother and I have an, ah, occasionally rocky relationship."

I nodded. I could relate to that. I liked this Thaddeus fellow already.

"She's fine," Lizbeth said. "Had a rough bout with her health a few years back, but she's strong as can be lately. She enjoys having her own place and visiting friends and her grandkids, of course. She also likes not having to work anymore."

I remembered Maddie on a Monday morning, bemoaning the fact that she had to start another week of work at the laundry. And I, meanwhile, was almost always climbing aboard a bus or a train to play ball. She never came to terms with that, though she gladly accepted the money I sent home each week.

"And what of Jacob?" I said, my stomach filling with acid even as the waitress dropped my overflowing plate in front of me. At some point I'd lost my appetite. I noticed that neither of them had ordered anything to eat, and I felt like a gluttonous fool.

Lizbeth looked down at her empty coffee cup. "He's had some, ah, troubles, Father."

There will be consequences, Worrell had said.

But Mack had said my family would be at an All Nations game. All of them, in one form or another. Was I a fool to even believe his predictions?

"Tell me about them," I said, struggling to keep my voice calm. This was my *boy*. If he was in trouble, why hadn't they contacted me?

Thaddeus patted Lizbeth's hand. He opened his mouth to speak for her, but Lizbeth shook her head.

"He never finished school," Lizbeth began. "Which wasn't all that strange, with all the work here in the city. But then he got... Distracted."

As she spoke, I saw Worrell leering behind Lizbeth. Somehow he'd crept from his hiding place in the kitchen to the booth behind us. I knew my daughter and her husband couldn't see them, though she was shivering and pulling her shawl tighter over her shoulders. I could feel the cold draft now, too.

"*Tell me*," Worrell whispered, leering over the top of the booth.

I really ought to leave. I couldn't let Worrell affect my family.

"How so?" I said at last. "Distracted in what way?"

Lizbeth took a sudden breath. "He fell in with a bad crowd and left the city. We lost touch. Mom was the last to see him." She glanced over at Thaddeus. "That's all I can tell you. I've probably said too much already."

"Lizbeth," I began, feeling the fatherly authority slip into my voice. "You can tell me. I'm your father."

Lizbeth pushed away her coffee cup and wrapped her shawl around her even tighter. That was answer enough. I hadn't been her father for a long, long time.

Once again I saw Worrell pop his damaged head up behind her, and now his pale hands reached for her shoulders and neck. I could've killed the damned ghost. And he didn't appear to be alone. At least two other figures sat in the booth with him, becoming more substantial with each passing second. Who in the afterlife would want to dine with Worrell?

"At least give me your mother's address," I said, trying to meet Lizbeth's gaze without distraction. They were getting ready to leave as well. "Isn't that part of the reason you agreed to meet me here tonight? So I could make amends?"

Lizbeth exchanged a quick look with her husband, and they nodded at the same time. I had to smile at that. She seemed happy with this fellow, and he appeared to be a good man.

Lizbeth wrote on a napkin and handed it to me.

"I do hope you'll write her, Daddy," she said, moving out of the booth and getting to her feet. "That will make all of this much easier."

I slid out of the booth, but before I took the napkin, I had to know something.

"Lizbeth," I said, turning my back on Worrell and looking down at her. She was the same height as Maddie, the top of her head coming to my chin. "Was your mother at the game today?"

Lizbeth answered only with a smile. She moved close and offered up her cheek.

I took a shaky breath and kissed my daughter's cheek for the first time in over twenty years, and the contact with her made my heart ache with faded, almost forgotten memories. I hoped the next kiss would not be so far off in the future.

As we walked to the door, a few steps behind Thaddeus, Lizbeth turned to me.

"I wasn't supposed to tell you this," she whispered, "but she did say to me, when she got home today, that you still look as handsome as ever in your uniform, Daddy. And she hopes your head doesn't hurt too badly."

With that, my daughter, all grown up now, along with her husband, left me standing there in the diner with a dumb grin on my face. I wanted to chase after her, to follow her home and see her mother once again, but I'd lost my breath, and I could scarcely move.

"*You don't have much time left, boy,*" Worrell hissed from behind me, accompanied by low, hissing laughter.

I shivered from the cold spilling out from that corner of the diner, though the air outside was still summer-time hot. I wanted to turn and confront Worrell and his cronies, but I thought of Maddie being there, at our games today, and had no trouble keeping my back turned to them.

That was all Worrell deserved, I thought as I followed Lizbeth and Thaddeus out the door, which I did my best to slam on the vengeful, persistent spirits mocking me and hounding my movements.

* * * * *

Back in the crowded hotel lobby, Mack waited for me. Somehow, the young man, whose skin was a deep red color tonight in the bright light of the dusty chandelier above us, was always able to find me in a crowd.

"Coach," he called out. He once again had a cigarette tucked into the corner of his mouth, though he didn't seem to be enjoying it. The ash of the thing was almost an inch long, about to fall onto the lapels of his gray suit.

I walked past Mack without a word, feeling a surge of pain in my skull, right where the ball had connected with it. The pain was lessened with the thought of Lizbeth's parting message to me, but I certainly didn't have the energy for my centerfielder's mischief tonight. Not after that look he'd given me today after the ball had struck me.

"*Coach,*" Mack said again, and something in his voice made me pause.

"What is it, son? I'm tired and sore and really need to get out of this suit."

"We aren't alone anymore, you know," Mack said.

A chill ran down my back, as sure as if Worrell was stabbing me there with a dead finger. I almost turned to see if he'd slipped into the crowd of hard-drinking fans and the occasional All Nations player.

"Why, Mack? Why can't you just enjoy yourself, son? It was a big day today. A glorious day. Why won't you just have fun and live in the present?"

Mack cocked his head at me like a curious dog. The ash from his cigarette dropped onto his hand, and he shook it away without even looking down.

"The present," Mack said, as if considering this concept. "No time for that, Coach. Not when the clouds overhead are massing. And the big game is approaching."

"Today's games weren't big enough for you?" I wanted to keep a jovial tone, to prevent Mack from soiling the memory of not only our victories today, but of my dinner with my daughter. "Mack, let me buy you a drink."

But Mack just shook his head.

"We may be able to outrun them for a while, but at some point we must confront our demons. You know this, Coach."

His voice grew loud enough to break through the din of the crowd. People stopped talking and turned to stare. Mack smiled at me around his stinking hand-rolled smoke.

I sighed, feeling the hint of a chill creep onto the back of my neck. I shuddered before I could stop myself.

"Good night, Mack," I said, grabbing the cigarette dangling from his lips on my way past him. With one last shiver, I stubbed it out on the sole of my worn black shoes. "We've got a long bus ride tomorrow. Go get some sleep, son."

With Maddie's address in hand, I was sorely tempted to go track her down the day after our victorious Fourth, but events conspired against me. We were due to play two games a day for the next week and a half as we worked our way west across Illinois and Iowa. We didn't even get the fifth of July off, as our first game in Naperville started at four today.

I'd told old Blount to have the bus ready to leave at nine this morning, but at half past eight, I was still stuck in my hotel bed, exhausted, with aching knees and a throbbing knot on the back of my head.

Donaldson and Mendez had already packed up and left the room, most likely leaving in search of breakfast somewhere. I hoped they were treated to a complimentary meal after yesterday's wins. My team had earned that honor.

At last, after half an hour of groaning and limping around my room, as I rinsed out my filthy uniform and packed my few belongings into my bag, I headed downstairs to the team bus. While I was hanging my damp uniform next to my window in the bus, I saw J.L. walk past. I nearly fell out of the bus in my hurry to catch up to our team's owner and find out about when we could collect our winnings from yesterday.

"Ah," he said from the shadow of the bus after I'd asked him. He was sweating already in the growing July heat. "About the money."

"Oh no," I murmured. I'd had a feeling this would all turn sour, with my luck. "What happened?"

"My cousins talked to the wrong bookies," J.L. began, nodding at my players as they slowly made their way into the bus. The truck bed squeaked in protest with each new person arriving and settling into a seat. Soon all the windows were decorated with sink-washed All Nations uniforms.

"And...?" I said, feeling my knees twinge as I stood there waiting for J.L. to continue.

"They wouldn't honor our bets. Said they wouldn't pay for anyone betting on their own team. They'd checked the rules or something. I'm sorry, George, but they won't pay you the money you bet. You and me both."

"Tell me they gave us the money we put down back," I said, though I knew the answer. Damn this crooked town.

J.L. shook his head. "We waited too long to place our bets and got stuck with the grifters. At least some of my cousins made some money with the bookies they used. Otherwise we'd be all done. I bet just about all my savings on those games. Look at the bright side—that's how confident I am in your boys, George. At least we have money for fuel to get us through the next week or two."

I was too apoplectic to say anything more to our owner. The best I could do was nod at him before I boarded the bus, knees shouting out a rude reminder of their injured presence, and find my seat in the cramped, moist, shadowy bus.

The bus engine roared to life, and we rumbled west past the tall buildings and honking cars of downtown. Moving on to the next town, the next game. I rubbed the back of my head and closed my eyes.

That address on the napkin stuffed into my pocket was the last thing I wanted to look at today. I should have trusted my instincts. I'd gambled and lost again. When would I ever learn?

Chapter Ten

Naperville to Aurora to Davenport, Iowa. We played all comers, fresh and well-rested Midwestern teams, all of them white, while we were all exhausted and miserable from sleeping in our tents, on the bus, or on a forgiving farmer's porch or barn. We were lucky to scrape together enough cash for lunch each day. My players were on their own for the rest of their meals.

After Davenport, we hit what felt like every small farm town in Iowa, every day for the next two weeks, sometimes two or even three towns a day, until we reached the western end of the state in Sioux City. With each game, the crowds seemed to diminish, which I could only blame on the toll taken by the war; people either lacked the money to pay admission for the games, or they lacked the time to attend, due to the absence of a son or father, off to fight overseas.

And so, on the twentieth of July, I watched with a tired sense of relief as Buddha and the rest of my team finished up the last innings of a twilight game against the Sioux City Meat Packers, yet another all-white minor-league team. I barely had the energy to consult my roster, not to mention my sparse records from the past few games to know which of my tired pitchers had the most rested arm.

Fortunately, somebody other than my distracted self had been keeping a record of the twenty-one games we'd played from Independence Day through today. Unfortunately, he wrote in a language that nobody else on my team could understand.

"What's this mean, Jiang?" I asked at the top of the seventh. I pointed at a tiny square symbol made with about two dozen strokes of ink, careful not to touch the paper. I'd been watching him keeping his notes while our team was at bat, and I'd quickly learned that each game he recorded perfectly filled a thick, lemon-scented page in his book.

"Error," Jiang said, his pink tongue caught between his teeth as he painted his symbols in a line marching down the paper. I found it interesting that all men, no matter what their skin color, always had the same color tongues.

"Whose error?"

"Mack, in center. He caught ball, but not *possible* how he caught ball. Had to be error."

"You mean when he ran all the way from his spot in center to the rightfield foul pole and caught it just before it curved away? While *you* just watched him run past from your spot in right?"

"Yes, uh-huh. Should be foul. Error."

"And you explain all that, here, in your words and pictures?"

Jiang nodded, his dark eyes focused on the field, where Art had been caught stealing second. Jiang hissed in a quick breath and began stroking out another black symbol on his scorecard.

Standing at the plate for us now was Boles, who batted— as always—at the bottom of the order. Just as I looked up from Jiang's calligraphy, our white pitcher was beaned. Again. This time he took the hit in his hip.

A mix of laughs and boos erupted from the all-white Iowa fans, jeering Boles as he stalked to first, the whole time staring down the hometown pitcher. I could see our young white pitcher was doing his best not to limp.

Jiang was consulting his previous pages in his book, along with my scribbled records from before he joined the team on the Fourth. I couldn't believe he'd found my notes and rosters from where I'd stuffed them under my seat in the bus. It was a kind of relief to have an official scorekeeper.

"Thirty-nine walks for him this season," he said, touching the non-inking end of his brush to his chin. "All hit-by-pitches. Not good for body *or* sense of self-worth."

I just laughed and shook my head. Someday I'd learn how to read what the young man from China's scrolls really said. Of course. Right after I had Mendez teach me Spanish.

"You're on deck, son," I said to Jiang. "Let's not worry about anyone's self-worth right now, except what you can earn with the bat. I'd like to finish this trip to Iowa with a win, and we'll need three runs to pull that off."

As I nodded at our young beaned pitcher at first and gave him the signal for a hit-and-run, I realized that like Jiang, Boles hadn't yet chatted with me about his beliefs about religion in general, and the afterlife in specific.

I almost felt disappointed. I'd gotten used to these talks with my players in the long hours between games. Each one gave me new insight into various faiths that I could take or leave as I saw fit. Either Boles was avoiding me, or he simply didn't value my opinion.

Reaching into my back pocket, I consulted my roster and placed small checks next to the players who *had* talked with me. I'd missed not only Boles, but Carrie Nation, Art Houdini, Jiang, and Buddha Rodriguez.

I'd been staying away from a chat with Rodriguez for fear of what sort of gibberish the deluded Mexican might tell me, while I'd been avoiding such a discussion with Jiang due to the man's difficulty with the language (I'd learned my lesson with Phil the Philippine).

I heard the echo of hollow laughter once more as I realized what the rest of the players who had avoided me—and me, them—all had in common: they were all white.

I could almost hear our former head coach now, reveling in my discomfort: "*Are the beliefs of your white players less important? Do you fear being taught the truth about life and death and faith, boy?*"

But instead of a cold hand on the back of my neck in response to my dark thoughts, a strange cry went up from the crowd, accompanied by a pounding of footsteps behind me that made the earth shake.

From the stretch of infield between third base and second base came Phil the Philippine's voice, speaking the only words from him that I'd ever fully comprehended:

"Oh shit. My *family*."

All thick arms and wide bodies and wild black hair, a trio of amber-skinned men thundered past me on their way toward my shortstop. Phil dropped his glove and simply waited for the coming onslaught, helpless, his mouth open. An instant later, the three burly men, shirtless and wearing only baggy white pants, tackled him. For a painful moment, my shortstop disappeared under a pileup of long-limbed bodies.

"No!" I shouted, recovering from my shock. The crowd, thinking this was just a gag or a novelty act between innings, broke loose of their shocked silence and began to clap and cheer. The three big men lifted Phil—struggling at last—up on their shoulders. They'd already pried off his spikes and his cap.

"No!" I shouted again, on my way out of the dugout. "You can't just *take* him!"

At that moment, I turned and was confronted by a woman larger than me, wearing a flowered dress. She wore her hair in a topknot the size of my glove, and she wasn't grinning.

When she began speaking in the same strange language that Phil had used to try to communicate with me during his three seasons on the team, everything became clear. I thought I caught her mentioning something about the sun being in your eyes and fire filling the land under us, but her message was clear: the time had come for Phil to rejoin his family.

I took a step toward the field, but a sharp fingernail, attached to the woman's hand, which was attached to her very large, well-muscled arm, poked me in the chest, stopping me in my tracks.

And before any of us could say another word, Phil's broad-shouldered brothers had toted him off into a waiting horse-drawn wagon covered in bright, tropical flowers. They thundered off amid the hooting and cheering of the oblivious crowd.

The All Nations had lost another player. I didn't even get to say goodbye to Phil, our crackerjack shortstop and base thief. I wonder if the young man would've even understood me if I'd gotten to say it.

A fter losing Phil, we lost the game by one run; we simply ran out of daylight and innings to stage an effective comeback. When most of the equipment had been packed up onto the bus and our traveling band had played their final song (led by Mendez, he of the healed right arm and the trusty cornet), I was intercepted by J.L. on my way back to the bus.

"Didn't see you here during the game," I said, giving the team owner a pained smile. "Sorry we looked like such duffers out there."

"Not at all," J.L. said, and then flashed his trademark smile at me. "I just got in for the last few at-bats."

"Ah. So you missed the kidnapping of our shortstop."

"Was that who I saw on that wagon we passed on our way here? Phil?"

I nodded. "His family wanted him to come back home, I guess. I wasn't going to be the fool to stop them. His brothers, not to mention his mother, are all business."

"Hmm," J.L. said. I could tell he had something else on his mind, because this news would've have turned his face beet-red otherwise. "That figures. At least it justifies our coming trip," he said, as if talking to himself. He looked up at me, eyes flashing in the fading daylight. "So George. How about you ride back with me, in my car? We have some talking to do."

I almost dropped my armload of bats at the question. A white man and a colored man in the same vehicle? That sort of thing simply never happened.

"George? Are you okay?"

"Yeah," I said. I walked over to the bus and grabbed my bag from the front seat. "I'd be happy to join you, J.L.," I added, surprised at how much I meant it.

I ignored my players' ribbing about how I was too good to ride back to Kansas City with them and Blount. Today's game was the last one scheduled for a week and a half, and the ride back was sure to be loud and boisterous. I'd already seen a few flasks being passed back and forth in the bus seats.

"I didn't think you'd mind a less bumpy ride back home," J.L. said once we'd both settled into the wide back seat of the big Model T driven by Gilmore, J.L.'s secretary. "I know you've had a rough couple of weeks on the road. A rough *season*, really, if I may be so bold. Let's move out, Quincy."

Quincy, I thought. That was the man's first name. How could I forget that?

The black car rumbled past the team bus and up a gravel road that lead to the main highway. We rode for a comfortable ten minutes in silence, heading south from Sioux City. The cool air whipped past us and the sky went from dark red to purple to black around us. The squeaking of frogs competed with the rumble of the sedan's engine.

I sensed that we would cross over the Iowa border into Missouri in less than half an hour, though I was unsure how I could have known or predicted such a thing in the dark. From our right, I could almost smell the mud from the Missouri River, whose course ran parallel to our path down the old roads.

"So what are your plans for the next week or two, George?" J.L. asked, waking me from a near-doze. The map of glittering stars emerging from the night sky had hypnotized me.

"Resting," I said, then cleared my throat. "Beyond that, I've no major plans. Hard to enjoy too much time off when money's tight, and there's no games to play, and you're all alone. Probably set up some practices with the team in a few days."

"I see. That's... understandable."

I'd never talked to J.L. about my family and their absence from my life, but I knew he was aware of my situation. Like so many men my age who'd lived with baseball all our lives, certain situations needed no further explaining.

"You've done fine work this season," J.L. began. "You've won far more games than you've lost. What's more, well, the team always draws a crowd. The All Nations puts on a *show*, every game. That's your real skill, you know, George. Pulling the best game from each player. It's quite a thrill to see. I'm almost positive you don't even realize you're doing it. That's good coaching, my friend."

I caught myself smiling at this unexpected praise. A firefly whizzed past the window, followed by three more, like shooting stars falling close to Earth.

"Just doing my job, is all."

"Well," J.L. said, "if you're interested, your All Nations have a chance to play someplace few ball clubs have ever been."

I sat up straighter in the hard leather seat of the Model T. "What are you saying?"

"What I'm saying," J.L. laughed, "is that on the strength of the All Nations' wins against Foster's Giants and even Jack Johnson, I was able to arrange the mother lode of road trips for the team. My investors' bets paid off from Independence Day—while we never got our money, they had better luck with the topnotch bookies. And those bets are going to get us to *Cuba*."

"Cuba?" I looked from the fireflies blurring by us to my boss, whose pale face was almost glowing in the moonlight. I'd forgotten all about his hints about a trip south a few weeks ago; I'd figured that had just been another of his wild ideas that never panned out. I sat there, gulping night air like a dying fish.

"Cuba, George! We'll be there for a two-week stint, playing and recruiting. And there's no war down there to distract fans of our great sport."

"But... Cuba? As in south of Florida?"

"That's the place. The folks down there are mad about baseball, just mad about it. It's a whole 'nother world down in Havana, my friend."

I was too dumbfounded to say anything more. I gazed back at the stars stretching across the sky, too many to ever count. Who would have thought that I'd ever face such prospects in my life? Head coach, the oldest first baseman ever, and now, international traveler.

"Havana!" I said, and I was laughing with disbelief and relief as soon as the syllables rolled off my tongue. The tightness in my chest I'd been feeling all day, just thinking about going back home to my empty house, began to fade.

"Unless you'd rather stay in Kansas City, that is."

"No," I said, my spirits suddenly rising. "I think I'd like to go to Cuba. I think I'd like that a lot."

"That's the spirit. We leave in two days. And guess what, George. We'll be *flying*."

Our driver chose that very moment to launch the Model T up and over a rise in the road. The split-second of being airborne was enough to make me lose my breath.

Ahead of us in the darkness, Gilmore murmured an apology.

"Flying?" I repeated. "Isn't that a little dangerous? I don't think they've taken all the kinks out of that mode of transportation. Those boys in North Carolina just perfected their little glider a few years ago, I thought."

"Are you kidding me? They've got planes going up by the dozens over in Europe, George. Dropping bombs. If only I were young enough, I tell you, I'd go fight them myself. That would truly be an *adventure*. Fighting for truth and honor against the oncoming German hordes."

I had a sudden thrill of fear as I remembered the nightmare that woke me the morning of the Fourth, back in Chicago. The dream that had ended with that unnerving sense of nothingness.

"Just as long as," I said, swallowing hard, "just as long as we're not flying to Cuba in a *zeppelin*."

J.L.'s infectious laugh rang out into the countryside, most likely heard only by grazing cattle and wandering deer.

"Of course not, George! My cousin down in Florida knows someone with a plane we can use to get there, and I've got another cousin who's a pilot. It'll be the sort of thing that people will talk about for years! And we'll be *living* it."

I couldn't help but grin at the idea of gangly Phil or burly No Small Foot on a plane, on their way into the air and out of the country to play some Cuban ball. Then I remembered with a pang that Phil was gone, carted off by his family in their matching white pants, leaving us painfully shorthanded again. If anyone got seriously injured, we'd be short a player out in the field, and that was with *me* already playing every game on my unsteady knees. We needed a recruiting trip like this to bolster our numbers.

J.L. knew me well enough to leave me alone to hash out the details and feasibility of the trip. I sat back and wondered how my players would hold up if they were all stuck together in another country, especially a place where most folks wouldn't even speak the same language as most of us.

You've got Mendez to translate for you, I reminded myself. You and the team will be just fine. And this trip could just be the glue we need—a voyage to another world to keep the All Nations from falling apart.

"What do you say, George?" J.L. said at last, as the car approached the warm white-yellow glow created by city lights against the darkness. Probably Omaha, or maybe

Council Bluffs. "Are you ready for the next adventure in your life?"

With darkened farmlands stretching out on all around us, I reached out to grasp the hand J.L. was holding out to me.

"I'm your man for the job," I told J.L., shaking on it. "Of course, you knew that all along, didn't you?"

I let go of his hand.

"But you'll have to buy me one of those Havana cigars as soon as we get there."

J.L. laughed, and we rode on in companionable silence though the cool night, the last barrier created by our diverging skin colors melting away almost to nothing.

Damned if I didn't feel good about this crazy plan. And I couldn't wait to tell my players about the location of our next set of games. I'd have them over tomorrow for lunch and break the news to them.

At close to one in the morning, according to the clock tower we passed outside my neighborhood, J.L.'s Model T rolled up to my small house on the outskirts of the city. I was home again, much sooner than if I'd ridden back on the team bus.

With aching knees and a sore back, I waved to J.L. and lugged my bag inside. I leaned my body against the inside of my front door and inhaled the stale, unused air of my house. Home again.

I looked at the meager contents of my living room—couch, chair, trunk, end table, wood stove, leaning bookshelf—until I became familiar with them again. The place was surprisingly cool for the middle of July. Usually this little shack was hotter than a furnace when I got home between trips in the summer. I felt something give inside my chest, a skipped heartbeat, a hand squeezing my heart.

Cuba. Havana, Cuba.

The names filled me with a thrill in my cool, empty house. Our trip south—farther south than I'd ever been in my years of traveling—simply couldn't come soon enough.

And then the hand gripping my heart gave me another, violent jolt. The chill in my living room intensified as I noticed a figure sitting in my old leather chair. That chair had been empty a few seconds ago.

"Worrell," I whispered. My words steamed in the air, which had grown even colder in the past few seconds. His absence in my life since Chicago had been a blessing. And now he was here, like a curse renewed.

"*I got tired of chasing your damned ramshackle bus all over creation,*" he rasped as he put his feet up on my old trunk. His spikes were glittering, razor-sharp. "*Figured I'd just come here and wait it out until your victorious return. I have plenty of time for such things these days. Vengeance hath no timeline.*"

My hands were fisted, and my heart, suddenly released from its grip of sadness, beat madly.

So that was what this was all about. Revenge.

"This is my home. You are not welcome. You can go now," I paused, choosing my words carefully, knowing I had to say it. "Coach," I added.

I hated appeasing him like that, but I was tired of him dogging my heels. He'd nearly ruined my reunion with Lizbeth, and he'd been haunting my sleep and distracting me in my waking hours for far too long.

"*Oh not just yet.*" Worrell gave a dry laugh. "*I don't think that would be fair,*" he said as he lifted a thin arm and gestured around my house as if he owned the place, "*to all the old friends I brought with me.*"

Impossibly, the air around me grew even colder, and the shadows stretched out and grew together in my already-dark house. I staggered back a step before I could catch myself. Cold air hissed around my living room, and then the hissing turned into individual voices. The voices began to speak, all at once, making my head spin.

"*This is the one.*"

"*The new coach.*"

"*New nigger coach, killed off a white man for the job.*"

"*They play while we fight for our lives in some far-off land.*"

"*They will pay.*"

"He's *the one who must pay.*"

First six, then a dozen figures crowded into my living room, as if pulling themselves free of the darkness. Their skin, like Worrell's, was translucent, and half were wearing old baseball uniforms. Almost all of the uniforms were styles I hadn't seen in decades, from even before my playing days.

The other figures coalescing around me were worse; bloodied and horribly wounded men in soldiers' uniforms, most of them missing limbs or portions of their faces or head, and worse. But their voices continued on, in spite of their wounds, damning me for things I hadn't done.

"*I have a feeling,*" Worrell said, grinning at me from my chair as his ghastly entourage fell silent at last, "*that this will be a long, long night. We have much to talk about. All of us old friends.*"

Not real, I told myself, but I couldn't stop shaking. I looked down at my hands and the worn floor below them. Anywhere but at the figures pressing close to me. None of these apparitions are real. They're not really here.

I felt my chest tighten up once more in the cold air, but I bit down hard on the moan that tried to slip out of my mouth.

This was my house, damn it. I won't be intimidated here. Not after all we'd been through already this season. After all I'd been through in this *lifetime*, for that matter.

"And none of you are really here," I said through gritted teeth.

I was rewarded with Worrell's shaking head, following by resounding laughter from almost two dozen ghostly voices, including one as deep as thunder. A voice I'd heard before.

I thought immediately of Shreveport. That was where I'd heard him last. As impossible as that had to have been, as he was also, like Worrell, dead. I unclenched my jaw long enough to sound out his name.

"Derby?" The chill seemed to leave my bare skin the instant I said his name. The spectral intruders in my living room stepped back, as if to make room for the big man at the back of the room, closest to the kitchen.

"I went to your funeral," I began, then my knees gave out, and I dropped into my old coach with a puff of dusty air. I heard Worrell snicker from somewhere behind me.

It was indeed Derby Molton coming toward me. I'd know those big hands and wide shoulders anywhere, though his face was swollen and sewn inexpertly back together after his violent death aboard the doomed train.

Derby wasn't laughing. I looked at the pale faces of the spirits around me before they faded completely into the walls. The spirits had been creeping away ever since I called out my old friend and former teammate.

All of them white, I realized. Derby was the only colored spirit in my house. Even Worrell had slipped away from my old chair while I'd been distracted by my friend's return.

That thought encouraged me, despite the pain in my knees and the shortness of breath still plaguing me. Hold on, I told my old body, with special emphasis aimed at my racing heart. I did not need it to stop now.

"What is this company you've been keeping lately?" I whispered. I extended a hand to the big first baseman standing over me, knowing he'd never be able to shake it. "This doesn't seem like your doing."

"*Your former boss has some pull, where I've been,*" Derby began, hunkering down over me so we were almost at eye level with one another. "*I didn't have much choice. Plus, if what he promised me is real, I'll be able to find rest, at last. I been paying the price for my sins for a long time, George. At least he got me away from the train tracks. I spent a lot of time haunting those tracks, but never got anywhere—*"

"Derby," I began. I'd forgotten how the big man could talk, once he got started.

My apartment was warm and empty now, with just Derby and me in it. The other apparitions had lost interest.

We could talk freely, if such a thing was possible between the living and the dead.

"So Worrell made you some sort of deal, did he? What's he want from me, other than to torture me for not telling him to get his bony white ass into the dugout back on April Fool's Day?"

"*He wants you to quit,*" Derby said simply.

"What?"

"*Stop traveling, stop showing up other teams, 'specially the all-white teams. Stop getting everyone's hopes up. There's a war on, don't you know? This is no time for playing games, George.*"

I felt myself gasping for air—not from infirmity, but from anger. What had taken the spine out of my old friend? Did Worrell do that?

"I hope you like wandering," I said at last. "Because there's no way in the world I'm stopping, not for that bastard Worrell. Making you do his dirty work for him. Derby, just *go.* You're dead, my man. Let go and get out of here."

Derby started to fade at that.

"*Wish it was that easy,*" he said, sinking into my floor. "*I really do,*" he added before disappearing completely into the ground under my house. "*The only one who can let us go now... Is you, George.*"

Chapter Eleven

Being host to a dozen restless spirits can put quite a damper on a person's enthusiasm for remaining at home. After a day of it, I was ready to get back on the road, even if it meant heading to Cuba early. With dead soldiers and players from the last few decades passing through the walls of my cramped little house at random intervals, I was about to go mad.

Never a quiet moment, and the chill coming off the passing dead was constant. And they always had a word or two to share before walking through the walls.

"*Some new coach, sitting around and reading.*"

"*New nigger coach.*"

"*Playing games while we fight and die...*"

"*Worrell says you are the one who must pay, nigger coach.*"

What kept my sanity was what Derby had said to me before he disappeared through my living room floor—"*He wants you to quit*"—coupled with my own desire to never again bend to Worrell's will.

They were simply trying to scare me. Wasn't that what ghosts did?

Wasn't that all they were *capable* of doing?

If Worrell thought he could sabotage my team just like he'd tried to sabotage my reunion with my daughter and son-in-law, he was mistaken. I'd show him a thing or two about deadly determination. Even if it killed me.

So I stayed home and ignored the spirits attempting to haunt me. They were quite harmless, overall, and the chill coming off them was thrust back with the roaring fire I kept stoked in my blackened fireplace, here in the late days of July.

I did treat myself to an outing on my second day back so I could gather my team and announce the trip to Cuba. The plan was met with both shock and elation by the players, who weren't expecting to make any money or travel anywhere for these weeks where our barnstorming games had dried up on us.

My players and I talked over a long, leisurely lunch, making plans for our departure in less than two days, and quizzing Mendez on the proper ways to curse in *Español*.

And then I returned home. To an empty house.

"Come on out," I called. "Show your dead selves already."

But the shades were open and sunlight filled the living room, the house warm and almost fragrant despite the months of accumulated dust. I dropped my hat on the couch and took a seat in the banged-up chair where Worrell's ghost had rested last night, before he slipped away on me while I was talking to Derby.

This is no time for playing games, George.

Derby. He was a man who had charged heedlessly into everything he did, never asking permission nor begging forgiveness afterwards. He once picked up another player by the ankles and shook him upside-down for half a minute for insulting another player's mother.

And there he was last night, asking *me* to do wrong so it would benefit him. I couldn't imagine what sort of promises Worrell had made to Derby—and all the other ball players and soldiers with him. I didn't want to even try.

Exhaling with relief at the emptiness and silence filling my little house, my gaze came to rest on the old trunk next to my chair. I reached over and lifted the dusty lid. The hinges let loose, leaving me holding the lid like the skin of a dead animal.

Curious now, I began lifting out all the various items inside. In the middle were loose-leaf pages wrapped in thin slices of wood that were easily three decades old, with yellow newspapers and clipped articles on the left. On the right side were letters.

Looking at those letters, my chest went tight. Some of the letters had postmarks on them, while others had clearly never been sent. At least one of the sent letters bore the delicate handwriting that can only be accomplished by a female hand.

I should put these back, I told myself. Or toss them into the fire.

Instead, I began reading.

The first one was dated June 13, 1894. The year they'd left. The content was brief and succinct. "We'd appreciate you sending a money order to this address before the month ends. The baby needs clothes, my son needs a winter coat. Don't make me get the law involved."

I dropped the letter as if it were covered in flames. Lizbeth was "the baby" and Jacob was now "her son."

Jacob had been fifteen the last time I'd seen him, and Lizbeth had been barely eleven. My whole time back home after that season on the road, my boy had refused to even pick up a baseball.

That refusal became too much for me on a day in March, after a long winter of working in the laundry between seasons, when I wanted nothing more than to play a game of catch with my son. Approaching forty, I knew I was facing the end of my playing years, and that knowledge haunted my every movement.

I was in this state when, after learning that Jacob had thrown away the glove I'd bought for him, I lashed out at my son and knocked him to the floor. I'll never forget the soft give in his cheek I felt when the palm of my hand struck it. Thinking about it now made me want to vomit.

With that one foolish, frustration-fueled act, that chapter of my life came to an abrupt close. Maddie and the children were gone before opening day of that year.

Blinking the soreness of unspent tears from my eyes, I looked over at the coals smoldering under the grate of the fireplace. No chills filled the room, and I needed to open the windows to let the summertime breeze clear the stale air. But I remained sitting, frozen by memories.

How had the years run past so quickly? And all I had to show for them was a trunk full of letters. And an old body worn out from too many years playing a young man's game.

A surge of anger filled me, and I contemplated lighting a fire with these letters. I could be rid of Maddie and Jacob and Lizbeth, and my memories of them, in seconds.

But before I could get to my feet to incinerate the letters, I was interrupted by a knock at the door. I let out a long, slow breath as my anger and sense of loss sloughed off my like dead skin.

"Coming," I called as the person outside knocked again.

Better not be a salesman, I thought, walking on legs filled with pins and needles from sitting too long. Standing on my tiny front porch was the last person I would've ever expected to darken my doorstep.

"Sorry to interrupt, Coach," my white pitcher Boles said, glancing over his shoulder. "But we have to talk."

After fighting the urge to simply slam the door on him and go back to my reading, I let the young man inside. Boles gave my ruined trunk and the piles of papers in front of it a cursory look before perching himself on my old couch. Our southpaw pitcher was sporting a new bruise on his cheek and a puffy right ear that resembled a cauliflower, evidence of either a recent beaning or a bar fight since our last game.

"So," I began, "can I get you something to drink?"

Boles shook his head. "I need to talk to you about Cuba."

"Ah, I see. I think this trip will be a helpful experience for you. Their pitchers can teach you a lot, and—"

"No, that's not it," Boles interrupted, fingering his swollen ear. "I'm just worried about the people down there. The Cubans. What if they don't like us?"

"Boles. Since when did you worry about anyone *liking* you?"

"Look, Coach, just hear me out, okay? I'm talking 'bout all those darkies, ah"—he caught himself a moment too late—"dark-skinned people down there. What'll they *do* to a white boy like me?"

I could only shrug in response, thinking of Boles' Southern-accented voice cutting through the chatter of the games, deriding the opposing pitcher and batters, especially with the colored teams, and occasionally teasing our own players before either I or No Small Foot would lean on him to shut him up.

I bit my lip on my way to the kitchen and let him talk on.

"Old habits die hard, Coach," Boles said, still sitting on the edge of my couch. "Old feelings, too. See, my daddy had this burning hatred inside him that killed him. Not just of colored folks, but Jews and Germans and Italians," he said, pronouncing the word "eye-talians."

I nodded and passed Boles a glass of water, while I drank one last cup of coffee.

"My daddy. Now there was a bitter man. I think I consigned him to an early grave when I didn't join him and his farming buddies in their group of men wearing bedsheets."

I almost choked on the coffee I'd just swallowed. I knew that group all too well. As did my uncle, run out of South Carolina by a gang of them who claimed to be protecting the land he was sharecropping with his son.

"That was in Arkansas, you see. But I said no. I couldn't—I grew up playing ball with Negro boys, and they weren't all that different from me. More or less. After I turned Daddy down, I had no choice but to run away from the farm. I was fifteen. Been living off my pitching arm ever since."

I nodded and sipped at my coffee. "What would your father think of you playing on *our* team?"

"Oh Lord," Boles said, his bruised face paling. "It would kill my Daddy to see me now." And then, to my surprise, the boy smiled. "That's why I'm so proud to play on this team."

"So you're doing it just to spite his memory?"

"Not just that. I love pitching, and I honestly like the people on the team. Well, most of 'em..."

Boles gave me a crooked smile then, one that opened up a whole new side of him. I almost would've believed the sour, grumpy young man had a sense of humor.

"Heck, Coach. Even old Art and I get along these days. Haven't heard a harsh word between us since Chicago, have you? We've gotten... *close.*"

The kid was right—I hadn't had to break up any more scuffles between the two of them. But something about that shine in Boles' eyes made me wary, like he wasn't sharing everything with me. Then I looked at him smiling again.

Him and Art? Why was he telling me this?

"We have to work together, you know," talking over my sudden discomfort.

Surely not, I thought. That wasn't natural. So I kept on talking.

"That's how we're going to get by down in Cuba. If you can't handle that, we'll leave you here. Or, if you have a problem while we're down in Cuba, we'll leave you *there.*"

Boles' smile faltered for a moment.

"I know I just got to learn to shut my mouth," he said. "I got a short fuse, especially when I'm not pitching and I can't do anything to help the team except run my mouth. Art's always telling me that."

He glanced at my clock on the wall and stood abruptly. He seemed flushed, suddenly. As if he'd said too much.

"Sort of like I'm doing right now. I 'd better go. But one of these days, Coach, we got to talk about that other thing. That thing everyone's been talking to you about. You know— dying and all that. That religion stuff."

"Yes, of course," I said as I walked him to the door.

"Thanks, Coach," Boles said quickly, as if it pained him to do so.

"Not a problem. Now go get your arm rested for our trip."

With the door shut and Boles back outside, I heaved a long sigh and wondered what sort of beliefs a young man like Boles might have, a boy raised on this side of the new century. Believe it or not, I looked forward to our talk. We'd have plenty of time to get to it before the season ended.

I was a fool to think such a thing. Time was one thing the All Nations team was quickly burning through, like a handful of paper on a crackling fire.

In the next two days before our upcoming trip to Cuba, as I got caught up on my sleep, not once did I hear Worrell's voice. Nor did I see him or his fellow malcontents loitering in my living room. Maybe they were content to have my team stuck here idle, not playing any games. I didn't bother asking the walls or the floor.

I sat down in my beat-up leather chair to read some of the newspapers that had piled up on me in my travels. But before I could read a paragraph of an article about our wins over the American Giants in July, a sharp knocking sound came at my front door.

Surely *this* had to be a salesman; I'd not had this many visitors so close together in ages. I wondered if Boles had come back. I hoped not.

I opened the door. Mack. Of course.

"You know, Coach," he said, talking as if our last conversation had never ended, "this trip to Cuba is going to make the All Nations stronger than ever. It may be enough to keep us together until the last game of this season. And if that's the case, you'll get your wish. I promise that."

"Won't you come in?" I asked as the young man hurried past me and took a seat on my couch. Today, Mack's skin looked light as Charlie's had, as if he'd gotten a tan somehow.

"Chief Tokahoma," I muttered as I sat down on my old chair. "Wonder what he's doing these days?"

"Do you *really* want to know, Coach?"

"No," I said quickly. "Let's talk about something other than our missing former players. What brings you here, son?"

"*My* future." Mack's dark eyes locked onto mine, unblinking.

"Shouldn't you know that already, Mack?"

After another ten seconds of staring, Mack blinked at last, and I looked away, letting out the breath I'd been holding.

"I know, Coach, of every possible outcome of the lives caught up in this world's turning. But I do not know the future of my *own* life. I guess that is my blessing and my curse, if you believe in such concepts."

I felt a chill breeze slip through my living room, as if one of Worrell's cronies had slipped back into the house.

"Can I get you something?" I asked, unable to sit still with Mack's strange words hanging in the air.

"I'm fine, Coach." He leaned forward on the chair. "I'm not afraid of the future. I just want to talk to you about it."

I waved at the newspapers on my table and my trunk with its letters. "The future is beyond me, son. I'm still trying to come to grips with the past. Or at least get caught up to it."

"I understand," Mack said, up and moving toward the door in one easy motion. "I'm interrupting."

I beckoned him back to his seat with both hands.

"Not at all. I think you're just the person I need to talk to right now, Mack. I've been doing some interesting reading the past few days, and I've learned a thing or two about the future of baseball. Who knows—maybe I can give you some hints about your future in the process. It's the least I can do, you know."

"Why, thank you, Coach."

"Look. Most of the sportswriters have heard of the colored teams we play—they call 'em blackball teams, usually—and they're *writing* about them. Wondering why hitters like 'Home Run' Johnson or John Henry Lloyd or pitchers like Cannonball Redding or our own John Donaldson aren't in the big leagues. I can't help but agree with them. People are at least considering the idea of a team being made up of more than just white men. Maybe we won't be the odd team out anymore. Every team will be as mixed-up and..." I searched for the right word, "as *colorful* as the All Nations."

Mack had been nodding along with my words, and when I quit talking, he stopped as well. He turned his gaze toward the fading sunlight coming in through my uncurtained living room window.

"But that's just my thoughts on the future," I said, feeling my face grow warm. "I know I don't have any sort of accuracy like you do, son, but... Mack?"

As I looked at the motionless young man sitting across from me, I could have sworn that Mack's skin grew white, then black, and then returned to its original tanned color. As if he were simply an empty container filling and emptying with a variety of colored liquids. Not once did he blink.

"Mack?" I said. "You all right?"

Finally, he clucked his tongue like a chicken three times and inhaled a long breath of air. On his young face was a look of sheer terror.

"Mack," I whispered. "What is it?"

"Something was here," he said, and my arms and legs went cold. "Something that's making the future hazy to me. This room is too full of the past Coach. You had—visitors? Men taken before their time. Soldiers and... Coach? Other players?"

Sudden guilt rushed over me, as if Mack had caught me cheating on my wife. I hadn't invited Worrell and his dead posse to my house. Why should I feel in the wrong about that? I was the one being haunted.

"Last night," I said after a long moment of deciding whether Mack deserved the truth. "A dozen men. Led by Worrell. None of them... alive."

"They were looking for me," Mack said, not a question.

"No, son," I said with a surprised laugh. "Didn't even mention you. They were just trying to strong-arm me. Wanted me to break up the team."

"I thought we were through with Worrell," Mack murmured. His eyes were dark as he stared into the black mouth of my fireplace. "This is dire news, Coach. Dire news. I never saw this coming. Never..."

I walked over to him, passing by the piles of papers and my trunk, and rested a hand on his shoulder. I almost pulled away, shocked at the tension filling him. I felt like I was touching a wild dog straining against a leash.

I thought of Mack's glowing eyes the day that Worrell was killed, and the way he'd gazed at me just before that foul tip knocked me flat earlier this month. I didn't know this young man at all.

"Mack," I said, my voice a croak. "What *do* you see? What's coming?"

Mack's only answer was to look up at me with a wide-eyed stare that traveled through me, into the dark, unknowable reaches of the future.

The third time I was interrupted from my reading by a knock on my door was two hours later, at dusk of that same day. This time, half a dozen of my players stood outside, dressed in their Sunday best, looking like they'd just gotten off the team bus and wanted to make a grand entrance at the ballpark.

"Time to go out on the town, Coach!" Donaldson called out, doing a quick dance on my crowded front porch.

"Get your coat, *Señor*," added Mendez. Art and Boles, I noticed, were standing side-by-side on my front porch. They nodded along with the others, while Buddha Rodriguez grunted his encouragement.

Mack was not with them.

"I think I'm just going to stay home and rest, guys..."

"Oh no, you don't," Boles said, coming from the back of the crowd to shake my hand and pull me part of the way out of the door. "Come have a drink with us and toast the start of the Cuban season with us. None of us can stand being cooped up at home any more. This team was built to *travel*!"

Before I could argue any further, I was led to the first of two old vehicles, a battered blue Model T owned by Donaldson and the other, a dilapidated truck belonging to Buddha covered with rust like polka dots. I sat in the passenger seat of Donaldson's car, glad to be spared Buddha's deathtrap.

"Where to?" I said in a resigned voice tinged with a hint of excitement.

"The Blue Room," Boles said from the back seat. Art flipped a coin in the seat next to him, catching it flat on his forefinger: heads. "You know, in Street's Hotel. They've got a great selection, if you're needing a little boost. And I think we all are, right, Coach?"

"Perhaps," I said, and then Donaldson hit the gas.

While the city rushed past me, I felt like I was being taken on a tour of my life up until now in the city. We passed the church where Maddie and I had been married, the building now twice its original size, adorned with a tall concrete cross five stories overhead. Two blocks later, the rows of black-owned stores rushed by—the clothing store where Maddie had shopped when we had our first baby, and the butcher where she'd bought her first ribs for the family dinner. Across the street was the new theater showing the latest moving picture shows, and another Baptist church two doors down.

The car rocked to a sudden stop in front of Street's Hotel. I'd only been here once before, during a hurried meeting I'd had years ago with J.L.'s man Gilmore, when they'd offered me the assistant coaching job. At the time, I never thought the All Nations concept would ever get off the ground, but I'd accepted the job anyway, expecting to have to find another the following fall.

We burst out of the car like a gang of boys out after curfew and poured through the hotel doors.

Usually, the people of Kansas City had a remarkable air of acceptance for the different races that passed through their river city town, but that Thanksgiving night at the Blue Room, I was aware of a sea of raised eyebrows and conversations hidden behind hands as I sat with my Chinese, Japanese, colored, white, and Mexican players. I ignored the looks and let my foot start tapping to the smooth sounds of the jazz trio next to the bar.

The bar was in the colored part of town, so the inclusion of the white men was most likely the source of the majority of the whispers and the glances, until the words "All Nations" spread between the patrons and servers.

"Just one drink, then," I said after Boles and Donaldson vetoed my attempt to order a tonic water from the waiter.

"Rum all around," Mendez shouted. "Why, we need to get used to the taste," he added, looking at me innocently.

Four rounds of rum later, I was telling stories about all the various teams I'd played for and then coached. My face glowing with the heat of the alcohol, I felt like I had so many stories, I couldn't tell them all fast enough. I was chatting faster than the drummer up on the stage could scratch out a beat.

I talked about the games with Moses "Fleet" Walker before Walker began to lose his mind and carry a knife with him wherever he went, just like Rube Foster now carried a gun with him along with his ever-present cigars, and how Fleet pulled the knife on a white man during an argument in a bar.

I talked about the rule changes over the years, how strikes had gone from four to three per hitter, and how pitchers once threw underhand. My players accused me of making it all up.

But I knew the real story of the game. I'd *lived* it.

Soon the rum made one story overlap into another, to the point where I couldn't keep the different teams named Giants straight.

"Why does everyone love that name so much, anyway?" I said, convinced I was slurring. "Kansas City Giants. St. Louis Giants. Everyone wanted to be the so-and-so Giants or some version of it. It all starts to get... to get... ah..."

"Confusing?" Art offered from my left, his nimble fingers rolling a shot glass down his knuckles.

"Confusing!" I said in a too-loud voice. "Thas' the word."

"We can't all be giants like you, Coach," Boles said from next to Art, and I gave him a long look. I couldn't tell if the young white man was making fun of me or being honest. Maybe Art had been a good influence on him lately.

Instead of thinking too much on that, I had more rum.

Half an hour later, after the band had packed up their bass, drums, and saxophone, and most of the other patrons had left the bar, our table remained full. Everyone was singing, alternating between drinking songs and hymns. The bartender shouted for last call, and I'd reached that unfortunate point of intoxication that led me to remember only the bad things in my life.

I turned to Art, who'd remained sober throughout the entire evening by pretending to down his shots of rum, dropping them into the potted plant next to him instead with a quick flick of the wrist. I was proud to catch him doing it.

I began regaling my third baseman, along with anyone else who would listen, about my absent wife, my aching knees, and most of all, my fear of dying. Being back here in Kansas City, not to mention my recent non-living visitors from my first night back, had brought those fears back to the surface.

"My time is so short," I said, vaguely aware that I was spraying everyone with a fine mist of spittle with each "s" sound I made. "You men don't realize how fast it passes you by."

Art nodded and patted my hand, prying the full shot glass of rum from my fingers. The potted plant absorbed another couple ounces of clear liquor.

"But Coach," Donaldson said, "haven't you come to some kinda terms with all that? After all we talked about with what happens after you... you know? I mean, haven't you talked to *everyone* on the team about this?"

I gave a nervous glance at Boles and then at Art again.

"Well, almost. Still some people I need to check up on."

"Soon," Boles said. "Right, Coach?"

I nodded, and the world shimmered as I felt a sudden rush of emotion.

You boys, I thought. *You boys are my family now. Even strange Mack.*

All of the young men around the table gave uncomfortable smiles or looked away, pulling at their collars or playing with their shot glasses.

"Um, thanks, Coach," Mendez said after a lengthy pause. "*Gracias.*"

With a rush of blood to my face, I realized I'd said my thoughts out loud.

I never saw this coming, Mack had said.

"Wait—" I began.

"That's okay, Coach," Boles said, making a big deal of pulling up his coat sleeve to look at his watch. "It's late, and we'd better get going."

"No, I just—"

"Yeah," Art said, catching Boles as the skinny boy stumbled. "I'll drive you gents home. Including this big lug," he said, poking Buddha Rodriguez, who'd taken one shot of rum two hours ago, and promptly passed out against the wall. Art got him up and on his feet in one neat movement, and then he, Boles, and Buddha clomped out the door.

"I'll get Coach," Donaldson said, waving off the rest of the players as if he were shaking off a pitch from No Small Foot. "See all of you bright and early tomorrow."

I took careful, drunken steps out of the empty bar and into the street, and the cool wind scrubbed some of the drunken lethargy from my mind.

"You've got a lot to look forward to," Donaldson was saying as we crept away from the curb in his car. The world wouldn't stop swirling. "Have hope for the future and all that's to come. Maybe even try reading the good book once in a while. It couldn't hurt."

Pop, I thought, remembering the sound of the ball meeting Worrell's skull. *Pop*. I thought I'd purged that memory from my brain, but the rum had brought it back again.

"Thanks," I said, shoulders hunched against the cool night air as well as the echoing sound in my brain. When we arrived in front of my house, I got out with more effort than I would've thought possible and waved at Donaldson until his car lights faded into the night.

I knew I needed to get to bed and grab a few winks before the team bus left at the crack of dawn tomorrow, but I felt the urge to do some *writing* once more. I hurried inside, stumbling once or three times, and found some paper.

"*Dear son*," I said as I began scribbling the same words onto a fresh sheet of paper, "*I know you have not heard from me in years, and it is possible that you do not want to hear from me now. But let me begin by offering my deepest apologies. My life has been full of regret since the day you left.*"

I had to keep wiping the tears that spilled from my eyes as sat writing and reeling in my chair. I told Jacob about my life and inquired about what he was now doing with his own life. I forced myself to stop long before I wanted to, knowing that I couldn't overburden him with too much information like this.

I looked at the scratchouts and inkstains on the page in front of me. This was unacceptable. Taking a deep, shaky breath, I took out another sheet of paper and began to carefully write the letter again. The room was still spinning.

After another hour (and three more attempts), I came up with a suitable version, free of blemishes and as readable as I could make it with my head throbbing.

I signed this version of the letter and lifted the lid of the trunk. Flipping through all the papers inside, I found the most recent envelope sent to me from Chicago, and I copied the return address onto an envelope. I even tracked down a loose stamp under some papers in my kitchen.

Only as I was folding the pages to put inside the addressed envelope that I noticed that this final draft was not addressed as "Dear Jacob" but instead, "My Dearest Maddie." My own writing hand, a traitor.

"Foolish old man," I said in a slurred mumble.

Still fueled by the encouraging words of my players and the shots of rum, I trudged out into the darkness. The post office was just six blocks away.

"Don't do it, boy," a hard but faint voice whispered on the wind, as if from a great distance. *"Not worth it, I tell you. You're just wasting time."*

Though it took quite an effort in my inebriated state, I was able to tuck the letter into my pocket and stop up my ears with both hands as I walked. A block later, the voice had dissipated like smoke.

"Take that, Worrell," I slurred. "You white bastard."

With much more effort than I could've dreamed possible, I slid the letter through the slot in door of the post office. I staggered home, pushed my way through my blessedly silent house, and crashed to sleep a mere three hours before I needed to get up for the long bus ride to Florida, and Cuba after that.

Chapter Twelve

The last time I'd been truly, utterly drunk, I was a young man and my wife had just taken my children from me. I'd gone out and spent all of my paycheck on cheap liquor and fortified wine in the back room of a restaurant downtown, a place that had been torn down a few months later.

I remember waking up outside the darkened restaurant, freezing in the late fall air, a cold so sharp it made me sick to my stomach. I stumbled home, fully expecting the house to be occupied again, that Maddie was simply bluffing. But after facing the toyless dressers, barren, closets, and stripped beds in the kids' room, I knew she'd followed through on her threat. I went to what used to be *our* bedroom and passed out next to the untouched bed.

I swore off drinking after that, and for all these years I'd kept my vow.

Until last night.

Getting me out of bed on the morning after Thanksgiving required the strength of three of my players, along with the promise of the biggest mug of coffee they could cobble together in my empty kitchen. My head was still throbbing as Rodriguez, Donaldson, and Mack pulled me to my feet, while the other players collected my bags. Luckily I'd packed before going out with the boys last night. With the room still spinning and my head full of white-hot pain, I would not have capable of doing so now.

I didn't start to feel like myself again until we'd left Kansas far behind in our chugging, wobbling bus, heading east into the orange glow of the rising sun. I had a nagging feeling I'd done something foolish last night, something more than just imbibing too much rum and talking too much, but I couldn't for the life of me remember what it was.

"They should just go ahead and outlaw liquor," I said as we crossed the Missouri border, croaking out my first words all day, "and be done with it."

"Don't give anyone any ideas," Donaldson said from his seat behind me as we bounced down yet another gravel road. "How else would we ever have any fun?"

"If that's your idea of fun," I groaned, "I am going to have to pass."

The rest of the players erupted into laughter around me, the loud noise setting off tiny explosions in my aching head. I couldn't get mad at them for my own lack of willpower with liquor last night. And in spite of my fatigue and aching temples, I had to smile. Everyone seemed bright-eyed and eager for our trip and the upcoming games, and the pent-up, nostalgic feelings that had been haunting me—along with other, less substantial entities—while I was back at home finally melted away.

I closed my eyes and slept off as much of my hangover as I could.

When we stopped to eat in Mississippi, none other than Carrie Nation took a seat on the picnic table across from me.

"I would like to tell you about my beliefs, Coach."

I nearly choked on my fried chicken. She had come up on me unawares, while I was still nursing a lingering headache. Carrie always kept to herself, so I was doubly shocked that she was coming to me with the rest of the team around us.

"Certainly," I said as soon as I was able to swallow my greasy mouthful of chicken. "I wanted to chat with you, too."

"My belief," Carrie said in a measured tone, ignoring the curious glances of her teammates sitting around us, at a careful distance, "is that there is nothing for us after this life."

I nodded too fast, filling my sore head with bright white pain. In that instant, I had a crystal-clear memory of the moment of complete nothingness that had accompanied my nightmare zeppelin crash. We hit the ground, and then, blackness. Silence. How would we even know we were dead?

"We simply *stop*," Carrie said in her clear, confident voice.

Sometimes I thought I caught a trace of an accent in her words, a thickening of certain words, but she worked hard to hide it, if it was there at all.

"We spend our lives here on Earth, and to ask for more beyond that time would be greedy, do you not think? Everything lives and dies, Coach, and that is it. If that was *not* the case, the world—the whole universe—would get pretty full, would it not? One life is all you get."

I toyed with my half-eaten plate of food in the warm sun. The rest of my team, along with Old Blount, had inched away from us.

"I can understand that being the case for this chicken," I said, setting down my now-meatless drumstick. "But people have minds for thinking deep thoughts. Souls, too."

I thought of Derby and his unruly band of accomplices in my house and shivered in the sunlight.

"Maybe souls. Doesn't that make us better than animals?"

"Coach," Carrie said, holding up the newspaper she'd brought with her from Kansas City. The main headline was once again about the war in Europe, along with a pair of smaller headlines on either side of it, one about a robbery and a suspected arson on the riverfront, the other about a murder just last night outside a dance hall.

"Coach," she said again in a softer voice, "do you really think we are *that* much better than animals?"

I spluttered for an answer, and simply dropped my drumstick onto my greasy paper plate. I'd lost my appetite. We boarded the bus and continued heading east, and Carrie's words rattled around in my head with each bump.

Her argument was hard to question, at least to her face, and she confirmed a hunch inside me that I'd been feeling for years. In the weeks following Maddie's abrupt, angry departure, I'd stopped attending church. I always figured I'd return to my religious ways again, after a short break. But too many games were now being scheduled on Sundays, and I simply lost the desire to listen to preachers tell me how to live my life. How could preachers be so sure about of heaven and hell?

One life is all you get, Coach, Carrie had said.

So make the most of it, Coach, I told myself. Don't waste a single moment.

As we crossed the border into the Florida panhandle, I tried to follow that advice as best I could by planning out the lineups for our upcoming games in Havana. Baseball was my strongest belief these days, and it had gotten me through many a difficult time.

I took a quick look behind me, at the tightly packed players from all over the globe sitting in our cramped bus. They had no idea what was in store for them down in Cuba.

Not even Mack, sleeping two seats back from me, could have foreseen any of it. Though after our recent talk, he didn't seem to be predicting anything anymore. He just kept to himself and kept his gaze directed firmly at the ground instead of on his usual focus, the sun.

At noon the next day, after a stopover in Tallahassee for the night and another painfully early morning, the team bus arrived in Miami. I'd managed to keep Old Blount from making too many of his patented shortcuts, so we actually got there on time. I was glad to see that I wasn't the only one who groaned as we got out of the team bus, which we'd filled from top to bottom with baseball gear and suitcases.

Massaging my knees, I realized that if there was such a thing as hell for me, it would be closer to how Donaldson had described purgatory, all those months ago—riding a cramped bus forever, without ever arriving at your destination. With no rest stops.

On the wide-open field at the eastern edge of Miami, a city filled with palm trees and deeply tanned white people mingling with Cubans or Mexicans with reddish-brown skin and jet-black, straight hair, the All Nations began emptying the bus. As much as I'd cursed the bus and its poor shocks and uncomfortable seats, I suddenly didn't want to leave it here. At least the bus never left the ground.

I looked around to see if J.L. had arrived yet. Maybe we could convince him to charter a boat to take us over to Havana. I already knew what J.L.'s response would be—we'd take the plane belonging to his second cousin from Miami and fly one by one to the island, saving us the boat fare across the ninety miles of ocean.

Once the team bus had been emptied, Old Blount drove off, tooting the horn and waving at us as if glad to be rid of the team. I hoped he enjoyed his two weeks off, driving around the southern half of Florida. I wondered if I could run after him and travel with him instead of getting on that damn plane.

The sun beat down on us, burning off most of the humidity we'd been suffering under in the cramped bus for the past day. Buddha and Donaldson began passing around gloves and bats, and soon everyone was playing catch or pepper on the far side of the smooth, grassy field.

You've had some crazy ideas in your day, J.L., I thought, recalling games my old friend had played in a dress or against teams dressed up as clowns, not to mention pulling together an independent team comprised of men (and one woman) from just about every race under the sun that I had heard of.

This had better be safe, J.L., I added silently.

My one-sided discussion with my absent boss was interrupted by the buzzing of an engine that quickly changed into a popping and spitting rumble. In the outfield, as soon as they heard the sounds, Jiang, Carrie Nation, and Mikado dropped to the ground with their gloves over their head. They'd probably heard about the death that rained down from attacking planes and zeppelins, and their instincts for survival outweighed their common sense.

They picked themselves up with sheepish grins as the gray plane wobbled down toward the landing strip, dropping with surprising speed. Boles and Mendez were able to get the bats out of the way just in time, and then the plane bumped down the landing strip, its propeller a lethal spinning disk. The faces of the lean pilot and his bulky passenger behind him were both hidden behind thick goggles and leather form-fitting caps.

"Not a chance," No Small Foot said, shaking his head so hard his black hair came loose from its ponytail. "Not a chance you'll get me on that. It's not natural. Man wasn't meant to fly. 'Least not *this* man."

I ignored him for the moment and gathered my players together. After traveling a hundred yards down the strip to slow itself down, the plane turned and it rolled toward us like a giant winged predator, smelling easy prey.

"I need a volunteer to go first," I began. "Remember, it'll take fifteen, maybe twenty minutes. You'll be there before you know it, and you'll have some great stories to brag about when you get back home."

"If we *get* back home," No Small Foot muttered. The rest of my team was uncharacteristically quiet.

"Or you can stay here and practice," I said, raising my voice to be heard over the growing sound of the plane's engine. I think we'll do some wind sprints next..."

"I will go," Buddha Rodriguez said, raising one hand and turning his cap backwards like a catcher with the other. His face was already shiny with sweat. "I hate the wind sprints."

"That's the spirit!" a familiar voice shouted down at us from above. "You won't want to miss this ride!"

J.L. sat in the passenger seat behind the pilot. He dropped to the ground as gracefully as he could, which wasn't very graceful at all. Getting to his feet and dusting himself off, he removed goggles and helmet and passed them both to Rodriguez.

"Told you I'd be here," J.L. shouted. He pointed up at the pilot. "This here's Amelia, just down from Canada, and she can't wait to meet all of you."

I knew the astonished, jaw-dropping expressions I saw on my players' faces were reflected on my own face. I'd never heard of a female pilot before, and the dark-eyed young woman sitting in the cockpit looked to be barely twenty years of age.

"A pleasure to meet you, Miss Amelia," Mack called out to her, doffing his cap and smiling up at the young pilot.

Amelia lifted herself halfway out of the cockpit seat and gave us a wave. Her dark eyes burned with an intensity and passion that lit up the rest of her face, making her look quite lovely indeed, even if she was checking her watch. She wanted to get back into the air again. Brave girl.

Buddha Rodriguez boarded the plane, grinning madly, and with a sudden roar of the engine, the plane was up and away.

"Amazing," No Small Foot said, staring along with the rest of us until the plane was just a tiny speck on the southeastern horizon. "But I'm still not going up there without a fight."

Every half hour, so accurate that I could've set my watch by it if I wore one, the plane would return, and another player would stow his or her bag and some of the equipment aboard the small plane. Then, with a nervous wave and either a big grin or a look of utter fear, the player would depart.

Even No Small Foot allowed the other players to pick him up and stuff his bulky body into the seat behind a laughing Amelia. I learned later that Donaldson had been sharing his flask with the surly Indian for most of the afternoon, hoping that would be enough to calm the big man.

Delayed only by three breaks for refueling, the landing strip was quickly becoming empty. As the western sky began to darken toward orange and red, only Mack and Goro remained with me, playing catch and talking about what our lives would be like in Cuba for the next month and a half.

"I would like not to be called Jap while I am in Cuba," Goro said, throwing the ball to me. "Don't like the way people say it. Hurts my ears."

"Me, I'd like to play in one game a week instead of one or two or even three every day, so my knees don't give out on me," I said.

"And I'd like to eat spicy food and win every game we play while we're in Cuba," Mack said, catching the strike I'd launched at him with ease, "and smoke some cigars, if I can."

Thinking about his strange aversion to my chewing tobacco, along with his failed attempts to smoke his own cigarettes, I gave Mack a curious look. But he said no more about it, and I didn't want to press him; this was the most he'd said since climbing aboard bus in Kansas City.

A few minutes later, Amelia swooped down to pick up Goro and his belongings. She gave me a smile, though her face looked a bit tired. I wondered out loud if she shouldn't wait 'til tomorrow to finish the rest of us.

"Oh, no sir," Amelia said, and dusting off her brown leather jacket. "I've flown much more taxing projects than this. And don't you worry about it getting dark. I've flown in the night more times than I can remember, and I can remember a lot. Even if I've only been flying for less than a year."

I tipped my cap at her, wishing I hadn't heard that last bit, and then they were off again.

"She's kin to J.L., you said?" Mack stood next to me, balancing the ball on the back of his hand as if it were a bug. The sky was turning dark much too fast for my taste.

"Yep," I said. "A distant cousin. Why?"

"I just... I have a strange feeling about her. You know, I can't really see what happens to her, beyond the next few months, when finishes her training as a nurse up in Canada, though her true love will always be flying. It's quite strange, though. Her future becomes blank to me after a certain point." Mack let out a long sigh. "I fear I'm losing my sight altogether..."

"Son," I said. "You're tired. You can't be a fortune-teller all day, every day. Don't worry about Miss Amelia. She looks to me like a very tough cookie."

"You're right," Mack said, his skin now sharing the same color as the deep red sky, a tone I'd never seen on him before. "You know, Coach, I'm looking forward to this flight. It's been a long time since I last took to the air. It will truly be an adventure, just as Mr. Wilkinson said."

Mack stepped away from me to gather up the last of the equipment before I could ask him when he'd flown before.

But my centerfielder had walked off to collect the last bits of equipment on the field, avoiding the subject until the now-familiar buzz of the plane returned. Amelia loaded him up and blasted away for Cuba again.

Just like that, I was left alone again.

Sitting at the edge of the field, I watched one of the men working at the landing strip carry a torch out to the edge of the grassy field and start working his way down it, lighting torches every thirty yards, until the strip was ablaze like a rectangular Christmas tree.

"Lights," I said. "That's what we need at our ball parks."

I couldn't remember how many twilight games I'd suffered through as a player, standing in the batter's box with the dying sun in my eyes, or worse, trying to see the white sphere of the ball coming at me in the growing darkness. Of course, the All Nations would need to get a home field before we could even think about lights. One step at a time. I'd have to talk to J.L. about this, maybe over rum drinks in Havana.

Just as I'd started to relax, the buzz of the returning plane chilled my blood. Surely it was returning too soon. Within minutes, it touched down and rolled up to me, motor rumbling and coughing.

"Are you certain it's not too dark to fly?" I asked before climbing aboard.

"Of course not, Coach!" she called down to me. "Stow your stuff and climb aboard. Trust me."

"You're sure?"

"Of course. I've got tons of flying time under my belt. Heck, I'm even thinking of going across the Atlantic to help fight the krauts with the Royal Air Force. My cousin J.L. said they need all the help they can get. There's only so much I can do, working at the hospital up in Toronto. I'm itching to do *bigger* things, see."

I fumbled at the latch holding the two pieces of safety belt across my chest. On my third try I got it buckled together, and I couldn't think of any response to my bright-eyed pilot looking back at me, other than to nod.

"Hold tight, sir, and mark my words: you're going to love flying!"

I remembered all the foolish situations I'd gotten into over the years—the night I'd been determined to have dinner at a whites-only restaurant with my colored teammates, the games I'd stood my ground at second base against the lethal spikes of sliding white players during exhibition games, the at-bats when I'd crowded the plate against overly aggressive pitchers, even the countless gifts of baseballs and gloves I bought for my uninterested son—but none of them came close to matching the feeling of foolhardiness I felt climbing aboard this fragile-looking airplane.

"Here we go!" Amelia called from the front seat, and then we were rushing down the torch-lit landing strip.

If I'd been a religious man, I would've said all the prayers I knew as the plane approached the end of the runway. According to Carrie, this life was all we got, and here I was, squandering what was left of mine.

Surely we were going to crash into the lake at the end of the strip. But then, at the last moment, Amelia pulled up, and we left the ground.

We were weightless.

I almost screamed, but even if I'd tried, all sound would've been eaten up by the wind and lost in the warm evening air.

I wondered if I'd left my body back on the ground, which was quickly receding below us, shrinking until the landing strip became a tiny row of white dots that soon blended together into a single line of light.

And then we were beyond it. The air turned cold, and I could smell the salty, fishy odor of the ocean. We were high above the water now.

Pain filled my knuckles and hands, and I looked down at my fingers locked to the rim of the hole cut into the plane for my seat. I counted to three and pried my fingers free, and that gave me the courage to look around.

High above, but much closer than I could have ever imagined, the stars pushed their way through the early night sky. I wanted to reach up and grab a few to share with my players later, but I didn't dare move any more than I had to. The night sky was so vast, and the engine of the plane was so loud, that I felt like I was falling into myself.

I risked a look down again and saw the distant lights of Miami spread out behind us like bits of glittering jewelry dropped and forgotten by a pampered, rich woman. In front of us, the jeweled lights were smaller but closer together, and fast approaching: Havana.

Below us was the deep, nearly endless blackness of the Atlantic Ocean. As I watched, the moon slid out from under the clouds and set the ocean ablaze with bluish-white light. I lost my breath once again, staring at the armies of waves under us as we shot through the air, and when I caught it again, I was laughing instead of screaming.

"You were right," I called out to Amelia. "I do love it! I love flying!"

Amelia had somehow heard me, because she flashed me a thumbs-up.

A few seconds later, the engine roared as we began our descent into Cuba. The flight was almost over, and it was much too soon for my taste. I'd just gotten used to the buoyant, joyous rush of it all. I felt intoxicated again, *more* than alive from the flight.

Oh yes, I needed to shake J.L.'s hand for this one.

So far, the trip to Cuba had been a great idea, and a true adventure for my players and me, just as promised. Flying beat the pants off doing shots of rum, you can believe me.

That newfound love of flying didn't stop me, however, from kissing the ground the instant we touched down in Cuba.

Chapter Thirteen

July 28th, 1918:
*   Cuba. The word seems to mean freedom.*
*   I feel it, as do all my players. We walk the streets, after barely three days here, and nobody tries to push us around or make us sit in back rooms. It sure beats playing the cornet to avoid a riot and dodging bottles thrown at us by drunk men in cars.*

*   And everyone knows who we are. The restaurants make sure we have the finest seats, and many of the meals are on the house. The young boys and girls of the city follow us everywhere we go, from the wide stone square with the women dressed in flowing red and yellow dresses to the wondrous church of San Francisco.*

*   Whenever I have a free moment, I've been going exploring. I set out from our hotel and pick a direction at random, and I start walking until I start to feel lost. Then I slow down and stop somewhere, whether it's an ancient church or a food stall in the marketplace or a tiny art gallery.*

*   Now, I've never been one for art to hang on my wall, but some of the galleries I've seen here have made me want to pull out what little cash I have on me and buy some of these brightly painted works. Art Houdini and Carrie have already started bartering with the artists and gallery owners on Miramar Plaza. I warned them not to spend too much, or buy anything too big to carry back on the plane, if that was how J.L. was planning on getting us back home.*

*   The plane. Part of me desperately wants to fly again, while the logical part of me doesn't want to push my luck for a*

second time. I still feel like I'm soaring between the stars and the ocean.

But back to this new city. So many churches and palaces are crammed into this area that I feel like I'm in one of the old adventure novels I read as a kid. Everything is here—we never have to ride in a bus or a taxi. Best of all, I can walk down the stone streets and nobody judges me, and nobody even looks twice at the range of skin colors on my team.

Freedom.

Though I must say, some of my boys are feeling a bit too free, especially when it comes to making new acquaintances at night, after our daily game.

Why, so many lovely women catch my eye during our afternoon games that I have to force myself not to look out into the stands until the last out has been called. Yes, they are that pretty (I'd ask Maddie to forgive me for such thoughts, but she is so very far away from me, and has been for so long).

When we do leave this island, I know I'll miss my room at the Bonita Hotel next to Tropical Stadium, with its rooms cooled by the breeze coming off the Gulf of Mexico. My players will miss the night life here, and I hope they'll realize how fortunate we all were to be able to travel here.

Ah, but before I stop writing, I must mention the food. My players complain about the tongue-burning spices—put the hottest spices on your favorite plate of pork barbecue and you're not even close to what it tastes like. The heat will knock you back in your chair. Personally, I love it, though it does a number on my old stomach more times than I care to admit.

Finally, the cigars. When in Cuba, you must mention the cigars.

Of all people, Carrie wanted to know where we could sample some on our first night in the city, after we'd all gathered at the hotel and Amelia had lifted off for the final time, heading north.

Usually Carrie was quiet as a monk when the team got together, but for some reason she seemed confident outside of

America. She wanted to try one of the Cubanos she'd been hearing about all her life.

She told me she'd been studying maps of the city the past few weeks, so she led us all, without a misstep, like a general down the boulevard to the most ornate restaurant I've ever seen. Even as Art and No Small Foot told Boles to quit talking—something Boles had been doing in his nervous, grating way ever since we arrived—I started to worry that we'd be turned away at the door. That was our usual reaction at establishments like this back in the States.

But led by Carrie with her dark blonde hair tucked up under her men's hat, we were welcomed into the restaurant by not just the waiters but the owner himself, who gave us a huge table next to the window that looked out onto the harbor. Then he came by with a wooden box filled with cigars.

Mack seems especially taken with the cigars. He claims they are so good, they'll probably make them illegal in the future. "Or for some other silly reason," he claimed.

Since we were inside and the sun wasn't around for him to stare at—he seems to get his fortune-telling power from it—I figure it wasn't a true prediction. I hope not, in any case.

He finished off at least five cigars over the course of the meal, and his strange, too-bright eyes got so wide I couldn't look at him anymore. The one cigar I'd smoked had made my head spin by the time I was done with it.

After the meal, I started to wonder where J.L. had gotten to, but No Small Foot and Rodriguez both claimed to have seen him walk off with some Cuban men in white suits as soon as he got in. J.L. was doing what he did best. Meeting and chatting with people, and recruiting new players.

(And, you know, that's exactly what he's done—we played our first game with our new rightfielder, Cristobal Torriente, today. Chief Charlie Tokahoma replacement, at last. Having Torri on our team to give our other outfielders a break has made the price of this trip worth it. The young man made Mack's job in center much easier, because nothing gets by big Torri—already Boles has become comfortable back on the

bench on his non-pitching days, instead being of a walking error in the outfield.)

But back to that first night in Havana, before Cristobal joined our team.

Sitting around that big table, we smoked and talked about the Cuban players in the major leagues, like Rafael Almeida and Armando Marsans. Art, with his photographic memory, reminded us of Cubans Merito Acosta and Jacinto Calvo playing for the Washington Senators, and "El Pajaro" Cabrera with the St. Louis Cardinals. So many names I can't remember them all.

Donaldson saw where this conversation was going. Usually he's a cool customer, but after he gets some liquor in him, his emotions flare up.

He saw the success of the Cubans as a chance for other colored men to break into the majors at last. The freedom we would come to know here in Cuba would surely spread to our own country, wouldn't it? He looked around for some backup for his argument, but I was the only other Negro man at the table—everyone else was from some other color-coded group.

Donaldson asked me point-blank what I thought about the big leagues opening up to colored players like him.

I almost asked Mack about it, to see if he had a prediction for us. But the guy was in his own world, leaning back in his chair, his skin dark and shadowy as he puffed away on yet another cigar.

"I don't see it happening any time soon," I said. In the awkward, abrupt silence filling the restaurant, I told my players that I thought the pros in the big leagues were scared of what the players on the All Nations could do, colored or white or Japanese or Chinese or Indian or otherwise.

"They don't dare play too many games against us," I said, forcing a smile, though I was thinking about Derby's words a few days back that night in my apartment. "We'd embarrass 'em too badly."

All bad feelings aside, the best part of the night was when I told my players what the plan was for the next twelve days.

How we'd play only one game a day, but make just as much money down here as we'd do in a tripleheader back home.

Getting to see all the shocked looks being passed around the table was priceless. I couldn't blame them; Cuba sounded like the Promised Land.

So far, after three games (two wins, one loss), nothing has happened to disprove that feeling. But now the hour is late, and I must check on my centerfielder one more time before I can relax and go to sleep.

I tell you, Mack says the strangest things while he smokes, and I find it disconcerting. Today he told me about the next man to be killed by a baseball during a game, something that won't happen for another two years.

Now, what do I do with this knowledge? Do I tell the man he named, a fellow named Ray Chapman, to avoid playing baseball in August of 1920? To not crowd the plate anymore, so he doesn't get beaned in the head and killed?

Mack never smiles when he shares these facts about the future, like the stories he tells about a tall, bearded pitcher from Cuba nicknamed "the Franchise," because of his impeccable control, but then he'd go and say that this pitcher named Fidel might go on to be some sort of revolutionary politician instead. He claimed it was hard to tell, sometimes, what would really happen.

I think the tobacco isn't agreeing with Mack. I really do need to keep a closer eye on him, along with the other the young bucks out running in the Havana streets at all hours.

And on that note, I must go. Until my next entry, ¡Adios!

When my team left Havana in early August, I carried with me three memories in particular that I wanted to preserve forever.

The first was the look on my players' faces as they won their final game in Tropical Stadium, surrounded by a crowd twice as big as their biggest group of spectators back in the States.

The second was the recurring images of fans during that game, rushing to the fence behind the All Nations dugout, stuffing cash into the fence after a home run by Mack or No Small Foot, or even a hitless inning by Mendez or Donaldson.

But the final memory I wanted to save forever, the only one I dared try to completely describe in my own personal journal, a book I showed to no one, was that of Isabel Maria Alejandro Prieto: her words, her smile, the touch of her lips. She truly turned my head around during my time in the heart of Cuba.

I wondered what sort of vast coincidence had led me to meet her at that point in my life, on a small island in the mixed waters of the Gulf of Mexico and the Atlantic Ocean. The whole encounter truly made me wonder: *Was* there some sort of higher power after all?

Or was it all some sort of cosmic joke, at my expense?

We met in the restaurant of my hotel on the thirtieth of July. With almost a week of Havana under their belts, my players were more than happy to go off on their own into the city, even though they'd spent most of the day sweating under the sun as we split two games with the two top Cuban teams, Club Almendares and Club Habana.

I was tired from today's games, and I'd grown spoiled. After just one game a day for the past five days, playing in and coaching *two* games in one day had worn me out. The four back-to-back games we'd played on Independence Day seemed like years ago, instead of weeks.

After seeing my players off, I'd decided to have a quiet dinner in the hotel by myself and listen to the three elderly guitarists sitting next to the bar, each of them playing a different sized instrument. Dressed in the plain white shirt and white pants favored by the Cuban men around me, I thought I'd rest my knees and maybe try writing a postcard, though I wasn't sure who I'd send it to. Maybe I'd just mail it to myself.

I'd finished my spicy pork sandwich and most of my pile of fried plantains, and I'd just flipped over the postcard I'd bought in the shop next to Havana Cathedral, when, as if on cue, a tall woman with skin the color of early nightfall walked past my table. The long sleeve of her dark blue dress brushed against my arm, sending my trusty fountain pen flying onto the tiled floor.

"*Lo siento*," she said, her melodic voice putting the music of the three guitars to shame. I felt something flip-flop inside my chest at the sound. She stopped and began to reach down for the pen.

"No, no," I said, bending down as well, trying to remember the few tidbits of Spanish I'd learned. "It's okay. Ah. *Es bien.*"

I plucked my pen from the floor, surprised at the sudden wave of heat coming to my face. When I came back up with the pen in my hand, gripping it far more tightly than I needed to, I was looking directly into the woman's face.

"You are Jorgé, the coach," she said, leaning toward me. "One of your players told me you'd be here. You coach the team from the America."

She smelled of fresh roses and sweet cigar smoke, and her dress was a deep red. Its low-cut front was covered by a shawl of the same color, which was fortunate for me, because otherwise I'd be staring right at the tops of her breasts. Her long dark hair was streaked with gray and white in a manner that made it seem to be constantly in motion from where she stood above me.

I nodded and relaxed a bit, glad to realize that this was just another fan of my team, and not someone interested in *me*. Glad at first, but with growing disappointment. This woman was stunning.

"Yes. *Todo el Equipo De las Naciones.*" I gave her a smile that felt as wide and heartfelt as the one on her lovely face. "Correct?"

"You have fine Spanish," she smiled. She straightened up and glanced around, as if remembering where she was. "You have a fine team."

"Thank you," I said, and with that she took a step back, ready to move on. At that moment, the thought of this woman walking away and exiting my life forever suddenly made me nearly panic. I wanted to ask her to join me, but couldn't dare. In spite of all that had happened, I was still a married man.

"Ah, *gracias*, I mean," I said, and I asked her to join me anyway.

The woman gave a quick nod and sat in the chair across from me. I glanced around the bustling restaurant, expecting all eyes to be upon us, possibly even pointing or whispering behind their menus, but the other patrons were paying me no mind. I may have caught a glint in the eye of one the three guitarists next to the bar, but that could've been my imagination.

"I am Isabel Maria Prieto," she said, her Spanish-accented words still trumping the smiling guitarists' music.

"George Grunion. *Jorgé*, right? You have a lovely city here, ma'am. I almost wish we didn't have to leave. Oh," I added, remembering her kind words, "and you have very good English, Isabel."

"Thank you. My sons teach me. Taught me. They are *muy* more smart than I am."

The waiter stopped by and took Isabel's order for a glass of wine, while I asked for more ginger ale. The waiter gave me a wink as he turned back toward the bar.

"Today I spend the game watching you," she said. "Not the pitchers or the hitters. You are a good coach, Jorgé. *Muy Bien*. My Domingo will enjoy playing for you."

I almost dropped my pen again as I realized who I was talking to: Isabel Maria was the mother of the second Cuban player J.L. had arranged to join the team, Domingo Prieto, a much-needed pitcher. I felt a wave of relief again, followed by another shimmer of disappointment. She was just checking in on her son's new coach. Little to do with me. I was a fool, through and through.

"So, do you like baseball?" I said, unsure of how to continue.

"Do *you*?" Isabel Maria countered, leaning forward. "Do you consider it your, ah, how do you say it... Your *passion*?"

I sipped at my ginger ale, considering the question.

"My passion? I've never thought about it that way, but yes, I do believe it is."

"Good. Then I'd like to hear you talk about it, if it is your passion, Jorgé."

The way Isabel said my name in her native language made me feel light-headed and short of breath all over again. So I started talking. You would've thought I'd had a series of rum shots already, the way I went on.

I told her how Cuban Pitcher Eustaquio "Bombin'" Pedroso blanked my team on our first game in Havana, and how I barely slept that night, thinking that this whole trip had been a huge mistake. I told her how every game at Tropical Stadium felt as crucial as our games against the Indianapolis ABCs or the American Giants, and how that pressure brought out the best in my players.

I made a point of telling her how important Domingo would be to my team, with his fastball and his control, not to mention his maturity, a sharp contrast to our other Cuban recruit, Torriente, who had a fiery temper. Then I told her how much the team had learned since coming here, mostly my pitchers, but also No Small Foot, who sometimes caught for the Cuban pitchers during non-All Nations games.

You would've thought my batters had never seen some of the different pitches coming at them. Half my guys were dumbfounded our first few games here, then they began to catch on. It was amazing to see.

I just kept right on talking, and Isabel simply smiled and nodded along with each sentence.

"And I've talked to my boss about it, and he said that more teams want to come down here to play in the winter, even the pros, the white men like Tris Speaker and Rogers Hornsby. But you Cubans are smart, only allowing select groups to come down, so that the island isn't flooded with too many Americans. And the way everyone loves the sport— what do you call it? *Pelota?*—you're going to have some strong, strong teams in the future. Teams that'll give American teams quite a run for the money."

I paused for breath. I'd long since paid the bill for my dinner and Isabel's wine, and the two of us had been unbothered by the waiter for the past hour.

I swallowed the last of my flat, warm ginger ale. I'd forgotten how fast time could fly in the presence of a beautiful woman.

"You know who I sound like?" I said, thinking out loud. "I'm starting to talk like my player Mack, making all sorts of crazy predictions about the future. Crazy. That's *loco*, right?"

"*Sí,*" Maria said with a laugh. "This is the man who plays in the middle field? The one who makes the catches impossible?"

"Yes," I said with a laugh. "That's Mack, in centerfield. He's amazing, simply amazing. Maybe even a bit *loco*, too. But Isabel Maria, I must apologize. I've been talking far too much. I have been rude."

Isabel's answer was just a smile, though I thought I could see something unspoken in her eyes. Maybe a touch of sadness.

"No, I enjoy listening to you talk." Isabel blinked and finished her glass of wine. "You remind me of my husband, Arturo."

I felt the heat rush to my head again, just as the musicians finished their final song of the night. The restaurant was nearly empty now, with just two other tables left with customers at them.

"Your *husband*," I said, the words burning as I spoke them. "I see."

"Jorgé, he pass away two and a half years ago. He would tell such stories about *pelota* and his job as a fisherman and the fishes he almost nearly catch every day. I never knew what to believe, but I loved to hear him talk."

I reached out to touch her hand. "I'm sorry. I'm... sorry you're sad."

Isabel shook her head. "But time has passed. I no longer mourn him, but remembering him always. What do *you* mourn, Jorgé?"

"Ah," I began. I almost told her everything, then. My lost wife. My children growing up strangers. My empty house back in Kansas. Mostly empty, that was, except for the ghosts.

The long, hard years behind me, and the dwindling years in front of me.

But I stamped on the words like a child killing ants. Without thinking, I'd retracted my hand and set it on the empty table in front of us. How could I answer a question like that? I sat there, staring at the table, tongue-tied.

"It is late," Isabel said at last, watching the musicians pack up their guitars and order a round of rum before the bar closed for the night.

I wasn't sure if I should offer to walk her home, or arrange to have a taxi come pick her up. So much time had passed since I'd last courted a woman, I no longer knew the rules.

Isabel reached out to touch my hand.

"Good night, Jorgé."

"Will I see you again?" I said, standing up.

"Of course," Isabel said. "I shall go to all of my son's games. I will watch for you."

"And I will do the same," I said, lowering my gaze for a moment, my face hot. So much I had left to say to her, and so many more questions to ask her.

But when I lifted my head, Isabel Maria was gone, leaving only the hint of sweet, smoky roses and the memory of her delicate touch.

Chapter Fourteen

I had more dreams than usual that night, as if I'd packed too much activity and sensation into one day, and my mind needed to spin out fantastic, sometimes horrific yarns while I was sleeping to unwind it all. Strangely for me, even after I woke, I remembered the events from all three of my dreams.

And that white bastard Worrell was in every last one of them.

The first dream was filled with images of battle—angry crowds of fishermen with dark skin and bare arms on one side, faceless white men (and one lone black man) in gray, mud-flecked uniforms with unreadable words on their chests carrying bayoneted rifles on the other.

And the All Nations trapped in the middle.

Armed only with our baseball bats, we tried to fight off the waves of angry Cubans and uniformed soldiers. Carrie and Art had already fallen, and Mendez and Donaldson were injured and fading fast. Goro and Jiang fought back to back in front of me, while off to my right, Buddha Rodriguez had turned into some sort of whirling dervish, spinning madly with a bat in each hand, deflecting bullets and bayonets. He was moving toward a rabid group of men swinging machetes and boards peppered with nails.

Boles, meanwhile, was hunkered down behind me, crying with his face averted. He kept trying to hand me his glove, but I pushed it away each time. Boles had seen where Art had fallen, I realized.

I saw Worrell lying face-down in the dirt next to Boles, unmoving, as if my players had never lifted his body up and packed it up into that pickup truck all those months ago.

The dream continued with Mack climbing onto No Small Foot's back and raising his long arms. That hypnotic white light once again began spilling from his eyes. I had to look away from him, because my dream-logic told me that when that light touched *me*, just like Worrell, I would die.

His light spread to the angry mobs surrounding us. Men of all colors flashed white for a painful instant, then fell like a strand of wheat hit by a scythe. Only to be replaced by two more for each that dropped.

As I turned my head, Mack's light hit Worrell, and the former head coach shuddered, then rolled over like a dog. He looked up at me with his bruised, dirt-encrusted face, and tried to stand. Slowly, *slowly*, he rose to his feet.

Of all the horrific images from my night vision, this one was surely the worst. My chest went tight, my vision reddened, and I could no longer breathe.

The odds were looking quite bad indeed for *Todo el Equipo de las Naciones* when the bells of the Havana Cathedral sounded through my open window, waking me.

I lay there panting in fear for a few moments until I remembered where I was. Cuba. No crowds outside the hotel, coming to get us.

Flexing my left hand, which had gone numb on me while I slept and navigated my nightmare, I gave thanks to the night-time bells for waking me. I fanned myself once with my sheet, closed my eyes, and fell into a new dream.

This one featured the most bizarre game of baseball I'd ever seen.

Counting the pitcher, who was perched on an oval-shaped white board in mid-field, only six players stood in the outfield. Clean-shaven men with pale faces played the game on an emerald-hued diamond that was a fraction the size of any regulation park. The grass of their shrunken park looked too short and unnaturally green, as if it had been painted.

The game itself was, like the grounds of the park, a strangely distorted imitation of the real game of baseball I'd played most of my life. I couldn't even smell hot dogs or grass clippings. Just the too-sweet sweat of out-of-shape men working up a lather around me.

The chubby man on the mound, dripping sweat in his white outfit that bore no team name or number, put his bare feet together on the wooden mound and lobbed the ball underhand toward the hitter. Waiting on the high-arcing ball, the hitter blooped a strange half-swing, half-bunt that dropped over the head of the squat second baseman. The ball hit the ground with a thunk.

"*Brilliant!*" called out one of the men from the sidelines in a simpering voice. "*Simply brilliant placement, I say.*"

It was Worrell in a loose-fitting white suit, clapping his hands together delicately. His smile was ghastly, even worse than his ruined left temple.

As the smattering of cheers continued, I looked around the field and realized at that moment that *all* the players were white. The stands were empty except for a handful of pallid women in short dresses, skirts, and pants that showed off a distracting amount of bare leg. They waved oversized fans in front of their pasty, expressionless faces, as if trying to hide their identities.

At the back of the stands, carrying a tray stacked high with drinks, was a colored man with bright white hair. Even from my distant vantage point, I could see that the servant had John Donaldson's eyes; framed by wrinkles, the whites yellowed with age.

He caught my gaze, face tight with concentration to keep from spilling anything on his tray, and I saw a silent plea in his expression. I didn't understand what he was trying to say to me.

I turned away quickly and looked back at the field, where the hitter had finally arrived, huffing and puffing, at first base.

"What game is *this*?" I said in my dream.

Everyone on the ridiculous diamond—the place reminded me of the snooty croquet fields at the all-white country clubs back in the south—turned on me, in one sudden movement. Worrell's dead gaze hit me like icy water.

"*Get that boy off my field.*"

Not again, I thought, clenching my teeth together with a grinding noise.

The players dropped their tiny white gloves and, moving calmly and silently, surrounded me as if I was a wild animal.

So many mobs of angry, violence-crazed people, haunting my dreams.

I pulled myself from the dream right before anyone could touch me.

Shaking my head in the darkness of my hotel room, I felt like I'd heard this before somewhere, most likely from Mack. Unless something was done, he'd said in one of his many predictions, the game of baseball would lose relevance. It could devolve into something close to that game in my dream.

That would be *truly* nightmarish. I couldn't let it happen.

Waiting for my pulse to return to normal, I stared at the formless shadows cast on the wall of my room, shapes formed by the lights outside. I watched them for close to an hour, until I'd pushed the images from my nightmares out of my mind long enough so I could fall back to sleep.

My final dream during that troubled night was a simple one, yet just as disturbing as the first two.

I dreamed Maddie sitting at a small café table with Isabel. The city could have been Havana or Kansas City or even Chicago. Guitar music played in the background, sometimes flamenco, sometimes jazz, as the two women discussed my shortcomings and failings, both past, present, and future.

I can't repeat all that was said there—the humiliation is too great, even now—but suffice to say, the two women who'd touched my heart had excellent insight into what made me tick.

"Oh, yes, he has a temper," Maddie was saying. "You should see him after he loses a game, or an argument."

But I'm better now, I wanted to say. And what arguments did I ever *lose?*

Isabel didn't give me a chance to interject.

"He does have passion in that respect," she said, her accented words adding a fascinating counterpoint to Maddie's soft Southern twang, which had faded from so much time in the Midwest. "But I wonder if that passion is in Jorgé for anything *else?* Something other than *Pelota, Pelota, Pelota?*"

A lanky waiter set down two oversized, steaming mugs in front of each woman. He bowed with a flourish, then turned to me and winked, pointing at the ruined left side of his head. Worrell. He never said a word. Never had to.

"Well," Maddie said without missing a beat, wearing that mischievous smile that I remembered so well from our younger days slipping onto her dark face. "Let me tell you..."

When they both began to laugh with a conspiratorial, gossipy familiarity, I woke myself once again, shaking not with fear this time, but with shame and embarrassment.

I heaved a sigh and rolled my aching body out of bed. My knees creaked as I lowered myself into the chair next to the open window, giving up on sleep for the rest of the night.

As I sat there gazing out at the quiet city and rubbing the circulation back into my aching left arm, I wished for the old reliable dream I used to have. The one that featured my death ride over Chicago on a doomed zeppelin.

At least I knew how *that* nightmare ended.

* * * * *

My team's time in Cuba had grown short, with only five days and half a dozen games left. We won a little over half of those games, but just barely. Better than the victories was seeing Isabel at every game, as promised. We would sometimes chat afterwards about the events of the exhibition games, as I steadfastly ignored the grins and pokes of my players passing by us.

I must admit, I felt more than a small amount of guilt, talking with Isabel Maria in such a friendly manner. I was still a married man, after all.

But I should have known better than to make such chaste plans. An hour after our game that day, as I was preparing to catch up on the sleep I'd lost the night before thanks to my dreams, my players hunted me down again.

Donaldson and Mendez, along with their new allies Prieto and Torriente, dragged me from my room, insisting that I celebrate our successful time in Cuba with the entire team, just like we did before leaving Kansas City.

Donaldson had wanted to take us all out into the wild night after our spicy meal capped off with more cigars. He wanted to go out where every storefront was lit up with candles and torches, and everyone you saw was dressed in bright reds and blues, enjoying their Friday night.

"This is good enough for me," I said, watching more people enter the hotel bar connected to the restaurant. I didn't need another hangover like the one I'd been saddled with the day we left. Donaldson gave me a pained look, then he ordered another round of rum for everyone.

Having learned my lesson, I stuck with ginger ale and delicately leaned my sore body back to light one of the fat cigars Mack had brought for all of us. Today's game had been an extra-innings win over the Havana club.

I'd played the entire game while Buddha Rodriguez meditated on the bench, complaining about headaches. Late in the game, I'd made an ill-advised dive for a foul line drive. I caught it, but landed badly on my right knee.

A few nips from Donaldson's flask of Cuban rum between innings had been required to take the razor-sharp edge off the pain, but both my knees were still aching. It was becoming a constant companion, this pain. That, and the shortness of breath that hit me even when I wasn't diving after baseballs.

Mack sat next to me, on my left, while Boles had taken up the chair on my right. I did my best to ignore the young white pitcher's complaints about Cuba—the food, the weather, the rough-and-tumble games, and of course, the people. Boles had been miserable the whole time we'd been down here, convinced the Cubans were treating him poorly because of his skin color. I wondered if he and Art had had some sort of falling-out.

Mack, meanwhile, was smoking silently on my left.

"Rum all around," said Mendez, decked out in his best black suit. "I want you all to leave Cuba with the taste of the best of my homeland—and Domingo's and Cristobal's—in your mouths." His smile faded the tiniest when he saw my dour look. "Ah, and one more ginger ale for our fearless leader," he added to the waiter.

The eye-watering smoke from Mack's stogie was starting to make my head spin.

"1918," he said with a sigh next to me. "A year that's already over half over. And our season coming to an end so soon."

I gave him a quick look, wondering if he was getting back to normal. He'd not made any predictions the whole time we'd been down here; when not playing ball, he'd kept himself entertained by strolling through the city by himself and smoking Havanas, his head down instead of gazing at the sun.

No Small Foot squinted at Mack from the other side of the table and made a frustrated sound. "Here we go again. Mack's got the crystal ball out."

"Hush," Art said, his eyes wide and his dark hair wild and unruly without his usual hat to tame it.

He'd been making a pair of coins dance up and down the knuckles of both hands, but he put them away now and leaned closer to Mack.

"What do you predict for the rest of the season, Mack?"

Mack puffed and puffed on his cigar, and then he spoke, the smoke spilling back out of his mouth like a strange form of punctuation.

"California and the Pacific Ocean. A team of Japanese, a team of Jews. Maybe even a team of clowns, but that seems doubtful at this point. Some of us go our own way, while other of us stay until the end—"

"Wha' 'bout the war, Mis'er Mack?" Carrie said with her cigar clamped in her mouth, her accent growing more pronounced. "Wha' do ye see wit' th' war? Will it end soon?"

I winced at the question, afraid of what Mack's reaction might be. But Mack simply closed his eyes and looked toward the window, as if trying to find the sun to help with his forecasting. He gave up and held up his cigar so he could gaze at its orange tip.

"You know, Miss Carrie," he said, his face pale, "the war will get worse in the coming weeks before it gets better. But it does get better. Only slowly."

Donaldson exchanged a look with No Small Foot, and they both nodded at the same time. They stood and circled around the table to pick up Mack, chair and all. Mack didn't even resist, but simply let them carry him outside, the smoke from his cigar trailing behind him like a quickly-disintegrating finger. Everyone laughed and resumed drinking in Mack's sudden absence, while Mendez began telling stories from his childhood in Havana.

"You got to do something about Mack," Boles muttered from my right. "The guy's losing his marbles."

"Right," I said, uncomfortable with Boles so close. "Be right back."

"Don't sneak off," No Small Foot said. "We need our fearless leader."

I pushed through the crowd, earning some slaps on the back as men recognized me as the All Nations coach, along with a kiss on the cheek from a tipsy female fan. I was having trouble breathing due to the smoke and the mass of people.

Before I could make it outside to where I figured Mack was still sitting with his cigars and his too-bright eyes aimed at the sky, I saw her.

Isabel Maria. It was as if she'd magically appeared to cut me off from my centerfielder. She sat at the table next to the exit, talking with a young man who looked so much like my new pitcher Domingo that he had to be her son. I pivoted on my heel, knees aching with pain, and walked up to Isabel's table.

Oh, Maddie, I thought, losing my breath suddenly. I'm sorry. I just can't wait for you any longer. Not now.

"*Jorgé*," Isabel said with a smile that cleared my head of all smoke, all guilt. "I'd like you to meet my son Miguel."

"A pleasure," I said as the young man stood up to shake hands. Thankfully, I'd caught my wind again and didn't gasp out my words.

"Nice to meet you," Miguel said. As soon as he let go of my hand, his gaze traveled over to the table where my team sat, close to the bar.

"*Por favor*, Mama?" he said to Isabel, nodding in the direction of his brother Domingo, who was leading the team and most of the other people in the restaurant in a fast Cuban song that I couldn't even begin to comprehend.

"*Sí*," Isabel said, and a moment later, I was alone at a table with the woman who'd been on my mind all week. My hand was already itching to reach out to her. The singing and music and talking around us faded away.

"You avoid me, Jorgé," she said, a statement instead of a question. "I hope to talk more with you, but your games keep you too busy for that?" This time she made her sentence into a question.

I gave a grudging, guilt-laced nod. "I'm sorry. *Lo siento.*"

"Why?"

"Why what?" I felt like a boy out on his first date, fumbling for comprehension. "Why am I sorry? Or why do I avoid you?"

Isabel Maria sipped at her wine, raised her left eyebrow and said nothing, as if waiting for me to figure out the answer.

I have a wife, I was about to say, but the words stuck in my throat.

"Your penance," Isabel said at last, "is one Our Father and three dances with me."

The smile that crossed her face as I stood up and reached for her hand made me fall for her like a boy falls for a girl after their first-ever kiss.

Three songs never went past so quickly. I felt Isabel's hand on my back, and her face was turned up to me, her eyes dark and mysterious and focused on me as the crowd roiled and danced around us. I knew the smile on my face was that of a young, young man. This woman so close to me, inching closer, had banished all my aches and pains.

I laughed along with Isabel as people bumped into us. The dance floor was full, and the music grew even louder.

She felt so good, her hands tight in mine, her hair brushing against my hands and arms as she moved to the music, that I simply couldn't hold myself back any longer. I tilted my head down and kissed her for what felt like far too short a time, but long enough the steal the air from my old lungs once more.

When we pulled away from each other, even as the rest of the crowd continued to dance, I felt a deafening silence fill my ears. My legs went wobbly, and not just from my bad knees. Already I wanted to kiss her again.

So I did. And she returned the favor. I have no idea how long that kiss lasted. I'm thinking extra innings.

And then, like a fool, I pulled away.

Still tasting her wine on my lips and smelling the smoky sweetness of her hair, I looked at Isabel's smile and felt her hand on my chest, but that wasn't enough to keep me from feeling a mix of guilt and wrongness.

I stepped back and limped out of the bar as fast as I could. I left the revelers farther behind me as I hobbled up on my way back to my room, alone.

My wife's name haunted me with each step.

Maddie. Maddie. Maddie.

Lo siento. Lo siento.

I kept moving until I was outside my door, key in hand, breathing loud as a horse at the end of a hard race. Another mistake in a life filled with them.

I couldn't put the key in the door and go inside. Standing there, gasping for air, I had a sudden memory, clear as a ringing bell.

Out of all the different life and death philosophies I'd heard this season, I kept coming back to what Carrie Nation had said to me on our way to Florida.

One life is all you get, she'd said. *One life.*

I surprised myself when I realized I was crying. Don't ask me why. Probably because I am a foolish old man.

"One life," I muttered. I wiped my face as best I could and slipped my room key back in my pants pocket.

Then I turned and nearly ran back down the stairs.

My knees threatened to betray me with each impact my feet made on the wooden steps, but I managed to stay upright until I hit the hard stone floor of the main lobby, and I went sprawling.

I saw red clay tiles come rushing at my face, then a pair of strong hands grabbed me and pulled me up just before I would have hit the floor. I turned to look into the darkened face of my centerfielder.

"Thanks," I said, trying to get my balance and get free of Mack's tight, unrelenting grip. My skin had gone cold with his touch. "Mack?"

"*Go.*" He released my hand and ambled back toward the outside doors which had been flung open to the brightly lit, crowded streets. "Dance the night away coach," Mack added, glancing back at me as he lit up another cigar. "I *know* you'll enjoy it."

"Is that another prediction?" I called out, but the only response I got was a shrug of his shoulders in his ash-covered sports coat, followed by a cloud of gray smoke from his cigar.

Well, I thought. That's that, I guess.

I focused on not looking like a hobbled man as I made my way back to the bar. For a long ten seconds I searched the crowd for Isabel, fighting off a sudden panicky feeling that she'd left already. And then I saw her next to the new, impromptu band setting up close to the bar.

Mendez was there with his cornet, along with No Small Foot and his flute and the three elderly guitarists from the night I'd met Isabel. They were playing a fast-paced tune that put a blessed lightness in my limbs. It made me even an old man like me want to dance.

When I was able to push through the crowd to get to the first woman in decades, she was doing just that—dancing with her son Domingo.

Surely the devil encouraged me to ask, "May I cut in?"

Domingo stepped back, and Isabel gave me a stern look.

"*Lo siento,*" I mouthed, the music making speech impossible. It was the best I could do.

To my shock and relief, Isabel's angry look evaporated, and she took me by the hand. Pushing her way through the crowd, she led me to the last open space left on the floor.

I would have never believed such a thing was possible, but I ended up dancing into the early hours of the morning with Isabel, never stopping once due to my bum knees. We barely spoke, didn't really even need to, even when the band stopped playing, and I was rewarded with a long kiss from Isabel.

Before we separated, before I could try to ask her up to my room—in spite of my utter physical exhaustion—Isabel pressed a piece of paper into my hand and walked out the door with her two sons. I followed her out of the hotel and stared out after her long after she'd turned a corner and disappeared.

At last, I looked at the address she'd scribbled onto the paper and smiled. Under the address were two words: "Write me."

Not even Mack's empty chair, surrounded by the butts of a dozen smoked cigars like spent bullets, could make my smile fade. I inhaled the night air, ears still roaring from the music and the dull roar of the crowd, then I breathed in the last lingering scent of Isabel Maria from my shirt.

"I love Cuba," I whispered out at the darkness, sinking into Mack's chair. "You know, we really should stay here, forever."

Chapter Fifteen

But of course, as always, we had to leave. We had the rest of our season to complete—there were always more games, and more traveling. We were forever leaving.

Though if I had known then that we had barely over a month's worth of games waiting for us back in America, I very well may have saved myself some trouble and stayed in Havana.

Instead of flying one-by-one from Cuba back to Miami, we boarded a rusting gray shrimping boat in the Bay of Havana. It was the eighth of August. Not only was I disappointed about having to leave, but the morning was made worse by the absence of J.L. and his distant cousin Amelia in her plane. This gray boat bobbing in the harbor did not appear very seaworthy.

I tried to raise my spirits by keeping Isabel's address in my right pants pocket, close at hand. I thought of the kiss we'd shared the last time we were together. If I knew what was good for me, I'd write her back.

That boat ride from Cuba was worse than anything I could have imagined. I felt like the violent rise and fall of the boat through the waves would never end. I'd heard men talk about being seasick, but I never thought it would affect me this badly. I spent most of the first half of our voyage leaning over the side, emptying my stomach whenever the sudden lurching got to be too much.

Luckily, my Chinese rightfielder was there to help me get through it.

"Deep breaths," Jiang said, his approach muffled by the roaring waves.

When I heard his voice, I felt a series of slight pricking sensations on the back of my neck. I risked loosening a hand from where I was gripping the rail of the boat to see what it was, but Jiang pushed my hand back down.

In the space of time it took two more waves to rock the boat, I felt like someone had just lifted a fifty-pound weight from around my waist.

I looked over at Jiang, feeling something brush against the collar of my sweat-drenched shirt as I turned my head. He still held my hand, his skin almost yellow against my dark brown.

"What did you *do*?" I whispered.

Jiang smiled. "This is how I live in harmony with natural environment, Coach. Beg pardon, but *I* did that to you."

He let go of my hand, and I lifted it to my neck, where six tiny nails were embedded.

Oh my. I felt my nausea returning, but not because of the rough seas.

"In English, called acu-punc-ture," Jiang said, the strange word rolling off his tongue.

"Ah. How long must I keep these, ah, nails in my neck, son?"

"Not much longer. I find pressure point, ease your sickness. Simple. All part of my training. My religion."

"Your religion?"

"You Americans call it Taoism," Jiang said. "Tao. It means... the Way. It makes up... everything." He held up a small brown root, sliced in half. "Eat this, feel even better."

"Tao." I really wanted to pull those pins out of my neck, even if they were making me feel better. It just felt wrong to be stuck like that, like a human pincushion. To calm myself, I took the root from Jiang and took a nibble.

"Can you tell me more?" I gasped, eyes watering. The root was like fire.

Jiang shrugged. "Tao can be talked about, but not Eternal Tao. Names can be named, but not Eternal Name."

My vision was starting to blur from my bite of the root. A name? I had a name for this feeling, but it wouldn't be a polite one. A gust of wind threw salty water onto us, clearing my eyes. The root slipped from my hand, but Jiang caught it neat as a pop fly.

At that moment, I relished the cold feel of the water on my face and aching arms, which were both gripped to the railing once more. I took a deep, cleansing breath, inhaling the salty, fishy odors of the water and feeling the warmth of the sun reach me at last.

When I turned my gaze back to Jiang, I felt another wave, this one coming from inside of me, filling me with peace. My nausea was gone.

"How did you *do* that?" I asked, a goofy smile on my face.

"Inner Alchemy. I learn from the strange men who try for immortality. Inner Alchemy teaches that all... elements of immortality are inside us." He pointed at his chest. "My body, your body—both are... reflection of universe."

"Hermits, shamans... immortality?" I couldn't figure out where to fit this newest belief system into all the others I'd heard this season from my players.

"All part of plan, for my immortality," Jiang finished.

I could still taste the fiery root on my tongue as I said, "To live forever?"

"Of course. We all have ability. Just takes some *work*."

"Now you tell me," I muttered, trying to catch a hint of the land mass of America somewhere ahead of us in the brightness.

"Okay," Jiang said, misunderstanding me. "I now tell you about it."

And so we spent the afternoon talking about *qi*, which Jiang pronounced as "chee," and how it gave us life and sustained everything around us. I also learned more about the sharp pins of acupuncture and the herbs Jiang used to restore his body's energy. He even practiced meditation, sitting and focusing on just one thought, which made me think that Buddha Rodriguez and Jiang needed to talk—maybe Jiang could help Buddha get his act together.

In any case, according to my Chinese outfielder, all of these different practices would enable a person to outlast death. I realized as he was talking in his careful, accented voice that the man truly believed he was never going to die. I couldn't figure out if that was something I should be jealous of or not.

How would it be to live forever in a world with so such problems as war and poverty and deprivation? And who'd want to spend eternity as an old man with bad knees? I wondered what Maddie would've made of such questions.

Jiang and I discussed these topics until the boat arrived in Key West.

"Jiang," I called out before he slipped away. "Can you, ah, take these pins out of my neck now?"

"Already did, Coach. Two hours ago."

I rubbed the back of my neck, half-expecting to find small bloody holes there, but all I felt was my own skin. I was whole again, no longer bristling with nails like some sort of porcupine.

At the harbor, which was just a series of wooden docks and a ramshackle train station a hundred yards back, over a dozen men waited for our boat to haul them across the water to Cuba. Some were colored, and some were white. I felt a stinging sensation when I saw that the two distinctly separate groups of men.

Welcome back home, I thought.

Like over-excited boys, our new recruits Prieto and Torriente pushed to the front of the boat to see who the waiting players were.

"Look—there is the one we call *El Fantasma*," Prieto said in an awed whisper, his voice reminding me of his mother with his melodic accent. He pointed at a young man that I didn't recognize.

"What's that mean?" Boles asked.

"The Ghost," I said before any of my three Cuban players could translate. "Ollie 'The Ghost' Marcelle. I've seen him play. The man has reflexes like a cat. Stands ten feet off the bag at third, but nothing gets by him."

As for the other men, I knew two of the colored men all too well: Rube Foster, owner and manager of the Chicago American Giants, and his star hitter John Henry Lloyd. How could I forget? Lloyd had hit over .500 against us during their series on the fourth of July.

I gave them both a big wave, and was rewarded with a pained look of recognition on Rube's face before he broke into his usual smile. So he hadn't forgotten those losses on Independence Day, either. We'd beaten him to Havana now, too, and hired two players he never got a chance to appraise.

Then I sucked in my breath as we began gathering up our bags and equipment. The group of white players below us included faces I'd only seen in photos on the Sports page. In spite of my long-held anger at the way the major leagues had kept colored men off their rosters for decades, I couldn't help but feel a flash of awe as I saw, up-close, some of the best players of the National League and the American League, right in front of me.

Of the over half-dozen white men, I recognized Tris Speaker and his teammate, sour-faced Ty Cobb, along with a somewhat older man who had to be Christy Mathewson. Next to Mathewson stood a big, dark-haired man with puppy-dog eyes that I knew was pitcher Babe Ruth from the Red Sox.

The boat rocked a few more times and blasted a long bass note on its horn before coming to a jarring stop at the dock. Black smoke filled the air, and I let out a deep breath of relief. We'd made it.

"You know, Coach," Mack said from behind me, making me turn with a sudden movement that almost made me lose my stomach again. I was relieved not to see a Cuban stogie in the young man's mouth as he spoke.

"That grown man they call the Babe will pitch over a dozen scoreless innings in the World Series next month and lead the Red Sox to a championship." The other All Nations players pushed past us, eager to get back on dry land as well. "But you know, Coach, there are two funny things about that: first, that win will be the last World Series title the Red Sox will win for decades; second, the man they call Babe will not be remembered as a pitcher, but a hitter. One of the best, ever."

"I can see that," I said as hoisted my bags and followed the others down the boat ramp. "The last part, at least. That fella is built like a brickhouse."

"Too bad we can't recruit him," J.L. chimed in from behind us.

"Where have *you* been?" I said as I stepped onto shore and immediately began wobbling. My legs were convinced the ground was swaying like the ocean, and I knew they'd give out on me any minute.

"Just making deals and, well, trying to get more players from Cuba to join us," J.L. said. I could see the dark circles under my old friend's eyes. "We'll see if it pans out," he added, then broke into a smile. "Now, did you see who's here waiting? Unbelievable, eh? Well, they must be sneaking off to Cuba for a long weekend. Even the pros are following our lead, eh, George?"

I nodded at J.L. as we walked up to the two groups of ballplayers getting ready to embark for Cuba. I set down my bag so I could shake Rube's hand and talk to the other colored players waiting at the boat dock.

"Hope you didn't beat those Cubans too bad," Rube said, squeezing my hand extra tightly. "We need a challenge while we're down there. Nice work on those games last month, George."

"You're welcome," I said, extricating my fingers from Rube's crushing grip with a smile. "Heard from the Champ lately?"

"Not since the fourth," Rube said. "He's living outside the country now. Last I heard was Canada. I don't think—."

"Say," J.L. called out, pointing at the grassy field separating the train platform from the landing dock, "what do you gents say to an informal game of ball while we wait for the boat to fuel up? The team leaving Cuba versus the team heading to Cuba?"

Cobb immediately snorted and spat from where he stood, a good twenty feet away with the other white players.

"No sir," he said, looking first at Rube and his fellow colored players, and then giving my All Nations a dismissive glance. "I don't play with niggers, or any of these other... types." He turned his back before anyone could respond.

Welcome back home, I thought again, feeling an odd tickle in my chest.

No Small Foot had taken two steps after Cobb before I stopped him with a hand to his chest. Donaldson and Rube Foster were right behind him.

"Let the hateful bastard go," I spat. "Forget we said anything to him."

J.L. stood between the two unbalanced groups of ball players, the All Nations and the colored players on one side, and the half-dozen white Major Leaguers on the other side. His face was red, and I felt for the man even as my own pride stung from Cobb's words.

"How about the rest of you gents," J.L. murmured to the other white men. The man was determined. "Do you feel up to, well, just a quick game?"

Speaker and Mathewson looked interested in the prospect, though Ruth seemed a bit doubtful about it. Before any of the white men could speak up, though, Rube cleared his throat and solved the predicament the only way he could have.

"Sorry," he said. "I just can't risk my men getting hurt in an unscheduled exhibition like this, I'm afraid. And it appears the boat's ready for us."

J.L.'s shoulders drooped, and he nodded. "You're probably right, Mr. Foster. It was just a thought."

He walked off in the direction of the train station, shaking his bald head.

"All right," I called out, too loudly. "Looks like the train's ready for *us*. Let's get our stuff loaded. And these *fine* players have a boat to Havana to catch." I aimed my last words at Cobb, who was walking toward the boat as if nothing had happened.

On my way to the train, I overhead J.L. talking with one of the men from the railroad.

"The bridges are still pretty new, so be ready for some bumps here and there," the rail man was saying. "And the wind's picking up, which could be a bit of a problem as we go across the bridges connecting the islands. Just as long as the wind doesn't reach fifty miles per hour, everything will be fine."

I let out a long, unsteady breath. As if the ride on the steamer hadn't been enough, I thought, wishing I'd not overheard the two men. Now we'd have to worry about getting blown off the train tracks. This is what I get for buying into J.L.'s so-called "adventures."

"Couldn't we just have Blount drive down and pick us up?" I asked J.L. after the rail man had hurried off in the direction of the train platform.

"And pass up a ride on a train? You must be joking. Plus, the roads from here to Miami are in rough shape. We're safer on the tracks. We'll meet up with Old Blount in Miami. Provided he remembers to pick us up, that is."

With one last look back at the group of players on their way to Cuba—I felt a surge of jealousy that they'd be so close to that fine, spicy food, those avid fans, and most of all, Isabel (though none of them had *dare* speak to her!)—I gave J.L. a weary nod.

"Right," I said. "Let's get back on the road."

* * * * *

By the seventeenth of August, I found myself once again in another world. I was in a ballpark, getting ready for another preseason game, surrounded by the familiar sounds and smells of the game, fried food, cut grass, and sweat, but those sensations were pretty much all I could recognize.

It was the women, I realized. I didn't know what to make of the women out here. They made me miss Isabel in her brightly colored dresses and her tasteful sense of propriety. I truly felt I was in another world.

Did I say Isabel? I meant to say Maddie—how I missed Maddie.

This world was called San Francisco. We were gathered in a ballpark next to the bay, with the sun beating down and the wind blowing out of left, and we were about to face off against a team made up of all Japanese men. For some reason known only to him, J.L. had scheduled games up the Pacific Coast for the rest of the month, on the opposite end of the country from Cuba.

The San Francisco Seals had just finished up their game at Rec Park, and I'd been watching storm clouds move in from the northeast all afternoon, coaxed along and then pushed back by the strange wind that seemed to come from everywhere in this park. Strange winds, strange women.

Some of them sitting in the stands around me, others marching on the grounds with signs and banners, the women chanted slogans about suffrage, working the crowd into a frenzy. I caught more than a few women taking nips from small flasks hidden in their long skirts, and almost all of them were smoking cigarettes.

Some of the skirts exposed more than a little ankle. I didn't know where to look without seeing something inappropriate. I felt like a corrupt and lascivious old man.

I knew that many women had taken jobs at the various military supply factories in the Midwest, as well as the shipbuilding plants on both coasts, taking the place of their soldiering husbands. These women had that look of hardened, determined labor about them. Behind me in the bleachers, Carrie Nation sat in her uniform with a look of amazed shock on her face. I figured at any moment she'd pull off her hat and join these other "modernized" women.

After the rally for women's voting rights ended and the drinking and smoking women settled back into their seats, the game got underway. Back in the visitors' dugout, I once again felt old, listening to these cries for change. All I wanted to do was make it through the rest of this season and see my family at the end of it, and maybe win a couple ballgames along the way.

Goro had been beside himself for the past few days, once he'd learned who we were playing here. So it was fitting that, as the game progressed, he got a hit in each of his at-bats.

Each time he was on the bases, I heard him chatting with the first baseman, then the shortstop, and then the third baseman as he made his way around the horn. He even chatted up a storm in his native tongue with the catcher, until the ump told him to get in the box for the next pitch.

"Mack," I called out during the seventh-inning stretch, recalling the shouted words of the suffragists demanding freedom from before the game. I had a strange hunch brewing. The odd glow in his eyes and the darkness in his demeanor had lessened the farther we traveled from Havana. Or maybe it was the fact that he'd smoked all his Cubanos and could think clearly again.

"Mack?"

I turned and looked at my players heading back outfield. Everyone, that is, except the other pitchers and Torriente, who was glaring at Goro. I knew Torri hated alternating games with Goro and Jiang in the outfield, but for the first time my team had a surplus of fielders, and I wanted to make sure nobody else got injured. So, as the new guy, Torri would have to work his way into the regular batting order.

Unless, of course, we lost someone else. But before I could think any further on that topic, Mack was there, standing next to me.

"Don't you wish you knew what they were saying?" Mack said, nodding at the other team. His eyes were wide with wonder. "Such an interesting language."

"Mack," I said. "Tell me what Goro is doing."

"Coach?"

"Come on," I said. "The game's almost over, and Goro's been talking non-stop to the other team. Tell me what he's *going* to do."

Mack looked once more at me, and his eyes seemed to ignite with that old, uncanny white light. He nodded at me and stepped out of the dugout as the ump was calling for both sides to play ball again. He looked up into the sky, but the storm clouds had moved in front of the sun.

"You know, Coach, there's nothing to worry about," Mack said, his eyes wide as he gazed skyward. "Goro has another good season with us this, at least," he added before blinking and shrugging his broad shoulders.

Before I could ask for more, Mack sprinted out to centerfield.

"Whenever you're ready, Coach," the umpire called out to me, voice heavy with sarcasm.

I nodded at him and stepped back into the dugout, still not convinced of Mack's prediction.

Thunder rumbled across the sky and echoed back off the water in the bay. The Japanese team loaded the bases, only to have Boles strike out the next two hitters on a mix of fastballs and his latest trick, a spitball Art had taught to him. I didn't really like him using it, but the spitter did its trick for Boles, just as it had for that sneaky, shifty Worrell in games past.

The next batter popped up, the ball arcing high in Goro's direction.

"Watch him miss it for his fellow countrymen," Torri muttered next to me.

"Careful, son," I said. I got to my feet, watching Goro set up underneath the ball. The wind sent the ball curving back, then forward, but Goro compensated, never letting his eyes leave it.

Just as he was about to catch it, however, he dropped his glove hand.

"*What?*" I hissed, and an instant later the baseball hit Goro "Jap" Mikami directly in the face.

One thing that J.L. and I had always disagreed on was the need for a team doctor to travel with our players to all our games. As much as he saw my side of the story, J.L. couldn't account for the expense of another person who'd need to have his room (or tent) and food paid for. Even after Worrell's death, J.L. would not give in to my demands for a team medic.

Which was why I had to shout out again for a doctor as I ran as fast as I could on my aching knees toward left field. My old heart thudded like a bass drum, and the distance to my injured man seem more like miles than feet.

I'd gotten some training in working with injuries over the years, but when I made it out to Goro and his bloodied face, I had no idea of what to do other than place the towel I'd brought with me over the young Japanese man's face. I didn't think Jiang's acupuncture or herbs would be of much good here.

Mack crouched next to Goro, holding the injured man's shoulders to keep him still. Mack stared up in the direction of the cloud-covered sun for a long moment. I shouted again for a doctor as soon as I had my breath back. The other players formed a circle around us, but when they saw all the blood, they kept their distance.

I turned back to Goro in time to see Mack pressing his hand against Goro's nose through the towel.

"Broken nose. Probably some damage to the eye socket as well."

"Mack?" I felt cold raindrops fall on the back of my neck as I bent over my stricken leftfielder. To my relief, Goro was starting to groan. Up until that point, he'd been unnaturally quiet, so quiet I feared he was dead.

An instant later, he cried out in a high-pitched squeal as Mack put a hand on either side of his nose and made a sudden twisting movement.

"Mack! What in God's name are you doing to the man?"

Mack didn't even flinch as rain dropped down on us in a sudden torrent. Under Mack's hand, blood soaked through the towel over Goro's nose.

"Have to set his nose, otherwise he'll never breathe right again. But I don't know what to do about his eye. I can't see—"

"Wait for the doctor, that's what you'll do," I said, pulling Mack away from Goro, who now was trying to sit up.

"Coach," Goro said from below us. His voice was weak and muffled by the dripping red towel and the pouring rain. "Coach, than' you..."

"What?" I leaned closer to hear what my injured player was saying, but I froze as a strong, cold hand touched the back of my neck and squeezed. I was standing up before I realized what had happened. I could barely feel anything in the rest of my body, just those cold fingers on my neck.

"*Solly*," said the small, gray-haired coach of the Japanese team. The rain was coming down even harder now. "We come help Goro. *Prease, a-row* us to help, sir."

I moved back as four Japanese players encircled Goro and slid him onto a blanket. Goro groaned, then reached out to me.

"Than' you, Coach..." he said again, his voice barely audible over the beating rain, "than' you for... not... calling me... Jap."

The four Japanese players carried Goro off the outfield. I took a step to follow them into the other dugout, but three more of the Japanese players held up their hands and stopped me.

"*Solly,*" they said in unison.

"But he's my *player,*" I began, standing shellshocked in the rain as Jap receded into the shadows of the home dugout.

And they just took him from me. Just like Phil. Just like my own boy, all those years ago.

I lost him.

I turned to Mack, but the young man was in his own world. He had his face turned into the pouring rain, his skin jaundiced-looking in the gray light. I watched as the blood from Goro's broken nose dripped off Mack's fingers and fed the hungry grass and dirt at his feet.

This game, I decided, was over.

Chapter Sixteen

Game followed game, the countless pitches blurring together until all I saw were white streaks across my tired vision. Every day I was either on the bus to another game or standing in the dugout of another ball field. Every night I slept—poorly—in a tent on the hard ground or stretched on one of the lumpy seats of the bus, listening to Old Blount's wheezy snoring from the front seat. The normally rewarding sound of the crowd became the same dull hum behind us as we traveled north through sunny California, headed for Oregon.

Ever since leaving Cuba, I'd noticed to my dismay—but not to my surprise—that No Small Foot was having trouble with his hitting. He was leading led the team in strikeouts. As much as I dreaded it, he and I were going to have a discussion. I hoped it wouldn't come to blows. He hadn't been the same since his fight with Charlie—Chief Tokahoma.

Something else I noticed as we moved up the Pacific coast was a surprising lack of discrimination on the road. In our six games in California, for instance, the stands had been more white than colored, and as far as I could tell, there were no segregated restaurants, hotels, or even drinking fountains.

If I were more like Mack, I probably would have made a prediction: if the current situation on the west coast continued and spread eastwards, the future of baseball would be exceedingly bright indeed, and my nightmare about the cramped field and Worrell's clumsy white players would never come true.

Normally I would have discussed all this with Mack, but ever since his erroneous prediction about Goro in San Francisco, I'd been avoiding him.

I kept my concerns about my odd centerfielder and my nearly blind catcher to myself for days, until I found my chance to talk to No Small Foot. With rain blowing down at us off the peaks of the Coastal Mountain Range, I decided to spend our dwindling funds on six rooms at a low, brick hotel wedged next to a craggy bluff.

I'd felt a tickle in my throat all day, and I knew a rainy night in a tent or on the bus was sure to turn into a full-blown cough. Hell, we *all* deserved a good night's sleep in a hotel room.

I made arranged to share a room with No Small Foot, even though I'd heard horror stories about his snoring and bouts of sleepwalking. I was willing to risk that if I could get his batting average back up above .100.

I was just hanging up my uniform after yet another rinse-wash when he arrived our room, which suddenly felt much smaller.

"Coach," No Small Foot said as he pushed past me, bag in hand.

The big, barrel-chested man dropped his bag and fell onto the first narrow bed, sending up a small cloud of dust. He put his hands behind his head and let out a long sigh.

"John," I said, sitting on the second bed and stifling a cough. "I think we need to talk."

"Had a feeling this was coming." No Small Foot turned and looked over at me, bad right eye slightly out of true. "It's my hitting, ain't it?"

"I think the biggest problem is you're not seeing the ball. It's your vision."

I paused, thinking of something Mack had said about Charlie, back in July. How the troubled man had gone on a *vision quest*. Where had that lost young man ended up?

I kept expecting an angry outburst, but the other man was quiet. So I pushed on, bracing myself for the worst.

"Your catching's been outstanding—I never have to worry about a ball getting by you or someone trying to steal off you. I don't know how you do it, but your fielding has been spectacular."

"Thanks," No Small Foot muttered. His black hair clumped up under his head, and from this angle I could see more than a few streaks of gray in it. I wondered how old the man actually was.

"How *do* you do it, John? How do you catch for our pitchers when you can barely see?"

The big man continued staring up at the waterstained ceiling, squinting enough to cause a web of crow's feet to form around his eyes. I waited for his reply, biting back another cough that threatened to slip out of my mouth.

"If I told you," he said at last, "I wouldn't be able to do it any longer."

I thought back to No Small Foot's anger at Charlie's charade of being an Indian, talking about the Great Spirit. I had to choose my words wisely.

"Is it some kind of... Indian magic?"

"You could say that," No Small Foot said at last, sighing. "Let's just say that I've trained the pitchers and infielders pretty well when it comes to runners leading off, and they give me a whistle or a shout if a runner's going. And I don't really have to *see* the base to make a throw there, do I? I mean, no matter what ballpark you're in, second base or third is always going to be in the same place every time, right? Our guy—or girl—just has to get there on time and make the catch."

I stared at him. Surely he was joking with me.

"As for catching the pitches, well, I'm the one who makes the call for each pitch, so I know where it's going to end up. It's up to the pitcher to put it where I ask 'em to. Instinct takes care of the rest. That, and my ears are pretty damn sharp, Coach. You can *hear* that pitch coming, if you listen close."

I inhaled the musty odors of the well-used hotel room, wanting No Small Foot to tell me more. Maybe there was indeed something magical about the man, and I'd just overlooked it all along. To not be able to see the ball coming at you...

"John," I began, thinking of how hard my pitchers threw, the blood on Goro's face. "I can't risk you getting hurt. You saw what happened to Goro—"

"Jap? Hell, coach, that fella wanted to join his countrymen so bad he was willing to bust open his nose and just about lose an eye to do it."

A sudden tightness filled my throat, and my left arm began to tingle with pins and needles. I let out a cough that I barely stifled with my right hand.

Than' you... for not calling me Jap.

"You're probably right," I said after clearing my throat. "I just don't want you to take a pitch in the face, son."

"Don't worry 'bout me," No Small Foot said with a barking laugh. "Plus, I don't think anyone'd be able to tell the difference on this old mug of mine if I took one in the nose."

"Be that as it may," I said, and I pulled from my bag a small metal case that I'd picked up in San Francisco. Inside the case were a pair of heavy-duty black spectacles, the frames thick as cables.

No Small Foot squinted at the glasses in my hand as if they were a weapon used to kill his father.

"No. I can't risk anyone in my tribe seeing me wear these things. I will look like a fool, or worse, like a..." he lowered his eyes, closed them. "Like a white man."

Without another word, I slid the glasses back into their case and set the it on the bureau. We said nothing more on the topic after I doused the light.

Like a white man, I thought, smiling in the darkness as I pulled off my clothes and climbed into bed. I remembered Worrell and his delicate reading glasses he'd pull on to read his bible between innings and on bus rides.

Worrell. I hadn't thought of him in days. As if the thought of him was detrimental to my health, I began coughing again. Damn this cold rain. Nothing worse than a summertime cold.

In the next few hours, I suffered through No Small Foot's snoring, drifting in and out of broken slumber. He was so loud, I wondered if he wasn't faking it to get back at me for attempting to help him see better.

I wrapped my pillow around my head and finally drifted off to a sleep blessedly free of any dead white men, only to be woken what felt like mere seconds later by the slam of our hotel room door.

I sat up, chest rattling, left arm numb. John was gone.

I rolled out of bed and stumbled for the door. I'd heard it was bad luck to wake someone who was sleepwalking, but I couldn't risk my catcher hurting himself as he took a stroll through the mountains next to our hotel, asleep.

I slipped outside and looked to the left and the right. The rain had stopped, and an early-morning fog crept in, allowing me to see just twenty yards in all directions. The cloying smell of the pines around me made my nose itch.

I held my breath and heard, ahead of me, the soft pad of bare feet. John No Small Foot wasn't in the forest; he was walking on the highway, in the fog.

I ran after him as fast as my sore knees would allow, biting back a groan. Did he do this every night? If so, it was a miracle he was still alive.

I finally caught up to him a quarter mile down the road from the hotel. The cool air was thick with humidity after yesterday's rain, sticking in my throat. Fortunately, the narrow two-lane heading north into Oregon was empty at this time of night, because my catcher was directly in the middle of the road.

Naked. Standing on one foot. And singing.

As the deep, low noises poured out of the big man, I felt something cold travel the length of my back, like the touch of a dead man's finger. Still singing, John lowered his foot, hunkered down, and began to dance in a circle that kept widening until he reached the shoulder of the road.

I shivered when I saw that his eyes remained tightly closed as he carried out his ritual. The sound of his voice brought a lump to my throat, and I felt like I was invading No Small Foot's privacy. I took a step back, prepared to return to our hotel room, when I heard the distant rumble of a truck.

A second later, twin beams of headlights emerged from up ahead of us, with my catcher dancing in between them.

I moved like I was chasing a line drive down the first base line, the muscles in my legs propelling me forward in spite of the old aches and the new pains covering my body. I was going after Jack Johnson's bullet of a line drive again, trying to make one more impossible catch.

The lights grew big as dinner plates around No Small Foot, then bigger. I wasn't going to reach him in time.

I dove, hoping to at least knock John far enough out of the truck's path to make the impact more of a glancing blow, but I was not close enough.

I was too late. I was going to lose him, too.

It felt like my body hung in the thick, wet air forever, my arms reaching out for No Small Foot. Then the impact occurred.

But instead of impacting the unyielding metal of a truck, someone grabbed me by my arms and pulled me forward. I went flying face-first onto the gravel of the far shoulder, and a roar filled the air as the truck flew past, missing me by inches.

I lay gasping and coughing on the ground for a full minute before I could sit up. My eyes refused to open, though I was able to pick half a dozen bits of gravel out of my cheeks.

"Heard it coming way off," No Small Foot said in a dull voice above me. He was still asleep, I realized. "Felt it on the road even before that. Still think I need those spectacles, Coach?"

I tried to answer, but a sudden lethargy had grabbed me. As my catcher padded off down the road toward the hotel, I rolled to my back on the gravel next to the road. The fog felt like spirits floating around me, stealing my air and my energy. Maybe Small Foot's dance had woken the dead, more ghosts to haunt me.

My eyelids drooped, and I stopped fighting it. I slept.

And like a bad, scratched penny, Worrell was there, waiting for me.

"Running," he said. He stood over me, appraising me like a pitcher from an opposing team, pale arms folded over his bony chest. *"Always running from me, you are."*

"Yes," I said in my dream, exasperated. I couldn't get up off the gravel below me. "You scared me out of Kansas City, possibly for good. You and your band of dead white men. Is that what you wanted to hear, Worrell?"

"I don't care for this lack of respect, boy—"

I found the strength to sit up, though even my dream body was sore.

"You talk to me about respect? After all those games of ignoring my advice, talking over me, dressing me down in front of my players? Me, with twice—no, three times—as much experience playing the game as you? Well, my disrespect is long overdue."

Worrell moved closer, the few stars in the cloudy night skies poking through his translucent body. He still wore the same All Nations uniform he'd died in, and that offended my eyes more than the fatal wound on his temple.

"So," he whispered, voice calm. *"You think you know more about the game than I, do you, boy?"*

The distant rumble of a truck filled the night around me, jarring me from this nightmare. Worrell was fading where he stood above me, but I could still see his cold grin and his calculating, beady eyes.

"I do," I muttered, feeling a cough coming on.

"I see," Worrell said. The headlights of the truck cut through him, dispersing him at last. *"And we shall see about*

that, all of my friends and I. We shall see, George Grunion. Head coach, indeed..."

And then the truck was almost upon me, lights exploding into my vision. I sucked in a jagged breath, but it was too late to scream. This time I was caught. I was going to die.

But when I opened my eyes, all that I saw around me was fog and an empty road. No Worrell, no Small Foot.

Alone again.

Getting up off the side of the road seemed to take ten minutes more. And when I sat up, the tickle in my throat had become a full-blown cough. Each sharp, barking cough felt like it would tear my lungs apart.

At last I limped back to the hotel room, wheezing from the effort of stifling my cough. Long before I opened the door to our room, I felt relieved to hear more of No Small Foot's train-engine snoring coming from inside. I certainly hoped *he* was having a restful night.

The next morning, I woke disheveled and aching, throat sore, feeling totally unprepared for the long, bumpy drive north ahead of us. We were leaving California after five sunny days, heading into Oregon.

Almost as soon as the team bus rumbled across the border, the rain began to fall. All the aches from my run-in on the road last night made me wish for nothing more than a hot bath and a couple hours to soak in it. At least I had only a few scratches on my face to show for my adventure out on the highway.

We had three games against a Portland semi-pro team scheduled at noon today. We'd get there in time for a quick lunch, Old Blount had told me, but he'd have to have to stand on the accelerator to get us there in time.

"No short cuts," I reminded him again as we roared down a highway lined with endless evergreens that marched right up to the shoulder of the road. "We can't afford to get lost again."

By the time we got to the Portland field, it was half past noon, so we skipped lunch and began playing. After half an hour of playing—Buddha was nursing a sprained thumb, or so he claimed—I kept getting short of breath, which I tried to blame on hunger and the rainy weather and my head cold.

I was getting too old for this—from my bad knees to my numb arm to the too-fast beating of my heart. Sometimes even my jaw would ache during a game. I hated to admit it, but my time as a player was running out.

I made Buddha Rodriguez and his sore thumb play the rest of our games that day. I refused to even listen to the bald Mexican if he complained. Part of my harshness with Buddha came from the fact that on the road to Portland that morning, he'd shared with me his fear of death.

Wearing a wide-eyed look of utter horror, he'd told me how his fear had led to his injury in the Mexican revolution over six years ago. He'd been part of a group of rebels who were planning on ambushing army soldiers in the middle of the night, but he'd panicked before the soldiers arrived. In his haste to save himself, he ran face-first into a tree. He hadn't been the same since.

Once he'd recovered enough from his humiliating injury, Buddha abandoned his friends and gave up being a rebel. He was too afraid of dying to risk running into either sides of the fight, so he slipped into America.

And so, with fat tears bubbling in his brown eyes, he told me how he'd concocted his story about a soldier clubbing him with a rifle. He thought he'd die from his injuries, and that had terrified him.

"What do you fear so much about death?" I asked Buddha.

He didn't even hesitate with his answer.

"It is so very... final, Coach. My people celebrate the day when the souls rise up from the body, All Souls Day, but I could never enjoy that day. Not after seeing dead bodies in the streets after battle. I did not see a single soul rise up after a battle. No, not a single one. Not at all. *Dia de los Muertos.*"

I had to fold my arms in front of me to ward off a sudden chill. The image of souls rising up made me think of the strange white light in Mack's eyes, the malevolent light that had distracted Worrell. The same light I saw at inopportune moments, like last night on the highway, after No Small Foot had pulled me from in front of that truck.

"That is why I had to leave behind my gun and knives and *mi amigos.* I could not be responsible for the deaths of... any more people. I..."

I swallowed, my harsh feelings softening toward Buddha.

"It's okay, son. You don't need to say more."

"No. I *will* tell you this. I must." He swallowed and wiped his face with his cap. His bald head glistened in the bright sunlight coming in the bus windows. "I saw a man die, at my hands. The life, it just... *left* him. Because of me, you see. His eyes just... went dark. I could never do such a thing again. *Nunca.*"

I could only nod, my mouth dry, as I watched Rodriguez get up and push his way through the crowded bus back toward his seat.

Dia de los Muertos.

I felt like a fool for even asking him if he feared death. What man in his right mind didn't?

Especially with so much in life to live for, I realized, thinking not of just my team and the rest of our season, but of a woman in Cuba and the piece of paper in my pocket containing her address.

With my harsh cough still lingering in my chest, I dreaded going back to my little house in Kansas City at the end of August, not knowing who or what might be awaiting me there. Would it be Worrell and his gang, all bluster and threats, or just Derby, sad Derby, ready to share his tale of woe from beyond the grave?

To my surprise, the house was silent and free of ghostly chills when I arrived. I didn't even bother unpacking, but just swapped my dirty clothes for what clean clothes I could replace them with.

Then I looked through the weeks of mail I'd accumulated while I was away. No letters from my family, as expected. And nothing from Isabel, not even a post card. That made sense, of course, as I'd not yet written her yet. She had no way of knowing my home address.

"Old fool," I muttered. It was up to me to make something happen. But I was too damn tired for such things. Or so I thought.

Along with my usual bills and newspapers, I found a letter from Goro. The Japanese team had indeed taken him in, and after his broken nose had begun to heal, he was back in the outfield again. He was considering going to college and studying mathematics once this season ended. He thanked me profusely for all I'd done, and I felt a surge of relief for the young man.

A little good news went a long ways, and I felt like I could handle the road trip beginning tomorrow. J.L. had arranged for more games against all-colored or novelty teams, explaining that white teams were too short-handed, with more men quitting their teams to either work in the factories or to go off to fight after enlisting to serve in the war.

The next two weeks of games could be quite chaotic, if not nightmarish. I remembered a rough game during the All Nations' first season when we played against a team dressed as clowns, and their red-nosed third baseman pulled a knife on Buddha after he'd belted a triple. Buddha had butted him with his forehead, and a huge melee had taken place.

To take my mind off my worries, inspired by Goro, I sat down on in my old chair and began writing—for the first time since my intoxicated night before we'd left for Cuba—a letter.

This one was addressed to Isabel Maria. I told her about the past few weeks, filling her in on all we'd done since leaving Havana—California, Goro, No Small Foot, Oregon, Idaho. Games, mostly wins, just two losses. Still no hits for me, though I was grateful to not have to play as often.

Then I gritted my teeth and plunged on, telling her how I still thought of her and all we'd talked about in our short time together.

I had five pages written in less than ten minutes.

And when I finished it, I actually considered *sending* it to her, no less. Had the enveloped all addressed and stamped, though in my hurry to leave the next morning, I swore I left it sitting on the end table next to my chair.

Maybe I did send it, after all. Or someone sent it for me.

As a result of J.L.'s creative scheduling, on a muggy, too-warm day in the fourth of September, the World's All Nations team ended up in Benton Harbor, Michigan to play the renowned House of David baseball team.

I'd heard plenty of stories about them, of course. The team's full name was the Israelite House of David. The players came from a religious colony just up the road from this park, where they all lived when they weren't touring the country and playing ball.

Every single man on the team had hair flowing down their backs and curly beards stretching to their chests. And the infielders made the ball *dance* while they were playing. Watching their double plays was like listening to Shakespeare being recited.

Between the first and second inning, while Jiang tried to steal a hit off of the pitcher—a tense-looking man with a pointed beard and hair like a black explosion on his capless head—I took a seat next to my third baseman.

"So," I began, "do these men share your religion, Art?"

Art swallowed suddenly and looked as if he was going to choke on the plug of tobacco he'd just put in his cheek. He'd been chatting in a low voice with Boles. I must've interrupted something.

"I'm sorry, sir?" he said, eyes wide. He looked guilty as a cat in a dairy.

"Well, I thought you were Jewish, like these fellas."

"I was brought up Jewish," he said with a shrug, arranging his tobacco with his tongue in his cheek and inching away from Boles. "And I still believe some of what Jewish people believe. But these House of David gents practice their own brand of religion, Coach. They're not Jewish like I used to be."

"I... I guess I thought it was all the same," I said. "Been meaning to talk to you about this, by the way."

"I know," Art said, his dark eyes moving from the action on the field—where Jiang had just stolen second far ahead of the throw from the long-haired catcher—back to me.

"So this team has its own set of beliefs. How so?"

"They consider themselves *true* Israelites, part of the so-called lost tribes. So they don't cut their hair or trim their beards because they want to be ready for the next coming of Jesus, for the millennium." Art smiled and shook his head. "They are not actual Jews, though. That's for sure."

"But you are," I said. "Or were, once."

"Yes. My father—my real father, that is, Harry's and my dad—was a rabbi, you see, so we discussed these things often, before Father moved away. My brother is nearly years older than me, so we were never close."

"So what happens?" I said, ignoring the last out of the inning as Jiang was picked off third base. "What happens when you die, according to Jews?"

Art picked up his glove and chewed on his tobacco, as if trying to decide whether to share the information with me.

"Okay," he said at last, with a tiny shrug. "It's like this: after you die, for three days the soul hovers over the body. It thinks about going back into it, but when it gets a good look at your lifeless face, after those three days have passed, it departs. That's why most Jewish people want to mourn all the time those three days, because the soul is so close by."

I thought of Worrell's soul lingering around me ever since our fateful game back in Kansas City and shuddered. If only I could've left *him* behind after three days.

We shall see, George Grunion. Head coach, indeed...

I felt another cough coming on, but I was able to stifle it.

"So, what happens after those three days?"

Art was about to answer when Buddha Rodriguez whistled at us from first, pointing at the unattended third base bag. Art was needed at his post.

"You mean the afterlife? Most Jews accept the notion of an immortal soul," Art said, talking fast now as he grabbed his glove and inched his way out of the dugout. "Just like Christians. But most of us believe that life is for the living, that we must be as good as we can during our short time here."

Art paused for breath, while the rest of the team yelled at him to get to third.

"Don't worry 'bout it, Coach. The afterlife will work itself out, you see," he called out over his shoulder. "Time is short enough as it is, Coach. Might as well enjoy yourself and play some ball, right?"

People in the stands shouted their agreement with Art's words, glad the game was back on again. Art sarcastically tipped his cap to them.

I sat down on the dugout bench, compiling and cataloging all the theories I'd gathered from my players this season. I thought Art's beliefs definitely made some of the best sense of them all. Should've talked to him long ago.

And so, over the next few innings, the game became more fun than I could have hoped as I tried out Art's theory.

I found myself laughing at the way the House of David team played, even as they befuddled our hitters and runners. When the House of David players were out in the field, the simplest of plays was turned into an eye-popping spectacle—the shortstop would dive and sometimes do a flip to snag a grounder, launching it to first at the last possible second, nailing our runner every time. The second baseman juggled the ball and his glove before tagging a runner out.

Life is for the living. The afterlife will work itself out. I didn't care if we lost. I hadn't felt this good since Cuba.

Even No Small Foot was feeling agreeable with the lightheartedness of the exhibition game. The first time he went up to bat, I saw him give a quick look around, then slip on the spectacles I'd given him. He got a hit at each successive at bat, too.

"You've been saving up these predictions for far too long, son," I told him with a grin. "But I thank you for them. Especially the weather report."

I felt as if my team was back together again, at full strength, and the new recruits were playing wonderfully— Prieto was working on a two-hitter against the House of David, and no ball hit in the outfield was left uncaught thanks to Torriente's range in left and Jiang and Mack's cooperation in right and center.

I wished that my feelings of hope and goodwill would stay with me for the rest of the day, the week, the rest of the season; but I knew, just like my tickling cough and the unending war heating up to a boil over in Europe—Mack's "storm cloud," no doubt—that my sense of peace was all too temporary.

Chapter Seventeen

I think I can safely say that, over the course of my long life, I've done more traveling than anyone else I know. On my trips to and from baseball games, I'd seen some amazing sites, including visits to the depths of the Grand Canyon and the heights of Yosemite as well as the impossibly tall, ornate buildings of New York City, including my favorite, the triangular Flatiron. Don't forget the endless lakes of Minnesota, the deserts and peaks of Arizona, the swamps of Louisiana. Each region—each town—had its own story, its own flavor.

And I can't forget our recent liberating visit to Cuba, where I'd tasted both spicy foods and the lips of a beautiful woman. A woman I doubted I'd ever see again. (Though one never knows—just this morning I'd dropped the second letter I'd written to Isabel Maria at the post office. At the time, I thought it was the *first* letter I'd actually put into the mail to be deliver to her.)

But I digress. I was talking about my travels, not my heart.

I felt like I'd seen it all as I hop-scotched across our country in the past forty or so years.

I was wrong.

Because there I sat, somewhere in the Upper Peninsula of Michigan, in the back room of a diner owned by yet another cousin of J.L., surrounded by plates of food and my players: Mack and Boles on my left, Buddha Rodriguez and the bespectacled No Small Foot on my right.

My three Cuban players stood above us, and they all— believe it or not—wore thick, dark robes they'd pulled from their traveling bags. Mendez held a pair of burning candles, Torriente held a live chicken, and Prieto gripped a nervous-looking pigeon in both hands.

"To *Olorun!*" Torriente shouted, lifting the squawking chicken in his hands.

"And the *Orisha!*" Prieto added, lifting the pigeon above the table in a flutter of wings and bird shit.

Yes. I am fully confident that I have never seen or experienced anything like this before in all my traveling.

"A blood sacrifice is needed," Mendez whispered, leaning down next to me and the other players. With a pair of hissing sounds, Torri and Prieto pulled knives from the rack behind us. "We don't have all the material to do a true *Santería* ceremony, so we must make do. Is fun, eh, Coach?"

I winced at the sound of metal meeting flesh, even though I'd killed more than my share of chickens on the plantation growing up. I imagined the last futile surging of the bird's muscles in Torriente's hands now that the head of the chicken had been separated from its body. The blood from the chicken squirted into a metal pan with a series of splashes.

The sickly sweet smell of fresh blood filled the small room, temporarily overpowering the thick cloud of incense and candle smoke from the shelves around us. I felt my throat try to close up on me, and my breath grew short.

Prieto was having more trouble with his pigeon. Every time he tried to position the gray bird on the table to lop off its head, the bird would either shit on his burgundy robe or bob its head out of the way of the knife. With a sudden burst of energy, the pigeon slipped out of Prieto's grasp.

Just before the bird got free, though, Buddha Rodriguez clapped his big hands around the struggling gray bird. With a murmured apology and a sudden movement, he twisted its neck.

"Shall we begin, *amigos?*" Buddha said.

"*Gracias,*" Prieto muttered, sheepishly.

The Cuban men began to mutter in Spanish over the tiny pair of corpses and the pans of fresh blood on the counter. Next to the bowls stood two faded portraits, one of Jesus and one of a robed woman that Mendez claimed was Saint Barbara. She was posed in front of a tower, holding a chalice and wearing a crown and a tentative smile.

This was their makeshift shrine, where I had deposited a biscuit and a slice of pie from the diner next to a range of bread and cakes brought in by the others. These were hungry gods, apparently.

I kept an eye on Rodriguez, who'd been eyeing the sweets ever since the ceremony began half an hour ago. Hell, we'd all been doing it.

Mendez leaned close to continue his lessons.

"You remember me telling you about *Olorun*, right, Coach? So you know how *Olorun* is the owner of heaven. He is creator of the universe, and he created the smaller guardians, called *Orisha*. Each *Orisha* has his own special color, food, and dance. The blood is for them. They are partial to chickens."

Prieto and Torriente circled our table as they chanted, cigars in hand, adding to the smoke of the incense and candles. I looked over at Mack next to me, thinking about his strange obsession with cigars and the detrimental effect they seemed to have on him while we were in Cuba. But he was just nodding along with the chanting, wearing a contented smile with his eyes closed.

"And *this* will bring us good luck?" I said, unable to believe I'd let them talk me into this after yesterday's late-inning loss against the House of David.

"You need to live in harmony with your destiny," Mendez told me, talking faster as he warmed to his topic. "You seem out of key, Coach. Something hangs over you. Perhaps that is why we lose more games lately. You can't know peace until you find it in *yourself*. This ritual returns harmony to everyone."

He pointed to a metal soup tureen sitting on the altar next to the dead birds.

"Inside that big bowl," he said, as Prieto and Torri waved their smoking cigars over it, "are the stones sacred to *Orisha* and the holy cowrie shells used for the shell oracle."

"Oracle?" I said, too loud, earning me an annoyed look from Torriente as well as a curious look from Mack. I felt sweat begin to form on my forehead and in my armpits. To cool myself off, I sipped at the thick, sour liquid called *chequete* in my chipped diner mug and grimaced at the bitter taste.

Torriente took a small bottle of his own from his robe and shook it over the table, splattering me in the face.

"Oh, he's got *aguardiente*, too!" Mendez said with a grin. "This stuff will knock off your socks. Usually they just spit it on you, so count your blessings."

Prieto gestured toward the altar while Torriente took out a glass container of what looked like mud.

"*Omiero*," Mendez said, "a mix of rain water, river water, sea water, and holy water, along with some secret ingredients that the *Orisha* love".

Oh boy, I thought, wishing we could've afforded a hotel instead of our tents tonight. I was going to need a bath after this so-called ritual.

Torriente gestured for everyone to move closer to the table with the altar. Once we were situated, Prieto held the container of *omiero* above us, then he held it to the north, east, south, and west, spilling a bit of it at each point, much to Boles' hissing annoyance when it hit him.

I waited for the young white man on the other side of the table to say something, but he was focused on the actions of his Cuban teammates. His eyes held a needy look, as if he were desperate for something good to come from this ritual.

I thought of the way he and Art had been talking quietly yesterday—right before I interrupted them—and wondered again about the relationship between them. Just how close were they? You never know. Maybe Boles just came here to help sharpen his fastball. Can't ever have enough luck.

Meanwhile, Torriente spoke in Spanish again as he drew strange symbols in eggshell on the table top, his finger crunching through the tiny pieces of white shell.

Prieto came back to the table, spilling three more drops of his *omiero*, and then he passed it around the circle. When it came to me, I took a small sip and saw stars flash in my vision. I took another eye-popping sip before passing it to Mack.

A soft drumming sound filled the room. I didn't want to pull my gaze away from the candles in front of me to find out who was making the noise—I was starting to *see* something taking shape in the light—but I guessed it was Prieto, probably using Buddha's drum. The flame-figures taking shape in front of me leaped and rolled and then disappeared.

The bottle of *aguardiente* was passed around again, and I took two more tiny sips. More constellations rocketed past my eyes before I could focus again on the shapes materializing in the candlelight. I could still smell the coppery odor of the bowls of blood, but I found the scent calming, somehow.

The drumming sped up, and Torri's voice began to go hoarse from his chanting. I could almost see a face in the candle's flame in front of me, and my hand ached to reach out to touch it. I felt like I was floating above the table now, looking down into the yellow outline of eyes and a mouth, smiling at me.

Just as I was about to reach down to the cold metal table in an attempt to ground myself, Buddha Rodriguez sat up straight, emitted a belch that lasted for close to five seconds, and then tipped over backwards in his chair.

"The *Orisha*," Mendez announced, "has arrived. Don't touch him!" he called out to Boles and No Small Foot, who were both leaning over Buddha, about to grab him.

On the floor, Buddha shook with some sort of strange convulsions that rippled up and down his round body. His leg kicked out, almost clipping Boles on the side of the head, And then, as suddenly as it had begun, Buddha farted, and his entire body relaxed.

When he opened his eyes again, someone else seemed to be in charge of my first baseman. That could be the only explanation—the man's eyes were rolled back, and his familiar lazy smile had been replaced by a hungry grin.

"Is he okay?" Boles hissed. He was leaning so far away from Buddha that was almost sitting in Mack's lap.

Prieto and Torri leaned over Buddha, and I could've sworn I heard them blowing on the Mexican's face and in his ears. They sat him back up again in his chair, and his grin widened.

"My *worshippers*," Buddha said in a voice that seemed to come from outside the room and above us.

He reached out for the headless pigeon and shoved it into his mouth. Boles hissed again, and I had to bite my lip to keep from doing the same.

"*Muchas gracias*," he mumbled with his mouth grotesquely full. Somehow he was still able to retain his grin as he bit down on the bird. I reached for the bottle of *aguardiente* and took a long slurping pull, hoping that would drown out the wet sounds of snapping bones and chewed feathers.

With more stars spinning in my vision, I passed the bottle to Boles and listened to the quickened breathing of the men around me, along with my own exhalations. I felt heavier now, as if the presence of the *Orisha* had broken my own half-drunk illusion of levitation.

I blinked the stars from my eyes and stared at Buddha, whose grin had gone away. Sweat now dripped off my forehead and nose, but I didn't dare lift a hand to wipe it away.

The *Orisha* did not look happy.

"What sort of foolishness is this?" Buddha said in that strange, outside-the-room voice. He looked at Prieto, then Torri. "You are no *Babalawo*. Neither of you."

He turned to look at Mack, and his frown intensified into a sneer.

"And what pale oracle is *this*?"

Torri turned to look at Mack with something like horror on his chiseled face. He tore his gaze away and looked over at Buddha's glowering face.

"We don't never ask him for any predictions," Torri added, pointing nervously at Mack. "You are the oracle true, of course. Do not get us wrong."

"We had to make do," Prieto said, reaching into the metal soup tureen. "But we bring you sacrifices and food. This is the only ritual we knew. All we ask for our gifts is that you grant us luck in the coming weeks. Luck for our team."

Mack simply sat there, his head wrapped in the smoke from the cigars behind him, and smiled at Buddha. His eyes narrowed to slits, unblinking, as he waited, almost daring the Mexican *Orisha* to say more.

Instead, Buddha reached for one of the smoking cigars and turned to look directly at me. The air fled from my lungs.

"So?" he said in his not-there voice. "You are the leader of this team."

I swallowed and nodded, my vision tinged with red. I felt a chill enter the room. I flinched as something touched the back of my neck, a grip cold as ice.

"Tell me. Why do you carry that spirit on your back in that manner?"

"What do you mean?" I said, my jaw quivering from the sudden cold. I knew who that was, though I couldn't believe he'd found me here.

"*Boy*," a dry voice hissed in my ear. I felt a cough try to shake loose in my chest, but I bit it back. "*Don't be foolish here. We're waiting on you back home.*"

"You let it *talk* to you?" Buddha said, his rolled-back eyes narrowing. My three Cuban players huddled together behind him like scared monks. "*Tell* me you do not listen to it nor heed its advice."

"Coach?" Boles said from across the table. "What's he talking about? Whose advice?"

No Small Foot stared at the space just behind me, squinting so hard behind his thick glasses that I couldn't see his eyes anymore.

"*Worrell*," he whispered. "He's standing right behind you, Coach."

"John," I said, not wanting anyone else to have to suffer through the indignity of Worrell's ghost. "It's just the liquor, making you see things—"

"Do not *deny* your visions," Buddha retorted. "You see the truth when I am with you. You must decide what to *do* about what you see, in the time you have left."

Without turning my head, afraid to get reprimanded by whatever it was that had taken over my first baseman, I peeked at Mack on my left.

He had a strangely satisfied smile on his face as he too gazed at something—or someone—behind me. If I had the strength to turn my body and my head around, I knew I'd see our former head coach in his soiled uniform, hovering over me with his swollen head and black, lifeless eyes.

"What the hell's everyone gawkin' at?" Boles wanted to know.

Mack reached out and patted Boles' hand, but the younger man hissed and pulled his hand away as if Mack's touch burned him.

"*This*," Buddha began, pointing at the space behind me, the being that had brought all the cold air and malice into the room, "is your responsibility. Your *guilt* attracts him like a moth to flame."

"But," I began, "I don't *want* him haunting me."

How the hell was this my fault, I wanted to ask him, but didn't dare.

"*Boy*," Worrell spat. "*What are you—*"

"What one wants," Buddha began, "and what one needs are two very distinct entities. But my time here is short, so I will assist you. For now."

Buddha's all-white eyes widened, and he twitched his bald head, once.

"Go," he said. "You are dismissed."

A sucking sound filled the room, coming from behind me.

"*No*," Worrell said from behind me, his voice going high as a woman's. "*Oh merciful heaven! No! Nooo—*"

With a snapping sensation, the chill that Worrell carried with him, along with his icy grip on my neck, disappeared.

Pop.

The dead man's spirit was gone, and I could breathe again. Feeling returned to my fingers and toes as I coughed for a good half-minute. All my players leaned away from me, staring at me as if they no longer knew me.

Everyone but Buddha Rodriguez, that was. He just watched and waited patiently for my coughing to stop. When it did, he nodded.

"*Bien*," the *Orisha* said with Buddha's mouth. "You will have to address that creature some other time. But now. I shall start with *you*."

I tried to blink to clear my vision, my head still light and reeling from Worrell's visit and sudden departure, blood in my mouth and filling my nose, but once my eyes closed, I could not seem to open them again.

I saw the stars from earlier in the ceremony, but this time I was out *among* them, weightless and spinning. The light of the stars went on into infinity, and as I stared, hypnotized, the stars turned themselves inside out, as if each star was the opening to a tunneled road. The roads pulled at me, beckoning for me to follow them all at the same time.

I felt stretched into too many directions. All those potential roads, all those *choices*, made my brain want to unhinge.

I wanted to scream, but instead of opening my mouth, I gritted my teeth and unfocused my eyes until the stars returned to normal and started shining again.

Finally, my eyes still closed, I saw a hazy image formed by the distant stars. I'd never been one to learn the constellations, so I didn't know if this was an actual design I was envisioning, like the Great Bear or the Big Dipper, but I knew right away *who* I was seeing.

"Maddie," I whispered, and just like that she was there, in front of me, the dark skin of her outstretched hand glowing with starlight. She was beautiful as ever.

I tried to raise my arms to embrace her, but my limbs were too heavy. Maddie's smile began to fade, though she nodded once and pointed first at the sky, then at the ground. Her face was contorted with pain in the instant before she disappeared into the whirling stars. She'd been trying to tell me something.

Why was she all alone? Where were our children? I needed to see Lizbeth, and more than anyone else, my boy. My Jacob.

Mack had vowed that they'd all show up by the end of the season. I'd put too much faith in his prediction, I realized now, too late. Mack was just a boy, not an oracle. He was only telling me what he thought I needed to hear.

After the vision of Maddie faded away, I felt a hand squeezing my heart, a claustrophobic agony that reminded me of how badly I missed my wife. She'd been so close to me, if only I could have reached out and held onto her.

And I was falling, falling.

I inhaled and saw another face: Domingo Prieto, my new pitcher, gazing down at me from a great height and puffing cigar smoke onto my face. I heard nothing but the rush of my own blood. Prieto leaned closer until his eyes filled my world, eyes that matched those of a widow in Havana who once danced with me for hours one hot summer night. I could not breathe.

I barely know you, I thought. But I miss *you*, too, Isabel Maria.

While my lungs began to scream for air, I looked once again into those dark eyes. I saw Isabel's sadness and loss there for a moment, mostly hidden by her intense curiosity and compassion. Then I imagined her smiling at me, making me ache to touch her lips again.

I still could not draw air, and the world went gray.

Panicking, I swung out convulsively, reaching for something, anything to stop the sensation of falling. I was rewarded by the solid thunk of my hand meeting the flesh of another person, followed by a tinkling of broken glass.

I opened my eyes. Seven pairs of eyes blinked down at me in unison and relief. After a long moment of confusion, I realized I was lying on my back in the cramped, smoke-filled store room.

"Coach!" Boles cried, pulling at my shirt. "You're okay!"

After I extricated myself from my toppled-over chair and Boles helped me to my feet, I touched my throat, still stinging from the potent sips of *aguardiente*.

Buddha reached over to steady me, and I pulled away from him.

"Coach?" he said, his face confused, though his brown eyes were remarkably clear and alert. His voice, I realized, was his own again. "You sure you are okay?"

I nodded, and Prieto and Torriente stepped closer, their robes now draped on their forearms like overcoats. Everyone else was standing, wiping their mouths and straightening chairs. Mendez was busy rinsing out the various bowls and pans in the big sink next to the table.

"Sorry nothing happened in our ceremony," Torri said with a sheepish smile. "We thought it'd be worth a try, but I guess the *Orisha* weren't hungry today. Or they weren't listening. Guess we have to make our own luck, eh?"

"At least we got to have a couple drinks," Prieto said.

I tried to say something about the stars and the visions I'd seen, but all of it was already fading from my memory. And hadn't they seen Buddha pointing at Worrell's ghost behind me, right before he banished him?

Maybe the sudden departure of that dead man's spirit had made me fall over. That was how I'd hit my head and saw stars. But when I reached up to check, I didn't feel any sort of bump on my skull.

"At least we will have some fresh chicken for dinner," Prieto said, winking at Torri. "Too bad Buddha tried to eat the pigeon. Think he had too much to drink during the ceremony, eh, Coach?"

"Ah, right," I said. "We'd better finish cleaning up in here."

The other players had already started picking up the food and portraits and cigars from the altar table, while No Small Foot bent down to pick up the bent frames to his broken eyeglasses.

"John," I said. "What happened to your spectacles?"

No Small Foot looked at me with annoyance as he pushed his thick black hair out of his face.

"*You* happened to 'em, Coach. Don't you remember? Smacked me right between the eyes just before you came out of your fit. They broke when they hit the floor. Guess I need to get some replacements now. There goes my batting average."

I muttered an apology and looked for a broom and dustpan. As I cleaned up the broken glass, I noticed that one of the players who had participated in the ritual—the *failed* ritual, according to Prieto and Torri—was gone.

Just like Worrell's ghost, Mack had disappeared.

"Pale oracle," I whispered, sending shivers up my spine and turning my sweat-soaked skin cold. I wanted to ask the others about Mack and where he'd gotten to, but they were too intent on cleaning up and getting out of the room.

He'd been right there at the table with me, smoking his damn cigar. But now I was wondering if Mack had been there at all. I shook my head as I watched my Cuban players rinse blood from the pan and wave the smoke out the back door.

Maybe I was just losing my mind. Unfortunately, that was starting to seem like the most logical answer.

The road and the endless series of ballparks scattered along its length called out to us once again, and we boarded the team bus an hour after the abrupt end of our Santería ritual. Prieto brought along a bag of freshly fried chicken from the ceremony, and everyone's spirits except mine were high as we headed north. Blount drove us over St. Mary's River, from Sault Ste. Marie in America to Sault Ste. Marie in Canada.

I was too disturbed by all I'd seen back in that diner to rest. Also, I worried that if I closed my eyes, Worrell would be there waiting for me. So I pushed my way to the back of the bus to find out what had really happened. I started with Boles, sitting with Art on his left—asleep—and Buddha on his right.

"I think you may have drank too much of their hooch," Boles said, winking at Buddha. "I don't blame you—the stuff was good. But it hit ya hard, Coach. You fell over like a ton of bricks got dropped on you."

"And while I was out, you didn't see anything? No... visions, or anything like that?" I looked from Boles to Buddha. They both shook their heads and gave me innocent looks. I didn't believe them for a second.

"Did *you*?" Buddha said, rubbing the faded white scar on the side of his head from his war injury. I still marveled at the sight of the bald man's clear eyes and the sound of his quiet voice. I couldn't forget his devilish grin during the ritual.

247

"I'm not sure," I said, and turned to No Small Foot in the seat behind them. "How 'bout you, John? What did you see?"

"Coach," No Small Foot said. "I didn't see a damn thing. You broke my glasses, remember?"

"Before that, though. Any visions?"

No Small Foot shrugged. "Not really. I think all the smoke from the cigars got in my way."

When I looked away from No Small Foot's frowning face, I saw that Prieto, Torriente, and Mendez were sitting huddled together in the seats at the back of the bus. Conspiring, no doubt.

I squeezed up next to them, hoping to catch some of what they were whispering, but they were talking softly and quickly in Spanish. I did hear the word *Orisha* twice before Mendez noticed me standing above them.

"Coach," Mendez said. "You okay? You took quite a spill back there."

"I'm very sorry about that," Prieto said. "We were just talking about, ah, what a bad idea that was. What do we know about running a good-luck ritual? We just thought it might be good for everyone to sort of..."

"Lift their spirits?" I finished for him, feeling a devilish grin of my own cross my face. "I think it did. In more ways than you could've predicted."

The three Cuban men looked at me, eyebrows raised.

"So," I said after an awkward silence. "None of you saw *anything*. Nothing happened to any of us," I said, watching their reactions. None of them even blinked. "Nobody was taken over by some kind of spirit, an *Orisha*?"

Prieto and Torriente gave me an identical double-take, while Mendez chuckled softly.

"No sir," Mendez said. "None of us have that kind of skill. To conjure an *Orisha*? No, that would've been much too dangerous. We're not that foolish. But at least the guys all had a good time, and got to get a taste of Santería, right, Coach?"

"Nothing happened," I repeated. This was getting ridiculous, and I was getting mad. The bus hit a rut, and all of us swayed back and forth for a good five seconds. "Guess I'll just check with *Mack* and see what he thought about it. He may have seen something that we may have... missed... What?"

The three men all stared at me with quizzical looks.

"Mack?" Prieto began. "But—"

"Coach," Torri said. "Mack did not come. He refused. He said, well, he said—"

"He said he did not want to tempt fate," Mendez said. "I am surprised you didn't hear him. Though that didn't stop him from borrowing our last few Havanas from us. Guy's been smoking them down to the nub again, he has."

My head had begun to hurt. Maybe I *did* hit it during our ritual in the diner, or maybe I was still suffering from the skull-popping hit I took during batting practice back in Chicago on the Fourth. I sighed, thinking about how badly I needed a bath, a shave, and a nap.

The team bus rocked over another hole in the road and turned east, putting the sun behind us, with Elliot Lake, Sudbury, and distant Ottawa ahead of us. As far as I could tell, looking out the window next to the trio of Cubans, Canada wasn't much different from Michigan or the rest of the Great Plains. The fields stretched out on all directions like a green blanket, broken up only by clumps of trees and huge lakes that seemed to spring up out of nowhere.

"Thanks, gentlemen," I said, moving back to my seat at the front of the bus, feeling a familiar tickle in my chest. My cough was coming back, just when I thought I'd banished it for good.

Swallowing hard, I glanced toward the front at Mack. I could just *ask* him.

But the pale-skinned young man was sitting sideways in Coach Worrell's old seat, puffing on a borrowed Cuban cigar he never took out of his mouth, blowing the smoke out of his window. Something kept me from approaching him. His used smoke curled back into the bus through the windows behind him, covering his fellow players like the tattered and smoking remnants of fever dreams, bad luck, and gray clouds.

Chapter Eighteen

On a cold, blustery day in Toronto less than a week later, with the wind blowing off Lake Ontario, we were about to start our final game in Canada when we experienced something completely new: our first-ever snow delay.

All day, the temperature had been dropping fast, to the point where everyone was huddled together in the dugout, bundled under our three team blankets. Carrie had already threatened Torri and Boles with bodily harm for getting too close. None of us had brought sufficiently warm clothing, and I wished J.L. was there for me to berate for this choice of scheduling.

And then, in the short break between games, the snow began.

It blew in like rain, falling in a white, sharp-edged sheet that rushed down at us from the north. This was gritty snow that stung my face and burned when it got in my eyes.

"Okay," I said, pulling down the brim of my cap. "I'm sure this will blow over soon."

"What was J.L. thinking, scheduling games here?" Boles moaned from where he sat sandwiched between Carrie and Art under the team blanket. "Here it is September, and it's *snowing*! It's like the end of the world up here."

"You'll be fine, Marty," Art said, and I realized he was talking to Boles. "Just don't think about the cold. Focus on something else. There are worse places to be than here, right now."

"Maybe," Boles muttered.

I glanced down the dugout bench at my players all huddled together under the blankets. Boles and Art were pressed especially tight to one another, unbothered by such proximity.

Friends, I told myself. Just close friends, staying close for warmth.

I gazed up at the gray sky, which had grown blacker in the cloud-choked north. I could smell the snow, an earthy, almost sweet odor filling my nostrils.

"Just be glad you're not pitching in this, Boles, Donaldson, Prieto, Art. Although maybe one of you could come up with an iceball or a frozen spitball up here. Maybe you should grab No Small Foot and start trying that out—"

I looked down the bench once more at my shivering mass of players, and my words died when I realized our Indian catcher was gone. Just Charlie Grant, simply walking off, without warning.

"Where'd he go?" I said at last. I hadn't realized how upset I was until I heard the quaver of my voice. This was tied into that Santería ritual back in America, I knew it. No Small Foot had seen too much in that back room. "And don't give me some story about a vision quest, either, damn it."

"Maybe he found someplace warm," Carrie Nation offered.

"Probably d-d-did," Donaldson added, teeth chattering. "If so, he's smarter than us."

"Wait a moment," I said, and I looked over at my centerfielder in the corner of the dugout. He sat wrapped up in the bag that usually held all the bats. I couldn't see his arms, though a cigar poked out of the top of the bag. Whitish-blue smoke puffed out every few seconds, as if he were a locomotive chugging uphill. I dared the cold and blowing snow to walk fifteen feet down the bench to join him.

As soon as I sat, a dozen coughs exploded out of my mouth. This cold was ensuring this accursed cough never left me.

"Mack," I said at last, staring out at the whitening field in front of us and rubbing my aching chest. "What's John doing right now? I mean, what *will* he be doing, a couple minutes from now?"

Mack wriggled his head out of the bag, his face strangely pale, almost blue from the cold. He took a deep puff on his cigar. He held the smoke in for almost ten seconds, savoring it. I knew the routine so well by now that I just waited for the young man to look up at the sun, even if it was hidden behind the black clouds. But Mack never raised his eyes.

"You know, Coach, he'll be coming back here," he said at last. "The snow will be melting by then."

"Where *is* he? Just answer the question, boy."

"Does it matter?" Mack said with a cough. "Does it matter where we are right now? Isn't it more important to know where we are heading? And where we end up?"

I looked down at my own hands and saw that they were clenched. I was close enough to Mack to reach out and touch him. Maybe it was the cold, maybe it was the soreness in my chest from all my coughing.

And maybe I was tired of his erratic behavior and failed predictions. I hadn't forgotten about Goro back in sunny California, and how Mack assured me the young Japanese man would be with us for some time. I felt manipulated and lied to.

When I looked up, I saw that the entire team was watching us from under their blankets and coats. I bit back the angry words I was about to say to Mack for not knowing where our blind Cherokee catcher had wandered off to between games.

He didn't deserve this, just like another young man who'd been the recipient of my anger, many years ago.

I leaned away from Mack and turned my face into the snow, letting the hard pellets cool the heat of anger on my face.

"You're right," I said to Mack after half a minute had passed. "I'm sure he'll be back soon."

As predicted, the freakish snowstorm was letting up, and the sun poked through the dark clouds overhead. The snow on the field was already melting. As the word passed through the crowd that the second game would soon be starting again, people crept back to the stands, brushing snow off the bleachers and bunching close together for warmth.

While the visitor's side remained empty, the home side of the stands was filling quickly. I was about to turn back to my team to check one last time if anyone knew where our missing catcher had gotten to, when a flash of white caught my eye. An unnatural whiteness, like a pale hand held high.

I never should've looked out there at the crowd, gawking like a rookie.

Worrell had found me, again.

His pale, bony fingers touching his bruised and swollen temple, the former head coach now sat at the front of the home bleachers. His face glowed whiter than the snow around him. He kicked his feet out onto the ground from the bottom bleacher, though his cleats made no marks in the snow. He leaned back, grinning at me with a knowing look.

An unnatural light that I couldn't blame on the sun bouncing off the snow filled the air around him and the men surrounding him. This was the same dozen men who'd passed through the walls of my house last month, gathering around Worrell as if he were some sort of spiritual leader. Four, no five, white men in American soldier uniforms stained brown and black with blood and mud. Half a dozen men in dirty baseball duds, the team names faded, their eyes dark and narrow as they glared at my players with what felt like jealousy.

And at the end of the row sat Derby, removed from the rest of the dead white men, his dusky skin also glowing, though his gaze was less a glare and more a look of curiosity, or maybe even apology. Derby nodded at me once before Worrell stopped him with a snap of his ghostly fingers.

"*Show us your best stuff*," Worrell said as a trio of fans walked through him on their way to their seats in the bleachers. He didn't even flinch as three pairs of boots stepped into the spot on the ground where his legs rested. "*I don't think your mad bald man from Mexico will be able to banish all of us, will he? So educate us in the niceties of the game... Coach.*"

My lip curled as I fought back an angry response. I sucked in a cold breath and, instead of saying anything, began barking out my ever-present cough. The Canadian weather had done nothing for my lingering illness.

Worrell and his group of men, all of them taken from this life too abruptly, let loose with a wall of harsh laughter. Laughter that only I could hear, as far as I could tell. No Small Foot wasn't looking in that direction, and Mack was still bundled up in the bat bag. I was on my own, it appeared.

What hurt worst was Derby's low chuckling, loud and clear to my ears, even from this distance. My old friend, now communing with Worrell.

You will have to address this creature, Buddha had said, under the spell of the Cubans' blood ritual, *some other time.*

No time like the present, I thought, swallowing another cough before it could slip out my throat. I stepped out of the dugout and into an icy blast of wind, fully intending to step right up to where Worrell and his laughing group of walking corpses sat.

But a hand grabbed my arm and pulled me back into the shelter of the dugout. Mack had slipped out of the bat bag, fast.

"*Look,*" he said, letting go of me and pointing down the first base line.

Wrapped in one of our old team blankets, No Small Foot trudged through the snow towards us. Something glinted on his face, catching the sun.

I could feel the collective sigh of relief pass through my players as he approached. I risked a look behind me at the stands behind the visitors' dugout, expecting to see Worrell and his team of spirits watching this latest scene of my team's instability unfold with bliss.

But all that covered that section of the bleachers was about three inches of untouched snow.

Meanwhile, our grinning catcher shook an inch of snow of his own from his long black hair before tying it back into a ponytail again. He was now wearing a pair of slender, gold-rimmed spectacles with round lenses. The dainty glasses made him look almost professorial.

"Game starting again?" he said, gazing brightly at everyone on the team with his restored vision. "Did I miss anything, Coach?"

Thinking of how close I'd been to grabbing Mack by the front of his uniform earlier, followed by my vision of Worrell and his lifeless, laughing posse in the stands, I could only shake my head at No Small Foot.

"Not a thing, John," I said. "Not a thing."

The September snow seemed to be a bad omen for my team's return to America. First, we lost our second game to the Toronto All Stars despite a heroic effort by Prieto, who pitched a shutout for the entire game, only to lose it in the twelfth on a wind-aided homer that slipped just out of Torri's long reach.

Then, on the way back into America early the next morning, our team bus was stopped by American soldiers. We all had to get out and let them search our bags, just as the skies opened up with more precipitation. At least it was rain this time instead of snow. By the time we were finally allowed back onto the bus, we were all wet, freezing, and irritable from the rain and from listening to the soldiers prattle on about spies and enemies trying to slip into America from all directions.

We didn't have time to stop for more than a few minutes at Niagara Falls. I'd been there twice before, but like the rest of my players, I couldn't help but gape at the roaring white falls. Even Mack put his odd, hermit-like behavior on hold long enough to admire the falls. Hell, he enjoyed them so much, at one point I had to grab the young man before he leaned too far over the railing and fell into the onrushing water.

Standing there, protecting Mack from the drop by positioning myself between him and the waterfall, I toyed with the idea of taking all my players back over the border into Canada to keep them safe from the war discussed by the soldiers at the border.

Or, even better, I decided, we could head south to Florida and then onto Cuba. I wondered if Isabel Maria had room for all of us in her home.

My warm thoughts of Havana were interrupted by a loud yelp from No Small Foot that carried over the roar of the falls.

"Everybody get down!" the big Cherokee shouted, waving his arms at his teammates and the tourists gathered around us. He had his new glasses on, and he was staring through them up at *something* high in the sky.

His next word sent all of us running for cover: "Zeppelin!"

A fat man in a bright yellow raincoat bumped into me on his mad dash past, but I kept my feet and looked up into the rainy sky. Following No Small Foot's pointing finger, I saw nothing but the flat gray nothingness of rain clouds. If there was a zeppelin coming in from the northeast, where my catcher was pointing, my old eyes were too weak to see it.

"*Coach!*" No Small Foot shouted. He and I were the only people left on the platform overlooking the falls. "Get under cover!"

I looked at No Small Foot's wide eyes, magnified to almost twice their size behind his new gold-rimmed spectacles. The man appeared to be tracking the slow progress of some sort of craft high above them.

But this was the same man who was blind in his right eye and almost sightless in his left. What in the world could he be seeing? How powerful must his new spectacles be?

Soldiers from the border patrol came running up to No Small Foot, rifles at the ready in case they needed to shoot it from the sky, if such a thing were possible. I had a sudden memory of my old nightmare of the crashing zeppelin, how the airship suddenly lifted up and over, followed by the long nothingness after the impact on the ground.

The memory of that nightmare took away my breath. I rubbed my chest, where my heart was pounding far too quickly. I started to cough once more.

No, I thought to my old body. Not now. Not yet. I'm so *close*.

I regained control of myself when I saw one, then the other soldiers, lower their rifles. The first one took out a small pad and scribbled down some notes, while the other three escorted No Small Foot back to the rain-slicked parking lot. The leader came up to me to make sure I found my way back, too.

"Crazy Indian," the soldier said. "I'd like to *see* those damn Germans try to attack us here," he added.

I swallowed and let the soldier, who could not have been more than twenty years old, lead me away from the falls. The young man let go of my elbow and turned to join his fellow soldiers without another word. As my heart returned to its normal speed, I followed No Small Foot onto to the bus.

Back inside, out of the rain and cold, No Small Foot refused to admit that he'd been seeing things.

"Not with *these* spectacles." He turned to look at me. "I know what I saw, Coach. You simply refused to see. All of you."

"Well, I'm glad you found a replacement pair," I said with a sigh, not wanting to argue the case any longer. Maybe there had been an airship high above us. But I'd had enough battles for one day, and I was ready for some rest and a little bit of warmth, out of the wind and rain.

Blount fired up the engine, and we left the falls behind us.

The three themes of our remaining two weeks of games were rain, war, and Worrell. Every game seemed to take place under cloudy skies and a light rain. The thunder was a constant reminder of the distant guns of war, growing louder each day.

And always in the crowd was Worrell, with his growing team of ghosts. He seemed to add at least one or two new recruits with each game. They watched every minute of our games, giving off their cold aura that kept their section of the home team's stand empty.

During those games, I'm ashamed to admit that I would sometimes let them distract me. Listening to their jeering, or simply feeling their dead eyes on me, I'd forget to flash my signals to the runners and leave man stranded.

Or I'd do what I just did now—let an opposing team's hitter knock one of Boles' fastballs over the fence, instead of showing the sign for a curve.

At the end of that two-run fifth inning by the Buffalo Bisons, No Small Foot came up to me, his catcher's mask still covering his face. I could barely see his dark eyes through the layer of twisted metal and his thick spectacles.

"You're letting him win, see," he said. He nodded his head at the crowd behind us. "Don't you understand he's scared of ya, Coach? That's why he's got all those other fellas with him."

My head ached from the pressure of clamping my jaws together for this whole game. No Small Foot's words were like a release valve. I exhaled, and then almost hugged the man.

"You see them, too?" I whispered instead, choosing the safer route.

He pointed at his eyes. "New glasses help. But I been seeing them since that damn Santa Claus ritual back in the restaurant. Never liked that fool of a white man. And now he has backup."

"*Santería*," I whispered. "What do you suppose they want?"

"To make us lose," No Small Foot said. He leaned close to me, the spikes of his mask almost poking me in the face. "Don't let them do that, Coach. You're a better coach than that."

I nodded, rubbing my chest to keep from another bout of coughing.

He was right. But I never got a chance to act on his advice.

"*Coach*," Boles said to me as soon as No Small Foot walked off to catch the bottom of the sixth for Prieto. "We have to talk."

With Donaldson dozing at the other end of the bench in our dugout and everyone else out on the field—our "mad man from Mexico" had played almost every game this month, saving me from risking my knees at first base—I gave Boles an awkward shrug and kept my eyes on the game from where we stood near the dugout entrance. This couldn't be good.

"Sure. What's on your mind, son?"

"We leave next Wednesday."

After watching Prieto's fastball slap into No Small Foot's glove a full second before the Bison batter could even twitch the bat on his shoulder, I turned to look at my young white pitcher. His eyes looked red, though his face was pale.

"No, we leave town tonight, soon as this game is over," I said, watching him closely. The doomed look on his face turned my skin cold with dread.

"No. We joined up. Me and Art. We're gonna go fight the damn Germans over in Europe and help save the world. We been talking about it all season, and Art can't wait any more. We leave to go to basic training next week."

So that was it, at last. I'd waited all season for the war to catch up to us. And these damn fool boys actually *chose* to enter the fray.

"I don't think you two have thought this through," I began.

Art was watching us at third between pitches, and Boles stared back at Art with an intensity I'd only seen when he was on the mound.

I sighed. "I'm not going to be able to talk you two out of this, am I?"

Boles sniffed suddenly next to me, as close to tears as he'd probably ever get with me.

After a long, painful pause that lasted three pitches— another strikeout by Prieto to end the inning, Boles spoke again.

"Please don't try," he whispered.

I coughed once, bit down on the ache in my chest and the tickle in my throat, and clapped Boles on the back. I nodded and said no more to him.

Two more. We'd soon lose two more players. Two more of my boys.

The echo of dry laughter filled my ears as Boles walked out of the dugout to meet Art at the end of the inning. With my hands balled up tightly into helpless, impotent fists, I turned at last to the section of the stands where Worrell and his growing team of the dead sat.

But as usual, he'd disappeared. Like everyone was doing to me in the past year.

Hell, for my entire *life*, it seemed. People were always abandoning me. And all I ever did was stand by and watch them leave.

Chapter Nineteen

The following day, as I was reading a Chicago sportswriter's broken-hearted accounting of yesterday's final game of the World Series—a game his beloved Cubs lost to the Red Sox—another one of my players gave me their walking papers.

Her walking papers. Carrie Nation was leaving the team.

I'd been keeping an eye on her statistics, now that Jiang had learned more of our language and started keeping them in English. Thought not as bad off as No Small Foot had been before his eyeglasses, she'd been in a serious hitting slump all season. No doubt the war in Europe had been affecting her playing all along.

"I must leave, to go serve my people," she told me after our game in Peoria, Illinois. A slight tremor in her lower lip was the only sign of her emotions.

"I am so sorry," she said, her voice again thickening with the traces of an accent. Was it German? French? I felt like I didn't know any of my players anymore.

"Where will you go?" I said. I almost handed her my handkerchief, but I was afraid she'd break my arm if I tried. I was so numb that I probably wouldn't even feel it.

"Into the heart of it," Carrie said, pronouncing *it* as *eed*. "My usefulness here in America has come to an end. I must infiltrate" (*eenfeeltrade*) "the Central Powers and learn of their plans for my people. With my language skills and my experience, I can do so much for—"

Carrie looked up at me with a shocked look on her face. She hadn't meant to say any of that.

"It's okay," I began. "I won't tell anybody."

"No, it is not okay," she said, her accent completely gone now. "I just received word today from home. My mother is... very sick. I must go back to England to help her... get better."

I nodded, thinking how, after all this time, I still didn't even know her real name, just J.L.'s nickname for her. And I had a strong feeling I'd never learn it.

"When will you leave? The end of the season?"

"*Now*," she said, and stood up.

She shook my hand and strode out of the dugout to pick up her bag from the front of the team bus. A black car rolled up behind the bus and did a sharp three-point turn to aim its nose away from the ball field. The engine rumbled, waiting for her.

"*Wait*," I said. "We still have more games. We need you—"

"Goodbye," Carrie called out, almost running from me so she could climb into the newly arrived car. "Farewell, brave teammates!"

The black car kicked dirt and gravel from its tires as it roared away from the ballpark, and I could only stare at the car as it pulled away.

The rest of my team and I were so dumbfounded by it all that none of us managed to wave goodbye to her except for Mack, who gave the car a sharp salute. Within seconds, the car had disappeared into the distance

Another one lost to the war. Another hole in my roster. Though my chest ached and my knees throbbed at the thought, I knew it was time for me to get used to first base again.

Barely a week later, after we'd traveled all the way across Illinois, hop-scotching always westward, creeping closer to our final game in Kansas City. Now that we were in Dubuque, Iowa, and the end of the season was approaching, I'd almost given up on Mack's predictions.

Soon I was too busy to even glance at the stands to see who might be there—family or former head coaches. It felt like all I had time to do was cough every few minutes. This cold had settled into my lungs like tar.

When I wasn't barking out coughs like a dog, I focused all my attention on this last game for Art and Boles. Before I realized it, we were beating this team of Iowa farmboys by seven runs. I imagined J.L. lecturing me that teams wouldn't be as likely to agree to a rematch with us later in this season or the next if we ran roughshod over them in front of their families and friends.

If he were here—the man had been noticeably absent for the past few months, ever since our return from lovely Cuba—I would simply nod and tell him I'd do my best not to try so hard. And keep on doing what I was currently doing.

Why? Because I didn't want Boles and Houdini to depart on a loss. When this game ended, they'd be on the next train out of Dubuque to start basic training in Kentucky.

Art was handling his imminent departure calmly, like the quietly confident young man I'd always known him to be.

Boles, on the other hand, was falling apart in front of my eyes. Ever since telling me about signing up a week ago, he'd lasted only three innings in his last two pitching starts. I took it upon myself to talk to the young man as our lopsided game against the Iowa team began to wind down.

"I didn't think you'd ever do it," Boles said when I sat down next to him in the empty dugout. "You've talked to everyone else on the team but me, haven't you?"

"Well," I said, realizing he wanted to talk religion. Life and death and what comes afterwards. "It's been a really busy couple of months."

"That's okay," Boles said. "I know I can be a little hard to be around at times. Got a chip on my shoulder and all that. But Art and I been talking, and he showed me the error of my ways. Well, he threatened to beat the tar out of me at first, but since then he's been a really good guy. Really good."

I smiled and looked at the baseball in my hands, feeling awkward again at the thought of Boles and Art, being so close. But who was I to judge?

"All right, Boles. Tell me about what's to come. What do you think happens?"

"Coach," Boles said, "I don't think I *have* any beliefs. That's what I wanted to tell you all this time, but I was too afraid to admit it. I don't have anything, not here," he said, tapping his chest, then his head, "or here. Not when you come right down to it. I'm just sort of empty inside. Hollowed out."

I flinched at Boles' words. I'd had those same exact thoughts, ever since Maddie and the kids had left me.

"Hell, coach. What if I die over there, and there's nothing left? It'll just end? That's not what I *want* to believe. But I'm afraid it's true." Boles looked over at me, truly looked at me for quite possibly the first time ever. "What do *you* think happens, Coach? Afterwards?"

I took a surprised step back, knees aching in response. Leave it to Boles. He was the first player to ask for my opinion on these weighty matters.

I'd heard so many different tales from so many religions from my players, but at that moment I couldn't remember the details. My memory was as full of holes as my roster.

I remembered something about a mockingbird from Goro, but Goro was gone. Something about nothingness from Carrie Nation, but she had just left less than a week ago. Heaven and hell and purgatory from Donaldson. The Orishas from Mendez. Great Spirit? That was from Chief Tokahoma, wasn't it? Along with Worrell, he was one of the first to leave us.

I was back to where I'd started on the day of Worrell's death. That sense of loss, followed by the fear of what was to come after that book snapped shut.

"Maybe it's all about expectations," I began. "If you expect that you're destined to go to hell and burn, that's what you get. If you're expecting angels and halos and harps, that's your game. If you plan on there being nothing, well, that's all you get. Nothing."

Boles nodded, his face twisted with uncertainty. "Yeah. I guess. Maybe."

"But I tend to think it's something more than that, too."

I mentally catalogued many of the wonderful experiences I'd ever had, playing ball and traveling, my past life with my family. The people I'd met, the places I'd seen, the kindness of strangers, and the magical, miraculous events that took place, without fail, on a baseball diamond.

Boles was silent and still for a change, waiting for me to continue. The game was over, and the rest of the team had packed up all the gear. They waited for us back at the bus. A train whistle sounded in the distance.

I took a deep breath.

"I think you have a choice, after you die. A million roads open up for you, places you could never go while you were alive. The number of trips you could take down those roads is endless. The afterlife is probably completely different from anything we could even guess at, but I'll wager it's amazing."

Boles finally cracked a smile and shook his head. "More traveling and trips, huh? Didn't I get enough of that playing on this team?"

I laughed. "That's just my take on it. Wish I had more for you, son."

"Don't apologize, Coach. You've given me something for Art and me to chew over while we're on the train. And on the boat to Europe, when that happens." Boles sighed. "But for now," he said, handing me his glove, "I need you to hold onto this for me. I plan on being back for it. I hope. No, I *will*."

"It's a deal," I murmured, the tickle back in my throat once more.

Boles nodded at that. He shook my hand, tears filling the corners of his eyes, and then the young man grabbed me and gave me a back-popping hug.

"Thank you," Boles said. He let me go and swiped at his red face. "I'll make you and the team proud, sir," he said, and turned to join Art, who was waiting for us outside the dugout. Art gave me a somber nod, and I walked over to shake his hand, and then hug him as well.

I watched my two now-former players gathered up their bags from next to the team bus and said their goodbyes to the other players. The sight of the two men walking off, suitcases in hand, after over four seasons of playing for me made my vision blur. I had to look at my shoes for a moment.

When I looked up again I fully expected to be able to see my two now-former players walking to the train station and Kentucky beyond that, but Marty Boles and Art Houdini had vanished from the parking lot as surely as if they were a part of one of Art's older brother's magic acts.

At that moment, Worrell's laughter returned once more to fill my ears. A sharp spike of rage hit me, more intense than the pain in my knees ever was.

I'd had enough of Worrell's shenanigans.

I turned to the stands, which had emptied of all the people who needed to breathe, people who never felt the urge to dog a man's every movement. My cleats dug into the dirt as I strode up to where Worrell and his two dozen laughing followers sat as if they owned the park. The wall of cold coming off these gathered entities felt like I'd walked into an icehouse.

I will not cough, I told myself, forcing down the ever-present tickle in my throat and fighting the urge to rub my chest. I hoped my players kept themselves busy loading the bus with Old Blount for a few minutes more so they didn't see me here, addressing the empty stands.

I stared down at Worrell, who still sat on the bottom-most bleacher, ignoring me. As I stood there, smelling the faint whiff of rotting meat and looking at the grass and the wooden boards through his translucent body, I realized that he must have had something to do with this. All of this.

As soon as Worrell started haunting us again with his crew of dead men, we started losing more players again. For all I knew, Worrell had pointed Phil the Philippine's family in our direction, and distracted Goro from that pop-up that crashed into his nose, too.

"We need to talk," I said to Worrell. I didn't bother raising my voice, though the spirits of the dead soldiers and ball players from years past roared with laughter and mocking applause at my words.

"*That's quite enough,*" Worrell said to his raggedy team. "*Can't you see my old friend and I need to talk?*"

As the other spirits quieted and receded into the growing darkness around us, Worrell seemed to take on a brighter glow than his usual pale fire. I thought of Mack's eyes and couldn't suppress a shudder.

Worrell gave me his patronizing smile.

"*Another impressive win for your team. I tip my hat to you,*" he said, though he wore no cap. He never had during his years as a coach, as if such a thing was below him. "*You'll have to share your coaching secrets with me someday. Boy.*"

"I have no secrets," I said. "Though I do have a request. I'll ask nicely, once."

"*Oh really?*" Worrell clapped his hands mincingly and held them together under his chin. "*Ask me anything. No secrets between old friends like us. Especially no secrets about those two players of mine you just scared off the team. The two who went sweet on each other since you killed me and took over the team. Such a nice job you did with those two. Now they're off to die on the western front.*"

Worrell dropped his hands and glared up at me, his left eye out somewhat out of true from his injury. Both light blue eyes darkened until they were dull and lifeless as old pennies, and the cold coming from him turned my fingers numb.

"*So please,*" he said in a voice that sounded as if it came from below my feet, six feet down, "*ask me anything, Coach.*"

I hunkered down over him, ignoring the shooting pain from my old, worn knees and the rattling in my chest. His stink of the grave and his dead man's glare only strengthened my resolve.

My players. I could only think of my players.

"I want you to stop following us. Just go away. Go to your eternal rest. If there is such a thing for someone like you."

"*Oh no,*" Worrell whispered. The fist-sized knot on the left side of his head seemed to throb as he glared up at me. "*There is no rest for me. You have seen to that, boy.*"

"No, I haven't. I'm just a coach. I have no hold over you."

Worrell just laughed until the hardness left his eyes. I straightened up, feeling nauseous from inhaling the foul smell he and his group of ghosts brought with them. I glanced at the stands around him and saw that his mess of players and soldiers had completely slipped away.

It was just Worrell and me. Out of the corner of my eye, I saw a few of my players standing in the dugout, watching. One of them was No Small Foot, and the other was Mack. I think they were both nodding at me.

I gave my knees a break and sat down next to Worrell.

"What will it take?" I asked him.

Even dead, the man seemed to dislike being too close to me, as if I carried some kind of disease in my dusky skin. He moved his barely-there body away from me a few inches. I advanced an inch or two.

"*Your soul,*" Worrell hissed.

My heart lurched at that, and this time I couldn't stop the cough from slipping from my lips. As nearly a dozen coughs exploded from my lungs, I thought of Carrie's belief that everything just stops with death, or Goro's belief in a new life starting when your previous life ends. Worrell's presence here, next to me disproved all of that.

Or his presence simply proved that I'd lost my grip on my sanity.

Worrell gave me a cold smile as I finished coughing and spat something bloody on the ground to my left.

"What value is my soul to you?" I said in a raspy voice, chest aching, fingertips numb.

"*It's good for exchanging. Your soul for mine, to the powers that be. My interrupted life for your long-lived one. Seems only fair to me, especially when you consider that you had every opportunity to prevent my death.*"

I shook my head.

"And I'll be cursed to haunt you forever, is that it?"

"*I go on to my eternal bounty,*" Worrell said, hungrily, as if unable to contain his excitement. "*What you do with your soul is not my concern.*"

I looked out over the empty baseball diamond in front of us, needing a reprieve from Worrell's damaged head and cold eyes. The chalk lines that started at home plate stretched out into left and right field like highways, continuing on in an invisible line beyond the wall, into infinity. There was a lot of world that could be covered in the space between those lines before a ball could be considered foul.

Over in the visitors' dugout, a small crowd had gathered. What was left of my team—No Small Foot, Mack, Buddha, Jiang, Donaldson, Mendez, Prieto, and Torri—stood there in a line, heads turned and eyes wide. My three Cubans looked especially horrified.

What did they see over here? An old colored man talking to himself? Or something more sinister?

Maybe they saw a man making a deal with the Devil himself.

With that thought, along with the low rumble of harsh voices and the doubling of the chill in the air, Worrell's team returned to the stands around us. I was surrounded.

"Will you take these poor men with you if I agree to this?" I said to Worrell in as low a voice as I could manage with my chattering teeth. I gestured at the broken soldiers and ruined ballplayers behind him.

"My will is all that binds them here. That, and my promise of their own salvation. Such things a desperate spirit will believe..."

I had to assume that once Worrell was vanquished, his men would be free of him and could find their own rest as well. I just had to get Worrell to depart. And I was willing to make that sacrifice. I'd lived a long life. My players deserved the same, free of the shadow of death dogging their every movement.

Before I could say anything more to Worrell, however, I was once more interrupted by one of my players.

"Coach?" a voice called from the dugout. I couldn't tell who it was, and I didn't dare look away from Worrell right now. "Coach!"

The gate clanged open, and footsteps approached. First one heavy set, then more. I saw No Small Foot again in my peripheral vision, but this time much closer. Mack and Jiang and the others were coming up behind him.

"Stay back," I said to my players. "Let me handle this."

"No," my catcher said. "You don't need to do this alone. We see what you're up against, Coach. We *all* can see."

I looked up at No Small Foot and the rest of the All Nations. They stood huddled together, as if we were up in Canada again, waiting out a snow delay, though this time their faces were filled with mingled looks of fear and disbelief.

"You all can see them?" I whispered. "All of you can see all of them?"

My players nodded, all but Prieto and Torri, who seemed to be on the verge of bolting like wild horses from their pen.

"Who are these guys?" Buddha said, gazing at the silent ball players and soldiers.

I followed his gaze and looked at the men gathered around us. Most of them suffered some sort of heinous wound, especially the soldiers, many of whom were missing limbs, some of them missing parts of their faces. I caught

Derby's agonized gaze, just for a moment, before he lowered his injured head.

"*Your next opponent*," Worrell announced with an abrupt chuckle.

The four hundred miles from Dubuque to Kansas City took us most of the day to traverse, and the deal I'd made with Worrell echoed in my head with every bump in the road and every swerving turn Blount made. I didn't think we'd ever get back home.

And I knew I had to be mad to agree to the terms set out by Worrell late last night.

The unexpected support of my entire team seemed to unnerve the ghost of our dead former head coach, if such a thing was possible. I doubted he'd ever experienced that kind of loyalty from the group of conscripted spirits he'd gathered around him.

"What do you mean," I'd asked him, shivering from cold, though the September night was still mild, "our next opponent? We play the Maroons as soon as we get back to Kansas City."

"*No. You will play my men. And the winner takes all.*"

I suppressed a shudder and looked at my men standing in front of the bleachers, shifting uncomfortably and strangely silent. Torri and Prieto looked to be on the edge of weeping.

"There's nothing for us to gain from a game like that. Would could we take from *you*, Worrell? You're all dead."

"*You will pay for that reminder*," Worrell intoned, "*at the game we'll play two nights from now, at twilight.*"

I balled my hands into fists, feeling like I was talking to Mack again, instead of Worrell, getting no answers to any of my questions.

"If we win, against this team of yours," I began, "will all of you leave us? Just disappear?"

Worrell's men grumbled and swore at that, but he nodded.

"And if your team wins?"

It was the All Nations' team to spit on the ground and curse.

"We take all, just as I said." Worrell gave his dry chuckle again. "We take your *souls*."

The team bus sputtered to a stop on the northern outskirts of Kansas City, interrupting my memories of the howls and shouts of my players at Worrell's direct, unflinching answer to my question. I hardly recognized the city in the weak daylight still left. My mind was still in the bleachers in Dubuque.

I tried to call off Worrell last night, to tell him to forget his mad plan. I couldn't wager the souls of my team and his over the course of one ball game.

"That's not my place—to risk anyone's soul but my own," I told him.

But it was Mack who stepped forward, always Mack the odd man out, speaking only for himself.

"I'll play in that game with you, Coach. I am confident in the All Nations."

Looking back now, I didn't remember specifically agreeing to playing in Worrell's game *myself*, but that was Mack for you. He saw things in his own way.

"Can't play without a catcher," No Small Foot said, taking a big step closer, never lowering his bespectacled glare from his former head coach.

"Or a p-pitcher," Donaldson said, his voice shaky but determined.

"First baseman," Buddha Rodriguez said, creeping closer.

"Second base," I told Buddha with a smile, feeling tears suddenly well up in my eyes at the sight of my boys, stepping up to the plate for me. "I'll be at first."

"And I am outfield," Jiang piped up.

"Short," Mendez added.

That left Torri and Prieto standing together behind Mendez, both of them silent.

"Guys?" Mendez asked his fellow Cubans. "*Amigos?*"

The two young men gave reluctant nods, and then nearly bolted as Worrell's men broke into applause and ghostly foot-stomping.

My last thought before Worrell and his team slipped away with one last burst of foul-smelling, icy air was that we'd all slipped right into the white bastard's trap.

The sun was already starting to set by the time Old Blount dropped me off at my place. The bus was empty now, and I shook the skinny old fellow's cold hand.

"You know where the lights are, right?" I asked him for what felt like the hundredth time.

Worrell had known about J.L.'s portable light system, which explained why he'd wanted the game to start at twilight. I didn't know what sort of attention the lights would generate, but I couldn't worry about that now. I needed to rest up for our last game.

Blount nodded. "I'll be sure and deliver 'em to the park. Just make sure you get some boys to meet me at my place so they can help me move 'em."

"It's a deal. Good night, Blount."

I slapped the side of the old truck that had been our bus for the past few years. It would most likely be decommissioned after tomorrow's game.

Exhaustion settled in on me as I rattled my key in the lock and finally pushed my way into my cool, dark house. After last night's conversation, during which he'd simply sat off to the side in silence, I'd been expecting Derby to rise up from the floorboards of my living room to greet me.

But I had no visitors that night. Just my memories and my growing disquiet about the game to come. A game that Worrell had surely been planning since his return to this world after his murder by foul tip. He'd not only been haunting me all this time, but he'd also been scouting my team, noting their weaknesses and planning this game for months.

This game. We had nothing further planned for the rest of the year, and with just six players left, I couldn't foresee much for the 1919 season, unless J.L. was able to work some sort of miracle over the winter. This would be the final game of the All Nations team.

What also haunted me was the memory from way back in April, when Mack had looked me in the eye and told me that my family would be at one of our games. *All* of them, unlike the game in Chicago that only my long-lost Maddie had attended.

They'd all be there at one of our games this season, he'd predicted. "Though not together in the manner that you might expect."

Always more questions and mysteries with Mack.

But how would my family know of *this* game in Kansas City? And if they made it to this new game we had scheduled, what would they actually *see*? Would they see Worrell's team of ghost players, or just the All Nations, running through some sort of false, one-sided farce of a game?

I left my bags on the living room floor and flipped through the jumble of mail piled next to slot in the front door. Nothing. No correspondence from Cuba or Chicago. Just bills, some magazines, and meaningless advertisements.

I picked up a loose piece of white paper and a pen. If I'd had any belongings worth anything, I would've spent this time composing my last will and testament. But the years on the dusty road had left me with nothing but a threadbare uniform and a pair of dull cleats. Even my house was worth next to nothing.

Instead, in the quiet coolness of my living room, with the roar of the road still filling my ears, I began writing one last letter.

* * * * *

*D*ear Isabel Maria,
    I do not know if this short note will ever reach you, for I fear I've been sending my previous letters to the wrong address. Or perhaps my return address has been illegible, which would explain your lack of response to those letters, if they did reach you.

But if you do actually hold this same sheet of paper in your hand on which I am currently writing, I just want you to know that I haven't forgotten you.

I also wanted to write to tell you, Isabel Maria, that your son Domingo is an excellent young man, and a perfect gentleman on and off the field. You should be a proud, proud woman for raising such a fine son. I am honored to have him on my team. I learn something new from him every day.

I must say, Isabel, that I've gotten so much insight from my players in this past season that I feel like I know now what I want to do with the rest of my life, no matter how short my time may be.

You see, I've learned that I have more to do in this life. I need to live it to the fullest. It's already halfway through September and the season will be over in a day. And I believe you and I may yet meet again.

I just hope I have the time to do these things.

Please know this, Isabel. I think of you often, and I cherish the brief time we shared during what feels like a lifetime ago. I remember your face, your words, and your lips. I hope we will see one another again.

Finally, I wanted to send this letter to you to let you know that this may very well be my last letter to you. We all have our debts to pay in life, and I fear that mine are coming due shortly.

If you never hear from me again, know that I spent what was left with my left attempting to do the right thing for my players. And for the rest of the world. If you don't get another letter from me, please tell everyone you know about the All Nations, and what we've done. That's all I ask.

I wish you all the best, of everything, and I truly hope to see you again, someday. In one fashion or another.

Sincerely,

George Grunion

Chapter Twenty

On the day of our final game, I woke to the news from Jose Mendez that we'd lost two more players—his fellow countrymen from Cuba. According to a very angry Mendez, who'd taken the disappearance of his fellow Cubans personally, they'd caught a ride on a truck headed to Florida late last night.

"They wanted me to go along," he said, still out of breath, as if he'd run to my place from his boarding house a mile away. "Told me we didn't dare risk upsetting the *Orisha* by playing this game with *el muerto*—the dead. I told them we had no choice. They still left, Coach," he said, angrily punching his open hand as if it were a glove. "They still left."

So we were down to six players, not counting myself—which I was unfortunately going to have to do in tonight's game against Worrell and his pack of over two dozen dead men. We'd faced worst odds in the past five seasons of the All Nations. Hadn't we?

"Thanks for coming to tell me," I told Mendez, who refused to come inside. He just paced up and down my sidewalk, cursing in Spanish. "And Jose—thank *you* for staying and playing tonight. *Muchas gracias.*"

The other news I got that later that morning was less of a surprise: the Kansas City Maroons, the team we'd traditionally opened and closed the season against, had to cancel their game with us. The young boy delivering the message to me claimed that the players had caught some nasty kind of flu, decimating their already-thin roster.

Exhaling slowly, I closed the door on my second messenger of the day and felt the familiar tightness in my chest return, along with my barking cough.

Worrell *had* to be responsible for spreading this sickness, everywhere he went. Starting with me up in the Northwest and worsening as we traveled to Canada.

The rest of the day passed speedier than a thought, and I was unbothered by any more visitors—alive or dead—all day. I rested and went through all the remaining papers and letters from my trunk, organizing them. I wished for a way to somehow contact Maddie, Lizbeth, and Jacob to tell them about what was most likely going to be my last game ever.

Instead, I re-read the letter I wrote last night to Isabel (including my glowing paragraph about her now-absent son, which I considered striking out, but didn't). What a loss, I thought, to never see her again. Even if she had yet to write me back. Hers was a face worth facing down the dead for nine innings.

Hoping against hope, I sent my letter to Isabel with that day's mail.

Soon night fell on Kansas City, and I gathered my glove, spikes, and roster for the walk to the park. Families gathered up their children from their front lawns and sidewalks and hurried them inside ahead of the slowly cooling evening.

The sky turned red at the horizon, then purple, as I walked, positioning my six players on the baseball diamond inside my head, moving Mack here, Buddha there, Jiang there, and so on, until I had the defensive setup just right.

An eerie yellow light covered Exposition Park, a buttery glow I could see from a block away. As I grew closer, breathing heavily with each step, I thought about recruiting Blount and putting him in the outfield, or maybe at second. But I quickly thought better of that plan when I saw him pick up a bat from next to the bus and nearly fall over from the weight of it. Bad idea.

It had to be my six young players and me against Worrell's ghostly two dozen. Unlike Blount, they had all agreed to play tonight, bless their hearts.

As soon as he fired up the five twenty-feet-high gas lights arranged in a half-circle on the other side of the outfield fence, aimed inward, Old Blount scurried off to the team bus. With a low roar and rattle of the bus engine, Blount disappeared into the night.

He must've seen enough ghosts the night before last. I never did see that skinny old fellow, or that beat-up old bus, ever again.

I dropped to the bench in the home dugout and let out a crackling breath that quickly eroded into more chest-wracking coughs. As I barked and gasped for air, I cursed myself for not getting Blount to give me a ride to the park. I was no good to my players like this.

At last the coughing stopped. I spat blood into the dirt at my feet and covered it quickly. Damn this cough.

To my eternal gratitude, the remaining half-dozen players of the All Nations team were already at the park, having helped Blount set up J.L.'s gas lights for him. Balls popped into gloves in the outfield as they warmed up, rawhide against leather, one of the most reassuring sounds I've ever heard.

A *night-time* game, I thought, breathing carefully and rubbing my aching chest. It just seemed so... unnatural.

Perfectly fitting for tonight's opponents, of course.

As the hissing lights bathed the green grass of the diamond in front of us in yellow light, I gathered my team around me in the home dugout for the last time. The field and the other dugout remained empty, as did the bleachers.

"Maybe they won't show up," Donaldson said, his voice hopeful.

"They better," No Small Foot growled. "We had an agreement."

"Have a seat, gentlemen," I said.

I gazed at what was left of my team and almost smiled. This was the core group here, the men with the fortitude to stick it out to the end. Jiang, Buddha, Donaldson, Mendez, No Small Foot, and Mack. Men from all around the world, gathered here tonight for what could be not only their last game for this team, but their last night, ever, on this Earth.

This game. It was just madness, wasn't it? What power did the ghost of our dead coach have over us—the living? How could he make a wager like that?

Just like everything spiritual I'd discussed with my team over this past season, I had no answers.

My back against the dugout fence, I stifled another cough and nodded at my players on the bench below me. I wasn't big on speeches, but tonight I could tell that they needed one to dispel the fear from their eyes. This would have to be their best game of baseball, ever.

"I know this has been a difficult season," I began. "I want to tell you once more how deeply I appreciate you being here, every one of you. So much hinges on the outcome tonight. But that's what we do, gentlemen. We're tired and we're hurting, we're shorthanded, but we do what we must. We play ball."

I dropped my arms to my side and hid the wince I felt trying to creep across my face from the pain in my knees. At least I didn't start coughing.

"We've seen and done some amazing things the past few years. Miracles, really. But what's most amazing is this *team*. Each of you, working together despite your differences. You made this team great. Historic, really."

I gazed at each player, taking in the different colors of eyes, skin, and hair. I stopped at Mack, waiting for his eyes to ignite with that white light I'd first seen on this very field, half a year ago. When they didn't, I pressed on.

"You are here tonight on your own bond, by your own choice. For that, I am in your debt. If you're heart is failing your right now, you can still leave, without shame. But if

281

you feel strong, if you have *confidence*, and if you are *with* me tonight, then give me a *'Yes.'*"

The voices of my six remaining players shouting out the affirmative stiffened my spine in a way that no prayer, no letter, no whispered confidence could have ever done.

Right in the nick of time, too. My players' voices prepared me for the sudden appearance of Worrell and his team of ghosts out on the field.

One moment the empty field was unnaturally bright in the gaslights aimed at it from beyond the fence. The next moment, nearly thirty men in gray flannel uniforms appeared in pairs all over the field, tossing lumpy brown baseballs to one another and bringing with them a chill so deep, even the lights seemed to dim.

Try as I might, I could not hear the sound of those baseballs hitting the gloves of the other team. Uncanny.

"*Forget something?*" Worrell said from barely three feet away, outside the dugout once more. I hoped nobody on my team saw me flinch at his sudden arrival.

Worrell pointed at home plate, where a short, squat white man dressed in black stood, arms crossed.

"*We brought our own umpire.*"

I looked closer at the slightly glowing man waiting impatiently at the plate. Old Judge Newsome, I realized, recognizing his gray hair and bushy black eyebrows. The most crooked ump from my own playing days. I heard he'd gotten shot three decades ago by his own wife for stepping out on her.

This was our umpire. I could've kicked myself for not finding an umpire of my own. Instead, I'd spent the day mooning over Isabel Maria and mourning the loss of my family, forever. That mistake could quite easily spell our doom. And it was *my* mistake.

"Let's play ball!" I shouted, angry. Worrell had completely set us up.

With every step I took on my way to first base, I kept my eye on him over in front of his dugout. I refused to limp despite the sharp pricks of pain in my knees, and I held in the coughing fit that threatened with each breath, not wanting to give Worrell and his horde of ghouls the pleasure.

All the players jammed into the visitors' dugout wore matching gray uniforms with a ridiculously ornate W emblazoned on the chest. At first glance I couldn't distinguish the dead soldiers from the dead men with actual ball-playing experience. Only the missing limbs and grievous injuries showed me who the lost soldiers were. Though like Derby's fatally damaged head, many of the former players taken from life too soon by accidents carried harsh wounds that would never heal.

These were all men who'd once had lives, and Worrell had ripped them from their searching and wandering in the afterlife for his own purposes. If we won, I prayed he would release them as well as leave my team alone.

I knew Jiang would be compiling his detailed record of the game—though I'd never be able to read it—yet I still wished we could've had someone in the stands to witness this. But even J.L. had been strangely distant today, not even asking questions when I got his permission to use his portable lighting system tonight. It was like the season was over to him, and my team dead to him already.

Tossing grounders to Buddha and then Mendez from my spot at first, I listened to Worrell bark out his batting order behind me—to the occasional groan and complaint from his too-full roster of players.

I'd put Mack in left and Jiang in right, while Mendez stood exactly between second and third, covering both bases. Buddha covered second from about twelve feet back, in shallow center. I played a dozen steps off from the bag at first, while behind the plate, No Small Foot's spectacles reflected the yellow lights from behind his mask as he gave the signals for the next pitch.

And Donaldson, the man with the best arm I'd ever seen, was on the mound, pitching one last fireball to No Small Foot before the game began.

The rotting smell of the ghost players and soldiers wafted over the field, along with the chill coming off their barely corporeal bodies, filling my mouth with the acid taste of bile. Already Worrell's team had started jeering Donaldson in their strangely deep, almost monotone voices.

His face gray and his eyes wide, Donaldson looked over at me before the first pitch. He was already getting unnerved.

I simply nodded and pointed at him, as if to say, "You can do this, son."

Donaldson nodded back, eyes set in determination, and turned to face their leadoff batter, a soldier with a bullet hole square in the middle of his pale white forehead.

Twenty-seven outs, I told myself. That's all we needed to get against this team of dead men. One out a time, just like any other game.

Now that the game was about to be underway, I wasn't sure how Worrell's team was going to manage picking up a bat, much less hit the ball. I wondered if their bats would even make contact with our ball. Donaldson's precise and powerful throwing, however, prevented me from learning any more.

One nine pitches, he struck out the first three ghost players.

Twenty-four more outs.

I jogged past Worrell's players, who'd stopped jeering and began grumbling and swearing louder from his bench. Nine of them gathered gloves in their ghostly hands and drifted onto the field.

A fleeting hope filled me—maybe this game had been a big bluff on Worrell's part. Maybe his spirits lacked the actual physical *presence* in this world to play ball. I remembered how their baseballs tossed before the game made no sound in their gloves.

That overly optimistic theory of mine was dispelled quickly in the bottom of the first.

Jiang swung hard three times but made no contact against Worrell's puffy-faced pitcher, whom I finally recognized as a white player I'd known in the 1880s as simply "the Gun." He hadn't made it to the 1900s, I'd heard, thanks to a kick in the face by a horse on his family farm. Despite the damage from that fatal kick (I could almost discern the imprint of a horseshoe on his cheekbones and forehead), the Gun's ghost could still throw with deadly heat.

After Jiang's strikeout—with the field growing even colder due to the surge in confidence by the ghosts all around us—No Small Foot stepped up to the plate with his scratched and well-taped bat. The bat didn't leave his shoulders for the first two pitches, the first one low and outside, the second inside and high. Both called as strikes.

I marched over to the entrance to the dugout.

"Come on, ump!" I called out. "Ever heard of calling a ball?"

"Calling 'em as I see 'em," Judge Newsome croaked from behind the plate with a laugh.

"All right," I said to No Small Foot, who'd stepped out of the batter's box so he could turn his body and gaze at me with his delicate eyeglasses, which made his brown eyes seem twice as big. "You know what to do, John."

He nodded and stepped back into place, only to be nearly struck right between the eyes by the next pitch. He'd ducked just in time.

I was halfway out of the dugout before Mack grabbed my arm. Still in the batter's box, No Small Foot simply raised his right arm and patted the air at his side, as if to say, It's okay, I can handle this.

At least crooked and blind Newsome called that a ball.

Before the next pitch, I happened to glance out at the stands, just for a moment, and saw maybe a dozen people sitting there, silently.

We had witnesses, it appeared. And were they *glowing*?

The pitch came, outside again. No Small Foot's big arms reached for it, snagging the ball with the end of the bat. Instead of the dull *thwap* of bat on ball, I heard nothing as the ball shot into the gap between first and second. The ghost team's ball had substance, though it made no sound.

And we had our first hit of the day.

Turned out it was the only hit of the first inning, however. Mendez got called out on strikes by Newsome, while Mack hit a noiseless pop fly that soared above the yellow blanket made by the lights for what felt like half a minute, only to be caught by the one-legged dead soldier playing centerfield.

Limp applause drifted over like rustling leaves from the bleachers, where the crowd had grown to at least fifty people now. All of them giving off the weak, tell-tale glowing light of the spirited dead, not to mention the low, rank odor and chill of the grave.

Jogging with aching knees over to first, I tried to shake off the cold they brought with them, and the cough they tried to inspire deep in my chest.

In the second inning, the crowd and Worrell's team became more agitated as Donaldson retired the side, one-two-three, without any hitters making contact. Not even a line-drive foul tip, Worrell's bane.

I wondered at the lineup he was fielding, if he'd put the weaker hitters at the top of the order for some reason, possibly to trick us into a false sense of security. These first few hitters almost felt like cannon fodder.

"Don't try to second-guess the dead," I told myself back in our dugout, watching Buddha Rodriguez step up to the plate for our half of the second.

"Pardon me?" Mack said from next to me.

"Nothing," I said quickly to the young man, whose skin had turned almost dusky in the glow of the gas lights. The lights seemed a bit dimmer to me now, as if they were already losing some of their heat.

"Coach," Mack began, and then I saw Buddha crumple to the ground at home plate.

You missed it, old man, I cursed to myself as I bolted from the dugout and ran to the plate. You took your eye off the ball, damn it.

Buddha was not moving when I reached him, and the rest of my players were right behind me. No Small Foot pushed away Worrell's three-fingered, smelly catcher as I went down on one painful knee next to our bald Mexican.

"Right in head," Jiang said from above us. "*Had* to be intentional."

"Rodriguez," I hissed. His eyes were closed, and his head rolled back when I tried to raise him up by the shoulders. I thought of his old head injury, and wondered why he hadn't moved out of the way of this pitch.

"Buddha!" I shouted, looking at the nasty bump now rising up from the man's smooth forehead.

Buddha flinched at that, a movement that nearly brought a cry of relief from my mouth. When he opened his eyes, though, all I saw were the whites. He grabbed me by the front of my shirt, aiming those awful eyes my way.

"I thought I *told* you," he growled in a voice that seemed to come from ten feet away, "not to listen to him or heed his advice."

"What?" I said, almost dropping him back to the dirt. "Who?"

Then Buddha flinched again and farted loudly. As everyone stepped back for air, he rolled to a sitting position, groaning and holding his forehead. When his eyes opened this time, he looked at me with normal eyes.

"*¿Qué pasó?*" he mumbled. "Wha' happened, Coach?"

Still shuddering at his words, which brought back the memory of our so-called good luck ritual, I helped him up as best I could. He was right, of course. I couldn't fall into the trap of following Worrell again. I had to stand firm.

"You got beaned," I told him, "and beaned good. You okay to play?"

"*Sí*, Coach," Buddha grinned, dropping his hand from the lump on his head. "It does not hurt anymore."

"Then take your base," I said.

As Buddha ambled off to first, I turned to glare at the umpire.

"If this happens again," I said, loud enough for Worrell to hear, "I'm taking my men off this field and down to the Catholic Church to talk to them about an exorcism or two."

The crowd hissed at that, to be sure.

Unfortunately, I was up to bat next. My hitless streak continued. I hit a silent dribbler to short that the three dead infielders—drowning to knifing to gassing—turned into an easy double-play to end the inning.

"Damn it," I said, the bat still in my hand as I passed in front of the glowing crowd. I thought I could see more than half a dozen former teammates out there, all of them white, though a few colored men and women sat together behind our dugout. Still separate, even after death.

Nowhere in the crowd did a see a sign of any living spectators, much less a sighting of anyone from my family. I had to look, though. Mack couldn't have been wrong about that. Could he?

Donaldson set down three more of Worrell's batters in the third, though these hitters each made contact instead of striking out. No Small Foot caught the first silent pop-up halfway down the first-base line, and I made an unassisted out at first by snagging a noiseless one-hop line drive and outrunning the limping hitter to the bag by two steps.

For the third out, Mack ran down a towering hit in deep center that seemed certain to be a homer. He caught it at the fence after crossing half the outfield in seconds, once again making it look easy.

"*Impossible!*" someone shouted, either from the crowd or Worrell's overstocked bench. As I walked back to my dugout, stifling a cough, I heard a few men murmur, "*Put me in, Worrell*," and "*Lemme play, Coach*,"

Worrell, in a surprisingly blunt voice, told them to shut up or go back where they belonged. I didn't want to get too hopeful, but he was starting to sound a bit flustered. I don't think he'd expected this game to be close at all.

Eighteen outs left.

After hitting one to the wall himself at the bottom of the third, only to see Worrell's leftfielder snag it (to the dull cheers of the crowd of ghosts behind us), Jiang sat down next to me to talk strategy.

Just like I'd learned to heed Mack's predictions, I'd come to respect Jiang's attention to the details of the game. He watched everything and recorded it all in his book, using his elegant pens to paint symbols up and down the pages, right to left, in a fashion that always left me bewildered.

"The pitcher," he began, "shake off curve ball when ahead in count. Always want to throw fastball. Before a fastball, he drops head. Watch cap."

With No Small Foot up to bat for us again, the tall ghost pitcher shook his head at his catcher, just as Jiang had called it. I watched the man on the mound, whose sallow skin seemed to catch the yellow lights and absorb it so I could scarcely discern make any of his features but his black eyes.

What brings a man's spirit like this back to this time and place? How does he feel about being here, pitching for his very soul?

A second before entering his windup, the pitcher dipped his head.

"Fastball," I said.

I heard the swish of No Small Foot's bat, then... nothing.

But our big catcher was now lumbering off to first, still watching the hit ball rise into the gaslit night.

"Come on," I said, watching Worrell's outfielders give chase. "Go over."

I took a second to glance at my players around me, on their feet now. They knew what this hit would mean, if it went over.

"Coach," Mack began, but I waved him off and watched Worrell's centerfielder run right *through* the outfield fence, chasing the dropping ball.

"What?" I spat. "*No!*"

The outfielder ran onto the dark grass outside the ring of yellow light and lifted a glowing, gloved arm high. The ball silently disappeared into his glove.

Home run. They'd *stolen* our home run.

The crowd applauded the catch, though the colored fans directly behind us complained about broken rules. Worrell laughed over in his dugout, while behind the plate, the ump signaled the out, sealing the crooked deal.

Both of them looked at me, waiting for me to charge out of the dugout to appeal the call. But instead of taking their bait, I just grabbed my glove and trudged off to first.

Though we should've led by one, I had confidence we would persevere, without resorting to such trickery and dishonesty. With six full innings—eighteen more outs!—left to play, we remained deadlocked at zero.

After a hitless, scoreless fourth inning, Worrell made his first replacement early in the fifth. With one out already, Judge Newsome had just allowed Donaldson's first base on balls, walking a batter on four pitches that would've been called strikes by any other umpire, living or dead. The batter hadn't even *tried* to swing his club at a single pitch.

This is it, I thought. The desperate times begin.

I had to stay close to the bag to prevent the runner from getting too big of a lead and stealing second. Which meant I had to breathe in the spirit's lingering odor of death and let his cold aura spill over onto me. He didn't try to talk to me like most opponents did; he simply looked at me and spat something from his mouth that never hit the ground.

On the next pitch, the foul-tempered runner tried to steal second. Mendez whistled as soon as Donaldson's pitch left his hand, and I didn't have time to yell a warning to No Small Foot. But our man behind the plate was already launching a bullet of a throw to Mendez, who caught it three inches from the ground and waited for the ghost runner's leg to slide into his glove.

It wasn't even close—Newsome had no choice but to call the fellow out.

Worrell burst from dugout to argue with Newsome about the inaccuracy of his call. After a few fruitless seconds of complaining, maybe even throwing a "damn" in there for good measure, Worrell showed the umpire his back.

The ghost of the dead coach looked over at me for some reason, then, and smiled. Not his usual patronizing smile, but a devious, sinister stretching of his lips over his straight white teeth.

I was so surprised by that look on his face that I started coughing. After a dozen loud barks and two bloody spits, I recovered in time to see that Worrell had arranged for a new hitter to stand in the on-deck circle. Worrell okayed the switch with Newsome the ump while I gazed at the new player.

His gray, custom-made uniform fit his tall, muscular body well. I motioned Mack and Jiang back in the outfield in case this strong fellow got a hold of one. I looked at the young man standing with his back to me and thought that something about him seemed different, almost familiar.

And then he turned to glance back at his coach in the dugout behind him, and I lost my breath.

Worrell had recruited the ghost of a *colored* player.

"Play ball!" Newsome shouted as Worrell walked back to the safety of his dugout, laughing under his breath in the sudden silence of the crowd.

My chest ached as I looked at the young man digging into the batter's box from the left-handed hitter's side. Dirt flew into the air in silent puffs under his gleaming spikes. With his hat pulled low over his brow and his back to from where I stood at first, I could scarcely make out his face.

Why? I wanted to ask him. Why would you ever choose to play for that white bastard?

"Come on, Donaldson," Mack called from deep in center-right field. "Retire this guy for us."

Mack's voice sounded much too loud in the now-quiet ballpark. The crowd of ghosts also seemed unable to fathom this young man's presence here tonight.

As soon as Donaldson launched his first pitch at the plate, the hitter leaned forward, bat still on his shoulder, as if eager to get hit by the ball. But Donaldson's pitch was too fast for him. It popped into No Small Foot's glove, a welcome sound instead of the silence that came from a ball pitched or hit by someone from Worrell's team.

I wondered if a ball pitched by Donaldson that hit this fellow would make any noise. I preferred not to find out, but on the second pitch, the batter leaned in sharply again. The fastball got past him again, and Newsome called a second strike.

Worrell and his bench shouted out their disbelief at the call, but I had to admit, Newsome was right—that was a strike. This poor kid that Worrell sent out like some sort of sacrificial lamb simply couldn't move fast enough to get beaned on purpose by one of Donaldson's fastballs.

"*I'm warning you, Newsome,*" Worrell called out. "*Make the right call, damn it. You know the consequences if you don't.*"

Newsome simply pointed a warning finger at Worrell before crouching behind No Small Foot.

"*You gonna take that, Coach?*" one of Worrell's players called out.

Worrell didn't answer. He just stared at the batter, who had stepped out of the batter's box to look back at him for guidance.

Worrell nodded, slowly, his left hand touching his own baseball injury on his temple.

The boy was already dead, I thought. Why put him through this?

From the far side of the crowd, behind out dugout, the growing group of colored fans—some of them dressed in the rags of slaves from decades past—had thought the same kind of thought. They booed and hissed, calling to the batter to swing away and play the game right.

I gave Donaldson a look as a shudder passed through me from the cold falling over the ballpark. Everything seemed colder and darker here as this game went on and on.

"You know what to do," I said in a low voice that was drowned out by the growing clamor of the crowd. Even some of the dead white fans had joined the chorus against Worrell's tactics.

Donaldson perched on the top of the mound, his handsome face strained with fatigue, but a tiny smile on his lips as he shook off the first two signals from No Small Foot.

Worrell's bench seemed to be undergoing some sort of unrest as they waited for the next pitch. Some were goading on the batter, while others were moving to the other end of the dugout, away from Worrell and the batter. Some seemed to have slipped away while their coach wasn't looking. He surely had no more than twenty players on his bench, along with his hapless colored young batter.

Finally, Donaldson got the signal he wanted from No Small Foot. He nodded, and the crowd rose to their feet on some unknowable impulse.

Instead of rushing past the young man with his elbows pointing wildly and his head leaning into the pitch, this time the ball seemed to take forever to reach the plate. The hitter had time to close his eyes, anticipating the impact of the ball against his skull.

And then the ball dropped, curving right under the batter's jutting chin to smack into No Small Foot's round mitt.

"Steee-rike *three!*" Newsome hollered, punching the air to his right.

As the batter stepped away from the plate, dumbfounded, I went over to clap Donaldson on the back.

His curve was something monumental to witness: the ball had broken a good two feet before it reached the plate.

Behind us, Worrell's dugout roiled with activity, as half his players prepared to take the field, and the other half pushed up to the fence, shouting at the ump and their own player. He'd lost a couple more men in the confusion.

Soon he'd be as depleted as us, I thought with a bemused smile, as I headed back to our dugout. I tried to get a good luck at the face of Worrell's colored player, to no avail.

I made it to the dugout just in time for another coughing fit that dropped me to the bench, lasting over a minute. When it was over, Worrell's colored player was now standing at his position in deep center field, his face a shadowed mystery.

O ver the next few innings, my cough sat perched inside my chest like a caged animal, waiting for the first opportunity to break free. I should've visited a doctor today to see if it wasn't pneumonia, but the clinic downtown had a line out the door. This cough would go away soon. I hoped.

Each time we took to the field, Donaldson's pitching kept us from having to work too hard. We managed to hold off any kind of rally from this team from beyond the grave, and Worrell's players were in a frenzy.

The fans were now equally split between white and colored. When Mack made his fourth nearly impossible catch for the third out in the eighth, the white stands nearly erupted in a Shreveport-style riot.

At the bottom of the eighth, No Small Foot passed me on his way to the batters' box, his cap still turned backwards from his time catching.

"John," I called out, limping on my way out of the dugout.

He turned, shoulders slumped as if the very action was costing him precious energy. "Yeah, Coach?"

"Your cap," I said, pulling the other man's bill around to the front. When I let go of the cap, I looked down into the gold-rimmed lenses of No Small Foot's spectacles. I sucked in a sudden breath.

"John," I hissed. "What's on your *glasses*?"

"Nothing. Look, Coach, you're holding up the game, and we need a hit."

"But," I said, unable to form the words I wanted to say.

The moon, I thought to myself. I could see the *moon*.

Except in No Small Foot's glasses, the moon was hundreds of times bigger than I'd ever seen it with my naked eyes. The white and gray surface I'd seen reflected in No Small Foot's glasses was peppered with strange holes, crevices that would surely make the Grand Canyon look like a ditch.

"What does he *see* with those spectacles?" I muttered, even as my Cherokee catcher knocked a line drive between the ghostly left fielder and center fielder. When he tried to turn it into a double, he was tagged at second.

"He sees untold miles," Mack said from behind me. "I saw him talking with a Mohawk Indian, a shaman, during our snow game in Canada. You know, Coach, John traded a year of his life for those glasses. He knew how important playing on this team would be. He had to be able to *see*. For our future."

"Mack," I said. "How can you—"

"I just hope," Mack continued, "that his vision won't hurt him the way mine has damaged me. I've seen too much. And Coach?"

Mack was looking directly at me, his eyes giving off a hint of their strange white glow. Once more, my breath went short.

"What, Mack?" I gasped. "What is it? Tell me. Please."

"You're *up*, Coach," Mack said, pointing at home plate. The umpire and Worrell's catcher stood there, hands on their hips, waiting.

I blinked, trying to forget the deep pockmarks of the moon reflected in No Small Foot's glasses. Too deep. Standing at second base, my catcher waved and pointed at the empty scoreboard.

"Yes, I'm up," I mumbled, rubbing my sore chest and shaking my left arm, which had gone numb on me again.

On my way to the plate, I looked over at Worrell's dugout. Only four players stood next to him now, with the other nine men out in the field. He knew what I'd felt like all season, losing players like this—starting with poor, unstable Chief Tokahoma. Either some of Worrell's men were seeing the error of their coach's ways, or he was simply losing control of their spirits as he fought to take the lead of this game. Possibly both, for all I knew.

I exhaled, grateful for the cool air in my lungs and the smell of grass in my nose. I dug my spikes into the dirt of the batter's box, savoring the sharp pain in my old, battered knees.

The pitcher looked at me for a long moment, assessing me while his catcher ran through the signals. The Gun shook his head once, then twice. He looked tired, but determined to finish this game with a W. His soul depended on it, or so Worrell had led him to believe.

Putting Worrell and the moon and my cough and everything else out of my mind, I focused on just the ball in the pitcher's gripped fingers.

The baseball was like a star, capable of going anywhere, at any time. The stars went on to infinity, just like the ball could be hit in an infinite number of directions here in the ballpark.

As I stared, the pitcher nodded his head.

Then the ball began moving as if of its own accord. The ball guided the Gun's hand, leading the man through the windup, instead of vice versa.

A million roads opened up to me—George Grunion, hitless for the past two decades—as the baseball freed itself from the pitcher's hand and threw itself toward the plate, moving through the air like a silent bullet, a falling star, a life passing; the ball, the star, the life, all of them almost passing me by.

Almost.

I felt like I'd been waiting for that pitch for half of my life. Before the ball slipped past me, I swung.

And I made blessed contact, though it made no sound.

The ball shot over the infield, rising and lifting over the centerfield fence, the ball still carrying upwards as it left the gaslit air on its way to what could've been another world. Even after running through the fence and into the darkness beyond the diamond, Worrell's rightfielder couldn't catch up to my hit.

I jogged the bases, laughing in spite of the sharp pain in my knees, laughing until it made me cough all over again. Then I laughed some more.

After all these fruitless at-bats and endless games in this hellish, wonderful, miraculous season, I'd *finally* gotten my hit.

Chapter Twenty-One

That impossible hit put the All Nations up 1-0 against Worrell's team of ghost players. I scarcely remember the rest of the eighth inning—I think Jiang got a single, No Small Foot struck out, and then a double play ended the inning. All I could think about that hit and the way the entire world had seemed to slow, just so I could clobber that ball. Even Maddie would've approved of my hit. And Isabel Maria would've been dancing in the stands.

Now we had just three outs to make against the other team and this game would be ours.

The first trio of batters Worrell threw at us at the top of the ninth were white men we hadn't yet faced in the game. I'm sure he thought of them as his secret weapons, his aces in the hole.

The first batter, a brawny fellow over six feet tall, sent four silent foul tips over the backstop, only to let Donaldson's curve bamboozle him on the fifth.

Two outs left.

Worrell stood behind the fence of his dugout and glared not at Donaldson or his own player, but at me where I stood ten feet off first base. I met his gaze, and I'm proud to report that not a cough slipped from my lips.

Just as big as the first batter, his second hitter man had a fast, slashing swing. He missed the first pitch, but sent the next into center. The ball hit Mack so hard on its second bounce that he bobbled it for a moment. That was all the hitter needed. Running like a bull released from a chute, he rounded first and plowed into second long before Mack's throw ever reached Mendez.

One out, and the winning run now in scoring position. Damn it.

Worrell and his dwindling band of players laughed at us from their dugout. Even the gaslights warding off the darkness seemed to be failing; I could scarcely see the outfield fence now. The collective chill from the gathered spirits had made my fingers go numb.

I considered a talk with Donaldson on the mound, but he shook me off before I could leave first base. I let out a long breath that steamed into the air in front of my face, knowing I had to trust the young man knew his limits. We had no other pitcher to turn to, anyway.

This hitter swung at each pitch Donaldson threw. The first two zipped past him, but he connected on the third, sending it right back at Donaldson.

Only instinct and self-preservation saved our pitcher, who was still off balance from completing his throw; his gloved hand lifted up to protect his face from the silently onrushing ball. He captured the ball there for the second out, and in my relief I let my guard down and started coughing.

The colored stands clapped and called out their congratulations for the catch, while the white fans simply sat and glowered, until the arrival of Worrell's next batter. It was the young colored player again.

I forced down any more coughs as I moved into position, keeping the runner at second in my peripheral vision. My knees ached so badly it felt like the pain was spreading up my legs and into my chest.

One out left. We needed to end this game, and soon.

Fortunately, the colored batter hadn't been ordered to get hit by a pitch this time. Worrell knew that much at least. All the kid had to do was knock it into a hole in our two-man outfield, and the game would be over.

The kid knocked the first pitch down the first base line, too far in foul territory for me to even attempt a play at it. I saw Worrell cowering in his dugout after that—that line drive had looked far too much like the hit that had killed him back on April Fool's Day.

Good, I thought, feeling a surge of confidence with potentially just two strikes left in the game. Stay there, Worrell.

My warm feeling evaporated when the batter stepped away from the plate and, for some reason, turned to look at me. I felt my heart skip a beat from the intensity of those dark eyes.

Who *are* you? I wanted to ask him. I swear I could almost place his face, if I could just see more clearly in this weakening yellow light.

But he turned his back on me and set up in the batter's box again. He shot Donaldson's next pitch down the third base line, just out of the reach of a diving Buddha.

That was too close for comfort. I motioned for No Small Foot to meet me at the mound with Donaldson.

"I know," Donaldson panted before I could even limp onto the mound next to him. The mound seemed extra high tonight to my tired legs. "You want me to give him another curve, right? I'm not sure about—"

"No curves, Coach," No Small Foot whispered as he huffed up to us, glasses glinting in the weakening light. "Everyone's expecting it. Give 'im a hard fastball, high and inside."

I heard both men, but my attention was focused on the batter. He stood to the left of the plate, half-turned toward Worrell, waiting for us. I could now get a better view of his face. So damned familiar.

"Coach?" No Small Foot said. "We got a game to win here, Coach."

A chill deeper than any cold emanating from all these spirits sank into my chest. This batter. It couldn't be him. Could it?

"John," I said. Both pitcher and catcher turned to look at me. "I meant you," I said, gesturing to No Small Foot. "Let me borrow your glasses."

With the white half of the crowd jeering at me along with most of Worrell's players in the dugout, I took the spectacles that my catcher grudgingly handed me and placed them on the bridge of my nose.

Through the glittering lenses, I felt the air leave my lungs as I looked at the batter once more. I saw his face as clearly as if he were standing right in front of me, even as the lights dimmed all around me and my vision blurred.

It had to be him.

He'd always had his mother's eyes, a deep brown color that hadn't been diminished by the unnatural glow covering his skin. He was taller, more filled out than when I'd last seen him, of course. He'd become a man in my absence.

"Jacob," I choked, still unable to breathe, and then I dropped forward onto the pitcher's mound, oblivious to my players, the other team, the crowd, and the rest of the world.

My son was here, as predicted, and he was dead.

For a long, numb moment, my world plunged into darkness.

My son was dead, I thought again, and then the darkness lifted, and I knew I was either dreaming or dead myself.

Above me, a flock of headless chickens and broken-necked pigeons took flight against a backdrop of zeppelins that were flying too high to be seen with the naked eye. But thanks to No Small Foot's powerful spectacles, I could see them clearly. And I heard their bombs—tiny explosions, popping in the green sky like prayer books slammed shut.

The moon grinned down at me with empty eye sockets, a face that looked like Worrell's, glaring down at me with anger and contempt, while fires sprouted up from beneath the empty baseball diamond where I now stood. I breathed in the smells of burnt grass and pine tar and tobacco and never once felt the urge to cough.

I truly must be dead.

The moon was so close, I felt like it was trying to block out the sun. I knew with my own strange dream-logic that I had to look up into the sun, even as it turned a bright, blinding white. So I did.

While I was gazing directly at it, I let myself fall backward onto the infield. The grass immediately burst into yellow-white flames, but I was not burned. On my back, I had unfettered access to that great ball of whiteness. I stared and stared, thinking of the afterlife and all my players' depictions of it, from nothingness to angels to mockingbirds, and more.

Was I finally going to find out the answer to what happens after you die?

Flames eating at me now, I felt my eyeballs begin to quiver and boil inside their sockets as the sun turned itself inside out, and I saw through it to the other side, to the thousands of roads that were all there, if only I dared to look hard enough.

I wanted to travel those roads, all those roads, but not just yet.

Not just yet. I had more to do here, tonight, starting right now.

I opened my eyes, and standing over me was my son, holding a baseball bat.

No. This was the *ghost* of my son. Jacob had, at some point in the past, unbeknownst to me, died. And nobody had told me about it.

Go ahead, I wanted to say, looking up at the bat in Jacob's big hands. Finish me off. If I'm not dead already.

Instead of following my silent order, Jacob squatted next to me. We were halfway between the pitcher's mound and home plate. The crowd had fallen silent once more, and I could see my players huddled outside our dugout, ten feet away, afraid to come any closer.

"*Your family,*" Jacob said in his low, dead voice.

I wanted to sit up, to get off my back so I could look Jacob levelly in the eye. But my body wasn't cooperating.

"What..." I exhaled. "What do you mean?"

"*You said your team was your family now,*" Jacob said, nodding with his glowing chin in the direction of my few remaining players. "*I was always jealous of that, Father. Jealous of them.*"

Despite my helpless position, I felt a surge of anger. If Maddie hadn't taken my family from me, I wouldn't have had to place all my heart into my players. But then, gazing up at Jacob's angry eyes, I knew that was a lie. Even before they'd left, before I struck Jacob, I'd been far too devoted to whichever team I was playing for.

"Jacob," I said, surprised at the weakness of my own voice. "That was years ago. I'm..." I drew in a sudden breath as my son looked down at me. I felt the rattle in my chest dissipate. "I'm sorry."

The crowd was starting to get restless, whispering and muttering almost nervously. Their mood had changed, from a cluster of people enjoying a close game to a gathering of nervous ghosts, worried possibly about their very existence, such as it was.

Worrell stood in the gateway to the visitors' dugout, a glazed expression on his pale face. None of this had gone his way, I realized. He was always was a poor strategist when it came to the deciding moments of a game.

"*Thank you,*" Jacob said at last, reaching down a cold hand to grip my shoulder. I flinched at first, and then felt my entire body relax at his touch. It had been so long since I'd felt his touch, alive or not. Far too long.

And already he was starting to fade.

"Jacob," I said, "why? Why are you playing ball? And for him, of all people?"

"*Worrell found me,*" Jacob said, still gripping my shoulder, though his hand grew more transparent with each passing moment. When he looked at me, his eyes, thank God, were no longer angry but content, almost relaxed.

"*Said he'd show me the way to eternal rest. He also said he'd let me play ball one last time. You gave me that gift, Father. I love the game.*" I tried to sit up at that, but Jacob's grip was too strong, even as his voice began to fade along with his ghostly presence. "*I was just too stubborn and jealous to play ball with you. I was playing for a team up in Canada, right up until...*"

His last words were drowned out by the angry shouts of Worrell's remaining players.

"*Eternal rest!*" one of the brawny white men shouted at Worrell. "*You promised that, to that nigger?*"

"*All you promised me was one more game,*" shouted another. "*Liar!*"

"*Release us, and all the others!*"

"*Let us go. We quit!*"

Worrell gave me one last pathetic look, followed by a hopeless glance at the scoreboard.

"*Go,*" he said to his players. "*I have no hold over you anymore, anyway.*"

A warm breeze seemed to blow through the ballpark as the twelve white players in the visitors' dugout simply faded from existence.

"*Coach,*" Newsome said from behind the plate. "*What about the game? Do you forfeit?*"

Worrell left his empty dugout, glaring at me as he stepped closer. I felt Jacob's grip on my shoulder tighten for a moment, then he stood up. I sat up, painfully, and watched the silent exchange between my grown son and our former head coach.

"*I quit too,*" Jacob said.

The colored stands erupted into applause. The white stands, meanwhile were emptying at a fast clip, following their disappeared players.

So many lives, I thought. I hoped they found some sort of peace as well. And some place where there was a game playing.

"*I have no choice then,*" Worrell said, voice shaking, "*but to forfeit.*"

I could hear my players' shouts of relief from a few feet away, but I focused all my energy on getting to my feet so I could look my son in the eye before he too left me.

"*Good game,*" Jacob said, extending his hand to me.

Now that I was standing, I could see that he'd grown taller than me, though the front of his uniform had a dark stain on it that made my stomach clench to look at.

I shook Jacob's hand, marveling that is was no longer cold. His grip was firm, and as we shook, I felt many of my years fall off me like so much dead weight on my back. I stood up straight and held tight to my dead son's hand, hoping I never had to let go.

"I love you, son," I whispered.

"*And I, you, Father,*" Jacob said.

Then his hand simply left my grasp.

"Wait—"

Jacob grew so faint I could see the gaslights poking through him. His final gesture before he left this world forever was to point at our empty dugout.

"*They're waiting for you,*" Jacob said. "*We always were. Farewell, Father. And thank you...*"

"You," I began, vision blurring once more. "You're welcome, Jacob."

Slowly I turned from where he'd been standing to look in the direction where he'd been pointing. The All Nations stood there, all six of them, watching with disbelief as well as relief written all over their faces.

But before I could reunite with my players, I had to get past Worrell. He stood at home plate, as if burning with the need to see what I would do after Jacob left me, forever.

Looking at the battered head of the glowing white man in front of me, I felt strangely grateful to him. I'd never spoken to a white man in the way I'd spoken to Worrell before. I felt like I was his equal now, not an inferior. I would continue that behavior with all *living* white men I encountered as well.

Also, I had to admit, because of Worrell, I got to see my boy one last time and do my best to make amends.

I caught myself before I dared thank the white bastard. Instead, I said:

"Worrell. You were a bastard, but you didn't deserve to die like that. I'm sorry you got hit, that I didn't warn you. But remember. That it was never my fault. I have no guilt about that any longer. So please, just go. I release you."With one last pop of air, Worrell simply disappeared, without a sound. Not even a dry chuckle or a final, whispered "*Boy...*"

I was finally free of him, so I turned to my remaining family. After surviving a bear hug from No Small Foot, then shaking hands with an exhausted Donaldson, I clapped Mack, Jiang, and Mendez on the back, and gave our sweaty Buddha a hug.

When I'd finished congratulating my players, I happened to glance over at our dugout, expecting it to be empty.

Instead, I saw who Jacob had truly been pointing at.

Mack," I whispered, my legs threatening once more to give out on me. "Mack, your prediction was *right.*"

Huddled together inside the home dugout, just as Mack had predicted, stood my wife Maddie and my daughter Lizbeth. My son-in-law stood behind them, shielding them from the quickly dispersing crowd of spirits.

They're waiting for you, Jacob had said. *We* always were.I forgot about my players and walked on my sore legs to the dugout, a trip that seemed to take forever. I nodded at Lizbeth and her tall husband, feeling a smile touch my lips, and then I met my wife's gaze. After all this time, she still made my heart pound.

Though her hair was now steel gray, clipped short as always, and her eyes had circles under them and crow's feet framing them, Maddie hadn't changed much at all. I know I'd put on a few pounds, carrying my old man's paunch like a medicine ball under my uniform, but she was as slender as the day she walked out of my life.

"Maddie," said, out of breath at the dugout, suddenly unsure of what to say after all this time. "You're here."

She nodded, and her face tightened.

"That was Jacob out there," she said, her voice making my head want to spin. I hadn't heard her in so long. "That was our boy, wasn't it?"

I nodded. My throat was too tight to speak. She never told me about Jacob. I bit back my words, not wanting to start another fight, despite my anger at her silence.

"He was playing ball up north about fifteen years ago," Lizbeth said, rubbing Maddie's arm next to her. "Like I said before, at our dinner that night, he got in with the wrong crowd." Maddie sniffed loudly at that. "The team was always short on money, never paid him enough, and he liked to impress people. One night he was up late, gambling. Someone thought he was cheating, or maybe just celebrating his winnings too much. There was a gun. I heard it happened fast. He didn't suffer."

"Thank you," I whispered. I felt tired now, tired and empty inside, thinking about Jacob dying like that. "Thank you for finally telling me this."

"He loved to play ball," Maddie began, then her voice betrayed her. "You... would've been... *so* proud."

My arms and legs felt too heavy to lift. I felt strangely exposed outside of the dugout, as if an attack was imminent from any direction. But I nodded and swallowed hard, glad to have seen my boy one last time, but still too angry to speak about not being informed of his death.

I looked at my wife, then, as the gas light far out at the edge of the field grew even dimmer. I saw the woman I'd fallen in love with, all those years ago, but I didn't remember—or perhaps I'd chosen not to recall—that hardness in her eyes.

She hadn't told me about Jacob intentionally, knowing it would hurt me when I found out. Did she think I didn't care? And why did she let him go in the first place?

I opened my mouth to speak, to put some of these swirling thoughts and jagged emotions into words, but my daughter spoke up first.

"You should move to Chicago," Lizbeth said.

I looked over at her and her husband in surprise, half-expecting that to be a joke. But they were nodding their heads in earnest. I couldn't for the life of me remember he husband's name.

Maddie's eyes had gone wide at the suggestion, then she nodded as well.

"It *would* be nice," she said, in a soft voice, "having you live close to us."

Behind me, the gas lights stuttered and popped. Their time was almost up, and the field grew darker with each passing second.

Close to, I realized Maddie had said. Not *with*.

"I'll consider that," I said. "I truly will."

And then they were walking out of the dugout and past the stands, ready to leave in Lizbeth's husband's Ford. It had to be long past midnight.

Thaddeus, I thought as I followed them out into the darkness. That was the name of Lizbeth's husband.

"Let me give you a ride home," Thaddeus said. "It's late."

I looked at the empty space in the back seat next to Maddie and shook my head. After all that had happened in tonight's game, I needed some time alone to go over it all in my head—the game as well as its aftermath.

"Thanks, but no thanks. I'll be okay." I swallowed with a clicking sensation. "I'll see you tomorrow, right? Tomorrow *afternoon*," I added over the rumble of their flivver, thinking of all sleep I needed to catch up on back home.

Once the rumble of the car faded, I turned back to the empty field. I'd been so enamored with my returned family that I'd let my team wander off, without any final words to them, or even saying goodbye. Some coach I was.

Or, I should say, some coach I *used* to be. It looked like I was unofficially retired now.

The lights fizzled one more time. I stepped into the dugout to grab my gear, only to get a coppery whiff of aftershave mixed with sweat.

I wasn't alone, after all.

Mack stood there in the dying light, silent as one of Worrell's spirits. He just looked at me, his dark face glowing with the brightness of his smile and the tears covering his dusky cheeks. Then the baseball diamond was blanketed in darkness again.

That smile is how I'll always remember Mack, to my dying day.

Chapter Twenty-Two

After that night in September, I'd never see Mack in the same way again. To be honest, after I'd said goodbye to Maddie, Lizbeth, and Thaddeus and promised to consider a move to the Windy City the next day, I rarely saw *anyone* from the team. It looked like Mack had disappeared, possibly for good.

A week after our final game, J.L. stopped by my place to tell me what I already knew—the All Nations team was no more. He was hoping to use some of our players in a new league he was working on that might start up in 1919 or 1920 at the latest, but he could make no promises. He wanted me to help coach that team, if I was available.

"Maybe," I told him. "But I think not."

By that point, I'd caught the same influenza virus that had crippled about half the city. Feverish and aching, I spent the rest of September in bed, too tired and feverish to read or write letters. I just slept and dreamed.

In my fever dreams, I saw Maddie again, looking young and pretty, but no longer angry at me for lashing out at Jacob, or for choosing baseball so many times over her. She kept asking me pointed questions about my life now, like what I was going to do next, but she never waited for my answers.

Then I'd dream of Isabel, passionate Isabel, her hair a gray-black waterfall falling through the darkened forest of my illness, her brown eyes burning with passion as she listened to my wild ravings and touched my brow with her strong, cool hand.

"You know, Coach," Isabel said in her musical voice, speaking in melodious Spanish that I could understand without the slightest effort, "your time has not yet come. You have something more to do, starting with someone who needs to find his way home."

With those words echoing in my head, I opened my eyes, feeling Isabel's touch on my now-cool brow. I could still smell her smoky, rose-tinted scent, and then I winced at the coppery, too-sweet smell of aftershave and the tangy odor of Cuban cigars.

At that moment, I knew what was holding me back from embarking upon my new life.

Mack. I'd never said goodbye to him.

With more effort than I'd expected, I pulled myself from my bed, mopping sweat from my body with my quilt. I wondered if I wasn't still dreaming, with my body still fighting the sickness that people now called Spanish Flu.

Everything felt like a hallucination from the past season, especially my memories of the All Nations. Had the team really existed?

My memories of this past year—dancing all night in Havana, the rainy games in the Northwest, the impossible catches Mack made in centerfield, even the fights and the injuries—were already growing fragmented and faint.

I had to go, now, and find Mack before I lost anything more.

I pulled on my clothes, grabbed my coat, and made my outside, trusting that my instincts, coupled with my hard-traveling feet, would help me find my lost centerfielder somewhere in this great big world of ours.

On a cool day in November of that year—a day that would soon be known as Armistice Day, the official cease-fire to the fighting in Europe—I found Mack.

I'd been tracking him for a month and a half, showing people my only team photograph, pointing out his face in the middle of the picture, a shadow between the multi-hued faces of his teammates around him.

When I found Mack, his skin was nearly as black as my own, and he looked painfully fragile and small, hunched there all by himself in an empty cornfield, next to a brown river no larger than a trickle.

He still wore his All Nations uniform, though his feet were bare, his toes muddy. With his long arms wrapped around his knees, he gave off just a hint of his old coppery, almost-sweet smell. His eyes had lost almost all of their unnatural brightness.

Mack began talking as soon as I walked up to him. As if he'd been waiting for me all this while.

"You know, Coach," he began, and I held up my hands to silence him. He looked so thin and so fragile I didn't want him to waste energy on speaking. Nor did I want to hear any more of his predictions. Not now.

"I have to tell you," Mack insisted. "There's something *more* coming, Coach. More than the constant fighting and bloodshed, more than the game itself. It's called segregation. Separate but equal."

"What's that mean? Don't we have that now?"

Mack shook his head and kept talking.

"We didn't reach as many people as we should have. The victories of our All Nations team are already fading. Memories fade like sunlight at the end of the day."

Mack paused, out of breath.

"Mack." I could hardly hear my own voice. I went down to my knees next to him, my legs betraying me once again. I had to lean close, inhaling his sickly-sweet smell so I could hear what he was saying.

"You have to remember *all* of it. The good... and the bad. Just don't let the... bad could break you. Coach. You have to... tell our team's story."

"Mack. Let's get you some food—"

"And that's all... I have for you, Coach," he whispered. "I thank you... for all of your faith in me over the years. You... kept me here much longer... than I thought I'd ever... be able to... manage."

I saw that old, ghostly light begin to fill his eyes. He turned his skeletal face up to gaze once more at the noon sun.

"And I'm sorry about Coach Worrell," he said, no longer pausing, as if the sun had given him an extra dose of energy. " I knew I had to distract him at that game. Some things had to be done, whether it was a white head coach's distraction or sending a letter in the middle of the night. But his death put everything in motion. I just... I never could have predicted all that would follow. His spirit was stronger in death than in life.

Mack sighed, eyes fluttering.

"I'm so glad... you let him go, at last."

I touched the wasted shoulder of the man that I only knew as Mack, and he looked from the sun over at me. That unhealthy, unholy white light spilled out of his eyes as if he was being lit up from within.

"You know, Coach," Mack said, for what would be the last time to me, ever. "You are a good man... You still have time... to do more."

I had no words to respond to that, so I simply nodded.

I'm trying to remember that moment now, that instant went Mack must have slipped away from me, but everything runs together in my head.

I *must* remember, I tell myself. But I can only gather the fragments of memory like the pieces of a broken window. Or a the remnants of a shattered bat, spread across a green ballfield in a halo.

There in that dead field in early winter of 1918, the light of the sun shone above me one moment, and in the next it came from Mack next to me.

I must have been relapsing into the fever dreams of the Spanish Flu, because what I saw in that field at that moment was impossible. I could brush off the countless visions of Worrell as quirks of an old man's guilt, but this conflagration unfolding in front of me was real.

I could feel Mack unraveling, the heat coming off him in waves. Within seconds, Mack, my centerfielder, had disintegrated into the light of the sun.

I tried to look into the whiteness that once was my star player, but my eyes refused. When I blinked, Mack's strange light had blended in to the more yellow rays of the sun.

All that was left of him was a new baseball, bright white and unadorned, sitting on the ground in the shadow of a cloud that slowly passed over me. I stood all by myself in the winter-stripped field with the combined scents of copper and cigar smoke lingering in my nose. I picked up the baseball, reveling in its perfect newness, and carried it gripped in my left hand all the way back home.

Little did I know I still had one last trip left in me.

Just before Christmas that year, I spent a snowbound afternoon reading and re-reading my way through the letters and cards sent to me by my former players.

My players. They'd done well since our last game.

No Small Foot had returned home to North Carolina, where he was given what he described as a "hero's welcome" in his one and only letter to me. I think he was still mad about me breaking his second pair of spectacles in half, but the last time I saw him, he'd managed to glue them back together.

Buddha and Jiang had struck up a friendship after the season ended, and they were doing something Buddha called "walking the world" together. The letter had come from somewhere in Africa, as best I could make out. I even got a letter from Boles, and now that the war had ended, he and Art had moved to New York to find work on one of the many ball clubs up there.

I'd hoped to hear from Carrie Nation or maybe even Phil the Philippine, but never did.

I still saw Donaldson and Mendez around town, and they always seemed happy to see me, though Mendez still hadn't let go of his anger at his fellow Cubans for running off.

Under the letters from my players sat a pile of accumulated newspapers from the past season. I reread the headlines about the war and, of course, the stories inside about baseball. Nowhere in those pages of newsprint did I see a single article about the All Nations. We weren't worthy of the reporters' time, apparently.

Was our contribution to the game so small, I wondered, so insubstantial? Were we being forgotten already, just as someone had once warned me?

Someone...

I looked at all the letters from my players from the past few months, along with my tattered rosters and letters, and for the life of me I couldn't find any mention of the person who'd warned me of that.

"Mack," I whispered at last. "His name was Mack."

At some point in the past few months, I'd managed to misplace the bright white baseball he'd left for me. I spent a good hour searching for it, only to find it buried in one more pile of unopened mail inside my trunk.

How the hell could I have forgotten Mack? In my various letters to and talks with my former players, I didn't tell any of them about what had happened to Mack. And none of them asked. It was as if he never existed.

With his ball tight in my left hand, I peered down into my trunk. Right where I'd found Mack's baseball, I saw the bright colors of a postcard.

My heart suddenly in my throat, I bent to pick it up.

At half past noon the following day I stood at the train station with Spanish running through my head. All of my most important belongings—precious few, I realized— were stuffed into the five bags next to me. My house was sealed up and locked.

In my coat pocket were two articles made of paper. The first was an envelope thick with pages that included the deed to my house and a copy of my will.

The other item was smaller, just a postcard, with my address, a return address, and one line written on it. The same postcard I'd found in my trunk. I looked at the image on the front of the card once again. The sun shone upon the Havana Cathedral, its dark stone walls pristine, the bells of its two unmatched towers in full motion. I turned the card over and read the sentence written on the back for the hundredth time since yesterday.

"*Deje su toma de la vida usted donde su pasión le conduce.*"

I'd made two stops on the way to the train station. The first was at the boarding house where Mendez still lived. He read the Spanish words on the back of the card, dated two months ago, and gave me a wide grin when he saw the name at the bottom.

"Let your life take you where your passion leads you," he translated.

I'd memorized the way Mendez had pronounced the words, saying them over and over.

"*Buena suerte*, Coach!" Mendez had said before I left to go directly to the telegraph office. I had them send a telegram to Isabel Maria, letting her know I was on my way. I was letting my passion lead me now, and I'd sleep on the streets of Havana if I needed to.

Waiting for my train, I ran a finger over the elegant words written in Spanish on the back of the postcard. I liked the way it sounded in Spanish. I was going to have to learn the language sooner or later.

After I boarded, I took from my duffel bag the record book Jiang had given me a few weeks before he began his own journey. He'd filled every thick page of the book with every minute detail of our games this year, along with a primer on the Chinese characters he'd painted in it.

I then pulled out the little notebook I'd picked up yesterday, a sturdy journal full of empty pages. As the train chuffed out of Kansas City, I took out my pen and thought about my team, and all we'd done together.

Where to begin?

With the burnt smell of coal ash in my nose and the cool air from the window on my skin, I heard from somewhere behind me a small popping sound, like a small book snapping shut. With that sound I knew exactly how and where my history of my team would start.

April Fool's Day, 1918.

As I wrote, I couldn't help but smile at the cold air in this train car. Havana would no doubt be lovely at this time of year. I just hoped I'd have enough time left in my life to write down all I had to say.

I set down my pen for a moment in the rocking passenger car.

In honor of Mack, my absent, far-seeing, strangely wondrous centerfielder, I dared to make a prediction: I would indeed have plenty of time, plenty of *life*, to do all I wanted to do, and more.

About the Author

Michael Jasper loves to explore the places where the normal meets the strange. In pursuit of this fascination, he has written and published over a dozen novels, three story collections, sixty short stories, and a digital comic with artist Niki Smith.

In the past he attempted bartending, teaching junior high, painting houses, being a secret shopper, working construction, and many more jobs; he prefers fiction writing. For his day job, he works as a technical writer.

He lives with his family in North Carolina, and his website is **michaeljasper.net**.